A WOMAN OF FORTUNE

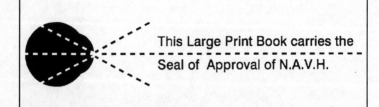

This Large Print Book carries the
Seal of Approval of N.A.V.H.

A WOMAN OF FORTUNE

KELLIE COATES GILBERT

THORNDIKE PRESS
A part of Gale, Cengage Learning

GALE
CENGAGE Learning®

Farmington Hills, Mich • San Francisco • New York • Waterville, Maine
Meriden, Conn • Mason, Ohio • Chicago

GALE
CENGAGE Learning®

LIBRARY OF CONGRESS CATALOGING-IN-PUBLICATION DATA

Gilbert, Kellie Coates.
   A woman of fortune : a Texas gold novel / by Kellie Gilbert. — Large print
edition.
      pages ; cm. — (Thorndike Press large print Christian fiction) (Texas gold
   collection) .
   ISBN-13: 978-1-4104-7216-8 (hardcover)
   ISBN-10: 1-4104-7216-7 (hardcover)
   1. Criminals—Family relationships—Fiction. 2. Swindlers and
swindling—Fiction. 3. Fraud investigation—Fiction. 4. Texas—Fiction. 5.
Large type books. I. Title.
PS3607.I42323W66 2014b
813'.6—dc23   2014021962

Published in 2014 by arrangement with Revell Books, a division of
Baker Publishing Group

Printed in Mexico
1 2 3 4 5 6 7 18 17 16 15 14

To my sister,
Jeannie Ann Cunningham,
a woman of extraordinary grace

PROLOGUE

Until today, Claire Massey had never been inside the walls of a federal prison.

She'd taken French cooking lessons in Paris, photographed the aurora borealis, and even dined with a president and his wife. But never in her wildest imagination could she have contemplated herself doing this.

She fingered the fine-grain leather bag in her lap as the car slowly moved through heavy metal gates and past the guard tower that strangely resembled a childhood fort.

"You okay, Mom?"

She startled at her son's voice. "What? Uh, yes, I'm fine." Her hand plunged inside her purse for her Dolce & Gabbana sunglasses.

Max took a deep breath. "You don't have to do this, you know."

Claire nodded, keeping her eyes averted from the razor wire that cut a line across the horizon. She slipped the glasses on, glad for the barrier between her budding tears and the harsh Texas sun reflecting off the building looming ahead.

She swallowed. Hard. This was no time to lose it.

After pulling one hand from the steering wheel, her son slipped his palm over her trembling fingers. "Please, Mom, let me go in with you."

She shook her head. "No, this is something I need to do. Alone."

Max circled the parking lot twice before finding an empty spot. He pulled the car between a pickup with wheels the size of her car door and a battered green sedan that had definitely seen better days. From its rearview mirror hung a rosary and a pair of red lace panties, the kind you might see on a Victoria's Secret model.

Her son cut the engine.

Claire took a deep breath. "I don't know how long this will take."

Something in Max's eyes dimmed. He scratched at his beard stubble. "I'll be here."

The line at the front door extended several hundred yards. Claire moved with caution into place at the end, behind a heavy woman clothed in a stained housedress and slipper-like shoes that dug deeply into swollen flesh.

She shifted uncomfortably in her own

wedge pumps, aware she'd made a question-able shoe choice. Why hadn't she thought to wear tennis shoes? The woman she'd talked to on the telephone yesterday warned Saturday was their heaviest day for visitors, cautioning the line would be like this.

Forty minutes passed before Claire reached the front-entry door and stepped into the large, old brick building and out of the baking sun, the inside air a welcome respite from the heat emanating from the concrete she'd been standing on. Despite the cooler temperature, sweat formed on her scalp. The heat perhaps? Or maybe nerves. She couldn't tell.

From somewhere in the line behind her, a young girl shushed her squalling infant. Claire couldn't help but think this was no place for a baby. But then again, would any of them be here if given a better option?

A woman officer dressed in a blue shirt, damp at the underarms, stepped forward. "I'll need your driver's license." She thrust a clipboard at Claire. "Sign at the designated spot and put the time next to your name." She tilted her head toward a large clock on the opposite wall. "And place your belong-ings in the basket."

Claire looked up. "My belongings?"

The woman sighed. "Rings, watch. You

can't take nothing in with you."

"But my purse —"

"Nothing," she repeated.

Claire swallowed and did as she was told. When finished, she held up the basket to the officer.

The woman pointed to a wall lined with lockers and handed Claire a key. "Over there."

As soon as she stored her belongings, she glanced around, confused about where to go next. An older black lady with white hair gave her a toothy smile and pointed toward a metal door with a sign posted above that read "Visitors Holding Room."

Claire gave her a token nod of gratitude and followed a crowd of people moving in that direction. After passing through the metal detector, she was patted down by another female officer, who smelled of cigarettes and maple syrup. "Wait over there," the woman said, pointing to metal chairs lined up against a pea-green wall in bad need of paint.

She nodded and scanned for an empty chair, then sat to wait.

A man moved past, mopping the floor. His shoes made a slight squeaky sound every time he sludged forward, slowly pulling the dirty-looking mop across the speckled linoleum floor.

Claire looked away, focusing instead on a fake philodendron wedged in the corner, a few feet away from a drinking fountain hanging from the wall. Anything to quiet the voices in her head. Especially Jana Rae's.

"What are you? Ten shades of stupid?" her friend had asked over the phone.

"Look, this is something I need to do," Claire explained.

"Claire, listen to me. This crazy idea is going to put you square on the wrong end of an intervention. You know what I mean? Haven't you been through enough already?"

That was one thing Claire loved about Jana Rae. Few people could truly be counted on in life. Her crazy friend with blazing red hair and a mouth snappy as a bullwhip had always been in her corner of the arena. Even now.

Claire leaned her head back against the cold, hard wall of the holding room, keeping her eyes closed so she wouldn't have to see countless young girls waiting to see their baby daddies. The sight was far too depressing. But then, she wasn't so different. A female who had stood by her man and looked the other way, failing to see things as they really were.

Funny how she'd always known the grass

11

was green — but never needed to know how or why.

She gnawed on her bottom lip, a habit she'd taken up as of late.

"Claire Massey?"

The booming voice caused her to startle. Claire glanced about the room as if there might be another woman with that name. "Me?" she asked.

The woman officer with the clipboard heaved a sigh laced with boredom. "Your name Massey?"

She nodded and stood. She followed the officer through the door and down a long hallway with windowless walls the color of the dried mud lining the pond out at Legacy Ranch, the one she'd gazed out at each morning while sitting in the breakfast nook.

The woman led her through a heavy metal door into a room less than half the size of her bathroom at home. Granted, the bathroom had been much larger than most, but this space felt cramped nonetheless.

A barrier cut the room in half, the upper portion made of glass grimy with handprints. The scene was straight out of a television episode of *CSI*.

Claire turned to thank the officer, but she was now alone. Nervous, she slid into the empty chair on her side of the barrier.

And waited.

Claire told herself to breathe. Her heart pounded wildly, and by the time the door on the other side of the barrier creaked open, every nerve fiber in her body was charged. It would take next to nothing to spark tears.

She trained her eyes on the doorway and vowed not to cry. Not here.

Then he entered, appearing older, more tired than the last time she'd seen him. Perhaps resigned to his circumstances. But he still looked at her with the same eyes — the ones she'd gazed into that night all those years ago at the Burger Hut. And so many times since.

Tuck quickly moved to the window and took his seat. With a guard standing nearby, he placed his shackled palm against the glass and mouthed, "I love you."

Claire blinked several times before picking up the telephone receiver and motioning for him to do the same.

He scrambled for the phone at his side, as though it were a line to the life he'd left behind . . . to her. He quickly nestled the black handset against his ear.

"Claire." He said her name with a kind of reverence, a tone you'd use with someone you cherished.

Claire swallowed against the dryness of her throat. She looked into her husband's eyes and steeled herself.

"I want a divorce."

1

Four Months Earlier

Claire wrapped the apron ties around her waist and gazed out the window. In the distance, a small army of men assembled large white tents. Catering trucks littered the horizon, and she could see smoke drifting from the barbeque pit, where in a few hours, beef briskets would be slow-roasted until tender, and hundreds of T-bone steaks grilled to smoky perfection.

Like in past years, come dusk, a steady stream of chrome-laden trucks and shiny black limousines would ease through the gate leading to Legacy Ranch, continuing well after uniformed servers marched across the lawns, carrying the first trays of lobster canapés. Snagging an invite to the Masseys' annual barbeque bash was akin to receiving the Hope Diamond in a Christmas stocking. No annual event in all of Texas — not even the Cattle Baron's Ball — was more

15

widely anticipated.

"Where would you like the flowers placed, Mrs. Massey?"

Claire turned to find a guy in a green and white T-shirt holding a clipboard. "Oh . . ." She wiped her hands on her apron. "Let's take them right on out back. Just give me one minute." She picked up a pâté mold from the counter and turned to her housekeeper. "Margarita, would you place this in the refrigerator for me?"

"Sure." Margarita stopped chopping, took the mold, and headed for the walk-in cooler.

"Here, this way." Claire waved for the young man to follow as she walked through the French doors leading to the back portico.

Every year, Tuck shook his head and wondered why his wife involved herself in these types of details. "Isn't that why we maintain a staff and hire caterers?" he'd patiently remind her.

He was right, of course. Margarita was fully capable of orchestrating all the party preparations, and Claire usually let her. But she didn't care what her husband and three grown children thought — even a woman of her financial means was entitled to spend time in the kitchen if she chose, no matter how many staff they employed.

Claire stepped into the morning sun and shaded her line of vision with a raised hand. "Was Mr. Larsen able to get the hydrangeas I ordered?" she asked the young man with the clipboard.

"Got the shipment this morning, in all the way from Oregon. Blue and white, just like you specified." He motioned a delivery truck into place, then jumped up on the landing platform and opened the truck's back door. He pulled out a sample vase filled with blooms and held them up for her approval.

Pleased, she awarded him with a quick smile. "They're perfect!" She pointed. "See the pillars on either side of the portico?"

"Yeah."

"That's where I'll want them. There, and on either end of the buffet tables and at each of the bars." Claire motioned to the manicured lawn, past the pool area, where the tables and equipment were being set up. "The smaller floral arrangements are for the tables where the guests will be seated for dinner." She reached out and caressed the bursts of periwinkle-blue blossoms.

"Sure thing, Mrs. Massey."

"You can call me Claire." She smiled and turned just in time to see her sleepy daughter step through the door, steaming coffee in hand.

"Isn't everything turning out lovely, sweetie?"

"Sounds like a small war going on out here." Lainie surveyed the activity and shook her head. "I still don't understand why you don't have a catering service do all this, Mother."

"Because I enjoy it. Your father is going to be so pleased, don't you think?"

"I think Dad has more important things to think about."

Claire swallowed the sting of her daughter's remark. "I just want everything perfect."

Out of the corner of her eye, she spotted Margarita in the kitchen marshaling a spur of activity. "Oh, good. The cake's here." Claire brushed past Lainie to where two women were entering through the service door, balancing a large multitiered cake frosted in white and covered in perfectly spaced dots the exact color of the blue hydrangeas. At the top, a replica of the Legacy Ranch logo was centered just so, surrounded by tiny cattle made of marzipan.

Claire clasped her hands. "Oh yes — that's just what I had in mind."

"Do you want the cake placed in the

cooler, Mrs. Massey?"

"Yes, but let's plan to set it out at least an hour before we cut it, okay, Margarita? I don't want everyone biting into ice-cold cake."

Lainie slugged into the kitchen, flip-flops slapping the tiled floor. "Morning, Margarita."

"Good morning, Miss Lainie." The older woman surveyed the girl in the baggy sweats and T-shirt, hair pulled back. "Looks like you stayed out a *leetle* too late last night." She wiped her hands on her apron and winked. " 'Bout time you kicked those heels up a little."

Lainie threw a loving but impatient look at their housekeeper. "I wasn't 'kicking up' any heels. Reece and I attended a fund-raiser gala for the Dallas Symphony last evening. Reece's mother is on the board. We joined his parents and the Mannings for dinner afterward."

Claire looked up. "The Mannings?"

Lainie took a sip of her coffee. "Major contributors to Reece's campaign."

"Ah-yee, amiga." Margarita waved her hand. "You need some fun in your life." The older woman turned and headed outside. Claire couldn't have said it better herself.

"Where's Dad?"

"He had to go to the office for a little while." Claire walked to the sink to wash her hands. "Would you call your brother later and remind him to be here by five o'clock?"

"What? Do I look like Max's keeper?" Lainie refilled her coffee.

"Oh, don't be that way. He'll probably get here in plenty of time. I just want to be sure." Claire opened the cupboard and drew out her own mug, walked over, and poured herself some coffee.

"I invited Reece's parents to stay over in the guest house after the party tonight. I hope that's okay." Lainie grabbed a banana from the fruit basket next to the coffeepot and turned to the door.

"You did? Well, sure — of course." Claire studied her daughter's back as she blew through the doorway and out of sight.

Great. Just what she needed. It wasn't that she disliked Andrew and Glory Sandell. It was that Reece's parents — and especially his mother — always seemed to have ulterior motives. Like her dad used to say, "Those coyote pups may look cute . . . careful, they're anything but."

That was how she felt whenever she was in a conversation with Glory Sandell. Lainie's future mother-in-law appeared charming enough, but Claire worried if she left her hand extended a little too long, Glory might just bite it.

By five o'clock, the party had barely started and the lawns were crowded already. Near the dance floor, Claire spotted a couple of Dallas Cowboys players, the producer of *Good Morning Texas,* and a stunning woman who had been Miss Texas in the mid-nineties, whose carefully doctored looks could still trump those of some of the much younger women at this party.

Several yards away, a slender brunette wearing five-inch stilettos and a tight silver dress waved. "Great party, Claire."

Claire raised her glass, barely able to hear over the helicopter landing on the pad behind the barns. "Hey, Sharon," she called back. She'd met the owner of the wildly popular exercise studio, Milana, in Dallas several years back after Tuck suggested they both might lose a few pounds before their trip to Aruba. Claire had made a weekly trip downtown for Sharon's popular yoga class, which Tuck teased was populated by women with air-brushed complexions who practiced born-again matrimony — leaving starter marriages behind to worship more lucrative marital prospects.

Speaking of Tuck, where had he taken off to? Claire scanned the crowd for her husband. Failing to spot him, she headed toward her oldest son. Garrett and his wife, Marcy, were talking with Sidney McAlvain, owner of a large gas and oil conglomerate headquartered in Houston. Sidney had his arm around a tall blonde nestled beside him. Rich men seemed to have no trouble finding what Lainie called *arm candy,* even short bald guys with cigar breath.

At one of the parties held in their Dallas Cowboys skybox, Sidney once bragged there was nothing more profitable than black gold. Tuck had laughed. "You're absolutely right," he said. "As long as that black gold has horns and eats grass."

Sidney must have agreed. Tuck later confided his friend had written a check investing nearly twenty million dollars, becoming the proud owner of several herds of Kansas Holsteins. Less than a year later, Tuck maneuvered his friend's investment into a tidy sum.

That was how Tuck operated. No one knew the cattle market like her husband.

Just last month, the host of one of those cable news networks reported few were more successful than Tuck Massey at turning a profit. After the show aired, the telephone never stopped ringing.

Not that she should complain. After all, she had a charismatic husband who loved her, and they'd raised three great children. Being Tuck Massey's wife came with a lot of perks.

"Hey there, everybody." Claire leaned forward and accepted a slight kiss on her cheek from her daughter-in-law, who was dressed in a pretty tangerine-colored sundress that offset her auburn hair. "I hope y'all are having a great time."

Sidney puffed heavily on his cigar, sending a cloud of smoke her direction that made her eyes water. Discreetly, she stepped back as the man's manicured fingers flicked ashes on the grass at their feet. "Claire, you and Tuck have done it again. I keep thinking this party can't get any better. Yet somehow you Masseys top the year before."

The blonde shifted her tight dress and let out a nervous giggle. "I can't believe I'm here. I mean, really. I've read about these barbeques for years. I'm so honored to attend."

Claire saw Marcy's gaze drop to the blonde's neckline and the surgically enhanced chest captured within the fabric. In a wise move, Garrett trained his eyes on the woman's face.

Amused, Claire gave Sidney's companion du jour a welcoming smile. "We're so happy you could join us." She extended her hand and paused. "Uh . . ."

Sidney pulled the cigar from his mouth. "Daisy," he said.

His date smiled broadly. "Daisy Anheuser. No relation to the beer family," she quickly added before leaning back into Sidney's arms.

"Where are you from?" Marcy asked, disapproval evident across her features.

"I'm from Ohio. Grew up around Cincinnati. But I live in Dallas now."

Sidney slipped an oyster from a tray being passed by one of the servers. "Where's my favorite cattle meister?" He blew cigar smoke, then slurped the raw oyster and placed the empty shell back on the tray.

Claire winced and placed her hand on Garrett's arm. "I was just wondering the same. Could you please excuse us? I have a missing husband to find." She gave Sidney and his date a pinched smile. "Enjoy the evening."

She hooked her arm inside Garrett's and they walked with Marcy past the pool. Claire's eyes scanned the crowd. Seeing no sign of Tuck, she voiced a not-so-subtle complaint. "Doesn't your father know we're hosting a barbeque? Where could he be?"

"I think I saw him head toward the office with his banker." Garrett slipped his hand onto Marcy's back. "But that was over half an hour ago, right, honey?"

Claire stopped walking. She jutted her chin. "During our party?"

A server stepped forward. "Caviar, Mrs. Massey?"

She directed her attention to the black beluga roe on the silver platter. Using the tiny pearl-handled spoon, she scooped a small mound onto a toast point and slipped the rare and very expensive delicacy into her mouth.

With a frown, Claire waved over one of the catering managers. "The caviar is several degrees too warm." She placed her hand on his forearm. "I'm afraid the outside temperature is working against us."

"Yes, Mrs. Massey. I'll certainly take care of that right away. My apologies." The man in the black tuxedo snapped his fingers at another waiter, then spoke into a lapel microphone. Seconds later, two men scurried from the direction of the house, carrying trays of shaved ice.

"Look, go check on your father, would you, Garrett? And if he's out there, tell him I send a message. This is no time for business. Not during the party."

Claire watched Garrett and Marcy continue on, maneuvering through pockets of guests. As they faded from sight, she packed up her angst and headed in the direction of the house.

"It's a shame Baker had to pull out of the race. Fighting cancer doesn't work very well on the campaign trail. But Reece Sandell will make a fine senator . . ." Governor Jackson let his words fade as Claire approached.

"Claire, dear — what a lovely party." The governor's wife clasped her hand.

"Thank you, Mrs. Jackson." Claire brushed the woman's cheek with a kiss before greeting her white-haired husband. "Governor."

Suddenly, Tuck was at her side. He patted Governor Jackson's shoulder. "Glad you could make it, John."

"Hey, there you are." The governor's eyes lit up. He extended a blue-veined hand and gave his host an enthusiastic handshake.

A huge grin on his face, Tuck waved over one of the servers with a wide swipe of his hand. "Now, you two, listen up. I don't want either one of you to be shy when it comes to dishing up for dinner." He leaned forward and lowered his voice. "In addition to the T-bones, we had several cases of the filets you raved about last year prepared special. And," he added, "there's a case for you to take home."

Mrs. Jackson eyed the barbeque pit appreciatively and rewarded her host with a smile before sliding a tall glass of sweet tea from the tray offered by a white-gloved server, who then turned to the governor. "Sir? Would you care for something to drink?"

Last election cycle, television pundits claimed John Jackson was past his prime, causing him to slip in the polls at a dangerous rate. Tuck stood up at the Cattle Baron's Ball and endorsed John as a friend to Texas ranching, garnering the wavering candidate enough support to win the election, just barely. The act placed Tuck on a pedestal in the governor's eyes, which should bolster Reece's run for election. "It's all about relationships," Tuck often reminded his boys.

Claire took in the scent of her husband's cologne as he leaned in and kissed her. "So, where've *you* been, mister?" Her voice teased, but she hoped her eyes sent a more serious message.

"Schmoozing." Tuck winked at the governor and his wife. "If you two will pardon us, Claire and I must greet a few hundred guests."

Out of earshot from the governor and his wife, Tuck apologized. "Sorry, babe. I didn't mean to get tied up. You know nothing could keep me from our party for long."

She squeezed his hand. "Yeah. Uh-huh. You've been spending way too much time out in the offices lately. Today is for you to relax and enjoy yourself."

As they neared the pit, the air filled with an intoxicating aroma of beef cooking over mesquite. Tuck patted one of the cooks on the shoulder. "Hey there, Charlie. Those steaks are looking mighty good."

"Thank you, Mr. Massey. We'll be ready to serve up the first round of this'n here beef in about ten minutes."

"Mmm, can't wait." Tuck gave the old pit master a smile of approval.

Claire felt a tap on her shoulder. "Mother, may I speak to you a moment?" There was an unusual urgency in her daughter's voice. Claire offered up an apology and followed Lainie.

Once they were a safe distance from being overheard, Lainie explained. "It's Max." She nodded over at the table where her younger brother sat, arm draped sloppily over the blonde seated to his right, who was looking a bit annoyed.

"Oh, goodness." Claire waved for Lainie to follow, but before they could make their way to Max, Glory Sandell wedged herself in between the two women and their destination, blocking the line of sight to where Max was more than enjoying the party.

"Claire, you're fixin' to put us all to shame. This party is" — she hesitated — "uh, quite the show."

"Thank you, Glory." Claire graced the woman with one of her most brilliant smiles, then looped her arm with Glory's and strolled a few steps, maneuvering away from the blasts of laughter coming from Max's table.

"Glory, I wanted to tell you about the new cake decorator I've discovered. He's wonderful." Glory tried to glance over her shoulder, but Claire pressed on. "You might consider him for Reece's upcoming fundraiser. In fact, Lainie, why don't you take Glory and show your future mother-in-law the cake?"

Lainie picked up on the opportunity. "Oh yes. You *have* to see this gorgeous creation before they cut it."

Claire took a few more steps with them, pointing out that the smart little bakery was located in the Market District, right next to the café they'd lunched at last month, the one that served the to-die-for risotto with chanterelle mushrooms.

With Glory Sandell safely commandeered, Claire scurried to Max's table, which thankfully was now vacant except for her son and the girl.

"Max?"

"Hi, Mom." He grinned up at her. "Mom, this is Bridget. She's the new love of my life." He snorted out a giggle. "I'm gonna marry her."

"Hi, Mrs. Massey."

"Bridget." Claire gave the young woman an apologetic smile before extricating her son's arm from the girl's accommodating shoulder.

"Do you need any help, Mrs. Massey?" Bridget asked.

Claire saw Margarita heading their way. "No, I think we're good."

Minutes later, with Margarita's help, Claire successfully wrangled Max away from the crowd mostly unnoticed, then across the side yard and into the door leading to the east wing of the house.

"Max, for goodness' sake. What if your father had seen you like this? Or worse, one of those reporters?"

"What do you think would happen,

Mom?" Her son hiccuped. "Oh, *that's* right. I might be the black sheep of the family. Baaa . . ."

Claire tightened her grip. "Max, that's enough."

"Get it, Mom? Black sheep. Like you said were on Grandpa's farm — in the old days?"

"I can get him from here, Mrs. Massey." The stout housekeeper slapped at Max's hand as he attempted to pinch her cheek. "Enough of you, young man."

"Margarita, would *you* marry me?" he teased, his words slurring.

"I'm gonna marry that hind end in a minute. You're not so grown I can't still bend you over." Margarita placed her more than ample arms around his shoulders and guided him past the leather sofa and down the hallway to the first-floor guest quarters.

Claire followed close behind. "Thank you, Margarita. I don't know what I'd do without you."

"No problem. Now get back out there. They'll be cutting the cake soon. Oh, and . . ."

"Yes?"

"Miss Lainie is nearly beside herself."

Claire nodded and assured her house-keeper she would report back to her anxious daughter as soon as possible that all was well. She gave Margarita a quick pat on the shoulder and headed back to the party.

What was Max thinking? Her son had never used this kind of indiscretion. She only hoped Tuck hadn't seen. Things were tense enough between the two of them as it was.

Tuck adored his son. But unlike Garrett, who rarely stepped outside his father's expectations, Max never measured up. As his teen years melted into young adulthood, he'd simply quit trying, instead finding his own path.

Max was a writer. A gifted one — despite the fact he was currently on his third unpublished manuscript since he'd dropped out of college over a year ago. He traded free room and board at home for a two-room loft above the offices of the *Longhorn Weekly,* a small alternative newspaper where he earned rent and a meager paycheck and authored a regularly featured editorial column on the dearth of contemporary politics in America — his destiny, she supposed, given he'd interrupted dinner one evening many years ago with the question, "Daddy, are we *democraps* or *repelicans*?"

While she and Tuck had concealed their laughter, Lainie had daintily placed her fork down, given her little brother a stern look, and responded, "We're *Texans,* silly."

Claire smiled at the memory, then slowed her pace as Tuck's voice drifted from the door of the study. He sounded angry.

"Tuck?" she said from the doorway.

Tuck glanced in her direction. "Look, I gotta go. I'll call you on Monday. Yes, uh-huh. We'll discuss all this then." He ended the call and slid his phone in his jeans pocket. "Hi, honey."

"Tuck, who was that?"

"One of our buyers from Amarillo. Nothing to worry about. Just business."

Claire studied her husband's face. He looked like an armadillo hit by a cattle truck. "You sure?"

"Oh, you know these guys," Tuck said a little too quickly. "Always complaining they don't make enough money." He slipped his arm around her waist and led her out into the hallway. "As if millions weren't enough." He forced a smile.

Outside, they made their way to their designated places at the head table, where Claire discreetly turned her attention to Jana Rae, who was seated at her right. "I'll tell you, there are times when managing this family is a full-time job."

Jana Rae nodded. "I don't think too many people noticed Max. Everybody's attention has been on pretty boy."

Claire followed her gaze to a table nearby, where Reece Sandell pulled out a chair for Lainie. A photographer clicked several shots of the couple. Claire nudged her friend's arm and responded in a low voice. "Shh, somebody will hear you."

"Well, it's true," Jana Rae whispered. "I mean, look at that guy. No doubt he's cut from a politician's bolt of cloth." She took the linen napkin and placed it in her lap. "If his teeth got any whiter, Lainie would have to wear sunglasses."

Claire whispered back, "You're only getting away with those remarks because you're my best friend. Besides, I've never seen Lainie happier."

After the last of the meal was cleared, the crowd made their way to the dance pavilion. Claire followed Tuck to the stage, where he cleared his throat and leaned into the microphone. "Excuse me, everyone. Can I have your attention?"

Their guests quieted.

"I'd like to thank y'all for coming out for the Legacy Ranch annual barbeque." Over a ripple of applause, Tuck slipped his arm around Claire's waist. "Once in a while, a fella gets luckier than he deserves."

"That's called *grace*," Pastor Richards

shouted from near the front of the crowd. Several people laughed, including one of Tuck's fellow elders at Abundant Hills Church, where Claire had chaired the annual missions gala for the last couple of years.

Tuck nodded. "Yeah, that's right. Can't believe the big guy upstairs trusted a guy like me with such a pretty thing." He gave Claire a squeeze. "Seriously, though, I want to tell y'all how much my family means to me. As some of you know, my oldest son Garrett recently took over the ranch operations here. And with any luck, he and that pretty wife of his, Marcy, will be making me and Claire some grandbabies soon."

Laughter broke out again.

"My son Max, on the other hand — he tossed my advice aside and joined the media. A fine profession, I suppose." Tuck cleared his throat in an exaggerated manner and pointed to the business reporter from the *Dallas Morning News*.

The reporter smiled and waved.

Tuck cleared his throat a second time, his eyes filling with emotion. "And now my baby girl is getting married. And to the future senator from Texas, no less."

A roar of applause erupted. Near the front of the crowd, Reece pulled their daughter tight against him.

"Lainie, sweetheart, may you always love one another as much as I love your mother." Tuck squeezed Claire before lifting his glass. "After nearly thirty years of marriage, my heart still skips a beat every time I look at this gal."

Claire leaned into the microphone. "And after thirty years of marriage, I can't believe that tired old line of his still works."

The crowd responded with laughter. Tuck took Claire's hand and led her from the stage. She cupped her left palm around Tuck's shoulder and placed her other hand in his. Together they held everyone's attention while they two-stepped around the dance floor as Lady Antebellum played their popular tune "I Run to You."

After the last note played, Tuck escorted Claire to where Garrett and Marcy stood applauding. Her husband grinned. "That's how it's done, Son."

Tuck lifted Claire's hand and lightly kissed her palm. The intimate gesture made her feel warm all over, or perhaps it was the balmy Texas evening — she wasn't sure.

The warm air carried the scent of blue bonnets mixed with —

Cigar smoke?

Across the dance floor, Sidney McAlvain

puffed away, sending plumes of blue-gray smoke into the air. He pinched Daisy on the backside, sending her into a fit of giggles. When she looked up and noticed Claire watching, she gave a little wave.

Despite what she was thinking, Claire smiled and waved back.

2

Lainie stepped from the dressing room, modeling dress number twenty-nine.

In Texas, finding the right wedding dress could be compared to hunting wild boars. Her daddy always told the boys, "You can shoot at any of 'em, but a trophy pig can only be found if you're willing to do the work to hunt one down."

"Oh, darlin'! That's the one," her mother whispered, sounding nearly breathless.

Lainie gazed at her reflection in the bank of mirrors, feeling very much the bride she would be in less than eight months. "You think so? I kind of liked the antebellum skirt with the crystal-studded train."

Her mom shook her head. "You've always been a bling child, but that dress with the big skirt makes you look like you stepped off the *Gone with the Wind* movie set."

"Oh, that's not true." Lainie looked to the boutique consultant for support. Unfortu-

38

nately, the woman peering over top her glasses knew who would be paying the bill and judiciously refrained from weighing in.

Lainie frowned. "It's pretty, but the dress doesn't send the right message."

Her mother raised her eyebrows. "Message?"

"I think I have something we just got in from Milan you might be interested in. The design is an Alvina Valenta one-shoulder ruffle gown made of oyster silk-faced satin with a modified A-line silhouette." The woman slipped the glasses up into her hairline. "I believe the style would meet both your tastes, especially if Alvina added a Swarovski crystal-studded belt and you wore a chapel veil, also scattered with crystals." She pulled her mouth into a tight smile and waited for approval.

Her mom clasped her hands. "Oh, that sounds exquisite." She looked at Lainie with a hopeful expression. "Don't you think, sweetheart?"

Lainie hated to admit it, but in the end, the suggested gown was stunning — and finally something both she and her mother could agree on.

They'd been a little at odds over this whole wedding business from the start, it seemed. Her mama had wanted to host the ceremony out at the ranch with Pastor Richards officiating, an offer Lainie immediately and adamantly declined.

She and Reece had wanted a dignified affair at the Dallas Country Club — that is, until Reece's dad reminded them over dinner how the club's membership admissions, particularly its often criticized by-invitation-only exclusivity, might give the wrong impression for a candidate who held political aspirations beyond the borders of the Lone Star state. "Did you forget how the press reacted when Dick Cheney's wife played a simple round of golf?" he cautioned. "Other areas of the country don't always view these things the same way we do here in Texas, Son."

Despite her rather healthy pout, her handsome dark-haired fiancé caved to his father, and plans had been amended. Only after Reece promised a Christmas season wedding at the Dallas Arboretum, with blowout fireworks over White Rock Lake, had she pulled in her lip and rewarded him with a smile.

To make her mama happy, a special Chihuly exhibit would serve as the backdrop when nearly a thousand guests gathered to celebrate her magical evening and — if the election went as planned — the night she would become Mrs. Reece Sandell, wife of the newly elected US senator from Texas, the youngest at only thirty-four years old.

And Lord willing, one day she'd raise her children in the White House.

Never mind she'd overheard Andrew Sandell tease his son he should be very careful marrying a girl whose daddy calls her Princess.

Well, she knew what her grandma, God bless her, would say to that. "If the glass slipper fits, wear it."

With the dress fitting finished, Lainie gathered her bag while her mother called for the car. "Mom, can you believe we only have eight months until the ceremony? I don't see how we're possibly going to get everything done."

Her mother slipped her sunglasses on as they headed for the front door. "Baby, I wish you'd reconsider and have Pastor Richards officiate. How's that going to look with Daddy an elder and all?" They stepped from the air-conditioned lobby into the warmth of the sunny May day. "Besides, proper etiquette dictates the bride's family chooses who performs the ceremony. Are we rewriting the laws of the South now?"

Lainie slid her own sunglasses in place. "Mama, don't start again."

41

Their driver opened the car door and her mother slid into the plush backseat. "What am I going to tell the ladies at Bible study? I'll be renounced as chair of the missions gala this year."

Lainie ducked her head and followed her mother into the town car. "Aren't you being a little overdramatic?"

Her mom pulled out a mirror and re-applied her lipstick. "Well, maybe a little. But seriously, Lainie, I don't understand why Pastor Richards can't do the ceremony."

Lainie checked her phone for messages. "We already went over this. The Sandells count on financial support from their own church members for Reece's campaign. I'm picking my battles, and this isn't one of them. If Reece wants his pastor to perform the wedding ceremony, I see no reason not to consent." She slipped her phone back inside her bag. "Besides, it's too late to change things now."

Her mom opened the door of the tiny refrigerator and retrieved a bottle of water. "Want one, honey?"

Lainie shook her head.

Her mother made an awful face. "Well, I don't like this pastor thing. Not one bit," she said and unscrewed the bottle. "Just promise me the ceremony will be dignified. Some of these wedding officiants love to hear their own voices and just go on too long. I hate when wedding ceremonies get too preachy. Takes the focus off the bride."

"Oh, Mama." Lainie sighed. "We've got the dress ordered. Now let's just focus on tonight."

Goodness knows only the Lord could help Lainie make it through the next months leading up to her magical day without killing her mother.

Claire parked her hands on her hips. "This won't work," she muttered out loud, despite being alone in the penthouse suite. "These pumps are the wrong color."

From the recesses of her mind, Claire could hear her mother's voice from years back. *Any woman can slip into a remarkable dress, Claire. A woman of fortune makes sure her shoes perfectly complement her outfit. Always look at a woman's shoes.*

Claire wrapped the tissue around the pumps and slid them back into their velvet-lined box. She tossed the container aside and made her way to the wall of windows overlooking the Dallas skyline, her feet padding across luxurious carpet. From the marble-topped table, she retrieved her cell phone and speed-dialed her personal shopper, peering out the window in the direction of the American Airlines Center while she waited for Tony to pick up.

"Hey, Claire. What can I do for you?"

"Tony, I need shoes. The pumps I planned to wear for the fundraiser tonight are the wrong shade of teal. Too dark."

"Well, girl, I've got just the thing. I received an email this morning that the Neiman Marcus buyers snagged two pair of Manolo Blahnik alligator boots. And one is in a shade of blue that will make the pattern in that dress scream!" He paused. "Be warned. They're pricey."

"They sound perfect! I'm at the Adolphus. Can you get them here no later than three?"

"Oh, absolutely." Tony chuckled under his breath. "Just wait until everyone gets a look at these boots."

Claire smiled with satisfaction. Tuck was totally devoted to her, but it never hurt to do everything possible to keep his eyes home on the range, if you get the picture.

After ending the call, Claire moved into the bathroom. She unscrewed the cap from the vanilla bottle she'd slipped into her overnight bag before leaving home. Carefully, she dripped the velvety brown liquid into the steaming bathwater, sending a

44

sweet aroma drifting up. Even though her dressing table at home was lined with bottles of every shape and size filled with some of the most expensive fragrances a woman could buy, she often still preferred this simple scent.

She'd learned the trick years ago while poring over beauty hints in her *Teen Beat* magazine. When Claire was growing up, her mother and her new husband had no problem jet-setting around Europe, leaving her to feed bum lambs with her dad every holiday. She'd needed some way to cover the hint of sheep hanging on her skin.

On the day they'd received the call that her mother had remarried, Claire heard her father crying in the middle of the night. Earlier in the day, he'd assured her nothing important would change. Nothing would alter his own love for her. In all the important ways, life would remain constant and Claire would be able to see her father as much as she wanted.

That was a lie, of course. With each passing year, Claire's mother found more excuses for keeping them apart, claiming summer travel was vital to her daughter's education, until finally Claire spent only Christmas holidays at her father's sheep ranch in San Angelo. There were, at that time, no cell phones, iPads, or Skype.

Her father died three weeks before Claire's graduation. By then, they barely knew one another. The days of climbing in her daddy's lap had turned to polite exchanges by telephone and across a dinner table. They lived worlds apart, in more ways than one. Remembering always left her feeling sad.

Claire stripped her clothes and laid them carefully over the sofa back for the maid to hang later. She grabbed her favorite lounging robe and draped the silk garment over her arm. Minutes later, she stepped into the waiting tub.

Ahh, the warm water felt good.

Leaning her head back, she let her mind drift to the details of the morning.

The gown Lainie had chosen for her wedding was stunning. By far, better than the one she'd almost set her heart on. She would have looked like Scarlett O'Hara dancing in that full-skirted monstrosity.

Sure, the Alvina Valenta was priced twenty thousand more. But the dress was worth every penny. Lainie looked gorgeous in it.

Now if she could only convince her headstrong daughter to reconsider Pastor Richards. Maybe Tuck could come up with something to sway her. If her husband could find time, that is.

In times past, Claire's husband would have endured her sharing details of the wedding. But last week she'd tried to ask his opinion about the seating arrangement at the rehearsal dinner, and he'd brushed her off and made his way back out to the offices. He'd fallen asleep on a sofa and hadn't returned to the house until late the next morning.

Claire closed her eyes and slid further down in the warm, scented water until her toes barely touched the other end of the massive tub. From this position, with just her face not immersed, the only interruption to complete silence was her beating heart — *thu-thump, thu-thump.*

No matter what Tuck promised, there always seemed to be more cattle to purchase, more futures to analyze, more clients calling at all hours. If anything, Tuck was at his desk more. When he wasn't roving Texas finding the next cattle deal.

Claire startled at the feel of fingers brushing across her collarbone. She threw open her eyes, then broke into an immediate smile.

Speak of the devil.

She lifted from the water, all disapproval scrubbed clean with one look into his deep blue eyes.

"You'd better be careful . . ." Her husband flashed a teasing smile. "We might end up missing the party."

Claire squeezed water from her dripping hair. "Well, mister. Maybe I won't mind," she bantered back.

Tuck grabbed the thick bath towel from the warming rack, draped it over his arm, and offered his hand. She stepped from the tub and leaned into him. As he wrapped the plush fabric across her back, Claire tilted her head and met his kiss.

After all these years, he still made her feel desired.

"How long before we have to make our appearance downstairs?" he whispered, his breath hot on her ear.

Claire slapped at his straying hand and tried to finish drying. "Your timing is a bit off. We can't — really," she insisted. "The gala starts in less than three hours, and the stylist still has to do my hair."

Despite her protestations, her husband pulled the towel away. Dropping it to the floor, he took her by the hand and slowly led her to the bed. "So, you wear your hair down tonight."

Claire smiled. She knew better than to argue. Tuck had a way of talking people into what he wanted.

■ ■ ■ ■

"Honey, could you zip me?" Claire backed up to where Tuck was sitting, drinking a glass of sweet tea while poring through the pages of the *Dallas Morning News.* He pulled the paper to his lap and looked over his reading glasses.

"Sure. Bend down."

"I spoke to Lainie again this morning about having Pastor Richards officiate."

Tuck pulled up her zipper. "And did you get anywhere?"

Claire knew a grin had formed on Tuck's face. "No, not exactly. But then, you know our daughter. Once she makes up that mind of hers, there's little I can say to alter her plans."

Of her three children, Lainie was definitely the most stubborn. She'd been born with six silver spoons in her mouth and knew it.

Once, when their daughter was nearly three, she'd climbed down the stairs still in her footie pajamas, rubbing sleep from her eyes with a sour look on her face.

"What's the matter, sweetheart?" Claire asked with her arms held out. "Did someone come take your happy away?"

Lainie frowned. "Are you gonna boss me today?"

Garrett, on the other hand, would melt into compliance with only a stern look from one of his parents. A pleaser.

And the baby — ha, now two decades old. A good scolding would only make him giggle. Max had found humor in everything. Still did.

Like most mothers of grown children, Claire constantly wondered how time had passed so quickly. And how three kids from the same parents could turn out so very different.

Tuck kissed the back of her neck, then patted her shoulder. "Well, Richards will understand. Besides, last week I placed a market order that netted the church a truckload of money."

Claire stood. "You did?"

"Enough to build that youth center the elders voted for last month. Honey, I think you're making too much of all this. Everything will turn out fine. You'll see."

She moved to the chest of drawers. "Ah, you're probably right," she said, putting the matter to rest in her mind. If Tuck wasn't worried about offending Pastor Richards, what sense did it make for her to keep stressing over the situation?

She glanced at the clock. "You'd better hurry, Tuck." She turned and gave her husband a pointed look. "We're a little behind schedule."

Claire ignored his wicked grin, grabbed the diamond and sapphire earrings from the dresser, and walked to the mirror.

In the reflection, she could see Tuck watching her.

She gazed at her image. Tony had scored again. The blue Vera Wang halter dress, coupled with the boots, was just right. Claire stepped back and posed in front of her husband. "So, do you like the dress?"

"Very nice." Tuck repositioned the newspaper and went on reading. From behind it, he added, "But, babe?"

"Yes?"

"I liked what you had on in the tub better."

Despite numerous extravagant hotels in downtown Dallas, including the new Omni, the Masseys preferred to spend overnight stays in the iconic Adolphus. *Lavish* best described the hundred-year-old cherished landmark, with its rich paneling, Brussels tapestries, and English Regency furniture.

Claire and Tuck stepped out of the elevator on the lobby level of the hotel, then rode the escalator past the famous ornate brass chandelier. They were running a bit late. In addition to the unplanned delay upstairs, Tuck's phone had not stopped ringing.

Inside the Grand Ballroom, Lainie rushed over. "Where have y'all been? We're minutes from being served."

Tuck kissed his daughter's forehead. "Sorry, Princess. My fault."

The room was filled with deep-pocket contributors from around the country, including more than one celebrity. Claire recognized several men standing near the bar — incredibly successful doctors and lawyers from Preston Hollow, many fellow members of the Petroleum Club. Over by the wall sat Lisa Blue Baron. Claire didn't know how the flamboyantly wealthy widow had possibly weathered those awful rumors of her husband's cover-up of John Edwards's affair with Reille Hunter. This town liked to place the rich on pedestals, then knock them off for sport.

Out of the corner of her eye, she saw Glory Sandell heading their way. "Well, you two. It's about time." Glory gave Claire a sweeping once-over, then leaned forward and exchanged cheek-to-cheek kisses. "Andrew and I were afraid some new cattle deal had pulled you away from the festivities."

She laughed tightly.

With his arm, Tuck pulled Claire close. "Not exactly," he said with a conspiratorial chuckle. She poked him with her elbow.

Glory's hand moved to the diamond-laden chandelier earring at her right ear. She arched her eyebrows. "Oh . . ." she murmured. "Let's get you seated, shall we?"

Tuck ignored Lainie's scolding look and placed his hand at the small of Claire's back as they followed Glory past tuxedoed servers in white gloves placing salad plates around linen-draped tables set with the finest china and crystal.

When they'd reached their designated table up front, Andrew Sandell stood to greet them. "There you are."

Tuck gave his friend a slap on the back. "Sorry we're a bit late," he said, taking his seat. Tuck greeted Garrett and Marcy with a nod before pulling a linen napkin onto his lap. "By the way, Andrew, I got the price locked in on those thirty weights in Amarillo. I think this deal's going to turn you a tidy profit, my friend."

Claire had turned her attention to her pear and arugula salad when Reece stepped into view and made his way to the podium. The crowd went wild with applause. Overhead, strains of "God Bless Texas" played while confetti rained onto the stage. In the audience, a crowd of tuxedoed and sequin-gowned people waved paddle signs that said "Reece Sandell: A New Way to Stay the Same."

"Thank you," Reece said. "Thank you very much." The dark-haired hopeful tried to settle the crowd by holding up his hands, but his supporters kept chanting.

"Sandell . . . Sandell . . . Sandell."

Grinning, the young candidate pulled his iPhone from the pocket of his tailored suit, and a large screen descended behind where he stood. The room quieted.

Reece cleared his throat and bent over the microphone. "Will y'all excuse me just a moment?" He ducked his head and worked his thumbs furiously.

On the massive screen appeared his tweet as he typed, "Stand 4 TX. Vote @RSandell. 2gether we will make a #difference!"

The supporters in the room exploded once again with deafening approval of the contrast of their candidate's youth with the ways of his much older forerunners — and his opponent, a crusty older woman known for her raspy smoker's voice and mean-spirited television ads.

Claire didn't normally follow politics. But if this crowd's reaction was any indication,

Reece was a shoo-in.

Tuck leaned close. "That boy has what it takes," he said, mirroring her own thoughts.

Reece finished his speech, whipping everyone into a frenzy of giving. Claire found herself pondering the very real notion that by this time next year, her daughter might actually be living in Washington, DC, as a senator's wife.

Just as easily, Claire conjured an image of receiving a White House Christmas card in the mail with a photo of Reece and Lainie standing in front of a tree in the Blue Room, with wide smiles and Reece's precise hairline touched with gray. Lainie, of course, would never turn gray. No respectable woman from Texas ever would.

Humor aside, the implication of what may lay ahead for her baby girl couldn't be denied. Claire swallowed the emotion building in her throat.

Tuck stood and clinked his glass with the tines of his silver fork. "Excuse me," he hollered across the room. "Could I have everyone's attention, please?" A campaign worker rushed over and positioned a microphone in Tuck's hand. "Thank you. I'd like to say just a few words."

Claire held her breath. She expected what might be coming.

"As this young man's future father-in-law and one of his most staunch supporters, I would like to be the first to make a contribution tonight. Son" — Tuck smiled broadly — "last week I instructed my attorney to file the necessary paperwork with the Secretary of State to start my own political action committee in support of you. Claire and I are kicking off this evening with a donation of one *million* dollars." He slipped a bank note from his pocket and held it high. He grinned. "Ah, why stop there?" Tuck pulled a second note from his other pocket. "*Two* million!"

Claire watched as Andrew Sandell's expression filled with astonishment. Reece's father tossed his linen napkin to the table and moved to where Tuck stood, patting him on the back enthusiastically, while on stage, Reece led the crowd in wild applause.

Glory forced a quick smile, then mouthed an appropriate "Thank you."

What some considered crass grandstanding, Claire knew was simply her husband's generosity, stemming from a heart fashioned from years of caring for his alcoholic mother. Often his belly had remained empty while his mother filled hers with pretzels and tequila at the local bar.

An only child, he'd once confided to her

in the quiet of their darkened room after a night of lovemaking that he'd been the one to find his mother dead with her Bible open to Proverbs 23. He was fifteen.

The morning after Tuck's confession, Claire waited until she was alone. She retrieved her Bible from her bedside table, lifted the leather cover, and flipped to the middle. Her eyes scanned across the open page before landing on verse thirty-five.

They struck me, but I did not become ill;
They beat me, but I did not know it.
When shall I awake?
I will seek another drink.

In some ways, Tuck was still hungry — and his hunger had nothing to do with food.

Claire glanced around. Small pockets of people were moving around now, chatting. Music played from the live string quartet on the stage. To the right, Lainie stood by Reece's side, laughing at something the bald man in front of them said.

Claire leaned to kiss Tuck's cheek when two men wearing dark suits stepped forward from the crowd. Another man with a camera hoisted on his shoulder followed close behind.

"Mr. Massey?"

Tuck turned, his puzzled look quickly darkening. He squinted against the bright light of the camera. "Yes? What can I do for you gentlemen?"

The taller of the two flashed a badge. "I'm afraid you are going to have to come with us."

Claire's heart skipped a beat. She reached for her husband's hand. "Tuck?"

A look of resignation crossed Tuck's features. He turned to Garrett. "Call Ranger Jennings on your cell."

Garrett quickly pulled his iPhone from his pocket. "Dad, what's going on?"

"Just call him!" Tuck said.

In the background, Claire could hear a hush fall over the crowd. The shorter guy in the suit stepped forward with a pair of handcuffs.

"Theodore Massey, you are under arrest."

3

Claire tried hard to focus on the man before her, not on the chaos she knew was still going on downstairs. "Ranger, what are you saying?"

Tuck's attorney glanced around their hotel suite, his hand fiddling with his felt cowboy hat. "Claire," Ranger began, his voice taking on the tone of someone speaking with a child, "from the looks of things, a federal grand jury has indicted Tuck on multiple counts of felony wire fraud, mail fraud, false representation, and criminal forfeiture."

Garrett paced the floor, his face flushed. "But what does all that mean?"

Ranger's features grew grim. He placed his hat on the coffee table and pulled a thick, stapled document from the briefcase at his feet. "I'm afraid the government believes your father engaged in illegal activity whereby he ran a Ponzi scheme of sorts."

"A what?" Marcy asked, looking quickly

at Garrett for understanding, then back at Ranger.

"It's alleged Tuck sold phantom cattle." Ranger cleared his throat and thumbed through the pages. "Another way of putting it is that he sold the same cows to multiple parties, each time collecting funds from buyers." Looking up, his eyes moved in Claire's direction. "I've only been able to briefly read the indictment, but as I see it, the grand jury findings also show Tuck managed to secure bank loans with the fake cattle and took money from investors to feed cattle that didn't exist."

Claire's heart pounded. She shook her head vehemently. "No — no, Tuck would never do something like that."

Ranger released a heavy sigh. "Look, the firm will get this sorted out. But I have to warn you, there must be substantial evidence for the grand jury to issue this indictment. Right now our focus will be damage control. I'm not going to lie and tell you this situation is not very serious," he explained, his face flushed with sympathy.

She swallowed against a knot forming in her throat. "Do they want Tuck to spend time in . . . in prison?"

"Let's not focus on possibilities we have no way to ascertain at this time. But I want

60

a lid on all this," he said. "None of you is to speak about Tuck's arrest or any of his business dealings to anyone when we leave this room, and that includes friends. Anything — and I emphasize *anything* — you say could be used as evidence against Tuck." Ranger paused. "We don't know how far all this might extend. Where is your younger son?"

Claire took a deep breath. "He's — uh, Max skipped this event. He's likely at his place. We'll alert him as soon as possible. But he'll know not to say anything."

Garrett paced in front of Claire. "Oh, c'mon, Mom. Max works for a newspaper."

"But this is family." She stood. "Look, these accusations are all a misunderstanding. You know your father would never do such things." Claire moved to the window, drew back the heavy draperies, and peeked out at the city lights. Likely most of the guests had left the gala by now, except for the hangers-on. The ones who wanted to enjoy the details of this sordid example of government gone wrong.

Claire whipped around and pointed her manicured nail. "Ranger, I want y'all to prepare a lawsuit. For defamation of character and — and whatever else you can claim. Throw the book at whoever is heading this up. I don't care what it costs."

"Mom, stop." Lainie's voice broke into Claire's tirade. "You don't get it."

Garrett flinched. He turned his attention to Ranger. "Where's Dad now?"

Ranger scratched at his sideburns. "I don't know exactly, but my guess is the US marshals transported him to FCI in Fort Worth."

Marcy looped her hand through Garrett's arm. "FCI?"

"Federal Correction Institution. A low-security holding facility. He'll be in no danger," he hurried to add, likely for Claire's benefit.

US marshals . . . holding facility . . . no danger.

Claire's conscious mind rejected these foreign concepts while a small voice inside her head argued. Her life had just become a roadside bomb with few survivors. "What do we do now?" Her voice cracked as she pushed the words past her dry throat.

"I've made some calls to my partners. We'll be meeting as soon as I get back to the office." Ranger Jennings slid his hat onto his head. "News will break soon. That'll mean increased security for all of you, and out at Legacy. In the meantime, the firm will work to prepare a statement for you to release at the appropriate time."

"What kind of statement?" Garrett stood and followed Ranger to the door.

Tuck's attorney paused, his hand on the doorknob. "At this early stage, we'll want to stay noncommittal. We'll simply say we're investigating and intend to vigorously defend Tuck against the accusations made."

Lainie leapt from her chair. "But wait! What do I tell Reece?" Her fingers slid through her hair. She moaned. "And his supporters?"

Claire's mind raced to the hundreds of people who had witnessed Tuck being taken into custody. With jaws clenched, she recalled the image of Tuck's hands behind his back — handcuffed.

She took a deep breath, trying to calm her wildly beating heart.

Surely none of this was true. Tomorrow she'd wake realizing she'd been caught up in some bad dream. She'd relay the surreal events to Tuck over eggs Benedict and sausages, and together they'd laugh. He'd torment her with a silly wink and blow her a kiss across the table.

Oh, Tuck, what have you done?

A hushed sob escaped Claire's carefully constructed emotional levee. She buried her head in her hands.

This wasn't a bad dream — this was a nightmare.

4

Ironic how the "nice" girls his mother pushed on him were often the most forward when it came right down to things, a fact Max argued with his mother on more than one occasion, before giving in to her constant attempts to manage his love life.

"You could come upstairs if you want. My roommate's staying over with her boyfriend tonight." The pretty interior design major from TCU put her hand on his arm, clearly signaling an invitation.

"Nah. I appreciate it and all, but I have to get up early. I have a deadline tomorrow and I need to get some shut-eye so my head will be sharp in the morning."

Max hated turning her down, but word would get back to his mother if he crossed the line with another of her friend's daughters.

Mom, bless her snooty Texas heart, would run tell Dad, creating one more wedge. The last thing he needed was to have to sit and listen to another of his father's thirty-minute expositions on responsibility and the Massey family image. Or worse, feel Garrett's disapproving stare-down while he stood in the corner with his arms folded, nodding in agreement.

Max doubted Garrett had stayed over with Marcy until after they were wed. Yup, he was sure of it.

And Lainie — well, he adored his sister. But hello, that girl could do no wrong. She had Mom and Dad wrapped.

"You sure?" The girl scooted closer, letting her skirt rise a little higher.

Max pulled her close and kissed her. The girl's lips were soft and anxious. Perhaps he should reconsider, face the consequences tomorrow.

In the background, a radio announcer's voice cut into the heat being generated inside the Jeep.

"In breaking news, a grand jury has indicted Texas financier Theodore Massey on multiple counts of fraud and racketeering. In a stunning move by federal agents, Mr. Massey was led in handcuffs from the Grand Ballroom at the Adolphus Hotel, where he and his family were attending a fund-raiser gala for US senatorial candidate

Reece Sandell. Sandell, who is engaged to Mr. Massey's daughter, declined comment at this time."

Max pulled back. The air inside his Jeep instantly felt weighted, as if he were breathing lead. "Turn it up," he shouted.

The girl frowned and straightened. "What?"

"Look, you need to get out now. I gotta go."

"But —"

"Now!" he barked. "Get out."

The instant he heard the door click shut and knew his date was a safe distance away, Max threw his Jeep into gear. The tires screeched as he tore down the oak-lined street.

From her seat in the helicopter, Claire scoured the ground below. Even in the blackness of night, she could see a tangle of headlights at the gate leading into Legacy Ranch.

She looked across at Garrett, who sat clutching his wife's trembling hand. Despite their wearing headphones to soften the sound, the loud whirr of blades drowned out any attempt to talk, even if they had wanted to.

Thank goodness Garrett had the good

sense to know driving home was no option. They'd never make it through the mass of reporters camped at the gate waiting for a glimpse of the family who'd just been harpooned in a very public fishbowl.

Claire wished Lainie had come home with them, but her daughter had vehemently refused. "I need to talk with Reece," she'd declared, her eyes wild with hurt and confusion.

"Honey, it's far too late tonight," Claire told her. But Lainie said she'd rather stay over in the hotel if necessary. Clearly, leaving her daughter alone had not been a good idea. But Claire had been too fatigued to fight.

As the helicopter descended onto the landing pad, Claire checked her phone again to see if Max had called or left a text.

Nothing.

Minutes later, she ducked and followed her son and daughter-in-law out the hinged doorway. The moving air from the propellers caught her hair, lifting her highlighted tresses into a wild dance circling her head. She'd often shifted a scarf in place to avoid that very thing. But tonight, what did it really matter?

Claire waved for Garrett and Marcy to follow her to the house. Her older son shook his head. "We're heading to our place," he shouted. "We need some time alone. To sort all this out."

She understood. The mountain of things to consider loomed higher than Mount Everest, and for a gal who'd grown up in the flat of Texas, that idea felt overwhelming.

She and Garrett would meet with Ranger again in the morning. By then, her husband's attorney might know a little more. She'd tell him she wanted to see Tuck. Obviously something had gone terribly wrong in Tuck's business, but she sensed things could get blown out of proportion. Especially by overzealous prosecutors and the media.

They'd have to hire a publicist — a good one. From the looks of the gate out there, reporters would no doubt spin this story into a frenzied mess. The Masseys needed to put out an official statement, and fast. Curb the public's appetite for a salacious story that simply was not true.

No doubt Reece's campaign had taken a hit. But with the right handling, the impact could be contained.

She rounded the corner. Both her feet and her heart stopped.

Their circular drive was littered with strange vehicles. Claire stepped closer to one of the black cars and eyed the license plate.

US Marshal Service?

The double doors leading to the entry foyer opened. Out stepped two men dressed in dark suits. They carried large blue plastic bins.

"What's going on here?" Claire asked, moving forward.

Margarita stood in the doorway. The older woman clasped her hands. "Mrs. Massey, I tried to — I didn't know what to do." Tears pooled and her housekeeper shook her head.

Claire held up a hand. "Don't worry, Margarita. I've got this." She turned to another agent carrying a computer in his arms. "Excuse me! What is going on here? Could somebody explain where you think you're taking our things?"

Even as the words left her mouth, Claire recalled a number of movies where she'd seen this very image played out. In her gut, she instinctively suspected the answer. Still, she drew a deep breath and continued in the strongest voice she could muster. "Do you have a warrant or something?"

At the same time, she pulled her phone from her bag and worked her thumbs, furiously texting a message to Garrett.

A man who seemed to be in charge

stepped forward. He showed a badge. "I'm Deputy Chief Hodges — US Attorney's Office. I head up the Fraud Task Force." He nodded to a second man who wore a jacket with the words "US Marshal" on the backside. The man with the jacket offered up a stapled document to Claire.

Hodges's liquid black eyes turned serious. "We're here to execute a warrant for search and seizure. You will be provided a receipt for all property confiscated pursuant to the judge's orders."

"Judge's orders?" Claire asked, her voice now timid. She didn't blink. She wasn't sure she even breathed.

Margarita looked to the sky and muttered, "Oh, sweet Jesus. Help the Masseys."

A deep trembling rolled through Claire's gut, and she swallowed a wave of nausea. Strangers had rifled through their personal belongings. In an agent's hands, she spotted their family photo albums. Her scrapbooks.

Oh, Lord, help.

Claire's knees turned weak and seemed to fold like cards beneath her. She plummeted to the shiny tiles of the front porch, next to a manicured shrub in a ceramic pot.

Margarita rushed to her side. When the agents tried to assist, her trusted housekeeper shooed at them with her hand towel.

"No, I've got *mi la jefa,*" she said, reverting to her native language.

In the distance, the sound of a car engine gunned. Within seconds, Max's yellow Jeep broke into view from the dark lane. His tires screeched. She heard a car door slam shut.

"Hey, what's going on?" Max rushed forward. Margarita stepped aside as he knelt beside Claire.

Claire glanced up, her eyes pooled with tears. Her younger son's arms enveloped her shoulders and he helped her to her feet.

Biting her bottom lip, she leaned her head against his shoulder. "Max, do something," she whispered. "Can't you stop them?"

As agents continued moving boxes into the waiting trailer, Garrett thundered up the steps. Marcy followed close behind, shaking her head wildly. "Garrett, didn't I tell you this would happen?"

"They've got a warrant," Max explained before his older brother had a chance to ask.

"A search warrant?" Confusion and anger packed Garrett's words.

The man from the US Attorney's Office stepped forward. "We've already collected materials from your father's personal office. We'll need access to the corporate office and your place as well."

Marcy's hand flew to her chest. "Our house?" She looked to Garrett. Raw fear quickly spread across her features.

Suddenly the implication of Tuck's arrest dawned on Claire. These enforcement officers were after blood. They wouldn't stop until her entire family festered in their sick attempt to take Tuck down.

If proven true, the allegations against Tuck held the gravity of a boulder rolling out of control. Everyone in the path could potentially be mowed under with the force.

Claire's mind replayed the panicked look in Lainie's eyes as the handcuffs clicked shut around her father's wrists, the anguish on Margarita's face, her sons now trying to hide their own surge of emotions. Garrett wiped tears from Marcy's eyes, quietly assuring his wife everything would be all right. In that instant, Claire knew one thing for certain.

Her family's world had forever changed.

5

Lainie sat in the back of her mother's town car, wishing momentarily she'd find the tiny cabinet underneath the darkened window stocked with those tiny bottles of alcohol. Unfortunately, except for rare occasions, the Masseys rarely drank — well, except for her younger brother. Max often broke family rules.

Lainie grimaced. Who was she kidding? No amount of liquor could make her feel better. Not tonight.

Her mother's driver looked in the rearview mirror. "You okay, Miss Lainie?"

She nodded and assured Henry she was all right. Which was a lie, of course. They both knew Lainie was anything but all right.

The evening had been perfect, right up until Daddy made his surprise contribution (something they'd planned together — not even her mother knew). She and Reece stood near the stage with Mr. Findley, a

Sandell family friend with a lot of influence and even more money. "That speech was magnificent," he'd said, when out of the corner of her eye, she saw men in black suits heading toward the stage.

At first she'd thought they might be security, and a slight sense of alarm flowed beneath her calm exterior. But worry turned to confusion when the men stopped at her daddy's table.

The next minutes were tattooed in her memory, each second inked with wretched precision, the image of her daddy's hand-cuffed hands indelibly piercing her soul.

Lainie closed her eyes against fresh tears.

She'd been sitting here in front of Reece's family home on Beverly Drive for nearly a half hour, paralyzed with emotion like a pathetic crazy person.

Like most of the residents in the posh Highland Park area of Dallas, Reece's parents lived in a stunning mansion. From the cars congregated in the circular driveway of the French Mediterranean masterpiece, Lainie could tell Reece was inside with his parents and campaign staff — all likely in serious damage-control mode. Even from across the street, Lainie caught glimpses of Andrew Sandell pacing in front of the massive arched windows.

After the arrest, she'd hurriedly followed Reece and his entourage through the lobby. Reece's father had been the one to suggest she stay behind.

"Your family needs you," Reece said in consolation as he allowed himself to be whisked down the escalators. His campaign manager folded in close behind, leaving her standing in her pine-colored Nicole Miller sheath with matching stilettos, feeling stunned and very much all alone.

What could she possibly be so afraid of? Reece loved her.

She should go inside. Lainie was, after all, soon to be Reece Sandell's wife. She deserved be there, by his side. Not pushed away like . . . well, like collateral damage.

Sure, no one would claim having your future father-in-law arrested in front of hundreds of your potential campaign contributors to be a good thing. But Bill Clinton's indiscretion with an intern never unseated him from the throne of public adoration.

So Reece would fall a few points in the polls for a week or so, or however long it took Daddy to get this mess straightened out, but then the spin doctors would play the scenario as nothing more than a candidate standing loyal by his fiancée and her family in their time of need. The worst thing — the media might reference the overzealous federal agents during their wedding coverage. But by then, all eyes would be on her and that strikingly gorgeous gown, especially the way the oyster-colored ruffles looked against her skin.

Britain had their Princess Kate, and soon Lainie Massey Sandell would go on display in Texas's state trophy cabinet.

Her daddy always said his little girl's star wasn't meant to just hang in the sky and twinkle. Nope, he claimed her quasar presence would streak across life's horizon, leaving a trail of sparkle in her wake.

Lainie wasn't sure she could believe him. Her biggest admirer was a tad biased, just by virtue of loving her since she was tiny as a minute. His words, not hers.

Even her grandmother had predicted she'd live larger than most.

The night Lainie had met Reece she wondered, perhaps for the first time, if her dad and grandmother might indeed be prophets of sorts. Perhaps her future would be delightfully bright.

Lainie dreamed of rocketing past her mother's social status to a whole other sphere. And admit it — a senator's wife, maybe even the first lady . . . Those titles held radiance few could outshine.

Lainie checked her phone again. Why hadn't Reece answered her texts?

She glanced at her wristwatch. Twenty minutes. She'd wait that much longer — then she'd march across the street and demand to be included.

Lainie's mother would scold that was too assertive. A proper lady would bide her time and let the man come to her. But she held a more progressive view. Hadn't her saucy nature attracted Reece Sandell from that very first night?

Lainie placed her phone on the seat and reached into the refrigerator for an ice-cold bottle of water. She unscrewed the lid.

It had been Christmas time, a year and a half ago.

Lainie, home on holiday break from UT-Austin, begged off going to the holiday pageant at Abundant Hills. Instead, she headed into the city to meet up with girl-friends, where they planned to check out the trendy Lizard Lounge in Deep Ellum. First they'd shop a bit in Highland Park and eat.

It was her idea to board the horse-drawn carriage and tour the elaborately decorated neighborhood, a tradition from childhood. At first the girls balked at the idea, but Lainie argued they had plenty of time. "Besides," she teased, "those little blue Christmas boxes I just bought will find their way back to Tiffany's if you guys fail to give in."

That night, the first time Lainie saw Reece Sandell, she thought he looked a lot like Tom Cruise. The early one with the clean-cut, chiseled jawline and short dark hair. Not the version often seen lately, his hair long and unkempt. She hated when celebrities didn't feel the need to keep up their appearance.

The tour was about to start when Reece rushed up to the carriage hand in hand with a petite gal dressed in tight jeans and salmon-colored furry UGGs. Lainie thought the girl with perky, short-cropped hair looked a bit ridiculous. Did she think she was spending the holidays in Sun Valley, or what? This was Texas, for goodness' sake. The only boots anyone wore in this state were cowboy boots. Besides, the outside temperature in Dallas climbed near seventy degrees, a southern standard in December.

The carriage barely rounded onto Beverly Drive when Lainie noticed Reece staring in her direction. He glanced away, seeming embarrassed at having been caught. To cover, he adjusted the collar of his button-down shirt and politely turned his attention back to Miss Perky.

The corners of Lainie's lips pulled upward as the carriage rolled past mansions decorated in holiday splendor. It was a well-known fact that Highland Park homeowners flaunted their wealth with LED lights and electricity this time of year.

Several blocks into the tour, the driver — a round gentleman with a bulbous nose — pulled the carriage to a stop next to a sidewalk filled with people strolling and looking at the houses. With his red-and-gold-uniformed arm, he pulled a cooler from the space near his feet. "Would y'all like some refreshments?" he asked.

He pulled several small, frosty bottles of Dr Pepper from the cooler, like those Lainie had seen at the Cracker Barrel Old Country Store. He stood and moved to pass them out to the six people inside the carriage. As he neared, Lainie caught an unpleasant whiff of alcohol. Apparently, the chap's drink was spiked with something stronger than what they were having.

"Oh, let's make a toast." Miss Perky held up her tiny commemorative bottle.

Lainie shrugged. "Yeah, okay." Her friends nodded.

Reece's date smiled as if she'd just won the stinking lottery. "Uh, let's see . . ." she began. "Oh, I know. I'd like to toast —"

Before she could finish, a full-sized poodle broke free of its owner and headed toward the carriage. The dog barked, causing the horses to startle. The buggy lurched.

The bottle slipped from Miss Perky's grasp, shattering when it hit the floor.

Lainie and the girl next to her both gasped.

Reece steadied himself. "Be careful," he said. "There's broken glass everywhere." He turned to his date. "Are you okay?"

The gal frowned. "I — I think so."

The carriage lurched forward again, this time with greater force. The driver stood and tried to gain control, but it was too late. He lost his footing and toppled back, landing against Miss Perky with his legs in the air and his own Dr Pepper draining into those pretty furry boots.

Reece's date shrieked.

He stood.

In what seemed like one movement, Lainie handed off her bottle to her friend, leapt up, and in two long steps maneuvered into the driver's seat up front. She grabbed for the reins and pulled back. "Hey, now. Hey, now," she said in a calming voice. The horses immediately responded and slowed to a clip-clop just before the carriage entered a busy intersection.

From a seat at the back, one of the passengers blurted, "Whew, that was close."

Lainie heard Reece ask if everyone was all right. She listened as he calmed his overwrought date, telling her she was safe. "But I'm all sticky and wet now," the girl whined as they passed a group of carolers singing "We Wish You a Merry Christmas."

Back in the parking lot, Reece thanked Lainie for her quick action. "You were amazing," he said, his grin releasing deep dimples. "I can't believe how fast you moved."

Lainie laughed. "Had a little practice."

"Oh?" he said, leaning forward.

"Are you coming?" Miss Perky asked, clearly annoyed with the way the evening was turning out, and especially with the exchange between her date and the Texas blonde who'd saved the day.

Before they parted, Lainie caught Reece staring again. Only this time, he didn't look away.

The following morning, Margarita knocked on Lainie's bedroom door. "Ah-yee, amiga . . . somebody got a special delivery."

Lainie pulled her sleepy head from the pillow and perched on her elbows. "What?"

Margarita held up a vase overflowing with deep red roses. Probably twenty or more blooms instantly filled her room with a sweet perfume.

The card simply read,

To the brave cowgirl who saved the day (or night, as the case might be). Would you have dinner with me? I'll be waiting at Wolfgang Puck's at the top of Reunion Tower — 6:00 p.m.

A year later, Reece and Lainie rode the carriage through the decorated streets again. This time, Reece brought his own bottle of Dr Pepper with a red satin ribbon tied around the neck holding a two-carat diamond engagement ring. "With my drive and your spunk, we'll take the world by storm," he'd said. That was the plan.

Until tonight.

"Wait here, Henry. I'll let you know if I'm staying." Lainie climbed from the car. She straightened her dress. The light from the streetlamp caught her ring. She counted that a good sign and headed for the Sandells' massive front entry.

She'd barely rung the bell when the door opened.

Glory Sandell's heels clicked against the

polished tile. "Who is it, Darla?" Reece's mom peeked around the uniformed house-keeper. "Lainie," she said, her tone curt. "Reece is upstairs. In bed."

"I need to talk to him." Lainie hated the childlike sound of her own voice as she waited to be invited inside.

"I — I don't think that's a good idea."

"What do you mean? He's my fiancé, and I want to speak with him."

Andrew Sandell appeared, entering from a doorway Lainie knew led to the dining area. His expression turned to stonelike resolve. He motioned Lainie inside but made their position clear. "Much has tran-spired this evening. Under the circum-stances, we think it's best if you talk things over with Reece later. He's been through an awful lot tonight."

"You have no idea the implications —" Glory added.

Andrew cut her off. "What Glory means is, we'll need to sort all this out. But not tonight."

So the Sandells were going to punish her — push her away, tell her to go. "Fine," she said bitterly.

And now came the regret.

Reece loved her. In the morning, they'd work all this out. But Lainie would never forget the way she'd been slighted.

Going forward, Lainie would pretend to overlook the Sandells' treatment. Even so, Reece's parents underestimated how deeply they'd marred their relationship with their future daughter-in-law.

6

Claire stepped inside her bedroom and closed the door. She leaned her back against the only barrier between this sanctuary and the now silent house. Her eyes traced the empty room, finally focusing on the clock on Tuck's beside table — 4:30 a.m.

No wonder she was exhausted. After hours of high tension, every cell in her body ached. First the arrest, followed by what could be termed pandemonium. The meeting with Ranger, as she hoped for information that still remained sketchy at best. Escaping home in the helicopter to avoid masses of reporters, only to discover strangers carting out boxes filled with personal records and belongings. Watching like a helpless spectator while life unraveled.

Claire's eyes filled with tears.

Tuck.

The look in her husband's eyes would haunt her forever. She would have expected a chiseled response to the indignity forced upon Tuck by overzealous prosecutors trying to intentionally ridicule. Strangely, by the time those awful men clicked the handcuffs on his wrists, her husband's shoulders were stooped in resignation. That was what confused Claire the most.

Few things Claire Massey could not afford, and patience was one. This legal situation would not be easily resolved, but the truth would come out. She'd insist her husband find out who was behind this public spectacle and demand he use his wealth and influence to set things right . . . eventually.

She slumped onto the bed. She ran her hand over the place where Tuck normally slept.

Where would he be sleeping tonight?

She leaned back and stared at the ceiling. It occurred to Claire how little she really knew about Tuck's business. After they'd married, he'd struggled to find acceptable employment. Accolades gained on a football field seldom translated into marketable skills, a fact her mother pointed out on many occasions, sometimes even to his face.

Claire had crossed her mother on only two occasions. The first time, she passed over an opportunity to attend Princeton, instead moving to Austin to participate in a culinary arts program at the University of Texas. The second was marrying a man from a family far beneath her mother's standards. "Muscles, charm, and the ability to play football won't provide financial security," her mother claimed, a position she maintained until Tuck's assets far surpassed her own.

Mother hadn't counted on Tuck's tenacity, his driven spirit to come out a winner no matter what. He'd always promised he would score in life as he had on the field. And he had — big-time.

The break he'd needed came when an elderly UT alumnus with no heirs realized he had no one to leave his very lucrative cattle trucking enterprise to. Liston Cliburne was in his eighties. Although he was worth millions, he still drove a fifteen-year-old green Chevy pickup. "The color of money," he'd told Tuck the night he offered to sell his business for pennies on the dollar. "I've watched you on that football field, son. You have what it takes to build on what I've started. With you at the helm, this legacy will last far after I'm gone. I'll even finance you, son."

Liston died two years later, leaving Tuck in full control of the necessary capital he needed. Tuck parlayed that trucking business into what was now Massey Enterprises, a business worth ten times what Liston handed him.

Or at least was . . . until tonight.

Max stood outside his mother's bedroom door, pondering whether or not she'd be up. Who was he kidding? None of them would sleep tonight.

He lightly rapped on the door. "Mom?"

"I'm here," she called. "Come on in."

His mother had never looked more disheartened, more haggard. Her red-rimmed eyes were filled with fear, despite her earlier claims this would all get worked out.

She held out her arms and Max moved into them, giving his mother a tight hug. "Ranger will get Dad home soon," he said. If he could, Max would wrestle rattlesnakes to fix this for her.

His mother nodded. "I don't understand. One minute Tuck is passing out million-dollar checks, and the next —"

"Don't think about that now, Mom. You need sleep. Why don't you get undressed and I'll go down and help Margarita. We'll bring you up some hot tea."

"Margarita's awake?"

Max gave his mother a tired smile. "She

started baking an hour ago." Their house-keeper believed food cured everything.

"Are Garrett and Marcy still up?"

He shook his head. "Nah, they headed back to their place over an hour ago. Garrett's really freaked out over all this. So is Queen Marcy."

"Honey, don't call her that," his mother said.

"Aw, fine. I won't," he said. "At least not to her face."

It'd been a standing joke between him and Lainie that their big brother's wife ruled Garrett like a small country. If his mom were honest, she'd agree.

But Dad couldn't have been more pleased when Garrett landed his trophy wife. "Success always looks better with a beauty on your arm," he'd said, pointing out how Marcy shared their own mother's good looks. Out of Mom's earshot, Dad also claimed he'd never seen a woman open her mouth more and say less.

Now, Garrett. He was a whole other story. His parents should have named him Garrett of Assisi, for no guy was better suited to be a saint.

Even so, Max hardly wished what had transpired tonight on anybody — especially his tight-gripped brother, who clutched life

90

like he was in the last second of a championship bull ride.

If you took somebody's worst nightmare
and tripled it, you would be halfway to the
look on Garrett's face as he escorted the
feds across the lawn to his place. Even
Queen Marcy remained silent as they
walked away.

On the bed, his mother rubbed her forehead. "Max?"

"Yeah, Mom?"

"Your dad couldn't have done any of these
things. Right?"

Max sat on the bed next to her and patted
her arm. "I don't know, Mom." He hesitated. He'd never seen his mother this
vulnerable. "I hope not."

She shifted back against the pillows. A tiny
tear pooled at the corner of his mother's
closed eye, then trickled down, eventually
getting lost in her hair.

The sight cramped Max's chest. "Uh,
Mom, why don't you try and get some
sleep. There's nothing more you can do
tonight by worrying." In an odd role reversal, he bent and pulled the shoes from her
feet. He grabbed the afghan from a nearby
chair and draped it over his mother. "I love
you, Mom."

With closed eyes, she whispered, "I love

you too, baby." Just before Max reached the door, she added, "Max?"

He turned. "Yeah?"

"Your father does too, you know."

He didn't respond. Instead, he gently pulled the door closed behind him and headed for his old room, carrying his mother's words with him.

Max knew a lot of things. But believing his father truly loved him was not one of them.

7

Lainie had released Henry for the evening and was in the hotel lobby when the text came from Max and she learned what was happening at home. She rushed to the concierge desk, ordered her car, and raced north from Dallas on Interstate 75, only slowing for the exit to the road leading to Legacy Ranch. After clearing the stoplight, she gunned the engine, sending her cherry-red Ferrari flying down the road, braking only when the gate came into view.

The horizon held a hint of pre-dawn lavender. No matter how dark the night had been, the sun always appeared, bringing a new day. One she hoped couldn't possibly be worse than what she'd just experienced.

The sound of her car woke the cameramen at the gate. Van doors opened and barely awake reporters scrambled out, clutching microphones. Security quickly opened the gate and she drove through a mass of cameras flashing. When she'd safely made it through, she geared down and drove slowly toward the house.

Max met her out front. He opened her car door. "Hey, Sis."

"Hey," she replied, hoping she didn't look as wrecked as she felt.

After leaving her overnight bag on the front porch, together they headed for the oak on the knoll to the right of the horse barns.

The tree had played many roles over the years, from the perfect Alamo when Max pretended to be Davy Crockett, to Lainie's Grauman's Chinese Theatre when she dressed in her mother's nightgowns and heels, and a Prell shampoo bottle became her version of the Oscar. Garrett teased and called his siblings silly, but one time they caught him up in the branches, flying the friendly skies as a pilot.

In later years, the oak served as the place where Lainie escaped to think, at times joined by her younger brother.

Like now.

Lainie leaned against the sturdy trunk, pressed against Max's shoulder, each lost in their own thoughts until an early cicada's screechy song broke the silence.

Lainie picked up a twig and drew a stick

figure in the dirt, barely visible in the soft light of early dawn. "Max?"

"Yeah?"

"Do you think Dad is a crook?"

He drew a deep breath. "Funny. Mom asked me that earlier."

"She did?"

"Uh-huh."

Lainie outlined a wedding veil on the stick figure. "What did you tell her?"

"I don't think I've ever seen Mom cry before." Max picked at his thumb while staring at the ground. "She's pretty scared."

"I am too," Lainie said. "A grand jury indictment is a big deal, isn't it?"

Max nodded. "Yup. A very big deal."

Another cicada's screech cut through the heated early morning air.

"The Sandells wouldn't let me see Reece." Lainie scratched at the dirt, erasing her drawing. She bit the tender flesh inside her cheek to keep from tearing up. "I — I think they're going to try to call off the wedding," she whispered. The admission, once voiced, made her ache inside.

Suddenly Max pounded the ground with his fist. "Did he even stop to consider any of us?"

"What are you saying, Max?"

He huffed in disgust and stared up into

the branches. "I'm saying I think our father focused on everything but his family. Sounds like he cut a lot of corners just to be rich, and we're all going to pay the price. Especially Mom."

"So — you think he did it?"

Her brother turned and looked at her, misery evident in his eyes. "What do you think?"

Dreams in the middle of the night were never more vivid than in the hours following real dreams left shattered. Claire woke fitfully, with visions of her life with Tuck sifting into her early-morning consciousness. While asleep, she'd dreamed of her honeymoon, the memories a sweet respite to a night knotted with dread.

Unable to afford much, she and Tuck had combed rice from their hair, packed up their sprouting devotion to one another and a few pairs of jeans, and headed for Jefferson, a quaint town in eastern Texas known for their antique shops and bed-and-breakfasts.

Tuck sold his treasured football jersey to an avid collector of Texas Longhorn memorabilia for the price of two nights at the Delta Street Inn, a quaint B&B on the edge of town. Claire giggled as Tuck carried her over the threshold and into their second-story suite decorated with a lavish brick fireplace, hardwood floors, and views of magnolia trees in bloom. They spent most of the two days nestled under a thick hand-sewn quilt or lounging in the claw-foot bathtub filled with bubbles.

On the last night, he'd lifted her toe from the warm suds and brought it to his mouth. His kisses sent tingles through her already sated body, making her long for her new husband again.

"Claire?" he said, his eyes filled with wonder. "You know I'd give you the moon if I could, don't you?"

"I don't want the moon, babe. I want to get back under the quilt," she teased.

His chin tilted at a curious angle. "I'm serious. I'm going to take good care of you, Claire."

Tuck was a good man. He'd provided a life most wives only dreamed of. Oh sure, there were matching Maseratis in the garage and stays at L'Albereta in Italy. But there were also s'mores cooked on a campfire on the bluff with the children, and Sundays spent in church with his arm around her shoulders.

How could she reconcile these horrible accusations with the man she knew him to be? Her husband was not a criminal. He was that guy in the bathtub making a promise to his bride.

Tears pooled in Claire's eyes.

And more than any sports car or vacation stay, she wanted him home.

8

By mid-morning, light streaming through the windows of the sunroom warmed Claire's face, creating the perfect environment for much-needed sleep. She sat on the sofa and dozed until she felt a hand on her shoulder and slowly opened her eyes.

"Mrs. Massey?" From the conflicted look on Margarita's face, her housekeeper hated waking her. "I'm so sorry. You have a telephone call — Mr. Ranger Jennings."

Claire let the coverlet slide to the Saltillo tile floor. "Thanks, Margarita," she said, slipping her feet into her flip-flops. "I'll pick up in here." She scrambled for the phone on the wicker table and pulled the receiver to her ear. "Ranger?"

"Claire, I just found out Tuck's detention hearing will be in front of Magistrate Rower at eleven this morning."

"But that's in less than two hours. I can't —"

"You don't have to be there. The entire proceeding will take less than ten minutes. I'll make the best case I can for home confinement prior to arraignment."

Claire rubbed her temple. "Arraignment? What does that mean?" She'd watched plenty of crime series on television, but this was all new to her.

"I know you have a lot of questions. Let's plan on you coming to the office early this afternoon. I'll have more answers then."

"Will Tuck be at the hearing this morning?"

"Yes. I know you're anxious to talk with him, but you wouldn't have an opportunity this morning. Don't worry, Claire. I'll get this handled." They ended the call with Claire clinging to Ranger's reassurance.

"Mrs. Massey, Jana Rae is out at the gate."

She moved to the window, watching the gardeners at work. "Go ahead and instruct security to allow her in."

"I told them." Margarita raised her hands. "But all those men want your personal authority."

Claire rubbed her forehead. "Okay, sure — with the media circus and all, Garrett probably tightened things up out there." She grabbed the phone and made a quick call to the entry gate. No doubt the security guys were safer standing in the path of a tornado than weathering her best friend's whirlwind tongue if she lost patience.

Twenty minutes later, Jana Rae stormed into the sunroom. "Why haven't you answered my calls and texts? I've been worried sick."

Claire turned from the window. "I'm sorry, I should've picked up when you phoned." She patted the seat next to her on the sofa.

Jana Rae had been there from the beginning, the night Claire had first met Tuck.

It was a Friday night, the first free evening after a week of grueling finals. "C'mon," Jana Rae urged. "Let's go eat, drink, and get completely inappropriate."

Claire shook her head. "I don't know. I'm really tired."

"Nonsense," she said. "How do you know? This might be the night you meet *the one*! The guy who'll pick you up and whirl you into a vortex of love that'll make you want to dye your eyebrows pink."

"Jana Rae!"

Her friend rolled her eyes in response. "C'mon, Miss Goody Two-shoes. It'll be fun."

In the end, Claire adjusted her "halo" and accepted the offer. Her over-the-top buddy had been right. Certainly not about the eyebrow-dyeing part — oh, heavens no — but she walked into the Burger Hut that night and spotted Tuck immediately, standing with several guys over near the jukebox. Dressed in crisp, pressed jeans and a white oxford-cloth shirt, the sleeves carelessly rolled up to reveal brown, well-muscled arms, the man who would become her world turned and smiled in Claire's direction. Instantly, she was reminded of the hunky guys in her daddy's *Western Horsemen* magazines she'd stared at for hours in her early teens.

She smiled back.

It occurred to her now that her heartstrings had been tied to Theodore Massey from that first moment.

Only four days after that night at the Burger Hut, Tuck claimed she was his soul mate and asked her to marry him, sending her heart soaring. She'd laid her usual caution aside and happily let her emotions take over. Less than a year later, he stood by her hospital bedside gazing into their infant's eyes. Choking with emotion, he leaned over and whispered in her ear, "Claire, I love you so much I can't breathe."

At that moment, she bought that pink hair dye, so to speak.

Jana Rae kicked off her boots. She sank down next to Claire and gave her a hug. "The story is all over the news. I got here as quick as I could."

Claire flinched and burrowed her arms at her sides. "Sorry about that mess out at the gate," she said in a poor attempt to redirect the conversation away from their embarrassing situation.

"Those goons? The reporters sitting out there on the hoods of their trucks don't know any more about what makes a good news story than my house cat." Jana Rae shook her head. "Tell you what, sister. Took everything in me not to run a few of 'em down with my car. And I probably would've, except Clark just had the ol' Pontiac waxed. And you know how the Urologist is with his cars."

Jana Rae often referred to her sweet-mannered husband as the Urologist. Always behind his back, of course. It was no secret she adored the man, but she often wielded her caustic sense of humor in his direction when he wasn't around.

Clark Hancock was Jana Rae's second husband. Her first marriage to a rock guitar player/tattoo artist ended when she saw his name inked on a blonde's right breast in a bar in Austin. "At least when Clark is look-

103

ing at some other naked woman, I'm getting paid," she'd said.

Claire watched her best friend stand and move toward the pitcher of Margarita's sweet tea on the tray on the end table. Jana Rae poured a glass and drank it down. "Whew, that's better. My throat was dusty as a Midland oil field." She turned toward Claire and looked her over. "By the way, no offense, but you look awful this morning. That flat head of yours resembles a truck-kissed armadillo."

Claire ran her hand through her long blonde hair. "Thanks a lot. I've had a few things on my mind besides blow-dryers."

Jana Rae's eyes softened. "Did you get any sleep?"

Claire pasted on a fake smile and nodded, maybe a little too assiduously. "A couple of hours. The rest did me good."

Her friend frowned and plopped back down beside her on the sofa. "Well, apparently, your body didn't get the memo."

That was what Claire loved about her best friend. Despite a few quiet surgeries neither of them ever mentioned, there was nothing plastic about Jana Rae. What you saw was what you got. They'd known each other for years, and she was the one friend Claire could always count on to be in her corner.

Back in high school, when Jana Rae didn't have her face planted in her history book, she busied herself making grocery lists and planning how to divide household chores between her two little brothers. After her mom left with some dude from El Paso, the mothering duties fell to Jana Rae. All the more poignant since she'd never had children of her own.

Even now, she crowed with pride over Mike, who pastored a small church in Waco with his two adorable girls — a far cry from her younger brother, Jay, who'd left the Texas landscape littered with illegitimate children. "That lazy piece of bones would need sixteen jobs to pay all that child support," she'd said more than once, while Claire knew Jana Rae quietly slipped checks in the mail each month to the various mamas. *And* sent a generous check to Jay every Christmas.

Good ones like Jana Rae were hard to find. Claire knew she was lucky. Like Jana Rae often said, "Not much a woman really needs besides the support of a good bra and a close friend."

Jana Rae tucked her feet underneath her. "Like I said, y'all are all over the news. Every station, even national. That Joel Knickerson on cable, I used to think he was so cute. Until I learned he buttered his bread with a fork instead of a knife."

"Jana Rae!"

"Oh, pooh. I'm just saying, that's all."

Claire gazed back out the windows at the vista above the river, trying to ignore the sound of news choppers hovering back and forth on the horizon.

As usual, Jana Rae sensed her mood. "I'm here, you know."

She nodded, swallowing emotion building in her throat. "We won't know the full story until our meeting with Ranger Jennings later this afternoon." Then, more for her own benefit, Claire added, "Tuck will fix all this."

In rare occasions where life dealt unpleasant situations, she always relied on Tuck to step in and make things right.

This time especially, she needed him to come through.

The heels on Claire's shoes clicked across the shiny tiled floors of her entry foyer. Outside massive double doors, a black town car waited with the engine running.

"I don't know when I'll be back. It's possible I'll stay in town tonight. If so, Margarita, you know how to reach me at the Adolphus."

Jana Rae followed close behind, purse in

hand. "Hey, trying to support you is like pulling a double-wide trailer with a scooter. Blast it, Claire, let me go with you."

The housekeeper dug her hands into her pockets. "*Vaya con Dios,* Mrs. Massey," she muttered.

Without a word, Claire stepped through the doors onto the landing and walked to the car. She settled into the plush leather backseat and waited for Henry to close the door. She lowered the darkened window and leaned her head out. "Well, Jana Rae, are you coming?"

Confusion briefly crossed Jana Rae's face. She glanced at Margarita and shrugged, then rushed to open the car door. When Claire rolled her eyes, Jana Rae grinned and said, "Oh, don't look at me in that tone of voice."

With Jana Rae settled inside, Claire knocked on the Plexiglas barrier. "Henry, we can go now." Minutes later, they were on their way down the paved lane lined with oaks.

The Masseys had called Legacy Ranch home for twenty years, moving to the spectacular thirty-two-thousand acre spread when Garrett and Lainie were young and Max was tucked safely inside Claire's swollen belly.

Of course, back then none of the outbuildings had existed, and they lived in the house Tuck's father had built for his mother when they'd first been married, a rather modest one-story ranch style made of Austin stone, with a sprawling wraparound porch complete with rocking chairs. In happier times, before Tuck's mom started drinking, his parents perched themselves in those chairs after dinner, watching spectacular sunsets on the horizon in back of the stock ponds.

Years back, Tuck's cattle brokerage provided the means to rebuild, and Claire fashioned the showplace they now called home. Their ranch house, now valued at over thirty-eight million, had been featured in *Texas Homes Monthly* and was built by the same architect who worked for celebrities such as Alan Jackson and Reba McEntire.

Tuck wanted a showplace, and Tuck always got what he wanted.

Both Claire and Jana Rae now sat silent, staring out their respective windows as they passed the turnoff that led to the stables and indoor arena, each lost in her own private thoughts. For over a mile, the car rolled along river frontage until the massive iron security gate leading into Legacy Ranch loomed ahead.

Jana Rae broke the silence. "Uh, that doesn't look good. It's gotten even worse."

Claire peered out the front of the car at the satellite trucks and news vans lined up at the gate. Reporters and cameramen scrambled into position as the car approached the entrance and slowed.

Henry reached for his OnStar button. "I have Mrs. Massey. We're going to need security backup at the gate."

Nearly twenty minutes passed before the town car successfully maneuvered the mass of media and headed south toward Dallas. Thanks to darkened windows, Claire wouldn't find herself splayed on the front pages of the *Dallas Morning News* looking like she'd just eaten shards of glass.

On the seat next to her, Jana Rae fidgeted and reached for the remote. She pointed toward the television mounted in front of them. With one click, the screen brightened and a voice filled the vehicle.

"In breaking news, cattle mogul Theodore Massey was arrested late last night in downtown Dallas after a grand jury handed down an indictment alleging illegal business activity stretching across Texas and the Midwest. Unidentified sources within the US Attorney's Office report that once the investigation is completed, the case might easily be the biggest livestock fraud in the nation's history."

Claire's stomach knotted as footage of Bernie Madoff flashed on the screen. "Turn it off," she said.

"Claire, you need to understand what is going on. Don't you think?" Jana Rae took her lack of response as permission and clicked to another channel. Like driving by an accident you don't want to see but you look at anyway, Claire found herself riveted to the information pouring from the screen.

The reporter interviewed a man whose face was contorted with anger. "My kids' college fund is invested with Massey. All of it."

Jana Rae scowled. "Claire, honey. This ain't looking so good," she said.

"Tuck's innocent," Claire protested. "All this will get sorted out." She ignored the strange look Jana Rae shot in her direction. "It will," she insisted.

Jana Rae clicked off the television. "Okay, if you say so. But don't think you can stick pansies in a toilet bowl and call it a garden."

The drive into Dallas took just under an hour, with heavy traffic on I-75 testing Claire's patience. Henry exited off the Woodall Rogers Freeway into downtown and headed directly for Elm Street.

Renaissance Tower, known for its distinctive double-X lighting and majestic spheres, was a well-known Dallas landmark. The top floors served as home to Mehlhaf Jennings, PC. Unlike the recognized international firm of Baker Botts, Ranger's boutique firm focused on a select clientele. Tuck was one of their A-list clients, throwing millions in billable hours into the firm's coffers each year.

Jana Rae agreed to wait in the car. She pulled her e-reader from her purse. "I'll be praying," she said.

Claire stepped off the elevator into the expansive fifty-six-story lobby with glass vistas overlooking the city of Dallas and marched straight to the receptionist. A stunning blonde looked up and smiled. "Good afternoon, Mrs. Massey. The team is waiting for you in the Magnolia conference room." She clicked her fingers, and a young man left the drink cart he was pushing and hurried over to escort Claire into the meeting.

Ranger Jennings greeted her warmly just outside the door and motioned her inside the crowded room, where stacks of files and empty mugs monogramed with the firm name littered the large granite table.

A tall man stood looking out the windows, his back to everyone. His hand rested on an empty leather conference chair.

Claire's breath caught.

She'd know that profile anywhere.

9

Claire quickly dropped her bag on the table. "Tuck?"

Her husband turned and opened his arms. She rushed over. "I didn't expect —" She buried her face deep against his chest, taking in his familiar smell and not caring if everyone in the room stared. She'd forgotten in the brief time apart how much strength she pulled from his presence. "I didn't know you'd be here," she said, reluctantly drawing from his embrace.

Tuck let out a nervous laugh. "Ranger arranged a temporary release."

"Let's everyone take a seat," Ranger said, motioning around the table. Only then did she see Garrett seated. Their eyes met and he gave her a weak smile.

After the legal team got settled in their chairs, Ranger made brief introductions, then opened a file that lay on the table before him. "As you know, we've pulled in all our markers with the folks over at the US Attorney's Office. Even then, we barely managed to construct this deal."

Claire's head jerked up. "Deal?"

Tuck's hand covered hers, sending a silent message. She sat back in the plush black leather, tension knotting the back of her neck. "Sorry, go on."

Ranger cleared his throat. "In exchange for Tuck's full cooperation and disclosure, and in consideration of the establishment of an immediate receivership, the authorities have agreed to a consent order in lieu of the expense of a full trial." He paused and glanced through the contents of his file, then focused back on Tuck. "As we explained earlier, your assets will be transferred once the judge approves the plea agreement." Ranger closed his file, his face growing more somber. "And finally, Tuck will remain on home confinement with a monitoring device pending a hearing on the consent order at the time of arraignment. I expect that to happen within thirty days, possibly sooner."

Garrett leaned forward. "Wait, hold on. I don't understand."

At the same time, Claire pulled her hand from Tuck's. "But Tuck didn't do any of this."

Tuck stood. "Everyone, if y'all could excuse us for a bit, I need a few moments alone with my family."

Nervous glances ping-ponged across the table. Ranger scooted back his chair and stood. "Of course."

Tuck's attorney motioned to the others, and Claire watched as the gentlemen sitting around the table stood and followed him to the door. Tuck shook hands with several of the men and thanked them on their way out.

As soon as they were alone, Claire turned to her husband. "Tuck, what's going on here? This is scaring me."

She and Garrett exchanged worried glances as Tuck moved into a chair across the table from them. He steepled his fingers and looked to the ceiling, as if the strength he needed for what he had to say might be found in the harsh halogen lighting.

"I've done something awful," he said, his eyes glistening with moisture.

Claire swallowed against the brittle dryness in her throat. "Tuck, what is it?" she asked. "Is all this true?" Her voice sounded foreign, even to her own ears.

"Yes," Tuck admitted.

Garrett slammed his palm on the table and stood. "I knew it! Dad, what have you done?"

Claire felt herself tremble. "Tuck, how bad is this?"

Tuck met her gaze. "The details aren't important. What you need to know is that I'm short. There aren't enough cattle."

Garrett's face grew dark. His fingers pawed through his hair. "You sold cattle we didn't have?"

Tuck nodded and scraped his hand through his own hair. "I had no choice. When gas prices rocketed a few summers ago, high feed prices followed. Cash flows got a little tight and I floated a few things. Only for a short time," he quickly added. He turned his gaze and stared out the window. "But things snowballed. And now the books don't reflect these shortages."

"But Dad, how much are we talking here?"

Tuck took a deep breath and looked at his son. "I've already said way more than I should've. If this deal goes south for any reason, you may get called to testify. The less details you both know, the better."

Garrett plopped down in his chair. His eyes filled with tears. "And the consent order, Dad? All our assets?"

Tuck's eyes held a pained stare. He rubbed his forehead. "I'm sorry. I — I'm so sorry."

Claire felt light-headed. She couldn't breathe. Trying to gain some measure of stability, she focused on her shoes. Somehow the small act slowed her racing mind. She folded her arms and cast a wary glance toward her husband. "What are you saying, Tuck? Are you telling me you're a crook? That you took people's money on purpose?"

Garrett stood. "That's exactly what he's saying." He slammed his chair against the table.

Tuck startled. "Son —"

"What about me? And Marcy? Did you ever stop to think about what this would do to us? To Mom?" Garrett shook his head and looked over at Claire. "I'm outta here." He slammed out the door, leaving her to face her husband alone.

She eyed Tuck with suspicion. "I don't get it. People have been making money. Where did all those huge profits come from?"

Guilt painted a haunted look on Tuck's pale face. "Claire, baby, I'm . . . I'm sorry. I was just trying to —"

Claire held up her hand as if to steady the world that teetered all around her. "You're kidding, right?" Anger twisted and meandered across her now tense shoulders. "That's it?"

"Look, I promise everything's going to be okay. I'll make this right."

A tight rap on the door interrupted.

"Yeah," Tuck called out, sounding annoyed.

Ranger peeked his head into the room. "I don't mean to rush you, Tuck. But we've got a lot to go over before our meeting with the feds at two o'clock."

Her husband gave a resigned nod. He looked over at Claire, his eyes pleading for understanding.

She lowered her head, drew a deep breath. Already she could feel everyone's eyes watching her every move as the attorneys filed back into the room and took their places, their judgment landing on her like a sheath of barbed wire.

Her heart pounded. In a matter of minutes, her entire world had tilted upside down. She didn't know how to respond, what to think. All she knew was that she had to get out of here . . . get away.

Claire stood and grabbed her bag.

Tuck reached for her arm. "Where are you going?"

She pulled away. How could she possibly face this humiliation with him? She swallowed a scream forming in her throat, feeling it collide with the ball of fear lodged in her gut. In a whirl of confusion, she stumbled for the door.

"Claire?"

"I have an appointment," she mumbled over her shoulder, clutching her belly with a tight fist.

"An appointment?"

The question hung heavy in the air. She cocked her head and drew a tangled breath, turned, and looked back at the man she realized she barely knew. She said the only thing that entered her mind.

"A hair appointment. To get my eyebrows dyed. I — I don't think I like the color pink anymore."

10

Claire stepped into the harsh sunlight and waited while Henry pulled from the parking garage. She pressed her sunglasses in place, trying desperately to numb her mind to the news she'd learned.

"Mrs. Massey? Your family is being dubbed the 'Texas Madoffs.' Care to comment?"

Her head jerked around. A young guy in a Smirnoff T-shirt hoisted a camera onto his shoulder and scrambled to catch up with her. *The creep needs a haircut,* she thought as Henry screeched to a stop. *And some manners.*

Claire yanked the door open and scrambled inside, the heel of her shoe momentarily catching on the floor runner.

Jana Rae looked frantic. "What's going on? Claire?"

Claire knocked on the Plexiglas and mouthed for Henry to hurry. She wasn't about to be the target of vermin looking to cash in her dignity for a scoop.

The car careened away from the curb, sending Claire and Jana Rae sliding across the seat. Henry's voice could be heard through the speakers, sounding out of breath. "Sorry, Mrs. Massey."

She nodded and pushed the intercom. "Henry, they'll likely try to follow. Can you lose the news trucks?"

"Sure thing," he assured her. He gunned the engine.

Minutes later, they were safely heading west on the Tom Landry freeway in the direction of Fort Worth. Granted, with less rubber on their tires, but they'd escaped. At least for now.

"Claire, what happened?"

Claire looked into the eyes of her trusted friend. She hesitated, trying to find the words.

As usual, she didn't need to.

Jana Rae slumped back into her seat. "Oh."

Claire waited. This is where Jana Rae would launch some sharp missile, hoping to blast the tension into pieces. She'd be clever and funny. Even in this. Eventually Jana Rae's sense of humor would lighten the moment. Together they'd find a way to see things differently, to find some hope to hang on to.

Instead, her friend rubbed the space between her brows. "Spill," she said.

Ignoring Ranger's advice not to talk about the situation to anyone, Claire took a deep breath and slogged through a recitation of Tuck's deluded belief he could somehow fudge the books and then make up the difference when the market turned, but then cattle shortages had snowballed, leaving a situation no one imagined their family would ever face.

"Jana Rae, say something." Claire examined her friend's face, which had suddenly taken on a detached look. "Jana Rae, what's the matter?"

"Claire, look, I need to tell you something. And I don't want to make things worse."

"What is it?"

Jana Rae made a rare move and averted her eyes. Her voice lowered to just above a whisper. "Last month, Tuck approached Clark with a deal too good to pass up." She paused.

Dread crept into Claire's conscience. Inwardly she groaned, knowing what was coming.

"We put our assets — we invested with Tuck."

"How much?" she dared.

Several seconds passed before Jana Rae finally answered.

"All of it."

11

Claire leaned back against a stack of pillows on her bed and stared mindlessly at a program on the History Channel. Both the Bwa and the Buna people of Burkina Faso wore masks during their colorful wedding ceremonies, hiding their true identities until well into the marriage.

Apparently, as Claire had recently learned, the custom was not limited to Africa.

"Are you going to talk to me?" Tuck unbuttoned his shirt.

She glanced at the bedside table. The clock read nearly midnight, far too late for any more drama. Reluctantly, she shrugged away the hurt and turned to him. "I am talking to you."

Tuck unhooked his belt and slid it from his pants. "Claire, you know what I mean."

Claire sighed and returned her eyes to the television. The people on the screen danced wildly around a campfire, ducking and darting to a loud beat.

She wasn't normally mean-spirited, but she had a strange need to counter her own misery by inflicting pain back on Tuck. Besides, did he think he could wreck their lives and come home to a smile on her face?

Tuck grabbed the remote from her hand, his face flushed. He clicked off the television. "Claire, we'll never make it through this if we don't —"

Claire threw back the covers, stood, and grabbed her robe from the end of the bed. "Okay, let's talk, Tuck. Why don't you begin by telling me what we're going to do now?"

"Baby —"

"Don't 'baby' me. Tuck, did you even stop to think about the consequences here?" She shot her husband a strained look. "Who is going to tell Margarita that after working for our family for nearly fifteen years, she no longer has a job? Where will she go?" She took a deep breath. "All three of our children might as well wear scarlet Ms on their foreheads. They'll go through life carrying the shame you thrust upon them. And Lainie? It's a no-brainer Reece Sandell will move as far away from our daughter as possible. You pulled her dreams right out from under her feet."

Tuck buried his head in his hands. "I

125

never meant to hurt my family. Claire, you have to believe me."

"And me." Claire's voice broke. "Did you think about me? What am I supposed to do after they cart you off and take all our things?"

Tuck reached for her. She yanked her arm away, anger now starting to push its way to the surface as she counted the cost of her husband's choices. "Maybe Jana Rae and Clark will take me in. Except you stole *their* money too." She swung around and planted her feet. "In the end, maybe Mother was right. Maybe you are just a football jock who scores by mowing people down on the field."

Claire winced, seeing in Tuck's eyes the wound her words had sliced open. Her shoulders slumped, and she sat on the end of the bed and stared at the dark television screen. Her voice dropped to nearly a whisper. "In the end, you knew this was going down. Yet you kept letting people — innocent people — invest, knowing they would never get any money back." She lifted her head and looked at Tuck. "How could you do that and sleep at night?"

"Do you have any idea the kind of pressure I've been under all these years?"

Claire turned. "Pressure?"

"Yes, pressure." Tuck's chin jutted. "Pressure to overcome your mother's disdain, to be somebody my kids could admire, pressure to keep up in the circles you were used to running in." He shook his head. "And in these last years, pressure to provide profits to a bunch of greedy investors who couldn't begin to count the millions already in their bank accounts."

"You're saying it's our fault?" Claire looked at him in disbelief. "Are you that out of touch? Most of your investors were people trying to build retirement funds or trying to —"

"Trying to get rich quick off some scheme cooked up to pad their bank accounts without them working for it," he said, finishing her sentence. "Besides, do you really believe people aren't suspicious of those kinds of returns? Don't you think they watch the news and see how Bernie Madoff and the Enron bunch pulled together wealth? Secretly they consider the possibility of a sham — but their desire for wealth pushes them to take the risk, hoping they won't be the ones caught when everything tumbles."

"I can't believe you are pushing the blame onto others for what you did."

"I'm not pushing blame onto anyone. I'm

127

simply saying I'm not the only one wearing black here."

"Really?" Claire scowled. "And what color am I wearing now that everything has tumbled?"

His silence angered her. "How am I to blame for any of this?" she asked.

"I'm not saying you *are* to blame exactly."

She stood and faced Tuck. "Then what are you saying?"

"Each year, those parties at the ranch grew bigger. The vacations we took more exotic. The clothes you and Princess wore more costly."

Fury invaded every cell of Claire's body. "You're kidding, right? I passed up Princeton for UTA. I didn't plan to be an attorney or some other prestigious profession. I studied culinary arts because cooking feeds my soul."

"You didn't have to. You were taught to marry well. And when you settled for me, I spent the next twenty years trying not to be your father."

In a flash, Claire raised her hand and slapped Tuck.

He grabbed her wrist, pressing it down to the bed. Her body had no choice but to give in to the pressure. She folded and lay looking up at her husband's contorted face. She tried to wiggle free, but Tuck's strength — and the naked look in his eyes — held her pinned.

He sank next to her on the bed and drew her to him, burying his face into her neck. His musky scent filled her nostrils, and her tangled emotions — fear, sorrow, and anger — all knotted together to spark unexpected longing.

Tuck tugged at her nightgown, his mouth claiming hers before he pulled back to reveal in his face a need that reflected her own.

Over the next minutes, their bodies communicated what words never could.

The last twenty-eight hours had torn their souls asunder, yet the two had long ago become one. For better or worse, they were connected at their core. Claire could no more separate herself from this man than she could sever her arm.

Later, when she lay against her slumbering husband, she tried not to think about the future. Instead, she let her mind drift back to that four-poster bed in Jefferson, Texas, where she and Tuck had started their journey nestled beneath a quilt.

The memory strengthened her resolve. Somehow she and Tuck would get through this — together.

Claire ran her foot down Tuck's leg, across the familiar landscape of skin covered with hair. Suddenly her toes caught on something cold and hard.

The monitoring bracelet.

12

Lainie stepped from the harsh Texas sunlight into the shadowed interior stables with concrete floors. For several seconds she stood in the comforting darkness, breathing familiar leather- and liniment-scented air before her fingers instinctively moved to the panel to the right of the door. She pulled the lever and light flooded the tack room.

After knotting her hair and securing the clip a bit tighter, her hands drew a blue bandana from her back jeans pocket and tied it at her neck. She made her way through the wash bay and headed for the stalls.

Overhead, a speaker crackled. "Miss Massey, do you need some help?"

Lainie glanced up at the security camera and nodded her head. "Thanks," she hollered loud enough so the intercom could pick up her voice. "I'm going to take Pride out."

"Sure thing, Miss Massey. I'll get her ready."

Minutes later, Lainie's boots slipped into the stirrups and she pulled herself into the saddle. As if by magic, her shoulders relaxed. Normally, she didn't let circumstances get her down, but she was feeling the strain of the past couple of days. Who wouldn't?

Lainie's philosophy was fairly simple. "You have to create the life you want to wear," she often told herself. Unfortunately, that notion neglected how easily things could unravel, leaving your soul bare.

She leaned forward and stroked the sorrel mare's silky mane. The horse nickered softly in response.

Both Max and her mother had accused her of not embracing the reality of this whole situation with their father. Frankly, Lainie found that idea frustrating. What, did they expect her to stack up on self-help books and sit in front of the *Dr. Phil* show in tears just because life got difficult?

Lainie wasn't one to cry. She was stronger than that. Even in this.

She pressed her heels into Pride's side, urging the horse forward and into the open arena. With a click of her tongue, Lainie drove the horse into a soft lope. Around and around she circled the wrought-iron panels bordering the soft footing, letting the motion carry her mind back to a better time.

Lainie was thirteen the summer she spotted a pickup hauling a horse trailer down the lane. Elated, she'd jumped from her canopy bed and raced outside.

Daddy climbed out from his pickup. "Hey, Princess," he said as she ran up and met him. He grinned. "What do you suppose we have here?"

"My horse!" Lainie clasped her arms around her daddy's waist, barely able to contain her excitement until the trailer slowed to a stop and she climbed the wheel well to peek inside. "Oh, Daddy. She's beautiful."

The champion-sired horse came from the King Ranch of South Texas, known worldwide for their cutting horse stock. Pride and Prejudice, named after her favorite book, became Lainie's closest — and perhaps only real — friend.

Over the years, Lainie had confided in her four-legged buddy, telling Pride private thoughts she'd never dare share with any human. "You know, I'm not like everybody else, especially not the girls at school."

Pride's ears had perked as if she understood.

Lainie grabbed the curry brush. "It's just, well — I think Daddy's right. I'm special." She pulled the curry over Pride's front haunch, working the stiff bristles over her coat. Lainie paused her strokes. "You know what I'm saying?"

The horse swished her tail. Lainie tossed the brush on the shelf, then turned and stroked Pride's side with long, tender sweeps of her hand. "You wait and see, Pride." A self-satisfied grin emerged. "Alaina Claire Massey is going to be really important someday."

That whispered dream was the first of many secrets buried in cedar shavings and sweet-smelling hay, nestled in the corner of the last stall on the east aisle. No one else could begin to understand but Pride — the only living, breathing soul she trusted now with the smoldering truth about how it felt to watch her aspirations crumble.

After several laps in the arena, Lainie pulled at the reins and guided Pride out of the massive structure with its high steel-beamed ceiling and into the open air, pointing her mare in the direction of the small rise that barely concealed the river from view.

By the time Pride's hooves crested the rock cropping west of the large oak, sweat trickled down Lainie's spine and she wondered why she'd slipped her dad's old flannel shirt over her tank top.

From this vantage point, the steel-gray river drew a sharp contrast against the purple-hued bluebonnet patches leading to the water's edge. Daddy had nicknamed the small river running through their ranch Little Brazos, after the longest and most known river in Texas. Early Spanish settlers had called the winding water that meandered through nearly the entire state *Rio de dos Brazos de Dios,* meaning "the River of the Arms of God."

Lainie didn't understand why exactly, but God's arms never seemed to stretch long enough. Especially in times like this.

Reece had not called back. Not answered her texts.

No doubt he'd followed the same news reports she'd watched all morning. Federal agents had investigated her father's business activities for months. A grand jury had found sufficient evidence to issue an indictment, and US marshals had shown up at Legacy Ranch and seized business records from the offices.

Worse, her father admitted he'd done those awful things.

Investors clamored for answers. And far

too often, photos of Reece and Lainie flashed on the screen with anchors pondering what effect the debacle would have on the Sandell campaign.

It didn't take a genius to conclude savvy campaign advisors were advising Reece to distance himself from this sticky situation.

Lainie bent forward and stroked Pride's side, then straightened. "Let's go, girl."

Pride flung her head back and whinnied. Given rein, the mare lunged forward and her ears pricked, her hooves cutting into alluvial soil lining the bank.

Lainie released her hair clip, letting the blonde length flow in the wind. She leaned into Pride's gait, sensing the growing movement of the horse's muscles. They rounded a bend, raced past massive oaks and scrubs.

Lainie's legs tightened their grip. She felt Pride's withers tense and release.

Why had he done it? Why had Daddy put her in this situation?

The horse charged faster and rounded a bend, cutting a bit too closely to the edge. Lainie winced as a honey locust branch tore into her leg.

Did Daddy realize what he'd done? He'd stolen more than money. He'd robbed her of her chance to be a senator's wife.

Following a trick she'd learned as a barrel

racer, Lainie whipped the reins into her mouth and gripped the leather with her teeth. She leaned tight against Pride to maintain balance, the saddle horn competing for residence with the knot in her gut.

With her hands free, she struggled to pull her father's flannel shirt first from one arm, then the next, fighting to rid herself of the garment.

She urged the horse on, matching her breathing to the sound of the hooves hitting the earth. Pride clipped down an embankment, causing Lainie to nearly slide from the saddle. She braced. Pride lunged, clearing a patch of saltbush. The horse raced forward.

News clips played in her mind as hot wind brushed her face. Lainie wadded her father's shirt.

In a stunning development . . .

Candidate disgraced when . . .

A consent order will still require prison term . . .

Lainie pressed the horse to go faster, harder — in an attempt to outrun the loss.

Finally, she reached out and tossed the shirt into the murky brown water swirling below.

And for the first time in years, Lainie cried.

13

Nights were the worst. Those endless hours in the dark, lying in bed knowing he was awake too, but neither of them acknowledging their mental anguish. Ultimately, Claire resorted to moving into one of the guest rooms, where the silence didn't mock her. Unfortunately, she couldn't escape the loudest taunt of all. The internal voice that kept pelleting her with one question.

How could she not have known?

The late nights. The tense phone conversations cut off when she'd walk in the room. The tension often hidden in Tuck's assurances.

Everything now made sense.

But like Ranger said, all that was behind them. They needed to focus on the future. Tuck had made huge errors in judgment, but she knew her husband was basically a good man, despite his failings.

Sure, she'd been pretty angry at first.

Outraged that Tuck had played so loosely with all their lives. Ultimately, though, she understood there was a fine line between hurt and anger. No amount of emotional daggers thrown at her husband could kill the truth.

They loved one another. And that was all that really mattered.

This whole cattle thing had gotten away from him, that was all. Like he'd said, economic situations out of his control hindered profits, and Tuck felt pressure to turn a profit for those who deposited money in his care, people who'd trusted him to come through.

He'd in essence robbed Peter to pay Paul, only until economic circumstances turned back around. Tuck never meant to defraud anyone. By some crazy notion, he'd believed he could ride the downturn out. In the end, he'd hoped to see this economic storm through, promising himself he'd get out at the first glimpse of blue sky.

She knew this man, the way he rubbed his chin when something bothered him. How his eyes brightened when the solution to the problem finally dawned. She knew Tuck had a large freckle on his right hip, oddly shaped like a motorcycle — similar to the first Harley he'd bought when they'd been married seven years and he'd made his first million-dollar cattle trade. She still warmed at the memory of his offering to take her for a ride, with a deeper meaning than gunning down the highway.

She knew how grouchy he got when suffering the slightest head cold, how he'd poke a thermometer in his mouth every twenty minutes and huff when he saw no change from the last time he'd checked his temperature.

He liked foot rubs — both giving and getting. And he was never happier than on Christmas morning, playing Santa under the family tree. One year, even though they easily could afford to purchase new Tonka trucks, her man had spent days in his shop making wooden pickup trucks and horse trailers for the boys. Custom painted with the Legacy Ranch logo.

That was the year he gave her the cream-colored silk nightgown from Paris, and later that night moaned in her ear as he slid the pencil-thin straps from her shoulders.

Claire stared into the darkness, feeling a tear trail toward the pillow.

How was she ever going to be able to wrap her head around all this?

Tuck Massey was a good man. A good man who'd done something terribly wrong.

But with God's help, they would make things right again — eventually.

Not everyone would get paid, but Ranger had a plan. Receivers would liquidate the huge amount of assets turned over in the plea agreement — their real estate, including homes in Sun Valley, Pebble Beach, and Bermuda. They'd relinquish equity holdings, stocks, and aviation assets — the Long Ranger helicopter and Gulfstream Lear. Tuck's luxury yacht, which he'd named *Touchdown* to commemorate his college football career, would have to go, and his envied gun collection. For her part, many of Claire's designer gowns and shoes would be sold, a small sacrifice given how infrequently she'd be invited to parties in the coming years. Those days were likely over, at least for now.

With the judge's approval, the Masseys would retain Legacy Ranch, three vehicles — each valued under fifty grand — and a half-million stipend to cover living and staff expenses. Margarita and Henry would be the only house staff left. Garrett would run the scaled-down ranch operations, keeping things going until Tuck's release. Then they'd rebuild.

The Massey dynasty was over, but their family must go on, despite the wounds.

Yesterday at an empty breakfast table, Margarita had wiped her hands on her apron more than once — a sign Claire knew meant she had something to say. "What is it, Margarita?"

She lifted the silver coffee carafe from the sideboard and walked to where Claire sat. She poured the coffee and her heart out. "It's not good for a family not to talk, not to forgive."

When Claire didn't respond right away, the housekeeper went on. "Mr. Massey did a terrible thing," she said, shaking her head. "His actions created much hardship. But you mustn't let your family break into pieces." She set the carafe down and placed her hand on Claire's forearm. "I'm sorry if I overstep, but there is an evil one who will use this hurt, and all this silence, to further destroy."

Claire knew her sage housekeeper was right. Since Tuck's release, Garrett and Marcy barely came out of their house. Lainie spent all her time in the barn, and Max suddenly found himself very busy at the paper.

If her children were feeling anything like her own struggle, their hurt and confused distance was understandable. But she couldn't let the situation go on too long, or

Margarita's fears would become well-founded.

She supposed she needed to set an example and focus on the positive.

Tuck would find a way to parlay their circumstances into a more quiet yet comfortable lifestyle. Maybe Max would finally get contracted to write that novel of his dreams. Publishers loved celebrity.

Perhaps investors wouldn't be made whole in one sense, but the firm's attorneys argued most of the money lost represented profits reinvested. People would ultimately be paid a percentage, most of which would restore original deposits.

Ranger said if Tuck complied with the federal agents' efforts and worked to make restitution, and if a few people of influence would be willing to testify at the hearing on Tuck's behalf, the judge would render a light sentence. Likely five to seven years. With good behavior, Ranger promised parole would likely come at the end of two years and Tuck could be home again.

Claire wasn't sure how she'd get through twenty-four months without Tuck, but she didn't have a choice. And certainly the legal aspect of all this could have been much worse, given how many were out for Tuck's blood.

The plea bargain would also end any further investigation of Garrett.

Pastor Richards often preached that God used all things for good. Claire could choose to believe that. The alternative would be to sink into despair, and that simply wasn't an option. Not for her marriage, and certainly not for their family. They'd all have to forgive and move on.

If Jana Rae were still talking to her, she'd say Claire was serving up jam on an idiot cracker. She'd claim she had a Pollyanna attitude and tell her to face reality. "Claire, a sinner who pokes his eye out can ask and be forgiven, but he'd still be blind."

Well, yes. Perhaps that philosophy was true.

But Claire needed to be optimistic. What was religion's purpose if not for getting you through the bad times?

She couldn't turn on the television without horrible things being said about Tuck and her family. Cruel remarks. Vicious, really. No one could understand the deep shame and embarrassment, how Claire's skin crawled the moment someone recognized her and gave her *the look*. If she dwelled on all that, or how things might *actually* go, she'd never climb out of this bed.

No, instead she'd try hard to follow the advice of that lady televangelist and take all thoughts captive. She'd stop the "stinkin' thinkin' " and lean on the promises of God.

Claire wiped at her damp face. In fact, she had a plan. Tomorrow she'd turn to Pastor Richards and ask his help to get them out of this mess.

Her body shifted, and she pulled the coverlet tight. Closing her eyes, she let the tension drain from her shoulders. And for the first time in many nights, Mrs. Tuck Massey fell sound asleep.

Claire stepped into the massive circular foyer. The reception counter was to the right of the water fountain, sandwiched between the bookstore and the staff offices. She cleared her throat. "Excuse me, miss. You're new here, aren't you?"

A fortyish woman with blonde hair clipped at the back of her head looked up from her magazine. The motion caused her earrings to swing wildly from her ears. "Well, hello there. What can we do for you today?" The woman strangely resembled the perky actress she'd seen in a recent commercial for feminine products, except a bit older. And maybe heavier.

Claire pushed the thought from her mind.

Whenever she was uneasy, her mind seemed to wander to strange places.

This church, probably the most prestigious of all the churches in northern Dallas, didn't get its nickname — St. Minks and All Cadillacs — by catering to the blue-collar crowd. She had no reason to be nervous. The Masseys had been members for years. She'd chaired the missions conference, for goodness' sake.

She glanced at the lady's name tag. "Uh, Shelly, I'm here to see Pastor Richards. Is he here?" She forced a smile. "Claire Massey."

The woman suddenly eyed her with suspicion. She slowly closed the magazine cover. "Can I tell Pastor Richards what this is regarding?"

She managed a weak smile. "A personal matter."

The receptionist nodded. "I see. Well, you wait here just a minute and I'll check his schedule." She pushed away from the desk and stood. "And see if he has time available," she added.

Claire watched the woman duck into the hallway leading to the staff offices. Minutes later, she returned, trailed by the pastor.

"Claire, what a surprise." Pastor Richards's eyes barely met her own as he stepped

146

forward. "What brings you here?"

"Could we talk? Privately?"

"Absolutely." He led her back to his office, a room appointed with fine furnishings and lined with bookcases filled with volumes of reference books and Bibles in various versions. Above the sofa, on the wall opposite his massive walnut desk, hung a huge mount of a cape buffalo head he'd shipped back from Africa, from a hunt Tuck had sponsored four years ago. A similar trophy hung in Tuck's office.

"I'm sorry I haven't called since . . . well, since the arrest." Pastor Richards motioned her to a chair. "But, well . . . you know how these things go."

No, she didn't. But Claire nodded anyway and settled her purse squarely in the middle of her lap. "No problem," she said. "I understand completely. Like Tuck often says, businesses don't run themselves. And I guess that would go for churches as well." She shifted in the chair, suddenly a bit nervous after all, although she didn't know why exactly. She'd known this man for years. "Pastor Richards, I'm here because I need a favor."

"A favor?" The heavyset man with a receding hairline planted himself in the large black leather chair behind his desk.

147

"Yes. You see, Tuck's attorneys have worked out a deal with the prosecutors, and a hearing is coming up where the judge will approve the terms of the consent order. Ranger — that's Tuck's attorney — well, he thinks we should line up some folks to testify about Tuck's character." She rushed to add, "It's just a formality, really. But we'd like for you to testify that you've known Tuck for years and that he serves on the elder board here at Abundant Hills. Kind of provide some context for Tuck's . . . uh, indiscretions. Tuck would have come personally, but he's . . . well, he's staying close to home these days."

Pastor Richards steepled his fingers. "I see."

Claire felt a shadowy change in the man's tone. She examined his face for some sign that might assuage her intuition, something that would reveal the man sitting opposite her was squarely in her camp.

"I'm afraid I can't do that, Claire."

"What? I — I don't understand."

Pastor Richards took a deep breath and straightened. "No, Claire, I don't think you do," he said, his voice laced with sadness. "Tonight the board is meeting to remove your husband from his position as an elder."

Claire's breath caught. "Remove? Well,

under the circumstances, I guess that's understandable. But . . ."

The pastor's eyes grew thoughtful. "Let me clarify the situation," he said, seeming to choose his words carefully. He braced against the back of his tufted leather chair. "Several years back, Tuck submitted a proposal asking that the elders place excess funds, including our building and benevolence money, in his investment program. Over the months, it's been no secret Abundant Hills has enjoyed some fairly healthy returns. But now . . ." He sighed. "Now this church is broke. If it wasn't for the generosity of a few wealthy members, we wouldn't be able to pay the electric bill next month, let alone buy communion juice — or anything else, for that matter. I don't think under the circumstances I could —"

"I understand." Claire's fingers fumbled around her purse as she tried to hide their shaking. She schooled her lips into an impersonal smile and stood, glancing over at the cape buffalo. "And I'm — uh, I'm sorry," she said, trying to mask her expanding shame.

Pastor Richard looked at her with pity. "We could — uh, the women's circle could deliver some meals or —"

She shook her head. "No — uh, that's

fine. We're fine."

Then she turned and silently walked from Pastor Richards's office.

14

"Dad took money from the church?"

"Garrett, calm down. Your father needs our support." Claire looked her oldest son in the eyes. "Now more than ever."

Lainie leaned forward from where she sat on the sofa. "I'm with Garrett on this, Mom. The less my photo is flashed in the news right now, the better. I mean, I want to help Daddy, but —"

"But nothing." Garrett's scowl grew even darker. "I'm not going to be in that court-room on Tuesday."

Max stood quietly out of the way. From the corner of the room, he ventured over and shook his head. "Hey, Bro, at least hear Mom out."

Claire moved and put a supportive arm around Max's shoulders. "Look, Max is right. Let's everybody take a deep breath. I understand none of this is easy. But the only way to move forward is together. Right?"

Max shrugged, whether from modesty or embarrassment, Claire couldn't tell.

"Oh, now *Max* is the family hero?" Garrett glared from behind wire-rimmed glasses, which he rarely wore unless his contacts bothered him. "How mucked up is all this, anyway?"

Max plopped back on the couch and locked his hands behind his head, fingers lost in the tangled mass of brown curls. "What are you freaking about, Garrett? So we all go to the hearing and tell the judge what a great guy our dad is? C'mon, let's stick by the old man, even though he bilked a bunch of people of their savings and screwed just about everybody we know. Huh, what d'ya say?"

Claire became tearful. "Okay, all of you. You're acting like spoiled brats. Stop it." She watched her children's faces, waiting. Not seeing the reaction she'd hoped for, she paced in front of the fireplace. "Ranger has worked hard to arrange this plea agreement." Claire pointed to Garrett. "And your father had to accept a longer sentence to keep you out of all this."

"I'm *not* a part of any of this." Garrett narrowed his eyes. "Because of what my father did, I'll never be able to work anywhere without suspicion hanging over my head. Even now, people look at me as if I helped Dad take all these people's money." He slammed his fist down. "And I was not involved in any way, shape, or form."

Claire moved toward her son. "Garrett —"

Garrett held up his hand. "Don't, Mom." His lip quivered and he seemed to fight for control. "The feds are going through every check, every debit transaction. I'm not going to that hearing, and that's final."

"Anything Tuck did, right or wrong, he did for this family. For all of us." Claire forced strength into her voice that she failed to feel inside. "I know this is hard. But we are all he has."

She looked past the sofa, surprised that Marcy now stood in the doorway.

Marcy's chin lifted and she moved into the room, looking every bit the beauty who won the Miss Texas pageant the year before she married. "Claire, your family is not all that matters right now," she said icily, her hand on her belly.

Claire caught the gesture and quickly searched Garrett's eyes. "Garrett?"

Garrett showed resignation, apprehension even, as he walked to his wife, placing his hand protectively at her back. "We're pregnant."

Lainie leapt from the sofa, rushed over,

and hugged her sister-in-law. "When?"

Max extended his hand to his brother. "Good move. We didn't see that coming."

Still guarded, Garrett let a slight grin form. "The baby's due right after the first of the year. We'd planned to tell everyone, but then all this with Dad happened."

Claire didn't know what to say. A new baby was welcome news, even if the timing pricked at her. Announcements of this sort shouldn't be shadowed by what this family now faced.

She could imagine Tuck's elated face when he learned the news. Under different circumstances, he'd claim he was too young to be a grandpa while picking up his daughter-in-law and twirling her. Then he'd whoop and pass out cigars to all the ranch hands.

The image sucked away any joy she felt and bound her reaction with rusty-wire emotion. Like so much of her life going forward, nothing would go as she'd imagined.

"Mom, say something," Max said. "This is great news."

Claire walked over and drew both of Marcy's hands into her own. She spoke slowly, with exaggerated sincerity. "Of course I'm thrilled. Congratulations, both of you." She brushed Marcy's cheek with a kiss and then patted Garrett's shoulder, trying to grasp that her baby would be having a baby.

Garrett's expression sagged, his jaw less sharp and angular. He swallowed. "Look, Mom. I didn't want to do this until Dad got back from his meeting with Ranger, but maybe it's best you hear this first." He looked to Marcy for reassurance. "Marcy's dad has hired counsel to represent us . . . uh, I mean me."

"Represent you?" Claire stared at the son who shared her own features, her warm brown eyes and high cheekbones. "What do you mean, Garrett?"

Marcy spoke up. "My father has arranged for an attorney in Houston to advise Garrett."

"Just what are you meaning?" Lainie challenged. "You don't think Daddy and Ranger will protect you guys?"

Claire held up her hand. This was no time for war to break out in the family. Taut emotions shouldn't supersede good judgment. "Garrett," she said, trying to get him to look at her. "Help us understand what you're saying."

Marcy rolled her eyes. "We aren't going to stand by and wait for the other shoe to drop.

Garrett's going to work for Daddy until all this is over."

Garrett shifted as if something was being asked of him beyond what he was willing to give. He held up his hand to silence his wife. "I've been advised to not talk about any of this with anyone except Marcy and my attorney. I've already crossed that line to some extent." He looked to the ceiling for strength. "I have to do what is best for us — for our new baby. I'm already under suspicion and my records have been subpoenaed. I can't take any chances, you know?" His expression grew even more somber. "Marcy and I are moving to Houston to stay with her folks. Just temporarily," he rushed to add.

"Houston?" Lainie asked. "But that's hours away."

Claire let out a quick, bitter laugh. "So you're bailing? On running Legacy Ranch, and your father?"

Garrett hesitated. He took a deep breath and shook his head. Tears pooled. "My father bailed on *me,*" he said, his voice clogged with emotion.

The raw pain in her son's eyes startled Claire. She nodded, frustration instantly tempered by an overwhelming sense of protection. This was her child, after all, and he was hurting.

For several seconds, everyone stood quiet, as if one more word might destroy the family structure already threatening to crumble at their feet.

Finally, it was Claire who spoke. "I guess I understand," she ventured, acutely aware she really had no choice but to support their decision. She did understand at some level.

Still, her chest cramped with sadness.

She looked directly at Garrett and then Marcy, desperately trying to hold back tears until she'd stated what clearly needed to be expressed. "There's something I want both of you to remember, no matter what. When all this settles down, your home is here. At Legacy Ranch."

15

Lainie counted Reece's invitation to meet at the Dallas Arboretum a good sign. Beyond providing the requisite privacy they needed, the botanical showplace was known as one of the most romantic places in the Dallas area — and it was the venue they'd booked for the wedding ceremony in December, with fireworks over the lake and everything.

Only last week, she'd thought Reece's silence signaled the wedding was off. But then the text had come, asking how she was doing. He missed her and needed to see her.

She'd obviously miscalculated Reece's intentions and allowed herself to become insecure, a state fairly foreign to Lainie. But the situation with her father had left everyone in the family unsteady. She was no exception.

Even at this early morning hour, the gardens were filled with visitors strolling walkways lined with carpets of pink and white impatiens, some posing for photos beneath pergolas dripping with soft lavender wisteria.

Lainie wore a tight-fitted blue sundress, meant to ensure Reece was really glad to see her. Before they parted today, she planned on doing everything in her female power to make sure her fiancé never again left her wondering where they stood, no matter what the polls and advisors dictated.

She made her way past the DeGolyer House and through Magnolia Alley, heading in the direction of the concert stage. As she walked, she considered how the air carried a hint of rose, promising the knockouts would soon be in bloom.

Then she saw him.

Reece sat on a bench, looking out at a sailboat skittering along the shoreline of White Rock Lake, his back to her. Lainie paused for several seconds, surprised at how dry her mouth had become. He turned and spotted her then. His face broke into a smile and he waved her over.

"Hey, Lainie." Reece stepped forward and pulled her into an embrace. The smell of his aftershave made her ache. She'd missed him terribly and whispered in his ear telling him so.

"I missed you too." He took her hand and guided her to the seat beside him. "And I'm sorry about . . . everything." Reece glanced around before slipping his Ray-Bans in place. "How's your mom?"

Lainie caught him up, told him about the upcoming hearing. Her parents seemed to be doing all right. They'd been in frequent meetings with Ranger and his firm, planning the turnover of assets to the receiver.

She didn't tell him she'd gone for a glass of milk in the middle of the night and heard her mother crying. Or that she'd pretended not to hear and slipped quietly back to her own room because she didn't know what to say.

She also skipped over Garrett and Marcy's surprise baby news, and that they'd picked up and moved to Houston to avoid what she also wished to escape.

Instead, Lainie tried to remain upbeat until finally she forced herself to ask, "So, how's the campaign?" She swallowed back nerves, waiting to hear whether he was really still down six points like the media reported.

"Slowly climbing back," he responded.

Relieved, Lainie searched his expression. "That's good. Right?"

Reece nodded. He looked out over the

water. "Yeah, the numbers are up. But funding is down."

"Look, Reece. I know this situation is bad. Believe me, I know." Lainie touched his elbow. "But you love me. We're going to be married. By the time the election rolls around, all this will have settled down in voters' minds. Many news cycles will have come and gone, and Daddy's business dealings will be ancient history."

"You're wrong about that, Lainie. Politics creates long memories. The fact your father bilked thousands of people will be used over and over by our opponents." Reece stood and ran his hand across the back of his neck. "How can I debate educational reform when facing the fact my future father-in-law single-handedly robbed hundreds of people of college funds?" He turned, his voice rising. "Think of how I'm going to possibly counter accusations that a mass of Texans now have zilch in their retirement accounts because of what your dad did."

"Yes, but — all that will resolve in time. Many candidates have weathered worse. At least you don't have a mistress and a hidden baby somewhere." She laughed, trying to lighten the tension.

"No, I don't have a hidden love child somewhere." Reece's tone grew sarcastic.

"But you need a reality check. Your father is a crook."

Lainie tempered her response, though she felt a flash of fury. "I'm perfectly aware of what my father did and how the consequences of his actions ripple." Despite her desire to remain calm, she stood and pointed her finger in his direction. "I drove here in a Toyota, for goodness' sake. Because heaven forbid how it might look if I zoomed into the parking lot in my Maserati." She huffed. "Less than two weeks ago, I ordered a wedding gown my mother now tells me we can't pay for. We've had to let our staff go, all our stable hands, the landscapers, my massage therapist — they're all gone. Margarita and Henry are the only ones left." Lainie flung her arms wide. "I'm plenty in touch with reality."

With shaking hands, Lainie straightened her dress, already sorry for her outburst. Reece was attracted to strength. Not an angry woman who loaded up her mouth and shot rounds of anger in the not-O.K. Corral. Besides, her fight wasn't with Reece. She loved him and knew his concerns were more than valid. "Reece, I'm sorry. I know none of this is good."

"Look, Lainie —"

She held up her hand. "No, stop." Lainie

bit her quivering lip.

Reece's eyes saddened and he rubbed his chin. "Lainie, please don't make what I have to say any harder."

Lainie blinked to clear hot tears forming at the backs of her lids. "I'll make it easy. You don't have to say it." She quietly slipped the ring off and set her cherished trophy on the seat between them.

Across the lawn, a woman sitting cross-legged on a blanket dipped a tiny plastic wand into a bright blue bottle, raised the wand to her lips, and blew. Her toddler giggled and chased the blast of soap bubbles. Each time he reached for a bubble, it popped.

Lainie slowly lifted her purse from the bench, knowing her own dreams had burst. She'd never stand before this man in a white gown. There'd be no fireworks over a crowd of well-wishers. No White House in her future.

Lainie wasn't the kind of girl who would beg or cajole, or the type who might manipulate with guilt. Her approach was much more direct. She simply bulleted a steely look into her former fiancé's eyes. "You've made a huge mistake." She stood and headed in the direction of the parking lot.

Alaina Claire Massey never once looked back.

16

On the morning of the hearing, Claire swept through her closet searching for the perfect thing to wear. Black seemed too somber. On the other hand, color signaled the wrong message — that she held no remorse for what her husband had done. She'd have to choose carefully. Nothing too elegant or sporty. Too flashy. An outfit that expressed confidence but didn't portray a woman overly self-assured.

In the end, she pulled together a smart ensemble that consisted of a taupe-colored crepe dress, sleeveless, with a classic drape and a flattering pintucked neckline. But she needed a jacket.

Her hands ruffled across a dozen or more blazers. The red one would look beautiful, but who wears red to her husband's hearing? Someone who wants the media accusing her of flaunting, that was who. She could see the headlines now: "Mrs. Tuck

Massey, in a Scarlet Letter Jacket . . ."

Claire ultimately decided on an aquamarine scalloped-front cardigan and a strand of pearls. Not the ones Tuck purchased in Sri Lanka, the ones they'd insured for nearly a half million. Those were in the safe and soon would be turned over to the receiver.

The strand she now wore, Claire's mother had worn when she married her father. Claire wanted Lainie to wear the keepsake pearls at her own wedding, but that would be some time off now. Lainie had never been given to dark or brooding moods, but ever since Reece broke off the engagement, Lainie's actions had been out of character.

When she wasn't riding Pride along the riverbank, her daughter spent most of her time locked away in her room, refusing to join the family for meals. Tuck wanted to go talk to her, but Claire cautioned against it. "Give her time. She's hurting and you might make things worse."

He opened his mouth in protest, but she placed her finger over his lips. "I mean it. Let her be for now."

It had been Max who talked Lainie into attending the hearing today. Claire counted the gesture a good sign. Her daughter loved Tuck. Eventually her anger would subside and she'd heal. It would just take time.

Claire struggled to clear her mind and tried to focus on the task at hand. In a few hours, she'd walk the steps of the courthouse, media cameras clicking. She needed to look just right.

She moved to her shoe racks, sliding her eyes across color-coordinated rows of stilettos, wedges, and boots, until finding the perfect pair of pumps in a dark shade that complemented her sweater perfectly.

She slid the Madagascar diamond-and-sapphire-encrusted ring from her left hand, another gift from Tuck — a little something he'd picked up on a trip to the south of Africa. "A treasure for the one I treasure," the card had read. Claire popped the trinket into a velvet-lined drawer. There'd be no diamonds, not today.

She paused, then slipped the pearls from her neck and laid them in the drawer as well. No reason to test fate, she supposed.

Before leaving her dressing room, Claire positioned herself in front of the ceiling-to-floor mirrors and examined her reflection. Satisfied, she grabbed her bag and headed for the door.

She was ready.

The hearing was canceled.

Ranger telephoned minutes before Tuck

and Claire left the house. "Tuck, what is it?" Claire asked, seeing worry cross Tuck's face.

Tuck quickly glanced at Max and Lainie, as if measuring whether or not to come clean and tell the truth. Claire knew him well enough to suspect he couldn't stand their looks of distrust. He lowered his head and stared at the floor. "There's been a bomb threat. At the courthouse."

"A what?" Claire felt the air leave her lungs.

"A bomb," Tuck repeated.

Her hand flew to her chest. "Oh my. Are they sure?"

"Mom, of course they're sure." Max slumped onto the sofa, looking at her as if she'd grown two heads.

This incident was not the first threat, Claire learned. There had been many others.

"I want to know everything," she said.

"Babe, I don't think that's a good idea," Tuck said.

"Everything," she repeated, reminding him that withholding information was no longer an option he could choose to utilize if he was to remain in her good favor. There would be no second chances if he breached this newly established boundary.

168

The most alarming menace had come in the form of a call to Ranger's office. The perpetrator told the receptionist he planned to take Tuck's attorneys out one by one and bury them alive. "Maybe those buzzards will know what it feels like to have your finances choked," the throaty warning threatened. "If those fancy-dancy attorneys get that crook off, they deserve to suffocate in dirt."

There had also been anonymous letters and a message posted to Facebook from a phony profile page, set up specifically for sending the warning that Tuck's life could be in danger. All these incidents were being followed by the US Attorney's Office — when they had time — and kept out of the news to avoid risking the ongoing investigations.

"I didn't tell y'all because I didn't want to worry you." Tuck rubbed the back of this neck. "Given all this, Ranger suggests we all stay close to home until after the hearing."

"Oh, great," Lainie said, staring at her father with disdain. "You do the crime. We all do the time."

"Lainie," Claire scolded.

Tuck held his palm up. "No, Claire. She's right." He turned to his daughter. "This isn't fair to any of you."

Lainie's eyes filled with angry tears. "Ha,

169

you think?"

Tuck reached for her arm. "Princess —"

She pulled away. "Don't call me that. You lost that right the first time you crossed the line and put this family in jeopardy."

Tuck's head dropped. "Lainie, I love my family. I'd do anything to make it up to all of you."

"Well, you can't. None of us can turn the clock back to our happy *before*. Everything is ruined. You did this," she accused. "And I hate you for it." She turned and ran from the room.

Max whistled. "Whew, she's hotter than a jalapeño," he said in an attempt to lighten the moment.

Tuck scowled at him. "Not now, Son." He turned and headed for the front door. But not before Claire spotted tears running down her husband's flushed cheeks.

She turned to Max, and sighed heavily, fighting her own tears. "How did my family become so broken?"

He leaned against the empty fireplace and let out a quick laugh. "Mom, this family's always been broken. Problem is, you're just now discovering the fact."

17

On Sunday afternoon, the day before the rescheduled arraignment hearing, the real bomb dropped when Ranger and a team of attorneys from his firm showed up at the ranch needing to discuss a recent development in Tuck's case.

Ranger stood in the Masseys' library, looking grim. "I've been contacted by Charles Jordan of the US Attorney's Office. He's threatening to withdraw the plea agreement."

Claire gasped. "Can they do that?"

"On what grounds?" Tuck said, crossing his arms tightly across his chest. "We conceded to everything they asked."

Ranger slowly rotated the brim of his felt Stetson in his fingers. "Jordan's not saying much at this juncture. He simply says they are weighing options." He turned to Claire. "I'm sorry, Claire. We're going to have to ask you to excuse us."

Her eyes widened. "I can't stay? Why?"

One of Ranger's associates cleared his throat. "Given the turn of events, you could get called to testify."

"Oh," Claire muttered as she backed up several steps. She glanced at her husband. Tuck's face had clearly paled at the news. "I — uh, I'll go then."

She moved from the library to the hallway, pulling the large wooden double doors closed behind her. Stunned, she wandered past framed photos lining the wall.

There were shots taken of Tuck with Governor Jackson at the prestigious Beaux Arts Ball. Another with Jerry Jones, owner of the Dallas Cowboys. And still another with Sidney McAlvain, Tuck's wealthy oil friend from Houston, taken at the Dallas Petroleum Club.

Midway down the hall, another large frame held a photo of the ribbon cutting for Abundant Hills' new church building. Claire and her husband had contributed heavily to the effort. She passed her fingers lightly across the faces of people she'd sat with on so many Sunday mornings. People she now couldn't bear to face.

She stopped at one photo taken of their family at their home in Sun Valley. They'd spent Christmas in Idaho, enjoying the snow. Lainie had spotted Maria Schwarzenegger walking the sidewalk in front of Pete Lane's, carrying a new pair of Rossignols over her shoulder.

Max, then age seven, wanted to know if the Terminator was with her.

Lainie rolled her eyes at her little brother. "No, silly. He's probably at home watching the children."

Claire shook her head. If news reports were accurate, the muscled philanderer had been spending intimate time with his housekeeper.

Maria, Elizabeth Edwards, Ruth Madoff — all members of a club of betrayed women. An exclusive club Claire had never wanted to join.

She wandered out onto the side portico. Above the large fireplace, a television was mounted on the stone. She kicked off her open-toed espadrilles and sank into the brightly colored cushions on a chaise lounge.

She clicked past all the news channels, not wanting to add to her already high level anxiety. Past QVC and a golf tournament. Finally, a woman with far too much makeup and blonde hair tinted pink popped onto the screen. Claire shook her head, fascinated.

"Oh, honey." The woman with the big hair leaned into the microphone. "If you are hurting right now, I've got good news to share with you."

Claire winced but turned the volume louder.

"God's Word tells us in the book of Isaiah, 'When you pass through the waters, I will be with you.' " The woman dabbed a hanky to her tear-filled eyes rimmed with running mascara. "Honey, are circumstances in your life flooding out of control? Do you feel about to drown? Jesus promises you are never alone."

She sighed and clicked off the television, remembering her meeting with Pastor Richards. *But what about when you let God down?*

Just feet away, behind closed doors, some of the best legal minds in Texas were trying to build an ark for Tuck to ride out the storm. Since the arrest, their lives had been swept away in a torrent of accusations and consequences that had left their entire family splintered. Claire desperately wanted to believe Tuck's actions had not left them adrift.

She was scared.

And she had never felt so alone.

18

In the movies, an actress in a pencil skirt and heels often rushed the courthouse steps, flanked by the protective arms of her attorney shielding her from overzealous media and flashing cameras. In the movies, the lens zoomed in on the main character showing an air of quiet confidence on her face. In the movies, the target of all the media attention didn't climb the steps and get spit on.

Seconds after the wet glob hit its mark against Claire's cheek, security created a human fence between her and the spectacle of onlookers, but not before Claire caught sight of the culprit wedged next to a reporter — a fortyish gal in a T-shirt that read "Don't Mess with Texas." Their eyes met and the woman hissed, "Thief!"

Claire's companion, a woman associate from Ranger's office, handed her a tissue. She lied and assured her she was fine. In reality, the encounter had shaken her to the core. As soon as they cleared the security scanner, she excused herself and darted to the restroom.

"Let me go with you," the young associate said, already following on Claire's heels. "You shouldn't be alone."

Inside the privacy of a stall, Claire stood fighting tears. Never before had she allowed herself to ponder the notion there were people who actually hated the Masseys. Not just Tuck, but his entire family. They hated *her*.

Lainie was right. From that first moment in the Adolphus, the click of her husband's handcuffs had imprisoned all of them. Tuck's arrest had placed the first stone on a monument of shame Claire had desperately been trying to ignore.

How could she disregard what that woman on the steps represented? Claire's future grandbaby would be born wearing a name connected to the largest cattle fraud in Texas, maybe even in the United States.

Despite her choice to look at the situation cup half full, some endeavors were destined to fail. No plea agreement would change what the family now faced.

"Mrs. Massey?" the associate asked. "The hearing will start soon. Your husband and the others are already waiting inside."

Claire wiped at her eyes. She opened the stall door and stepped to the bank of sinks, avoiding the young woman's stare. After she refreshed her makeup, she turned. "Okay, let's go."

The doors to Courtroom 211 were located conveniently across from the ladies' room. Claire crossed the hall, feeling a bit buoyed by the knowledge she'd be reunited with Tuck for the first time since that morning at breakfast. He'd suggested they travel in separate cars to the courthouse. He'd needed to talk privately with Ranger over the telephone. Again she was pushed into the role of an outsider.

Claire had only been inside a courtroom twice before, once as a potential jurist and the other for a minor traffic violation. Not hers. Max had rear-ended someone while texting a high school classmate. Both occasions were a long time ago.

This courtroom was relatively small by most standards. And fairly utilitarian. None of the magnificent marble columns and architectural elements found in older courthouses.

Despite strong public urging, this would be a closed hearing today. Thankfully, the judge recognized the potential for a media circus and limited attendance to only the parties and counsel, which extended to anyone working with the attorneys. If that incident out on the steps was any indication, recently increased security would be served as well by the judge's decision.

The associate guided Claire to a pew directly behind the defense table, next to Max. Lainie had decided not to attend this time. Ranger greeted Claire and quickly returned to reviewing a paper in his hand. The team, as Tuck referred to them, sat in benches around her and nearer to the wall. She recognized some of the folks from Monty Dickman, the crisis management firm Ranger had hired after Tuck's arrest. Others had been at the ranch yesterday.

At the opposite table sat Charles Jordan, the head of the white-collar crimes unit in the US Attorney's Office and the chief prosecutor in Tuck's case. In the weeks leading up to the hearing, the man with the precise haircut had been grandstanding on the news. "Some criminals murder people," he'd claimed in front of the cameras. "Theodore Massey murdered wallets. But make no mistake," he said, pulling on his starched cuffs. "Massey left victims, and the US Attorney's Office will do everything in its power to bring justice."

Mr. Jordan also had a bevy of helpers in the courtroom today, sour men and women in dark suits, appearing as though they'd swallowed a box of government-issued paper clips.

A bailiff approached the defense table and said something to Ranger, who then nodded. The bailiff spoke into a lapel microphone. Minutes later, a side door opened and another bailiff entered, leading Tuck into the courtroom.

Tuck joined Ranger at the defense table. When he turned and spotted her, a familiar repose crossed his face. She ventured a quick smile, which Tuck acknowledged by lifting his chin.

For the briefest moment, Claire questioned Ranger's advice. Was consenting to all this really in Tuck's best interests? But then again, they had no choice. Not really. It was doubtful Tuck would end with a better situation if they made the US Attorney prove his case. In fact, as Ranger explained, Tuck would no doubt be found guilty of many of the counts in the prosecutor's complaint. And the sentencing would be much harsher, she supposed. There was no escaping the fact Tuck would pay for what he'd done.

This way, everyone would win — or lose,

whichever way you chose to spin the situation. By Tuck falling on his sword, no one could argue that he wouldn't come out of this eventually looking contrite and with an opportunity to reinvent his image, at least to some extent. Or so the crisis managers claimed.

These were the thoughts that ran through Claire's mind as her eyes followed her husband's every movement. He looked extraordinarily handsome in a suit and tie that had been selected by the folks at Monty Dickman, who were experts at manipulating public sentiment. In a meeting early last week, an impeccably poised young woman explained Tuck needed to wear brown — a color that imbued warmth and likability. There would be no jury, and even though the judge was not to rule with bias, she was human and could be swayed by impressions.

"All rise," the bailiff announced.

Claire took a deep breath and sent up a quick prayer. She grabbed her youngest son's hand for support.

"You may be seated."

Claire followed the legal team's instructions and kept her face without expression as she listened to the judge's clerk read off the case name and number. Ranger said Judge Herrick was a no-nonsense adjudicator, fair but expedient in doling out justice.

Judge Herrick dispensed with prerequisites she might otherwise have afforded had the hearing not been closed to the media. Instead, she looked over her glasses at the counsel. "Good morning, everyone. Before we begin arraignment, I'd like to know where things stand. Has anything changed since the proposed agreement was lodged with the court?"

Charles Jordan stood. "If I may, Your Honor."

Judge Herrick nodded. "Go ahead."

"This case is extraordinary, Your Honor. As the record reveals, our office has brought charges alleging Theodore Massey perpetrated the largest cattle fraud this nation has yet seen. The federal violations we've outlined in our pleadings show how far-reaching the actions of Mr. Massey's illegal activities are. We have hundreds of victims. Millions of dollars are at stake. The Office of the US Attorney is committed to seek justice. However, as you are well aware, Your Honor, we must balance that justice with what is also in the interests of the public and of the victims. The US Attorney's Office agrees to stipulate to the terms set forth in the consent order currently before this court, knowing the victims in this matter —

the creditors — would never be made entirely whole. It was our belief that the proposed consent order renders justice and creates the best opportunity for Mr. Massey's assets to be distributed to the victims at the earliest point possible."

Claire shifted in her seat, her heart pounding. She wished she could see Tuck's face.

Judge Herrick looked at Ranger. "Mr. Jennings. Do you have anything to add?"

"Only that my client, Theodore Massey, has fully cooperated with the US Attorney's Office. It is his desire to use his considerable assets in the interest of his investors, most of which made considerable money over the years. As far as sentencing goes —"

Judge Herrick held up her hand. "I believe your position on sentencing is clearly stated in your written statement. The court recognizes Mr. Massey's past contributions and that this is his first encounter with the legal system. However, these charges are substantial." She looked out over the courtroom. "Let's cut to the chase. Are all counsel in agreement?"

Both Ranger Jennings and Charles Jordan nodded.

Judge Herrick scanned a couple of documents. "I'm not inclined to sign off on the retention provision as proposed. The current residence represents assets that far exceed any homestead exemption. Therefore, I'll allow Mrs. Massey to live in the current residential house for a period not to exceed ninety days. At the end of that time, the ranch and house will be sold and proceeds will be distributed to the victims. Mrs. Massey will retain one vehicle not to exceed fifty thousand dollars in value, personal effects and furnishings not to exceed two hundred fifty thousand, and the same amount in cash. Everything else will be immediately turned over to the receiver and liquidated for the benefit of Mr. Massey's victims."

Claire tried to remember to breathe, though the air suddenly grew thick and clotted in her nostrils.

Mr. Jordan held up a finger. "Uh, one more thing, Your Honor."

"Yes?"

"We'd like Mr. Massey remanded into custody within twenty-four hours."

Max's arm instantly went around her trembling shoulders as she scoured the courtroom in wild confusion.

Ranger jumped up from his seat. "Your Honor —"

Judge Herrick held up her hand. "Save it. I agree with Mr. Jordan. There is no good reason to postpone incarceration." The judge looked around the room. "Anything else?"

Ranger and Mr. Jordan shook their heads.

The judge nodded to her clerk. "Then let's go on record."

Over the next hour, Tuck was formally arraigned on the original charges. Claire's heart thumped painfully in protest as the plea was read into the record, and Tuck gave affirmative responses confirming he understood and agreed to the consent order, including the judge's revised retention provision.

At the end, Judge Herrick pulled her glasses from her face. "I'd like to thank everyone for their cooperation. It is my sincere belief that justice has been served here today." She looked at Tuck. "Mr. Massey, you are to report to the US Marshal's office no later than noon tomorrow. At that time, you will be transported to the Federal Correction Institution in Bastrop, where you will begin serving the agreed-upon five-year sentence. This court is now adjourned." She hit the gavel.

"All rise," the bailiff bellowed. Judge Herrick stood and left the courtroom.

Claire lifted from her seat, fighting back tears. This was a bad television episode —

and she a helpless spectator.

Tuck turned.

His gray eyes revealed a fragility that was new to her, a crack in his confident demeanor. Their depths gave a quiet peek into the boy with the alcoholic mother. Despite all Tuck had done and all that was ahead of them, tenderness flooded Claire's heart. In that instant, this man was as important as her next breath.

Despite having lost nearly everything, including their home, it took everything inside her not to move into his arms and whisper that everything would be okay. Together they'd get through this.

Somehow.

19

The gravity of what had happened at the hearing did not hit Claire until she was home. She'd left the courthouse with Tuck and his legal team and sat emotionally numb in Ranger's office, trying to listen to a myriad of details. At times, the voices seemed to fade off, or maybe she did.

Bastrop is a low-security facility. Many white-collar inmates. Four hours from Dallas.

Asset turnover would happen fairly quickly. Ranger would supervise.

Disappointing ruling regarding ranch. Public outcry demanded. Will allow fresh start. Parole possible in two years. Maybe live outside Texas when Tuck is released.

Upon arriving home, an exhausted Tuck retreated to their bedroom for a quick nap. Glad for time alone to collect her thoughts, Claire pulled on a pair of boots and headed for the riverbank, where she hoped to walk out the sour feeling in her stomach.

As her boots cut into the dry dirt path, she could smell the day's heat, feel the setting sun at her back. To the east, the horizon blackened. Northern Texas weather was often filled with contradictions, especially in early June, with hot days shifting to thunderstorms at night.

Claire walked until she could barely make out the house. She wished creating distance from her troubles were as easy.

Overhead, a red-shouldered hawk dropped from the sky low enough for her to make out its sharp eyes scanning for prey. A mouse darted from behind a large oak several feet ahead, making a critical mistake. The hawk screeched and dove.

After a momentary scuffle, the raptor flapped its massive wings and lifted. Its spiked claws held tight to the tiny rodent struggling to be free.

She averted her eyes and collapsed at the base of the oak, leaning back against the brittle bark. One critical mistake and Tuck had lost his freedom. In a few short hours, they would have to say goodbye.

Claire's eyes surveyed the ranch she'd called home. The last two decades of her life stared back.

In her youth, she had ignored the popular voice of Gloria Steinem known for telling young women, "A liberated woman is one who has sex before marriage and a job after." Neither did she embrace her mother's philosophy that a woman's key goal should be to marry well — and in her mother's case, switch shoes when the first pair didn't fit.

Claire's marriage had been the perfect blend of light, crisp Chardonnay grapes mixed with the complex Pinot Noir variety. Water turned to fine wine, despite how their lives had recently soured.

Tuck meant to give her the world, even if by illicit means.

She couldn't hate him now.

True, she had much to consider. She'd be out of a home in three months and would need to find a new place to live and a means of support, because two hundred fifty thousand dollars wouldn't last forever. She'd never been employed. Could she even get a job at her age?

Thunder boomed on the horizon, startling Claire. She glanced toward the house and calculated the distance. She'd never make it back home without getting drenched. If she remained underneath the cover of this oak, she might be able to wait until the storm passed. Weather was unpredictable, and the disturbance may even pass around her.

She pulled her knees up tight and wrapped her arms around her legs, wishing she'd thought to bring along a jacket. Especially now that the sky had started spitting little rain droplets onto the hard, thirsty ground.

Garrett used to be so afraid of storms. In the middle of the night, he'd leave the security of his warm bed and pad his little jammied feet into their room, climbing in between her and Tuck and hiding under the covers for safety.

Now he hid in Houston.

She didn't blame him. She'd like to hide too.

The rain came harder now, and the air felt electric. The sky flashed and a loud crack followed seconds later.

Soon Marcy would be showing. There would be sonograms and baby showers, picking names and nursery colors. Unless something changed, Claire could easily miss it all.

Lainie was hiding too. She'd retreated behind a wall of silence. Max's face often showed stunned confusion.

Her children were hurting. She was hurting.

Rain pelted the ground. Every few seconds, pea-sized hail smacked the limbs above her head, making an eerie sound as water pellets tore through the leaves. Claire huddled closer to the trunk, nestling into the gnarled roots deeply wrenched into the ground.

Before her daddy left this world, he'd written her a letter. Across plain lined paper, he'd scrawled a message, asking her to remember two things.

The first: *What does it profit a man if he gains the whole world and loses his soul?*

And the second: *Remember, I love you always.*

Claire may have lost her jewelry, vacation homes, wealth, and status. But she couldn't bear to lose her family. Margarita was right. As she faced the dark days ahead, she must do everything in her power to keep her family intact.

Otherwise, none of the past years of her life would mean anything.

Suddenly the entire sky lit. A loud boom knocked her forward. A heavy crack sounded above.

She looked up. A large limb came crashing down, landing less than a foot away.

Her body involuntarily jumped and she let out a yelp.

"Claire!" a voice hollered.

Lightning illuminated the sky again. A

silhouette moved forward. "Claire, don't move."

Within seconds, Tuck was by her side. He pulled her chilled body into his warm coat and she leaned against his beating chest.

Together they rode out the storm.

20

By morning, the violent weather had passed and storm clouds of a different sort appeared on their doorstep.

Tuck joined Claire in their closet, where she had an open suitcase on the floor. "Honey, don't pack so many shirts. I won't need them," he said gently.

Claire tossed the folded button-down back in the drawer and slammed it shut with her hip. "Excuse me if I don't know how to pack for prison." She regretted the words the minute they left her mouth and apologized. The building tension was getting to her.

Tuck's hand touched her arm. "Let's have Margarita finish this. Ranger will be here in less than an hour, and I want to have breakfast with the kids."

Downstairs, the family gathered in the breakfast nook. Even Lainie, but not without argument. Her twenty-three-year-old daughter, who might once have been a senator's wife, now acted like a pouty teenager. One who didn't quite know how to process her raging emotions and made everyone around miserable by her cranky behavior.

Max, on the other hand, had really stepped up. With Garrett gone, he was no longer the irresponsible baby of the family, even at age twenty. He'd temporarily moved back into his former room, somehow sensing how much Claire needed him right now.

Sitting at the table, Claire found the lack of conversation a bit surprising. She'd have expected — or maybe wanted — them all to use this time together to . . . she didn't know, maybe reminisce or create some verbal solidarity. *Something.*

She made several attempts to start a lighthearted discussion. When every effort was met with silence, she finally gave up and pushed her cold eggs around the plate like the rest of them.

Margarita filled their coffee cups, her eyes brimming with tears. When she finished, Tuck slipped his napkin quietly onto the table. He cleared this throat. "I have something I'd like to say before Ranger gets here."

Margarita moved for the door.

"No, Margarita. Stay. I want you to hear

this as well." Tuck's voice grew thick with emotion. "In a little while, I'm going to begin paying society for what I've done. But in a million years, I can never make up for what I've done to my family." His broad shoulders shook and his lip trembled. He struggled for control. "I love you all so very much. And I'm sorry — for everything."

Lainie burst into tears. She slammed her chair back and ran from the room, sobbing.

Claire stood to follow until Tuck motioned for her to sit back down. "Let her go, Claire."

Margarita stood in the corner, her hand furiously working a tiny metal cross Claire knew was hidden in her pocket. Their housekeeper's lips moved in silent prayer.

Outside, a helicopter flew overhead. The media circus had begun.

The sound of a car engine drew her attention to the window. Outside, Ranger climbed from a large black sedan and headed for the front steps.

"Well," Tuck said, scooting his chair back, "looks like it's time."

Max and Claire followed Tuck to the front foyer, where Tuck's bags waited.

Claire hadn't slept last night. While nestled against her husband, the last time in possibly five years, she'd told herself she was ready. But now she knew she'd needed to tell herself that to make it through the night.

She watched Tuck hug their son. Her husband kissed Margarita on the forehead, told her he'd miss her cooking. His hand slipped an envelope on the table with Lainie's name across the front. Somehow he'd known his daughter wouldn't be able to say goodbye.

Then he turned to her.

Tuck pulled Claire into a tight embrace, burying his face in her hair. "Don't visit me in that awful place. At least not for a while," he whispered. "Promise? And give me a few days to settle in before we talk on the phone. It'll be easier, I think."

She swallowed against the baseball-sized lump in her throat and nodded. She tried to say something but choked on a sob. She squeezed her eyes closed, trying to cement this moment in her memory. His smell, the way his cheek felt against her own.

This last physical contact would have to last.

She felt him pull away. Suddenly terror filled her. She couldn't do this. No — she couldn't.

She clung tighter, sobs clambering up her throat as her heart ruptured.

Claire wanted to be strong.

She couldn't.

Max's arms folded around her. "I've got her, Dad," he said, gently pulling her from Tuck's arms.

Claire opened her water-filled eyes to find tears also streaming down her husband's agonized face. He turned for the door.

Then he was gone.

21

Claire wanted to believe the worst was behind her. But the process of turning over assets to the receiver brought a new emotional low.

There'd been back-to-back meetings with Ranger, with her signing quitclaim deeds and paperwork. Relinquishing interest in the company assets was hard enough, but turning over their personal property left a bad feeling in the back of her throat. "These are just assets," she told herself, but secretly she resented the implication that everything they owned had been acquired by stealing. She alone was audience to all those years of Tuck's legitimate hard work. His recent bad decisions had erased it all.

Ranger slid the deed to their vacation home in Sun Valley across the conference table. With her pen poised, Claire couldn't help remembering Christmas ski holidays spent there, especially the year Garrett broke his leg.

He'd been fourteen. Or had he been fifteen? She couldn't remember exactly.

She made plans to meet a friend for brunch at Gretchen's, a quaint restaurant inside the Sun Valley Lodge, named after Sun Valley's own legendary Gretchen Fraser, the first American to win an Olympic gold medal in skiing. Tuck and the children headed for Baldy, wanting to take advantage of the fresh powder.

The waitress had barely placed the eggs Benedict on the table when Claire's cell phone rang. She answered, wondering which of them forgot their ski pass this time. "Tuck?"

"Claire, Garrett's all right, but you need to meet us at the hospital."

"Hospital?" Claire dropped her fork. "What happened?"

"He's fractured his left tibia," Tuck said. "X-rays will confirm the extent of the injury, but more than likely this is a simple break."

Despite Tuck's attempt to sound calm, Claire heard alarm hidden in his assurances that their son's injuries were minor. She grabbed her purse. "Look, I've got to go. It's Garrett," she said, offering her friend an apology. They hugged briefly, and Claire bolted out into the lobby.

At the hospital, Tuck, Max, and Lainie sat in the emergency waiting room. There Claire learned Tuck had talked Garrett into following him down Exhibition, one of the more difficult expert runs.

She gave her husband an indignant look. "Tuck, what were you thinking?" she said with a raised voice, one of a few times she'd ever spoken to her husband in that manner. "Garrett had no business trying to make that expert run."

Tuck thrived on taking risks, but no way would she allow him to place the children in danger. She opened her mouth to argue that point, then noticed Max and Lainie sitting in stiff orange plastic chairs, watching the rare exchange with wide eyes. Claire clamped her mouth shut. Nothing would be gained by arguing in front of the children.

Only now did she realize how often Tuck took risks. Maybe if she'd protested more over the years, things would be different. Garrett and Marcy wouldn't be living in Houston with her unborn grandchild, for one thing.

She'd called her oldest son after Tuck left, asking when they were coming home.

"I don't know that we are, Mom. Marcy's dad got me a job at his engineering firm,"

Garrett said.

"But you can get a job here."

"Mom, no one is going to hire me. Not when my only employment history is working for Dad," he said. "I have to provide for my family. I have no choice but to stay here right now."

He was right, of course. All their lives had changed, and each member of her family would be forced to start over in some manner.

Claire scribbled her name across the deed, and Ranger's assistant stamped the document with her notary seal. "Is that it?" she asked.

"For now." Ranger slipped the stack of documents into his briefcase.

"Good." Claire pulled her reading glasses from her face, thankful she no longer had this task to dread. Although the Masseys' lives would never be the same, at least they were one step closer to reconstructing them. When Tuck got paroled, together they'd decide how to move on from this humiliating experience. They'd rebuild, refashion themselves in some manner. No matter what Tuck's actions had done financially and socially, they still had each other and their family. That was what really mattered.

"Oh, one more thing." Ranger reached for

the water carafe and refilled his glass. "The trustee would like to pick up the horse. He'll have a transport truck at Legacy on Monday."

"The receiver already has the horses, Ranger. Tuck arranged for delivery before he left."

Ranger frowned and pulled a file from his briefcase, quickly studying the contents. "Yes, I see that, Claire. The only remaining inventory is a mare originally purchased from the King Ranch."

"Pride and Prejudice? But that's Lainie's horse. Pride isn't included in all this." Claire's hand swept the air.

She watched Ranger's expression turn solemn. "I'm afraid that horse is worth a lot of money and is technically part of the assets to be turned over."

Claire steadied herself. "But Tuck would never let —" As the words left her mouth, a sinking realization pushed the idea aside. She'd been in that courtroom and heard what the judge said. "Ranger, you have to do something." She failed to curb the confrontational tone in her voice. "That's Lainie's horse."

She couldn't stand by and let Lainie's heart be broken — not again. Ever since Reece ended the engagement, her daughter

201

had been like a blossom plucked and left in the blistering sun.

"There's nothing I can do, Claire."

She stood and grabbed her bag. She gave Tuck's attorney her most indignant look.

"Then I will."

Claire left Ranger's office and headed straight to Jana Rae's house in Fort Worth, a forty-minute drive in good traffic.

Jana Rae lived in Overton Woods, an upscale neighborhood bordering the Trinity River. Even though the home was not near the stratum of Claire's, Jana Rae's house had been called "a stunning example of authentic Old Texas architecture" by *Fort Worth Magazine* and reflected the high-level success of Clark's medical practice. "Incontinence has been very good to us," Jana Rae often claimed.

Claire nosed her Escalade into the circular drive and parked. She took a deep breath, knowing what was ahead. Clearly she had no choice. She needed Jana Rae's help.

Waiting at the door, she reminded herself how tightly she and Jana Rae had woven their friendship since high school. Their relationship was like a favorite robe, the one you'd slip into every time you had an urge to curl up into something well-worn and familiar.

Claire had worried how the soured invest-ments might change things between her and Jana Rae, but they'd weathered the issue — barely — by placing their friendship above all else. Which is why today's visit held so much risk.

The massive wooden door with beveled glass opened, and Jana Rae's eyes widened with surprise. "Well, Claire Massey." Her friend glanced at the Escalade parked in the drive. "Look at you, all grown up and driv-ing yourself and all."

"Yeah, and I've learned how to use a GPS and everything," she bantered back.

"Well, get your backside on in here before I faint dead away." Jana Rae led her inside. "I bet you're famished from all that steer-ing. Let me get you some sweet tea."

Claire followed Jana Rae into the kitchen, where the smell of fresh cinnamon filled the air. Only then did she notice skiffs of flour on Jana Rae's arm as she moved for the refrigerator. "What? Are you baking?"

"Cinnamon rolls," Jana Rae called back over her shoulder with an air of confidence. "I had to do something to keep myself busy when you went AWOL," she said. "Why haven't you answered my texts or calls?"

Claire slid onto a barstool and dropped

her bag on the marble countertop. "I'm sorry, Jana Rae. I just had so much going on."

"Which is why I didn't press the matter. I watched the coverage on television. You handled yourself with grace and dignity, my friend." She washed at the sink. After toweling off, she moved to Claire and gave her a quick hug. "I've missed you." Jana Rae grabbed a mug off the counter. "You want some coffee and a roll?"

Claire shook her head. "Neither. But I'd go for that sweet tea you mentioned." She watched her friend move for the refrigerator. "So, what's up with all the cinnamon rolls? You suddenly develop a sweet tooth?"

"Well, one pan is for my brother Jay. What's family for if it can't take care of its losers?" She grinned. "The rest are for the bake sale at Mike's church."

"In Waco?" Claire watched Jana Rae pour two glasses of tea.

"No, for his church here." Jana Rae set the glasses down on the bar. "My word, maybe I forgot to tell you, what with Tuck's hearing and all."

Claire reached for her glass and jiggled it gently until the ice loosened. "Forgot to tell me what?"

"Mike was offered a church in Fort Worth

— Trinity Grace, that new church that opened up last year over on Camp Bowie, near the Amon Carter Museum."

Claire drew her napkin around the glass to catch the condensation that had formed. "I'm a bit surprised your brother would leave . . . well, where he lived with Susan. Isn't that where all their friends and support are?"

Jana Rae nodded. "But Susan's parents live here in Fort Worth. Bev — that's Susan's mom — has spent a lot of time down in Waco helping Mike out, but this will be easier for all of them, I think. And I can spend more time with his girls too."

She nodded and sipped her tea. No matter what difficulties life dealt, there was always someone worse off. Jana Rae's brother Mike and his wife Susan had been so happy, and then breast cancer robbed them of their future.

Claire and Tuck had suffered a blip on their horizon, but at least they still had one.

She let a slight grin form. "Is Mike prepared for how often his sister will be over there? I mean, between both you and Susan's mother —"

Jana Rae waved her off. "Oh, don't give me that. I'm familiar with boundaries, you know."

"Uh-huh. Familiar with how to mow them down."

"Well now, that might be true," Jana Rae said. "Just last week, I was telling a neighbor gal who seems bent on getting her a man that you can't make someone love you. All you can do is stalk them like crazy and hope they panic and give in."

Claire laughed. "I rest my case."

"Not that my advice is going to work for that poor gal. You could park a car in the shadow of her behind, know what I mean?" Jana Rae laughed, then added, " 'Course that man she's after fell down the ugly tree and hit every branch on the way down — so maybe things will work out after all."

An easy silence followed their banter as Jana Rae checked the timer on the stove, one that allowed Claire to ponder how to broach the subject looming ahead.

Jana Rae had a fine-tuned baloney meter. The best way to approach the subject was to just straight-up explain the circumstances and ask.

Jana Rae looked over the hot batch of cinnamon rolls with satisfaction. "These are going to be the hit of the bake sale, if I say so myself." She slid another tray inside the oven and set the timer. Finished, Jana Rae turned and leaned against the counter. As if sensing Claire's mental struggle, she folded her arms. "Okay, spill. Something's bothering you, I can tell."

Feeling like a deer caught in headlights, Claire started to argue. "What? I need an excuse to come see my best friend?"

Jana Rae's gaze lasered on her. "Gossips are like roaches around here. For every one you see, there's a thousand more."

"Why? What are you hearing?"

"A lot. But the better question is why I'm not hearing any of it from *you*."

Claire stared at the counter for several seconds. When she looked up, she let an apology form. "I'm sorry, Jana Rae. I know we haven't talked —"

"In weeks."

"Yes, a few weeks," she reluctantly agreed. "But it's not like I haven't had my hands full."

Jana Rae moved onto a barstool. "Well, let's start with Garrett. Why did he and Marcy hightail it to Houston?"

Claire reminded herself Jana Rae was on her side and launched into an explanation about how her older son had retained counsel, that he'd been advised to distance himself from this mess, and that he had a job with Marcy's dad. "And if you haven't heard, yours truly is going to be a grandmother." She grinned despite herself.

"What?" Jana Rae popped off her seat and hugged Claire. "Oh, honey, I'm so tickled." Her face sobered. "How did Tuck take the news?"

She fingered her glass. "He was delighted, of course. But sad."

Jana Rae nodded. "Can't be easy knowing he's going to miss all that." Her friend checked her watch and moved for the oven.

There would be no better time for Claire to pose her question. She drew a deep breath. "Jana Rae, I have a problem." She laughed — a bit tinnily, she knew. "I mean, I have another problem. And I need your help."

Jana Rae opened the oven door and pulled the tray out, then set it on the counter. "What problem?"

Heat from the open oven drifted across the room, and Claire found herself sweating, despite her loose clothing and the air-conditioning blowing down from the vent above her head. She felt her smile stiffen. "I wouldn't ask, but I have no one else."

She explained about complying with the terms of the plea agreement, and that on Monday a truck would show up to confiscate even Lainie's horse. "I can't let that happen, Jana Rae," she said, dabbing at the corner of her eye with a fingertip in bad need of a manicure. "My daughter's been through so much already. Her entire life changed the night they handcuffed Tuck and led him away."

"Lainie's a big girl, Claire." Jana Rae shut the oven door.

Claire forced a smile back in place. "Yes, I know that. But under these circumstances —"

"Look, Claire. I can be either your best friend or your worst enemy here. But someone needs to help you drink some truth juice."

Claire's insides grew brittle. "What do you mean?"

"I mean, the higher a monkey climbs, the more it shows its backside. And I think when it comes to Lainie, you're often climbing the wrong tree, Claire Massey."

Claire grappled with Jana Rae's words. Either her best friend didn't notice her growing irritation or she didn't take it seriously. "Tree?"

"You're coddling her." Jana Rae crossed her arms firmly over her chest. "Seems to me you have bigger financial worries than whether or not Lainie gets to keep an expensive horse. When are you going to start thinking about *you,* and what *your* future holds? Your life has not been put on a temporary pause until Tuck is released."

Claire's nostrils flared. "I'm trying my best to hold my family together," she said, sliding her glass of sweet tea back across the counter. Clearly she'd misjudged her best friend's willingness to move past what Tuck had done. "Look, I just need a loan. I want to buy the horse from the trustee — for Lainie. I won't be able to pay the money back right away, but when Tuck gets out and we're on our feet again, you know I'll make sure you get *every* penny back." Despite her carefully rehearsed plan, the request came out sounding pinched.

Jana Rae let out a quick laugh. "Added to the quarter of a million? Get real, Claire."

"Well," Claire said, only then noticing how little air had been moving in and out of her lungs. She shook her head. "I guess all the cards are on the table now."

Jana Rae quickly moved to her. "No, I didn't mean —"

Claire lifted her bag from the counter, feeling an indescribable weight descend on her shoulders.

"Yes, Jana Rae. You did."

22

The headline in the Monday edition of the *Dallas Morning News* read, "US Attorney Broadens Investigation into Massey Fraud."

"What do you know about this?" Frank Leonard folded his arms and waited.

Max frowned at his editor-in-chief, a bald, sniveling nebbish of a man with a bloated gut, resulting from countless late nights spent downing greasy drive-in hamburgers and black coffee laden with powdered creamer. A tacky polo shirt with the paper's logo printed on the pocket added to the often-misguided illusion that Frank Leonard headed up a two-bit weekly paper because he couldn't land a real editor job at a respected metropolitan paper. Not true.

"What do you mean? What do I know about what?" Max pulled the paper across the metal desk and quickly scanned the article. When he'd finished reading the few scant details, he slid the newsprint back. "I haven't heard anything about any of this."

"You're a Massey, aren't you?" Frank pressed.

"All the more reason the feds aren't going to march up and report what they're doing."

A copy editor not much older than Max stepped forward. "Frank, would you take a look at this mock-up?"

"Not now," he barked. "I'm busy."

The girl retreated, but not before Max caught the embarrassed look on her face.

He stood, ignoring the pounding in his chest. "Look, this report doesn't make sense. The plea agreement is set." He grabbed his cell phone from the desk. "But I'm on it."

Frank's eyes narrowed. "Those bottom-feeders at the *Morning News* aren't going to scoop us on this. Not when Massey's son sits in one of my news chairs."

As Max made his way to his car, he couldn't help wondering if Frank remembered he wasn't an investigative reporter. He wrote political op-ed pieces, weighing in on the weekly controversy du jour. How was he supposed to find out what was going on with a federal criminal investigation, especially one that involved his own family?

Still, he appreciated the heads-up. He

needed to uncover what this so-called further investigation entailed, for his family's sake.

If he'd learned anything in his line of work, it was that prosecutors often dealt from the bottom of the deck, so to speak — especially those with higher political aspirations. And Max knew that Jordan fellow wouldn't think twice about using his family's back to step up a little higher.

Right now, he'd keep all this to himself. He wouldn't call and alarm his mother. Not yet.

No matter how strong she tried to appear, Max knew these past few weeks had taken a huge emotional toll, especially Dad's hearing, where he didn't have the heart to tell his mom she'd only put mascara on one eye.

He slid into his Jeep and blasted the air-conditioning on high. While waiting for the interior to cool, he dialed and pulled his phone to his ear.

"Good morning. Mehlhaf Jennings Law Offices."

"Is Ranger in? This is Max Massey."

"I expect Mr. Jennings within the hour," the receptionist on the other end of the line reported in a pecan-pie kind of voice.

Max tempered his annoyance. "Tell him I'm on my way. We need to talk as soon as possible."

"Will Mr. Jennings know what this is regarding?"

He sighed. "I sure hope not."

"Lainie, stop. Listen to me. Where will you go?" Claire followed on her daughter's heels as Lainie pivoted from the dresser drawer to the bed, tossing clothes in a suitcase.

"Look, Mom. I'm done with all this. I've got to get out of here." She tucked pairs of socks in between jeans and T-shirts. "I'm sick to death of everything that's happened. And I'm not going to stand by and watch them take Pride." Tears rolled down her daughter's face.

Claire plopped on the bed. "Sweetheart, I understand. I do. But running away isn't going to solve anything. Where will you go?" Unable to help herself, she reached out and straightened the contents in her daughter's bag.

Lainie turned, misery displayed across her features. "I'm not like you, Mom. I can't forgive Dad for what he did and what he's putting us through." She slammed a drawer shut with her hip.

"Honey, your father loves —"

Lainie clenched her fists and stomped her foot. "Oh, would you listen to yourself? He broke the law, Mom. He stole from our friends, humiliated us, and we're losing everything because of what he did."

On the dresser, Claire spotted the opened letter from Tuck. She reached for Lainie's arm. "Honey, I'm trying to work something out. Ranger has asked the trustee to hold off disposing of — uh, selling Pride. At least until I've had a chance to raise some money to purchase her back." Even though Lainie pulled away, Claire continued. "This is only temporary, baby."

Despite the confidence she forced into her voice, doubt boiled like acid. Who was she to promise anything? Where in the world could she get enough money to stop the sale of that prized horse?

"Mama, please understand. I love you, but I can't stay." Lainie clicked the latch of the suitcase and pulled her bag to the floor.

"But this your home," Claire argued.

Lainie glanced around at the sand-colored walls lined with riding trophies and memorabilia. "Not in ninety days, it won't be." She walked out, leaving everything behind.

Claire followed her daughter down the stairs, past a wall of family photos. At the bottom, Margarita stood shaking her head. She opened her arms and Lainie hugged the old woman. "Ah, Miss Lainie — *vaya con Dios.*" Their housekeeper wiped her eyes with the corner of her apron.

Lainie turned to Claire, and they embraced. "I love you, Mom. Don't worry about me," she whispered.

As she drove down the lane, she took Claire's heart with her. First Garrett and now Lainie. Claire's family was crumbling one by one.

"She'll be back, Mrs. Massey." Margarita placed her arm around Claire's shoulders and led her inside. "Let me get you some tea."

"Not right now, Margarita." She patted her housekeeper's hand. "But thank you."

She wandered into Tuck's office. The walls were nearly bare now, stripped of the hunting trophies and art her husband had collected and proudly displayed. His desk, normally stacked with document folders and *Cattleman* magazines, seemed a sterile shadow of its former clutter.

She slumped into Tuck's leather chair, leaning her head back into the place Tuck had so often rested his. A deep loneliness enveloped her. In times past, she'd run to Tuck to talk over problems with the children. Together they'd piece together a solution. Often their conversations would end with him reminding her she was a wonderful mother.

Now their only telephone conversation, meant for her to see if he got settled and to assure him the kids were okay, was filled with prison-line static and a fifteen-minute timer measuring every moment. Even though Claire had so much on her mind and craved his perspective and advice, she'd taken her cues from Tuck and kept to surface conversation.

She'd told him she'd helped Margarita make corn tortillas, instead of sharing that she feared the money allotted in the plea agreement wouldn't support their living expenses *and* their housekeeper's salary. She'd already let Henry go. How much longer could she pay Margarita before money ran out?

She mentioned how the front bedding area was filled with pretty lantana blooms, but failed to disclose she'd had to cut the landscaping services, that the high grass and weeds in the yard around the stables looked disheveled and abandoned.

She recounted how she lay in bed at night and watched old movies. Rarely did she reveal she couldn't help but click to news channels and how mean the media reports were . . . still.

Just the other night, a broadcast included

a clip from a female investor saying, "It pains me so much that my husband worked hard so that Tuck Massey could buy his wife a Cartier watch." On the screen flashed a photo of Claire at the Legacy Ranch barbeque, and the camera zoomed in on the watch on her wrist, the one the trustee now held and would likely sell for pennies on the dollar.

It would certainly pain Tuck to learn of Lainie and the horse, that Garrett had decided to remain in Houston. Tuck sat in prison. Why add more to his anguish? Especially after her husband had come clean and done what he could to get all this behind them as quickly as possible. Instead of making the government fight to prove him guilty, he'd confessed, allowing assets to be sold and distributed to his investors more quickly. What Tuck had done to keep them afloat was wrong, but Claire sensed honor inside her husband that still made her proud.

Despite the fact she no longer attended church after the debacle with Pastor Richards and the elders at Abundant Hills, Claire knew forgiveness was available to all. And Tuck was sorry.

Disciplining herself to remain positive had seemed logical under the circumstances.

218

But lately, in the short time since Tuck left, cracks had formed in her happy facade. With every passing day, Claire found it harder to hold on to hope and keep a smile planted on her face.

Lainie claimed acting like Pollyanna wouldn't get her through the next two years. Jana Rae didn't buy her act either. She'd certainly made that clear that day in her kitchen.

Tears welled.

Claire ran her finger across the desktop, tracing the grain of the wood on the desk. What choice did she have? If she focused on everything she'd lost since that night at the Adolphus, she'd end up in a puddle on the floor.

She couldn't give in to despair. What good would that do her family?

"Knock, knock. Anybody home?"

She swiveled the chair to find Jana Rae standing just outside the office. "What are you doing here?" She swiped at the tears. "And how did you get in?"

Jana Rae tossed her purse on the sofa against the wall and slid into one of the guest chairs in front of Tuck's desk. "Margarita let me in."

"Remind me to fire that old bat tomorrow."

"Ah-yee, I heard that." Margarita's voice drifted from the front foyer. "I told Miss Jana Rae you were busy. But she's pushy."

"You can say that." Claire brought her gaze in line with Jana Rae's. "What do you want?"

"I want you to go get those roots done. You have at least an inch of gray showing." Her friend waited, probably hoping Claire would volley a smart remark back over the net.

Instead, Claire spiked. "Seriously, what do you want?"

Jana Rae leaned forward, her eyes pleading for understanding. "Look, I'm sorry. It's just — how was I going to lend you more money when the Urologist is already wetting his pants over what happened? Pun intended."

She leaned back in Tuck's chair and steepled her fingers. "You don't have to explain. I understand."

Jana Rae rubbed her forehead. "Now, don't go getting all understanding on me."

Claire dropped her hands and took a deep breath. "Jana Rae, what do you want from me? I mean, I get it. A quarter of a million dollars is a lot to lose."

Jana Rae shook her head, sending her gold earrings swinging wildly. "You don't get it.

It's not the money." She lifted her chin. "Okay, it's the money. But Tuck was our friend. He didn't just lose our retirement — he lost our trust."

"He — or we?" Claire challenged.

Before Jana Rae could respond, Claire's cell phone rang. She held up a finger. Using her other hand, she grabbed the phone and pulled it to her ear.

"Mom?"

She continued to stare into Jana Rae's face. "Max? What's up?"

"I'm with Ranger. I'm afraid I have bad news."

"What do you mean, the US Attorney's Office has extended their investigation?" Claire paced the conference room, waiting for Ranger to answer.

Max tapped a pen against the granite table. "Mom, calm down."

"Don't tell me to calm down. I don't understand." Claire turned and faced Ranger sitting at the head of the table. At either side sat other attorneys from his firm, their faces grim. "They have Tuck. Very soon they'll also have everything we owned. What more could they want?"

"Charles Jordan isn't showing all his cards at this juncture. But like I explained, he's issuing subpoenas, and I suspect he plans to reconvene a grand jury."

Claire tried not to emotionally jump off the cliff's edge that had become her life. "A grand jury?"

The gentleman sitting at Ranger's left, a thin-faced man with wire-rimmed glasses, set the document he'd been reading on the table. "Jordan is fishing, but you can bet somebody has handed him bait."

Ranger looked at Claire, and just for a second she thought she saw anger in his features, which scared her. The sand beneath her shifted. She needed a firm place on which to anchor her emotions. "Ranger, please be honest. What's going on here?"

Ranger folded his hands on the table in front of him. He drew a deep breath. "Well, it's obvious the US Attorney's Office has learned something that makes them believe Tuck has not complied with the agreement. I suspect they think he's not been forthcoming with information. Or —"

"Or they think someone else is involved," Max said. "Like perhaps my big brother."

In unison, the men flanking the table scribbled furiously on their yellow pads.

Claire's face tightened and she felt her insides splinter. Garrett — soon to be a father.

Oh please, don't let him be involved in this.

Ranger slid back his chair and stood. "Let's not jump ahead. We'll know soon enough what the government intends. Until then, there's very little we can do."

"That's it?" Claire said. "We're supposed to sit around and wait for Charles Jordan to make his move?" She slammed her chair against the table. "Sorry, that's not good enough. This is my family."

Ranger's face grew sympathetic. "Our hands are tied. Grand jury proceedings are highly secret. The only information we're going to get is what Jordan leaks."

Claire scowled. "You mean, like to the *Dallas Morning News.*"

"Yes, exactly. And sometimes these matters can take months, even years, to conclude. In the end, there's no guarantee a grand jury will issue findings that would allow the US Attorney to bring additional charges. This really is just a waiting game."

Ranger escorted Claire and Max through the lobby and to the bank of elevators. "If I hear anything, I'll immediately be in contact," he said.

The elevator dinged. Max shook Ranger's hand and thanked him. Claire followed suit and pasted a simulated smile on her face.

She needed to talk to Garrett. And soon.

They stepped inside the elevator and Max pushed the button to the ground floor. Slowly the elevator descended.

To their shock, waiting television reporters swarmed as they stepped out of the elevator into the lobby of the Renaissance Tower. A cameraman with helmet hair pointed his lens, and his sidekick reporter shoved a microphone into Claire's face. "Would you like to comment —"

She shook her head and felt Max take her arm, pulling her through the crowd. On the outside, she fought to remain composed.

But inside, Claire's emotions began their own descent.

23

Max hit the gas, keeping his eyes on the road while Claire pulled her cell phone from her purse. Her thumb scrolled to Garrett's number and dialed.

Several rings later, a familiar female voice picked up. "Hello?"

"Hi, Marcy, it's Claire." Her face pulled into a confused frown. "I — I meant to dial Garrett's number. It's urgent that I talk with him."

"This is Garrett's old phone. He's not here." Her daughter-in-law's tone sounded more than a little chilly.

"Where is he? I really need to —"

"Look, I know why you're calling. We've been told not to talk to anyone — not even you. Especially now."

Claire caught the fear in Marcy's voice, as if she walked a dangerous path and didn't know where to safely step. She tried again. "I understand the caution, but honey, I need you to have Garrett call."

"Can't your family just leave us alone?" Marcy's tight voice escalated. "Do you realize what y'all have done to my husband? To both of us?"

Claire flinched. "Honey, you don't understand —"

Before Claire could finish, the phone clicked off. Confused, she looked at Max and slowly lowered the phone.

He let out a brief, uneasy chuckle and swung his Jeep onto Stemmons Freeway. "Let me guess. Queen Marcy has closed her embassy."

After her encounter with Marcy, the rest of Claire's day felt unsettled, as though a dust storm had blown in, adding to a day already ruined by the sweltering news they'd received in Ranger's office.

Max talked Claire into trying to get some rest. Rather than argue she couldn't possibly sleep, she'd grabbed an afghan and headed for the sunroom to collect her thoughts and try to make sense of things. Despite the quiet solitude, she found herself jumpy and unable to concentrate on anything but the fact her family was at risk.

She'd said goodbye to Tuck, believing the worst was over. Now Claire faced the agonizing possibility Garrett was also the target of the government's investigation.

How could Garrett possibly be involved in criminal activity? She'd been in that conference room with him when he'd heard, as she had, Tuck's confession. Garrett had been furious. He was as surprised as anyone when Tuck was arrested. Still, the US Attorney's Office seemed willing to stir the pot to feed a bloodthirsty public.

Marcy's voice on the telephone replayed in Claire's mind. *Can't your family just leave us alone?*

What was that supposed to mean exactly? Marcy had always been a bit high-strung, but Garrett's family certainly wasn't the enemy here. They would always be by his side. Nothing, no one, would alter that fact. Not even her son's wife.

Claire would see to that.

When Garrett married Marcy Karstan, everyone had agreed the union was a match made in heaven. Claire wasn't sure.

Marcy had grown up in Houston, the only daughter of Jack and Emily Karstan. A former astronaut, Jack had moved on from his aeronautical career to build a successful engineering firm. He thought his stunning daughter, who won the Miss Texas title in 2001, rode stars to the moon.

Like Tuck, Garrett had played football and enjoyed popularity. Tall, handsome, and a rich up-and-comer, he was president of Sigma Alpha Epsilon, drove the best car, and made the dean's list every year. And when Garrett graduated, he'd been given a promising career waiting on his daddy's silver platter.

Claire adored her oldest son, but she couldn't deny her children were privileged. Especially Garrett, who walked straight out of knit booties into his daddy's cowboy boots.

And what could she say about Marcy? Well, the best way to describe her daughter-in-law was by how she chose friends. If you drove a Mercedes? You were in. A Lexus? Maybe. A Honda? Never.

You can imagine the instant attraction the little darling felt toward Claire's son and his silver Maserati Spyder, a gift from Tuck in celebration of Garrett making the Texas college all-star team his senior year.

Claire loved her daughter-in-law, but like Jana Rae often said, her son's wife boated on the shallow end of the bass pond.

Still, she wanted to give Marcy the benefit of the doubt. Tuck's actions had changed all their lives, and she understood the fear plaguing Marcy right now, knowing Garrett might be the target of an investigation. Claire shared that same panic.

But make no doubt, the little Botox beauty who only ate spinach salads with broiled chicken and a splash of dressing could never shove Claire out of her own son's life.

Never.

She punched the stiff cushion behind her back in an attempt to make it more comfortable.

"Mrs. Massey? I'm sorry to interrupt you. There is a woman at the door. I told her you were resting, but she insisted."

Alarm rang in Claire's head. Financial considerations had forced severe reductions in security, to almost nonexistent. "Who is it, Margarita?" she asked, praying the media hadn't gotten through the gate.

"She says she's your mother."

24

Claire blinked in surprise. At the door, across the shiny tiles of her front foyer, stood a stylish woman with perfectly coiffed hair, looking eerily like Shirley MacLaine stretched tight as Joan Rivers.

"Sweetheart," she gushed, extending her arms toward Claire.

"Mother?"

"Claire, darlin' — come give your mama a hug." She wiggled her fingers.

Claire had no choice but to move forward into her mother's embrace. In her arms, she caught her mother's signature fragrance, Shalimar — the heavy amber patchouli scent popular with women over five decades ago. She still thought it stunk.

After giving her mother a quick pat, Claire pulled back and let her in. "Wow. How long has it been? Five years?" She found it hard to keep the scorn from her voice.

Her mother stared back, wide-eyed. "Oh,

that's impossible," she said, waving off the idea. "I visited when Max graduated high school."

"It was Lainie's graduation, and that was —" Claire stopped and mentally counted. "Yup, five years. And you only came in for the ceremony but couldn't stay for the party. I think you had a plane to catch, to Bali, I believe."

Her mother nodded. "Oh yes. That's right. Honey, you need to go to Bali sometime if you haven't been. In addition to the powder-soft sand lined with lovely palms, that little island has such culture. Talented artisans and dancers." She glanced around the two-story foyer. "Your home is lovely as ever. But what happened to everything on the walls? Looks a bit bare, dear."

Inwardly, she grimaced. It wasn't that she and her mother had a distant relationship exactly — well, okay, they had a distant relationship. If you knew Eleanor Cooper Webster Hilderbrand Wyden, you'd stay at arm's length as well.

Ellie Wyden had made a career out of marrying well. After her second husband died, she quickly said her graveside good-byes to Jack Webster and married Lawrence Hilderbrand, owner of a well-known chain of resorts in the Caribbean islands. Sadly, he dropped from a sudden heart attack within the year, forcing her to move on to her last husband, Ari Wyden. Ari had serious money — the Kennedys from Hyannis, Massachusetts, kind. He owned a yacht company and named the company flagship the *USS Ellie.*

To her mother's dismay, Ari suffered a stroke and lingered for nearly ten years before passing. "Do you know what long-term care costs these days?" her mother had written in her Christmas card just before he died. What she didn't say is that he'd placed a good share of his money in a benevolent trust, leaving her without the extravagant retirement she'd planned.

No doubt her mother now hoped to hunt down another wealthy husband before she herself kicked the bucket. Despite tubs of Retin-A and other expensive wrinkle creams, Claire's mother wasn't getting any younger.

Claire looked past where her mother stood to the open door, just to make sure she hadn't already bagged another victim and forgot to tell her. Finding her mother hadn't brought along an unknown stepdaddy, she forced a smile and motioned her mother into the living area. "Well, this is a surprise."

To her mother's credit, she waited until

dinner to bring up the subject of Tuck's incarceration. "When I saw the news, I simply couldn't believe it. I was humiliated for you, darling."

"Yes, it's been really hard," Claire said slowly. "I've learned life can change on a dime."

Her mother wiped the condensation from her glass of sweet tea with a napkin. "Sounds like it was quite a few dimes, dear."

Claire sighed. Might as well open this conversation instead of waiting for her mother to unfold her inquisition. "Tuck made a huge error in judgment. And now we're all paying for what he did." Claire stared across the table. "Please don't say you told me so."

Her mother straightened. "Give your mama some credit, Claire. I'm the last one who would pour salt on your wound." She swirled her tea, sending the ice tinkling against the glass. "Counter to my predictions, Tuck proved to be quite the businessman. None of us saw this coming."

Claire's eyebrows lifted. "I'm surprised to hear you say that, Mother."

"Well, you shouldn't be. The returns your husband made were remarkable. Even I invested."

Her heart gripped. "You — you put money

233

with Tuck?"

Her mother's face turned grim. She placed her glass of tea on the table. "Yes, unfortunately so." She shrugged. "And now I'm afraid I'm broke."

When Jana Rae learned of the unexpected visit, she nearly choked on her sweet tea. "Wow. I can't believe your mom just showed up at your doorstep. Is she still just a mess in a dress?"

Claire smiled. "Too early to know for sure, but all indications point that direction."

Jana Rae knew Claire often made light of her relationship with her mother, but she'd also been audience to the times Ellie Wyden had hurt her only child.

Twenty minutes prior to Claire's wedding ceremony, the church had been filled with guests. Claire turned to her maid of honor. "Is she here yet, Jana Rae?"

Her best friend gave her a quick hug. "Not yet, but don't worry. She'll be here."

Unfortunately, Jana Rae hadn't counted on Claire's mother laying over in New York to catch a Broadway hit. The clock read nearly two o'clock in the morning when her mother called, waking the newlyweds. "I'm so sorry I didn't make it for your little ceremony, sweetheart. I hope you had a nice time."

Claire rubbed sleep from her eyes. "What happened? You said you'd come."

She could hear her mother take a drag from her cigarette. "I'm sorry. I should have called. But Jack got his hands on tickets to *A Chorus Line.* Frankly, I think some of those dancers were too heavy for those costumes," she said, oblivious to the fact she'd called at such an awful hour. "Of course, I don't judge."

That was laughable. Her mother judged everything. Well, maybe not everything, but she didn't seem to hold back when it came to Claire.

Honey, those shoes don't go with that outfit.
You'll never find a good husband at that school.

Claire, you mustn't eat bacon. It'll go right to your hips.

And her classic: *Don't marry that boy. He'll never amount to anything.*

In the library, Jana Rae pulled strapping tape across a box, sealing it. "Tell me you're kidding." She lowered her voice. "You're going to let the old bat live with you?"

Claire dropped the books in her hand into an open box. "What choice do I have? I can't very well turn her out on the street."

235

She pulled several volumes from the shelves and added them to the others. "Besides, she's out of money because of my husband. And it's only temporary."

Jana Rae shook her head, looking unsure. "Well, you'd better sharpen your skates, because you-know-what just froze over and it's going to be a long winter." She lifted her box and stacked it on top of the others by the door to the library. "What are y'all going to do with these books?"

"Donate them," Claire said, pulling more books from the shelves. "Before long I'm moving into a much smaller place. Guaranteed I won't have space for this kind of library."

Jana Rae dropped on the sofa and wiped her brow with her sleeve. "What do you hear from Lainie?"

Claire straightened and rubbed her sore back. "My daughter seems to have fallen off the face of the earth. When I talk to her on the phone, she tells me she's staying with a friend. Not to worry about her."

"What's this about Lainie?" Claire's mother swept into the room, her hair wrapped up in a pink turban that perfectly matched the hibiscus in her tropical print caftan. Two tiny Yorkies in pink bows followed close behind.

Jana Rae raised her eyebrows. "What are those?"

Ellie Wyden stopped. "Well, you're that nice girl Claire was friends with in high school." She scooped up her dogs. "Now, what was your name, dear?"

"Mama, this is Jana Rae. You've met several times."

"We have?" She shrugged and turned to her daughter. "Such a shame our Lainie isn't marrying that man who is running for senator. Now *he* would've been a catch."

Claire could see Jana Rae suppress a giggle. When her mother turned away, Claire scowled and gave her friend a warning look.

In an apparent effort to redeem herself, Jana Rae asked about the dogs. "What do we have here?"

Claire's mother beamed. "These are my little darlings — Puddin and Nutmeg." She bent and kissed her long-haired babies.

Claire felt a pulling sensation in her gut. Apparently her mother was capable of affection after all. "Are you hungry, Mama?"

"No, I had juice and a muffin earlier."

Margarita rushed though the French doors, pulling at her apron. "Mrs. Massey, you need to see the television."

Claire hurried over to the coffee table,

grabbed the remote, and clicked the on button. "What is it, Margarita?"

Before her housekeeper could answer, a
live shot popped on the screen. Kelly
Thatcher of WCBA-TV had caught up with
Deputy Chief Hodges of the US Attorney's
Office and was running alongside him. She
extended her microphone. "Sources are telling our station that your office has reopened
your investigation into the Massey fraud,
that others may be involved?"

Hodges brushed the reporter off with a
smile. "I can't comment on any investigation."

Kelly Thatcher pressed. "We're hearing a
grand jury may have been reconvened?"

"No comment. As you know, Kelly, grand
jury matters are not public." He slowed and
looked into her camera. "But I can assure
you and the public that the office of the US
Attorney, together with the Federal Bureau
of Investigation, won't rest until we've
explored every avenue, turned over every
rock. If there are others involved, we'll bring
them to justice."

The screen switched to a shot of Garrett
with a voice-over.

"Theodore Massey's oldest son, Garrett,
insisted through his attorney that he was
unaware that his father's successful cattle

brokerage business was really a multimillion-dollar Ponzi scheme, and in a written statement he said of his father, 'There's no way to explain what he did, the damage he has caused. What possible explanation could there be?' "

An image of Tuck being escorted from the Adolphus in handcuffs appeared.

"Massey was sentenced to five years in the Federal Correction Institution in Bastrop for orchestrating one of Texas's, if not the country's, largest cattle frauds in history. Victims include many well-known names and institutions, including Massey's own church, where he served as an elder. Despite Massey's claims he acted alone, sources tell WCBA-TV that his oldest son is currently being investigated."

Claire's hand flew to her mouth. For an odd second, she felt her life had turned into one of those annoying jingles that kept playing in your head even after the commercial ended.

"What does all that mean?" her mother asked, bending and letting her dogs jump to the floor.

Claire barely suppressed the emotion welling up inside. "It means my baby is in trouble."

Only then did she notice one of the Yorkies crouched and peeing on her floor.

25

Lainie leaned against the back of the plush hotel sofa, one hand holding her cell phone in place. With her other, she picked at berries on the room service tray. "Is Mom okay?"

Max's voice came quick. "Define *okay.*"

"Yeah, I get it. But seriously, Max. How's she taking the news?" Lainie popped a blueberry in her mouth. "It's been on every blasted channel since yesterday."

"Mom's been trying frantically to reach Garrett. But Superboy's been in hiding and won't take anybody's calls. That attorney Marcy's dad hired has got him scared spitless and he's afraid to talk — even to us."

"Cut Garrett some slack, Max. You would be too if you'd been working for Dad. Look how they came after Madoff's sons."

"If that's the case, I should be heading for the hills too, I suppose."

Lainie reached for a crescent. "Ha, with

the car you drive, no one would believe you were stashing money."

"Look, Lainie, I think you need to come home. Especially now that our grandmother showed up."

"I will. Just not yet."

"But Mom's going to need you."

Lainie wedged the phone with her shoulder and buttered the flaky roll. "She's got you. And Jana Rae." She took a bite and chewed, not caring that it was rude to talk and eat at the same time. "Have you talked to Dad?"

"Huh-uh. You?"

"Nope." She set the roll back on the china plate. "Frankly, I don't know what to say to him. I mean, he just ripped life out from under our entire family."

Several seconds passed. "You there?" Lainie asked, sadness creeping into her voice.

"I'm here." Max sighed on the other end. "Lainie, where are you anyway?"

"Don't worry about me right now. I'm going to be fine." She forced a brightness, one that didn't quite feel authentic. "You know me. I always land on my feet." Lainie moved the tray onto the sofa table. "Look, Max. I — I've got to go."

"Okay, but stay in touch. And Lainie?"

"Yeah?"

"I love you. So does Mom."

Lainie slapped her phone shut and tossed it on the table, trying to ignore a twinge of guilt. She was the older sister, but like so often, it was her little brother who sensed her need and filled it.

She had been only three when her mother became pregnant again. Even at that early age, Lainie resented another kid coming on the family scene. Garrett already scooped up much of her parents' attention. Clear through high school and into college, he was the one who did everything they wanted. Student of the month. Thrilled their father with Hail Mary passes and eighty-yard runs to win the game. Her parents had produced the perfect child.

But Max changed everything. He drove all of them crazy with his antics. He wasn't naughty exactly, but Mom called him "the inquisitive one." He took Dad's computer apart to see how the thing ran. On the internet, he learned how to make a potato gun and shot out all the stable windows with large Idaho russets.

Max never sat still in church, his shirt never stayed tucked in. On his sixteenth birthday, he broke the family rule and got a tattoo. A heart — sliced, with blood dripping.

Garrett would never break a family rule. And her? Well, she was the pretty one.

Lainie stood and moved to the window. She opened the drapes, revealing a view of Reunion Tower. She'd pictured her life much differently today. If that awful night at the Adolphus had never happened, she would've been knee-deep in wedding plans, worrying about rehearsals, blush-pink tulips, and the society pages. She'd be practicing how she'd stand by Reece on election night, smiling just right for the cameras.

Now all those dreams were gone. Thanks to her father.

Sure, she was sorry for her mother. For all her annoying habits, she was a good person. She didn't deserve any of this. Even though Lainie loved her mother, she had to look out for her own future now. She turned from the window and closed her eyes.

They'd even taken her horse. But she'd have Pride back by the end of the week. She'd made sure of that.

"Lainie, who were you talking to on the phone?" a voice called from the private balcony off the far side of the penthouse suite.

"Uh, just my brother. Nothing important." Lainie opened her eyes and forced a wide smile, telling herself she'd made the right decision. Everything would turn out okay.

She peeked her head out the sliding doors. "Coming inside for breakfast?"

Sidney McAlvain grinned as he stood and set his cigar in an ashtray. "Not yet. This hot tub is calling my name."

He dropped the towel from his robust middle, adjusted his trunks, and climbed in.

26

Claire closed her cell phone, stunned.

"What is it, Claire?" Her mother looked over top her sunglasses, licked a finger, and flipped a glossy magazine page. "You look like you just bit into a sugar-dusted beignet filled with blue cheese and codfish."

Claire lifted from the chaise lounge and walked to the edge of the portico. She looked out at the pond, where a turtle basked on a slimy green log, soaking up the sun.

In the background, her mother chattered. " 'Is There Life after Fifty?' What kind of article is that? I should have moved to Europe, where they appreciate women of age and what we have to offer." She paused. "Claire, what are you doing?"

She slowly turned. "That was Tuck's attorney. I've been subpoenaed to testify before the grand jury. So has Max."

"Tell that attorney to get you out of it.

Isn't that what you pay him for?"

"Doesn't work like that, Mama." Claire moved for the French doors and headed inside.

How had her life become such a sinkhole? Seemed she'd been sucked into a hole filled with media innuendo and legal threats that felt endless, leaving her drawn down, left to talk to her children on the phone with snippets of cheer, masking the pain of knowing she couldn't scoop them all back home and nestle them under her protective feathers.

She was a captive to a life she never planned with no way to escape, sorting and packing while her fluffy-slippered warden read magazines.

In her bedroom, she opened the bedside table drawer and retrieved a manila envelope filled with the papers Ranger's secretary gave her when Tuck left. "This is the family packet," she'd explained.

Claire opened the clasp and slid out the contents, which contained a booklet from the Bureau of Prisons. She thumbed to the section titled "Telephone Calls."

The bedside clock indicated she'd hit the window of time allowed for contact just right. With shaking fingers, she dialed the appropriate number and pulled the phone to her ear.

After three rings, the phone clicked and someone picked up. "Bureau of Prisons. FCI Bastrop." The abrupt voice startled Claire. "Inmate number?"

"What?" Her hand riffled through the papers. She lifted what appeared to be an information sheet that contained Tuck's number. She recited his eight-digit identifier into the phone.

"Name?"

"Tuck — er, I mean, Theodore Massey."

"Hold."

Several minutes passed before another click. "Hello?"

Claire heard Tuck's familiar voice. Her breath caught in her chest. "Tuck? It's me, Claire."

"Hey, baby."

Tuck had been away nearly six weeks. In that time, they'd only talked one other time, and then briefly. In the recesses of her mind, she found it easier to pretend he was out of the country instead of behind bars. Calling made the horrible situation more real.

And if Claire was honest — a part of her felt like punishing him.

"Tuck, Ranger called and —"

"Claire, these calls are monitored. Don't tell me about your conversation with Ranger," he said.

She drew back. Of course, what had she been thinking?

"Uh, a *situation* has developed," she explained, talking in code.

"I'm aware. Ranger was here yesterday. I'm allowed private meetings. Attorney-client privilege and all."

"Oh." Claire rubbed her chin. "Then you know what I'm facing."

"Don't worry. Just tell the truth. Everything is being taken care of." Tuck's voice was gentle and reassuring. "How are the kids?"

He'd changed the subject. Her cue to move on.

She brought him up to speed on everyone and told him she was deep in the process of packing. "Oh, and Mama is now living with me."

Silence.

"Tuck, why? Why my mother?" No matter what Claire did to mentally reconcile Tuck's actions with the man she'd known, she came up short.

"I'm sorry, Claire. In the end, I was desperate. I don't know what else to say."

Claire examined the drapes. The intricate way the swirls of color blended to create a perfect pattern.

She took a deep breath and bent her head.

Yes, Tuck had been under pressure. But that was no excuse.

In the aftermath, she'd hoped to move past what he'd done. She wanted to find a place in her mind where she could safely store what had damaged her soul. But she could no long obscure the lines between right and wrong. Nothing could justify many of his decisions.

She thought of television footage she'd seen of First Lady Pat Nixon. In front of the cameras, the sad-faced blonde stood by her husband, the president. But, like Claire, did she find affection slipping with each new revelation of wrongdoing?

Claire loved Tuck — and always would. But could she stay *in love* with a man who held others in such disregard, despite the pressure he claimed he'd been under? Every time she hoped things had settled down, another telephone call or newscast filled her with dread, or another family member's well-being was threatened with a subpoena.

She was human, after all. Claire tired of her cheerleader role, trying to keep everyone rallied around a man who had walked right over a line others would never dare cross. Every new layer of deceit tarnished her affection. How much more could she take before tossing down her pom-poms?

It'd only been weeks since their goodbye, and it already seemed a lifetime ago.

She wound a lock of hair around her finger. "Look, it was good talking with you. But I've got to go."

"I love you, babe." Tuck's voice sounded desperate.

Claire stared out the window. "Yeah, me too."

Was there anyone in America who hadn't watched hours of courtroom proceedings on television or the big screen and hadn't thought the legal world was fascinating?

As of today, Claire would not be one of them.

She shifted in her chair, knotted her hands in her lap, and stared around the tight hearing room, so unlike the courtroom where Tuck had been arraigned. The grand jury hearing room was small, with chairs upholstered in earthy tweed fabric and walls covered in outdated wallpaper spattered with tasteless art prints framed in cheap wood.

The court reporter sat near the window next to a tiny table on rollers, which held carafes of coffee, Styrofoam cups, and a little basket filled with packets of sweeteners, creamers, and red swizzle stirrers. The woman looked to be in her fifties and had a pinched face and sausage-like fingers that plunked the machine in front of her, taking down every word uttered. She looked bored.

The sixteen jurors, men and women sitting stiffly at oblong tables arranged in a U-shape, didn't lead Claire to believe they were having fun either.

The only person in the room who seemed eager was Charles Jordan, the lead prosecutor — the one who had appeared at Tuck's arraignment.

Directly across from where Claire sat in the cramped witness box, Mr. Jordan leaned forward as if she were about to serve up his favorite sirloin. "Please state your full name for the record."

"Della Claire Massey. I go by Claire."

"Ms. Massey, are you married?"

She looked at him. Was he serious?

"Are you married?" Mr. Jordan repeated.

"Yes. I'm married to Theodore Massey."

He looked over top his reading glasses in her direction. "Also known as Tuck Massey?"

Claire nodded.

The court reporter frowned. "I need an audible response. For the record."

"Oh, sorry." Claire reached for the water carafe and filled her Styrofoam cup. "Yes.

Theodore is also known as Tuck." She took a quick sip, wetting her dry throat. She wondered where they had Max waiting, then mentally scolded herself and remembered she needed to pay attention.

"Listen to the questions carefully before you answer," Ranger had said earlier. Unlike a courtroom proceeding, there would be no attorneys present during a grand jury proceeding. Only jurors and the prosecutors. And, of course, testifying witnesses. "Respond only to what is asked, nothing more. Don't expound," he'd said. "That can get you in trouble."

Mr. Jordan asked how long they'd been married and how many children they had, and went through the history of Legacy Ranch. Then his questioning turned. "Ms. Massey, in your own words, describe your husband's business."

Claire looked at him, confused.

Mr. Jordan scribbled on his yellow pad, then glanced at the jurors. "For the record, Claire Massey is listed as a corporate officer on the records at the Secretary of State office." He looked back at her. "Do you need the question repeated?"

"No," Claire said, her stomach rumbling with nerves. "My involvement in Tuck's business was extremely limited. But as I understood things, Tuck primarily ran our ranch located northwest of Dallas — Legacy Ranch," she clarified. "We owned livestock, cattle, and horses, mainly. The ranch is approximately four thousand acres, including over six miles of river frontage."

She took another sip of water before continuing. "The ranch includes our main house, two duplexes, a manager's house, an indoor arena, a round pen, a hay barn, an equipment shed, stables, and fifty acres of irrigated hay field. Oh, and a helipad."

"And the receiver appointed by the court has confiscated all the cattle and horses?"

"I believe so, yes." Against Ranger's warning, Claire added, "We turned everything over according to the terms of the plea agreement. Even my daughter's personal mare."

"Yes. Now, let's talk about the brokerage end of things." Charles Jordan leaned back in his chair, steepled his fingers. He drilled his gaze at Claire. "To clarify, do you have an understanding of your husband's brokerage business?"

Glancing at the jurors, she slowly responded, "Yes. A very basic understanding."

Mr. Jordan pulled at the bottom of his jacket sleeve. "And what is it? Your understanding, I mean."

"He bought and sold cattle," Claire said into the record.

Mr. Jordan whispered to a lady sitting next to him. She reached into a folder and brought out a set of stapled documents and handed them to him. He quickly glanced over the documents and presented a second set to Claire. He waited until his associate had passed duplicates to the jurors. "I'll represent to you that this is a set of the year-end financials we obtained for Massey Enterprises. The second page is an income statement that shows a substantial profit. Could you tell me how the corporation made that profit?"

"Not exactly. But like I said, it's my understanding Tuck bought and sold cattle for people. For investors."

"So, if Investor A had cattle to sell and Investor B wanted to purchase cattle, your husband would broker the deal and take a commission?"

Claire nodded, feeling the jurors staring at her. One woman's pen scribbled furiously on the yellow pad on the table before her.

"Audible response, please," the court reporter reminded, jerking Claire's attention back.

She apologized. "Yes, that was one way. Another was for Tuck to purchase cattle at one price, hold them, and them sell to another party at a later time for a profit. Beyond that simple explanation, I don't know details."

"I see." Mr. Jordan shifted the financials to the court reporter. "Could you mark these as Exhibit A?" He turned his attention back to Claire. "Now, who fed these cattle? The ones held for later sale?"

"What do you mean? I suppose we did. Until they shipped." Claire scowled. "We had two feed lots — I think one was west of Lubbock and the other a bit south of San Antonio. Truly, I'm not sure about any of this."

Mr. Jordan pressed on. "The ranch operation grew hay?"

"Yes."

"But feed was also purchased, isn't that correct?"

Claire didn't want to guess, but this line of questioning was a bit ridiculous. Of course Tuck bought feed.

Mr. Jordan handed her another document. "Perhaps this will help. Can you identify this document for the record?"

She frowned. "No, I've never seen this before."

Mr. Jordan had the exhibit marked. "Ms. Massey, are you familiar with the Chicago

Board of Trade, also known as CBOT?"

She shook her head. "No."

"How about the Chicago Mercantile Exchange — the CME?"

"No."

The jurors darted looks at each other, then stared back at her, waiting. Claire could sense the tension in the room building.

"Were you aware you were listed as an officer of a grain cooperative?"

She didn't like where this questioning was heading. "No."

"You didn't sign these Articles of Incorporation?"

She peered at the neatly written signature, one that clearly was not her own. Her heart hammered inside her chest. "No, I didn't sign that."

Mr. Jordan pulled the document back, but not before Claire noticed Garrett's signature on the document as well. Her scalp turned damp and her throat chalky. She reached for her water.

Oh, Tuck, no . . . What have you done?

"Ms. Massey, do you know what the term *hedging* means?"

"No — no, I don't."

"How about *stop-loss orders*? Are you familiar with that term?"

"No."

Claire drew a deep breath, trying to ease her churning nerves. Even the court reporter seemed engaged at this point.

Mr. Jordan displayed three sheets of paper before her. "Now, Ms. Massey, have you ever seen any of these documents? Not these exactly, but perhaps documents like these?" Mr. Jordan rubbed his chin. His eyes sparkled ever so slightly. "One is a bill of lading, the second is a shipping manifest, and the third is an invoice." He flipped the third document around and checked it. "To an investor, for eighty hundred weight of grain." He turned to the jurors. "We've blacked out the name. The identity isn't necessary to this proceeding."

Claire's head now pounded. She was unsure where this line of questioning was going, but clearly it was nowhere good.

She answered Mr. Jordan's questions as best as she could. She was unfamiliar with the documents.

Finally, Mr. Jordan smirked. "Fine. That's all we need."

"I'm done?"

He nodded.

Claire stood and made her way from the room. Before reaching the door, she passed the woman who had been taking notes, and

Claire couldn't help but wonder whose coffin her testimony had just nailed shut.

Tuck's . . . or her son's?

27

Claire pushed through heavy glass doors into the sunlight with a myriad of questions swirling. Before she could ponder a single one of them, her cell phone rang. She pulled it from her bag and held the phone to her ear.

She slipped her sunglasses in place and listened as Ranger questioned her about her testimony. "Jordan is asking about hedging and stop-loss orders," she said. "And about feeding cattle that didn't exist."

"Well, we should know very soon what all this is about," he said. "But I'm not going to sugarcoat the situation. This line of questioning does not bode well. The US Attorney is onto something."

Tell me what I don't know, Claire thought. She may not have understood how to protect losses in the commodities market with hedging and such, but any dummy could assume the feds had discovered more wrongdoing.

It appeared her husband had thrown his entire family under the bus. Perhaps even their son. And for what?

Like a simple fool, she had initially stepped right into the role of "stand by your man." What had she been thinking, for goodness' sake?

She hadn't been thinking — that's what. While she struggled to keep a stiff upper lip, hoping for the best given a horrible situation, Tuck sat on yet more secrets. More deceit.

Anger roiled up inside and the emotion became too much. Claire wanted to hit something — smash it to pieces.

Why, Tuck?

Tuck had bilked innocent investors of millions, their church even. Ripped her mother of her security and taken her best friend's retirement account. Now he may have put Garrett in jeopardy.

Ranger cleared his throat. "The terms of the plea agreement were clear. In exchange for a lighter sentence, Tuck was to cooperate completely. All indications are Tuck failed to disclose all the elements of his crime."

Claire felt familiar dread return. "So what happens now?"

"Well, you won't be involved in what happens going forward unless they try to include you and allege you were complicit. We'd fight that, of course."

"The prosecutors don't think I was involved?" Claire's hand instinctively went to her chest. "I — I had nothing to do with any of this." She didn't know which made her feel more sick — the thought she'd face criminal charges of some sort, or the fact her own husband had placed her in this precarious situation.

"You have little to worry about," Ranger assured her. "If necessary, we'll hire a handwriting expert who'll prove you did not sign those documents."

Feeling dazed, Claire headed for the parking garage.

At least Ranger was on her side.

The truth? She was as surprised as anyone at what Tuck had done. She certainly wasn't a part of any scheme that involved hedging and stop-loss agreements. And she felt sure Ranger would prove that, if it became necessary.

After some thought, she was almost certain Garrett knew nothing of all this either. Claire's gut told her Tuck had also forged their son's signature, an act that took Tuck's desperation to a brand-new low.

She opened her bag and fished out her

parking stub. She could take the elevator to the third floor, but after sitting all day, she headed for the stairs. The exercise would be good for her. She could walk off some of these angry feelings.

She climbed the first series of steps and rounded the landing, thinking for the first time she was glad Marcy's dad had convinced Garrett of the need for separate counsel so early on. At first Claire felt he'd intruded and pulled her family apart in the process. But clearly Tuck had no compunction about risking both their well-beings. She could relax somewhat knowing Garrett's legal matters were in good hands.

This time, Tuck deserved whatever came his way.

Out of breath, Claire reached the floor where she'd parked and pulled the heavy stairwell door open. Her footsteps echoed as she crossed the concrete to where she'd left her Escalade.

She was thinking she needed to walk the river daily, like she had before Tuck put in the gym, when her phone buzzed. She pulled it from her bag and glanced at the face.

Max.

"Hi, baby." Did her voice give away how emotionally exhausted she felt?

"Mom, we need to talk."

With her free hand, she fished in her bag for her keys. "Yes, I know. Where are you?"

"My appearance was just canceled. I'm heading for the Stockyards."

She moved past a row of cars. "Canceled? You don't have to testify?" What could that mean? Regardless, she was thankful her younger son had been spared that stress.

"Why don't you meet me at Riscky's?"

Claire reached the third row of cars and turned. She walked past a little green sedan and then a dark blue Suburban blocking her own car from view. "I suppose I could be there in about an hour."

She stopped, stunned. "Oh!"

Max's voice came through her phone. "Mom, what is it? What's the matter?"

Claire swallowed and walked slowly forward. "Someone — uh, somebody egged my car."

The attractive young black woman holding the clipboard was better suited to a pretty dress and some bling, Claire thought as she watched the uniformed police officer scribble on the report. "So, what happens next?"

The officer scowled. "Now, you're sure you don't know who might have done this to your car?"

She shook her head. "No idea."

A second officer, a short guy with stubby legs, stepped forward. "The guy at the entrance confirmed there are no security cameras. He provided a list of license plates from cars entering this structure in the hours since you arrived." He nodded. "Probably, though, somebody just walked up the stairs."

The woman clicked her pen shut. "We've taken down the information. That's really all we can do at this point, unless a lead develops." She ripped off a copy of the report and handed it to Claire. "Massey — now why does that name sound so familiar?"

The short guy scowled. "Hey, wait a minute. Ain't you that rich lady I been seeing on the news? The one with the crook husband who weaseled all those people outta their money?"

The female officer cocked her head. "What's this?"

Claire confirmed she was Tuck Massey's wife. "I suppose this could be the work of a disgruntled investor."

The short guy agreed. He looked at her with scorn. "My grandma bought into your family's scheme . . . lost everything."

She rubbed her forehead. "I'm sorry. I . . ."

The female officer made an additional note on her copy of the report. "This is certainly relevant. Unfortunately, these facts still don't identify the perpetrator. Like I said, we'll get in touch with any leads." She looked at Claire. "Better get yourself to a car wash before that mess dries. It'll ruin your finish."

After texting Max she'd be a bit late, Claire headed for the nearest car wash. She slowed and read the instructions on the sign, then aligned her front tire with the metal railings where indicated. A heavyset woman with wiry hair and thick glasses stepped forward.

Hoping no reporters were parked with zoom lenses pointed in her direction, Claire lowered her window. "I'd like a wash, please."

"You want wax?"

She confirmed she did and passed her last twenty-dollar bill over to the woman, who adjusted her earphones before providing change and a receipt.

The woman tilted her head and looked at the mess on the car's exterior paint. "Looks like somebody was mad at you or something. You want to ride through?"

"Huh? Oh yes — that'll be fine." Claire had not been through a car wash in over ten years. She raised her window. The pulleys caught and she felt the car jerk forward. Water sprayed the sides of her Escalade. Out of another nozzle, water jetted onto the windshield, temporarily blocking her view.

Claire pressed back against the headrest, hoping the rhythm of the conveyor and the spraying water would lull her away from all that had transpired.

Regardless, her thoughts still drifted back to Tuck.

No matter how she tried, she couldn't reconcile this new knowledge of Tuck with the husband she'd lived with all those years. She'd believed him when he said he'd gotten in over his head with the cattle investments, felt pressure, and cut some legal corners. Never intending to defraud anyone but hoping to buy time until things turned around.

But now? What was she supposed to think now?

The same guy who'd lost that grandma's money had rocked her babies to sleep. The man who forged her name, and Garrett's, to legal documents had sat with her in church more Sundays than she could count. He was an elder, for goodness' sake.

He'd lied. Not only to investors, to his family . . . but to the court.

Nothing about this made sense.

When given the chance, he could've come clean. The judge had made that requirement completely clear at the sentencing. What would Tuck's reckless decisions mean for all of them now?

Soap squirted the windshield and mixed with the egg, creating little yellow rivers running down the glass. Through the blur, a yellow light flashed.

It was true. She almost hated him for what he'd done. But another emotion also churned. She couldn't help herself.

With little effort, Claire recalled her husband's nightly touch. Like the flutter of butterfly wings, his fingers stroked her cheeks, swept downward against her bare skin, to places only he knew.

An ache formed, one she'd felt often since his arrest.

Big rollers of fabric strips beat against the windshield. *Slap, slap, slap.*

She missed his smell, the way she thrilled when his eyes met hers across a room with the promise of what awaited when he finally got her alone. There were times she'd give anything to feel him against her again, his breath hot on her neck.

Helpless, Claire closed her eyes against tears.

She hated Tuck.

And, heaven help her, she loved him.

28

Claire slipped inside the doors of Riscky's over an hour late. Immediately, the tantalizing barbeque aroma hit her nostrils and her stomach contracted. Had she even eaten today?

She pulled off her sunglasses and surveyed the noisy restaurant, with its raw wood beams and floor, until she spotted Max checking his watch. He looked up and she waved, then followed the hostess to his small table by the window.

"About time, Mom."

She slid into the wooden bench and dropped her purse on the red and white checked oilcloth covering the table. A wire basket held plastic squirt bottles of ketchup and mustard and a set of disposable salt and pepper shakers. "I know. Sorry."

"What'll you have, darlin'?" An aging waitress in tight jeans and a tighter tank top stood with pen poised on a small tablet.

"Uh, let's see." Claire's eyes scanned the stained paper menu. "I'd like some brisket, please. And a Dr Pepper."

"Dry or wet?"

Claire focused on the question, thankful to think about something as mundane as which rub she wanted on her beef. "Half and half, please."

"Gotcha." The waitress winked and scurried away in the direction of the kitchen.

Max took a drink of his root beer. "I can't believe somebody egged your car." Scowling, he set the frosted mug down. "Did you report it?"

"Yes, the police took a report. But there's nothing they can do, really. We'll probably never know who did it."

"Please be careful, Mom. There's a lot of nutcases out there. More than a few hate our family now."

She nodded in agreement, trying not to dwell on the possible danger.

Max leaned forward and lowered his voice. "Mom, I'm scared for Dad. I think he's in some serious trouble."

Claire looked into his thoughtful eyes and released a heavy sigh. "I know, Son."

"The scoop in the newsroom is that the feds are pulling back the agreement. Strangely, Dad is pressing to amend instead of forcing their hands and making them prove him guilty at trial."

"He is guilty, Max." Her voice was barely audible above the music blaring from overhead speakers.

They grew silent. The waitress stepped up to the table and slid platters in front of them. Starving, Claire buried her fork, and her thoughts, in the thin slices of fire-roasted meat.

In her mind, she again examined the turn their lives had taken, this time from the perspective of the young man across the table from her.

How does a kid, only twenty years old, cope with the knowledge his father is a criminal? Claire's heart sank, knowing she was impotent to protect him. No doubt scars would result.

As a little boy, Max often viewed life proudly perched on his daddy's shoulders. Sadly, being Tuck Massey's son was no longer a badge of honor.

"Mom, the prosecutors are catching flak for not discovering the additional fraud, and heads are rolling at the US Attorney's Office. Investor groups are threatening a public protest that the government failed to catch the commodities fraud scheme earlier."

"No doubt your dad's sentence is in jeopardy. But let's not get too far ahead of ourselves. We'll likely know soon where all this will lead." Claire feigned a quiet resignation, even though she felt like putting her hands over her ears and groaning.

She finished off the brisket and downed the remaining Dr Pepper. With a flicker of guilt, she reached across the table and covered her son's hand with her own. "Dad brought all this on himself. We can't save him from what he's done, the choices he alone made. All we can do now is move on from here." She smiled at Max with genuine fondness. "Son, you'll meet a girl someday. Fall in love. Marry." She patted his hand. "Together you'll build a life and all this turmoil will be left behind. You'll be happy."

He looked unsure. "What about you?"

"I'll be okay." Claire tried to assure him with a weak smile.

When they'd finished their meal, she reached for the sales ticket, then followed Max as he picked his way through the tables and headed for the front counter. She passed a guy with a scrubby chin wearing a button-down shirt and jeans. He lifted his beer bottle and eyed her with appreciation. She quickened her step.

At the cash register, she handed the clerk

her credit card and focused her attention outside the window at the famed Stockyards cattle drive. Slow-moving longhorns sauntered down the street, followed by a cowboy in chaps and a wide-brimmed cowboy hat, riding a chestnut-colored horse. A little boy on his father's shoulders clapped.

"Uh, ma'am?"

Claire glanced back at the clerk. "Yes?"

The man hesitated and smoothed his mustache before handing the sales ticket back. "I'm sorry to tell you this, but I'm afraid your credit card has been declined."

29

Two weeks later, word came from Ranger that further fractured Claire's heart, leaving her to wonder if she'd ever feel whole again.

She stood at the riverbank as the sky darkened and the first stars twinkled in the Texas sky.

"Everything will be okay," Tuck said when they'd talked on the phone, although she did not understand how he could make so grand a statement. Clearly he underestimated how little control he had over the situation. He'd orchestrated a multimillion-dollar cattle fraud, and now they'd learned he'd committed securities fraud, manipulating the commodities market. Did he think he'd go unpunished?

Even so, when Ranger's call came confirming her worst fear, the bottom fell from Claire's world. This changed everything. No longer could she hold on to the hope Tuck would be released in two years, that they'd be able to pick up and go on, even if differently.

Now he'd also pled guilty to multiple counts of security violations, and this time the admission would cost him dearly.

Claire's first priority was her family — her children. She called and told them to come home, even if just for a brief visit. Garrett and Lainie both argued, but Claire wouldn't take no for an answer. They needed each other right now. Better said, she needed them.

She stuffed the ache further down. Ranger said she had less than a week before the new deal was official and news would break. She didn't want her children hearing from anyone but her.

She turned and looked out over Legacy Ranch, the stables and outbuildings all dark now. Weeds grew at the helipad landing.

She closed her eyes, conjuring visions of the barbeque they'd held in the spring — the crowds and the laughing. She and Tuck had danced under these same stars. She could almost feel his arm at her back, see him gazing at her.

Claire slumped to the hard ground.

How could someone she loved wound her so deeply? Every lie, every betrayal sliced her soul.

She'd tried her best to stand by Tuck. Tried to believe in him. What was she to think now?

The evidence proved her husband had masterminded a scheme to purposely make money through fraudulent means. Unlike with the earlier charges, Tuck's back was not against the wall. These crimes were by choice, motivated by pure greed.

That revelation left Claire feeling sick inside.

She shook her head in disgust. How had she trusted so blindly?

She loved him. That was why.

No matter what he'd done, he was still her mate of nearly thirty years, the father of her children. Was there a way to vacate that history so anger could fully move in? She wasn't sure.

In the meantime, she'd have to survive financially and emotionally — especially emotionally. Right now, every breath hurt. Each time Tuck broke her heart, her chest cracked with deep, jagged crevices that gouged Claire's very core. She didn't know how to move on with her life — or if she even wanted to.

Claire looked to the star-filled sky and whispered a desperate prayer.

Please, God, help me.

■ ■ ■ ■

Lainie dropped her coffee mug to the table and glared. "What are you saying?"

Claire took a deep breath and looked at her children. "I'm saying your father consented to a twenty-year sentence with no possibility of parole."

"Twenty years? That's — that's like he's never getting out." Lainie's face contorted into a ball of fearful anger. "Why would he do that? Did he even think about us?"

"Do you think Dad had a choice?" Max asked, eyebrows lifted.

Garrett cleared his throat. "Yes, he had a choice. The first time he decided to phony the books and scam someone, he made his choice."

Shaking, Claire held up her palm. "Look, what matters now is that we're still a family." She looked around the table. "None of us can alter what your father did. All we can do is rise above his actions and move on. Together."

"Cut it, Mom. Realistically, do you actually believe this family can just move on?" Garrett challenged, his voice an ax chopping at Claire's carefully constructed plan. For emphasis, her oldest son snapped his fingers. "Just like that?"

Max leaned back in his chair. "Oh, and this coming from the guy who just picks up and leaves."

Garrett huffed. "What was I supposed to do? While you had your arms draped around another bar bimbo, I had my wife to consider — and my child."

He rolled his eyes. "Oh, here it comes."

"What's that supposed to mean?"

Color heated Max's cheeks. He shook his head. "This is where you make yourself out to be someone we all know you're not."

Lainie looked across the table at her brothers, apprehension filling her eyes. She glanced at Claire as if to say "stop this."

Claire's internal alarm was sounding as well. "Boys —"

"Mom, stay out of this," Garrett said. "I want to hear what Little Boy Wonder has to say."

She threw her napkin to the table in tears. "Knock it off. Both of you."

"Little Boy Wonder — that's classic." Max smirked. "Especially coming from a guy who says he *never* smoked pot, *never* had sex before he was married, *never* sold out his father to save his own neck."

Garrett's face drained of color. He squinted his eyes but said nothing.

"Tell them," Max said. "They all deserve to know why Dad isn't ever coming home again."

Claire's gut squeezed tight. The conversation around her dinner table had become a car wreck. But like any onlooker, she couldn't turn away no matter how bloodied the victims.

Lainie voiced what she could not. "What . . . we deserve to know what?"

Garrett dropped his head. "I — I had to think about Marcy. And the baby."

Claire's heart thumped inside her chest. "Garrett?"

Her mother burst into the dining room, a Yorkie in each hand. "What's all this yelling down here?"

"Nothing, Grandma," Max said, never pulling his attention from his brother.

"Garrett?" Claire repeated. "Talk to me."

Her son raised his head and met her gaze. When he spoke, his words were choked, his guilt-filled eyes glazed with tears.

"Please, Mom, don't hate me."

30

Lainie leaned her head against the bark of the oak tree. "How did you know?"

Max looked up at the sky filled with storm clouds, making the early evening atmosphere even darker. "The newsroom. An anonymous source."

Despite her tough show at the table, Lainie's insides ached. "I know what Garrett said, but I don't understand. What is *substantial assistance*?"

"When Dad forged Garrett's signature on those papers, the feds came after Garrett. All I heard is he remembered seeing an order for feed he knew had never been delivered. He must've put two and two together. Dad would make money selling fake cows, then charge the investors to feed them. He'd use those funds to place orders for massive amounts of grain in the futures market, and hedge the price by selling that same feed back with stop-loss orders in place." Max lifted his chin. "All on paper, of course. Nothing in Dad's world was real. A great way to make a lot of profit until the markets turned and cash flow tightened."

Lainie frowned. "But that still doesn't answer why Garrett would rat Dad out. Especially when he knew the information would blow Dad's earlier deal."

Max closed his eyes, seeming lost in his thoughts. Finally, he answered. "Garrett got immunity."

"Well then, I don't blame him, especially if Garrett didn't do anything." Lainie stood and brushed off. A gathering wind blew her long blonde hair. "Dad sold us all down the river. Garrett had every right to protect himself. I just hate that he snuck around behind all our backs to do it." She huffed. "That's so Garrett."

"You're kidding, right?" he asked. "Did you see Mom's face? Did you even stop to imagine what this has done to her?"

She grabbed her hair and knotted it at the back of her neck. She didn't need her little brother pointing out the obvious. "Yeah? That doesn't mean we don't all have lives, Max. That we don't have to do what we can to survive this humiliation."

She wasn't going to let him pull her moral ground out from under her. If she needed to get Pride back and secure a future by hooking up with Sidney McAlvain, she would. "I'm not taking Garrett's side here, but if I was facing prosecution, you better believe I'd do the same." She started for the house, then turned back. "You know, Max, I love her too. But none of us did this to Mama — Daddy did."

Claire followed Garrett into the front living area. Her mother trailed behind them, dogs in her arms. "I think the heat is getting to Nutmeg. She's dropping hair, and Yorkies don't shed."

Claire turned. "Mama, could you give us a few minutes?"

Her mother frowned. "Sure," she said. On the way out she bent her head to her dogs and mumbled, "They keep sending me out of the room, and then they wonder why I don't visit more often."

As soon as they were alone, Claire moved to Garrett. She drew him into an embrace, noticing that he failed to hug back. "I'm your mother. I'll always love you, Son."

He stepped away. "But you think what I did was wrong."

"Not wrong," she said, choosing her words carefully. "I just don't understand why you didn't come to me — to Ranger.

Maybe we could've figured out another way." She bit the tender spot inside her lip. "Twenty years, Garrett. Even though what your father did was wrong, that's a long time."

"My attorney urged me —"

"He's not your family," Claire gently corrected.

Garrett moved to the massive window overlooking the front drive and gazed out. "Do you know what it was like, Mom? Always trying to live up to his expectations?"

Claire drew a deep breath and dropped onto the sofa. She kicked off her shoes and drew her legs up under her, all the while watching Garrett at the window. "I remember you being happy."

But did she really?

Images of Garrett bent over his desk, studying into the wee morning hours, flashed in her mind. "Honey, it's late. You need to get some sleep. You have a big game tomorrow," she'd said to the younger Garrett, ruffling his hair.

He never looked up. "I will. But I've gotta ace this test or else."

Or else what? What did her son think would happen if he got a B on one lousy exam?

Claire remembered the disappointment in Tuck's eyes as he patted Garrett on the back after he'd lost a game his freshman year at school. "Don't worry, Son. With a few laps added to your daily routine, you'll pick up speed. You've got to be fast if you're going to quarterback on a college team."

Garrett had added those laps. And he'd come within inches of adding a Heisman Trophy to the shelves in Tuck's office.

Maybe she should have noticed the pressure back then. But she didn't.

And then there was that time in Sun Valley, when Garrett pushed past his skiing ability and ended up with a broken leg.

Claire yearned to make sense of all this for her son, even when she didn't quite understand it herself.

"Garrett, your father meant well," she offered, regarding her son with compassion. "Tuck carried a lot of demons from his own childhood. He didn't have much available to him growing up, and sometimes I think he simply wanted us all to have the world. Especially you." She felt the unexpected sting of tears and wiped her eyes. "He only wanted the very best for you."

With a heavy sigh, Garrett looked up at the ceiling and put his hands behind his head. "Thanks for the pep talk, Mom. But you'll never understand." He sniffed before dropping his arms.

Claire winced. She hadn't meant to sugarcoat his pain. "Garrett, what your father did was wrong." She watched her son warily, checking to see if what she was saying had any impact. "But that doesn't mean he didn't love —"

The blaze in her son's eyes stopped her midsentence.

"The line between love and hate can become very narrow," he said. "And I wonder — which side will he be on when he learns what I did?" What little color he had left drained from his face. His eyes dimmed with grief. "I took the only possible path. But I still can't look at myself in the mirror."

Claire's heart thudded painfully. The sight of her boy standing there, his arms hanging at his sides in resigned despair, tore her apart.

Outside, rain spattered the glass.

She supposed in some ways they'd all followed Tuck down the same mountain. He'd taken unbelievable risks and raced toward destruction, leaving them all broken and unable to walk.

Especially Garrett.

More than a doctor would be required to

286

heal their crippled lives. Her family would need a miracle.

31

By ten o'clock the following morning, every station in the Dallas area carried breaking news of Claire's new plight. Based on recent developments, the US Attorney's Office had reopened the matter of *The United States v. Theodore Massey*.

Claire's unanswered phone rang for the twelfth time in less than an hour. With remote in hand, she clicked off the ringer and tossed her phone on the bed, diverting her attention instead to the screen mounted on her bedroom wall.

Deputy Chief McAlroy and the lead prosecutor, Charles Jordan, stood at a bank of microphones, a large Department of Justice seal in the backdrop.

McAlroy was the first to speak. "Good evening, everyone. Thank you for being here. I understand you have a lot of questions, but first let me make a few remarks, and then I'll open it up."

He cleared his throat. "On May 14 of this year, a federal grand jury indictment was issued charging Theodore 'Tuck' Massey with multiple counts of felony wire fraud, mail fraud, false representation, and criminal forfeiture. These charges resulted from a Ponzilike cattle scam whereby Mr. Massey defrauded investors, creating massive financial fallout.

"Mr. Massey was remanded into custody, entered into a plea agreement, and is currently incarcerated in the Federal Correction Center in Bastrop, Texas. In addition, pursuant to the plea agreement, authorities confiscated property and assets belonging to Mr. Massey — estimated value at half a billion dollars.

"Recently our office was made aware of another scheme prompting further investigation. This effort revealed a complicated commodities fraud where Mr. Massey manipulated grain prices through an intricate scheme of cooperative trading that created false profits.

"Yesterday at 9:00 a.m., Mr. Massey consented to plead guilty to additional charges. The amended agreement will include an extended sentence of twenty years, without the possibility of parole."

Claire stared at the screen. She blinked

several times, trying to focus. Hearing the news in a press conference somehow made everything more . . . *real.*

"First of all, let me reiterate that this office is committed to bringing justice in these kinds of situations, and all of us in the US Attorney's Office remain acutely aware that real people have been hurt. Grandmothers living on Social Security placed their savings accounts with Tuck Massey. Fathers and mothers invested their children's college funds. By not proceeding to a lengthy and expensive trial, restitution will be made much earlier, with more expediency and less burden on taxpayers.

"Now I'll open it up to questions."

Claire pointed the remote and clicked off the television. She slumped onto the bed, struggling to form valid thoughts.

She had to remember to breathe. *In . . . out. In . . . out.* Her heart pounded.

Her eyes swept the familiar surroundings. Their bedroom with cream walls and gold sconces. The chintz settee and armchairs. The ivory fireplace opposite the bed — her and Tuck's bed.

A bed that would remain empty for twenty years.

An involuntary trembling began in the pit of Claire's stomach, extending through her groin, her legs, her arms. She couldn't stop shaking.

Her skin grew clammy — cold and hot all at the same time. Fear, unlike any she'd ever known, caused her teeth to chatter. The room grew milky.

Her hands grasped the bedcovers in an attempt to steady herself.

Suddenly, in a wild fit of panic, Claire rushed for the bathroom. She latched onto the sink and spewed her emotions in chunks, retching over and over.

Her hands gripped the cold, hard porcelain edge as she thought of handcuffs, hearings, and subpoenas. Her mind formed images of the judge, of television screens filled with angry investors spouting their hatred, of Garrett and Marcy getting in the car and driving away. She remembered the scene on the courthouse steps and felt the spit on her cheek, remembered telling the children about the additional crimes and the extreme pain in Garrett's eyes.

From deep inside, her stomach expelled pain until no more came and nothing remained but her emptiness.

Quietly she collapsed to the floor, exhausted. With her cheek pressed against the hard, cold tile, Claire tightly closed her eyes and tried not to think.

A hand pressed against her shoulder. "Mrs. Massey?"

She raised her pounding head. "Margarita."

The buxom housekeeper folded to her knees and cradled Claire's dampened head to her chest. "Everything will be all right, Mrs. Massey."

The maternal tenderness was more than she could bear. Her emotions broke and tears spilled. Slow at first, then turning to torrents of sobs. She cried and cried.

Margarita smoothed her hair. "There, there . . . let it all out. That's right."

Several minutes later, completely spent, Claire swallowed and struggled for control. She pulled back and looked into the eyes of her trusted housekeeper. Her breath hitched from crying. "You know, Margarita," she said, "at some point in our years together, Tuck became an essential part of me, like an arm or leg."

Margarita's eyes filled with sympathy. *"Sí,"* she said, nodding. "Two became one."

"Yes," Claire said. "But in so many ways, our intimate connection was a lie. In truth, my husband was nothing more than a stranger." She swiped the back of her hand across her wet cheeks. "I've always treasured the notion of myself as strong and brave,

but I'm none of those things, Margarita."
With a watery smirk, she added, "And I
guess the life we built together is over.
Everything is different now."

"In these hard times, God will carry you,
my friend."

Hugging her arms tightly around herself,
Claire dropped her gaze to the floor and
said weakly, "I hope so, Margarita. Because
I've never been this scared."

32

Claire pulled from Knox Street into the parking lot and found a spot at the back not far from a Pottery Barn. PB (Jana Rae's nickname for it) was her friend's favorite store. But today Jana Rae wasn't interested in shopping. She'd decided they both could use some exercise.

Never mind it was August in Dallas. Never mind Claire owned several pairs of running shoes but never wore them. And especially never mind she was not, nor ever had been, a runner.

She slipped from her car. Jana Rae spotted her and waved. Claire watched as her friend jogged over, looking stunning in a white and robin's-egg-blue running ensemble. With her red hair pulled into a ponytail, she could pass for Lainie's age.

"Hey, you are going to *love* the Katy Trail," she claimed, running in place. "And you might want to warm up."

"Warm up?"

"You know, do some stretches."

Now her friend was speaking her language. Running always seemed such a hot and nasty form of exercise. Claire preferred her personal gym at the house and working with Koen Van Wygeurt, a Belgium trainer Tuck had hired for her when she complained her size 6 pants were getting snug and the yoga classes no longer seemed to be working. According to Koen, dynamic stretching performed in sets of eight to twenty repetitions was the foundation to his custom plan for strength building and his weight-maintenance program.

She followed Jana Rae to a park bench, where she began her side bends while Jana Rae squirted a long draw of water into her mouth from a stylish bottle that matched her tank top.

Claire's own outfit consisted of a cute little exercise set in tangerine, one of the things the receiver passed over when he'd done his inventory. She'd suffered many humiliations since Tuck's arrest, but watching a team of pinched-faced men paw through her closet topped the list. Thankfully, she'd been able to keep most of her wardrobe. But gone were the Valentino and Dior gowns, Jimmy Choo pumps, and Prada duffels — anything considered couture was bagged and logged and taken away.

Not that it really mattered. She'd never be invited to lavish parties or travel to Paris again. That life was over.

Jana Rae closed her bottle and clipped it on her belt. "You ready?"

Claire followed Jana Rae onto the running path. She wasn't a runner, but she could learn to love this runner's park. She remembered a fund-raiser sponsored by Friends of the Katy Trail, where Tuck had written a large check contributing to the construction effort.

Once abandoned railroad tracks, the trail consisted of an over twelve-foot-wide concrete path for pedestrians and cyclists that ran several miles through the Uptown and Oak Lawn areas of Dallas. Next to the concrete path, a soft, recycled-rubber track was built parallel for runners.

This was the first time Claire had actually used the lovely path lined with gorgeous perennial grasses and native Texas trees and plants, including chinquapin and lacey oaks.

They ran for about a half hour before Claire pooped out. "Jana Rae, I've got to take a break. You're used to this. I'm not."

She'd done a lot of running lately, none in athletic shoes. She'd run from television cameras and from investors who believed she was Bonnie to Tuck's Clyde. More importantly, she had run from the truth. That mind-set was now over.

She bent over and tried to catch her breath.

"Lightweight." Jana Rae pulled the towel from around her neck and swiped her brow. "You know, lack of exercise is as bad for you as smoking."

Claire straightened. "Does Clark know you spend your afternoons with Dr. Oz?"

"The Urologist has no room for complaint. He's in love with *The Good Wife.*" A look passed across her face as she realized she'd just mentioned a television show that mirrored Claire's life in so many ways.

She watched a blue jay flutter in the branches of a nearby tree. "Mama thinks I need to get a divorce."

Jana Rae didn't respond immediately. Instead, she pulled out her water bottle and squirted the back of her neck. Finally, she looked at Claire. "I'm not sure what to say."

They started walking.

Claire paced her steps, and her words, carefully. "Well, I agree with her at some level. I'm too young to be alone."

"You're not alone, Claire. You have your children. You have me."

She rolled her eyes. "You know what I mean. Besides, I'm learning I focused too much on Tuck over the past thirty years and didn't see things that were right under my nose. And I'm not talking about Tuck's crimes."

"What things?"

Claire told her about her conversation with Garrett, how her inability to see how much her son was hurting had left him feeling torn in two. She'd never forgive herself for failing him.

"Now my son's gone," she told her friend. "Garrett and Marcy plan to raise the baby in Houston. Three hours away."

"Mike lived in Waco until just recently," Jana Rae reminded her. "I saw him all the time."

"Still, I wonder if Mama is right," Claire said, ignoring her friend's attempt at another way to see things.

Her mother had seen the news coverage and made her position clear. "Seems to me the curtain has closed on this production. Take it from me, darlin' — you had a good run with Tuck, but it's time to close down the show so you can get out there and audition again."

Jana Rae spoke carefully. "Is that what you want?"

"I don't get what I want, Jana Rae. Apparently, for years I've lived with blinders on, not seeing things that were happening right in front of me. Now I have no choice but to face reality." She shook her head. "He's gone. Twenty years."

"That doesn't mean you necessarily have to divorce."

She stopped walking and turned to her friend. "I'm surprised you say that. I thought you'd be the first to push me to a fresh start."

"Eh, I think a bit differently about these kinds of things." Jana Rae looked at Claire, her eyes steady and sure. "Divorce is overrated, Claire. I know from experience."

Two young guys sprinted by, sweat drenching their shirts. They looked determined, as if trying to finish a race. Claire and Jana Rae stepped aside to let them pass.

Claire frowned. " 'For better or worse' doesn't include a twenty-year prison term, Jana Rae. I have a right to try to be happy, don't I?"

"I'm not advocating women shouldn't get out of marriages when abuse or unchecked infidelity is involved. But . . . well, I guess what I'm trying to say is that I've been there since the beginning, when you and Tuck first met and fell in love. How do you just stop feeling that for one another?" Jana Rae wiped her brow with her arm. "Look, I do want you to be happy. Just be really sure before you head down that particular path."

"Well, it's nothing I have to decide right this minute," Claire said, giving Jana Rae a weak smile as they stopped at a water fountain and filled their bottles. "I have enough on my mind. My focus needs to be on finding a new place to live and a job."

The credit card incident at Riscky's popped into her mind. Funds were running out, and she needed to get employed.

Soon.

On the morning of her forty-ninth birthday, Claire donned a sleeveless white top over peach-colored capris and slipped her feet into a matching pair of Ralph Lauren flip-flops. After days of no makeup, she moved into her bathroom and applied foundation powder, colored her eyelids with a light shade of amber, liner, and mascara, then smoothed a pretty coral gloss across her lips.

She examined her image in the mirror. The woman looking back didn't match the one who'd been packing all week, hair up in a clippy. Margarita was a huge help, but she was only one woman and, at her age, tired easily. Certainly Claire's mother had been useless in the effort. "Why don't you hire someone?" she'd suggested, forgetting Claire's current financial situation. So, much of the work of sorting and loading boxes fell to Claire, a far cry from her depending on the large household staff at her beck and call all those years.

She ran a comb through her long blonde hair. Satisfied, she headed downstairs. In a couple of hours, she'd be meeting Jana Rae in Fort Worth.

At first Claire argued she just wasn't up for a celebration, even a quiet dinner out with her friend. What if the media caught wind and cornered her again? But Jana Rae wouldn't take no for an answer. Tonight was her treat at the new Brazilian steakhouse. The one with great lobster bisque.

Claire asked her mother to join but learned she had an iPad and knew how to use it. She'd found a group on Meetup called Yorkie Lovers of Dallas. Tonight was their first meeting.

Claire didn't mention it was her birthday. Neither did her mother.

Last year, Tuck had flown friends in and surprised her with a party at their home in Pebble Beach.

Tuck wasn't much for golf, likely because he preferred custom leather Luccheses over shoes with spikes. Even so, they'd purchased the sprawling vacation home with amazing ocean views five years ago upon the urging of an investor, the owner of one of the largest real estate investment trusts in California.

She'd learned Tuck had planned her party for weeks, and indeed, she'd been shocked to arrive to a house filled with guests.

"Surprise!" they all yelled when she stepped inside the door.

Claire's hands flew to her mouth. She looked at the children's smiling faces, then turned to Tuck, who stood beaming. "How — when did you?" She kissed his cheek.

His arms moved around her waist as he said to her and to the crowd, "Ah, you know me. I'm filled with surprises."

She wondered if any of those people thought of that now — especially those who had heavily invested in Tuck's cattle program and lost everything. He'd surprised them all.

Claire grabbed her bag. "I'll be home late, Margarita."

"Go, go." Margarita shooed her out the door. "You need some fun."

From the rearview mirror, she watched Margarita wave. Today was supposed to be filled with celebration. Despite Claire wanting to feel happy, sadness descended as her thoughts played back on telling her housekeeper of over fifteen years that she could no longer afford to keep her on.

"I'm so very sorry, Margarita," she'd explained with a choked voice. "I just don't have the money."

The wise old housekeeper hadn't seemed surprised by the news. She'd watched as others had been let go, and she'd seen Claire's valued possessions carried away by men with badges. But Claire knew the turn of events had shaken the woman. Although she'd seemed excited to join her daughter and grandchildren in El Paso, a look connected her and Margarita each time they walked past one another. This was not what either of them had expected . . . or wanted.

This year, with her family scattered, Claire was forced to celebrate her special day quietly, with Jana Rae. Garrett was in Houston. Lainie was nowhere to be found, hiding out until she felt ready to face their new life. They'd both called with birthday wishes, and Max sent a bouquet of her favorite blooms. Delicate purple irises, which many say symbolize hope.

And Tuck had not forgotten.

Claire had received her first letter. He'd called since the new charges and revised plea agreement, but she could never bring herself to answer. Now he had reached out again. On her birthday.

With trembling hands, she'd opened the single sheet of lined notebook paper.

My dear sweet Claire,

I know you are hurting. My heart breaks each time I think of how my actions have caused you pain. I love you so much. Never did I mean for any of this to get so out of hand. I hope to explain these recent developments to you face-to-face. Will you come? I desperately need to talk to you.

Oh, Claire. I miss you so much. I lay in this bunk at night and ache for you. If I close my eyes, I smell your hair and the sweetness of your skin.

You are, and always will be, the love of my life.

T.

Claire slowed the engine as the entrance leading to Legacy Ranch came into view. This time next week, she'd exit that gate a final time.

A lump formed in her throat. She swallowed and thought of Tuck, and the letter.

For all that had transpired and the wrongs

Tuck had committed, she knew he'd placed his heart on that paper. Claire believed he loved her, which made what she had to do so difficult.

She decided she had to go to him.

33

A woman dressed in an official prison uniform led Claire through a heavy metal door into a cramped room. A barrier cut the room in half, the upper portion made of glass grimy with handprints.

Claire turned to thank the officer, but she was now alone. Nervous, she slid into the empty chair on her side of the barrier.

And waited.

It had been two weeks since her birthday and Tuck's letter. So much had happened in that short time, and often she'd pondered the future, wondering whether she was making the right decision. But in the end, she had no choice, really. She had to move on.

She'd taken Margarita to the airport and said goodbye, promising to visit her in El Paso. Before she left, Claire's mother helped Margarita open a profile page on Facebook so she could share photos of her grandchildren with Claire.

"I don't know, Mrs. Wyden. I'm an old woman. Hard to learn new things."

But when Claire's mother showed Margarita how to check her daughters' Facebook walls, her housekeeper's eyes lit up. "Ooo-eeee! Now, tell me. How do I hit 'Like' again?"

Ellie Wyden grinned. "Wait until I show you Pinterest, Margarita. That'll blow the ties right off that apron of yours."

Last Tuesday, the movers had arrived. In less than a day, everything Claire now owned was crammed into a van the size of the motorhome she and Tuck used to park out at the Texas Motor Speedway for tailgating at the NASCAR races. Everything had been placed in storage, waiting until she decided her next move.

Not so unlike her life in general.

Both Claire and her mother had moved in with Max temporarily. Only until Claire located an apartment, which was next on her list. Right after this visit to Tuck.

A distant noise from beyond the Plexiglas window pulled Claire's thoughts back to the present surroundings, and why she was here.

Even though she told herself to breathe, her heart pounded wildly. By the time the door on the other side of the barrier creaked open, every nerve fiber in her body was charged. Claire trained her eyes on the doorway and vowed not to cry. Not here.

Then he entered, appearing older, more tired than the last time she'd seen him. Perhaps resigned to his circumstances. But he still looked at her with the same eyes — the ones she'd gazed into that night all those years ago at the Burger Hut. And so many times since.

Tuck quickly moved to the window and took his seat. With a guard standing nearby, he placed his shackled palm against the glass and mouthed, "I love you."

Claire blinked several times before picking up the telephone receiver and motioning for him to do the same.

He scrambled for the phone at his side, as though it were a line to the life he'd left behind . . . to her. He quickly nestled the black handset against his ear.

"Claire." He said her name with a kind of reverence, a tone you'd use with someone you cherished.

Claire swallowed against the dryness of her throat. She couldn't waffle. This had to be done. She looked into her husband's eyes and steeled herself.

"I want a divorce."

■ ■ ■ ■

Claire leaned against the headrest and closed her eyes as Max pulled onto TX-95 and headed back to Dallas. She appreciated the coolness of the air-conditioning blowing from the vent, a stark contrast to the sweltering August sun and the different kind of heat she'd felt inside that prison.

No matter how she tried, she couldn't erase the memory of the look on Tuck's face. He'd visibly winced at her words. He understood her decision, he'd said. But she'd caught the quiver in his chin and knew she'd thrown him a harsh blow, wounding him with those four words far more than anything physical could have.

Even as he stood before being led away, he'd looked at her and whispered, "I love you."

A knot formed in Claire's gut. He had no right to put her through any of this. *His* decisions and choices had poisoned all of their well-being. He'd left her with no other viable option.

Claire had never pictured herself ending her marriage. But she was making the only decision that made sense, given these circumstances. Tuck was a criminal, incarcerated for twenty years. He'd betrayed her trust. Lied even. She was doing the right thing.

Wasn't she?

"You okay, Mom?" Max flashed the blinker and changed lanes.

She opened her eyes and gave her son a weak smile. "I will be."

Max's hand left the steering wheel and he lightly patted her hand. "You're welcome to stay with me for as long as you need. Gram too."

"Don't worry. Jana Rae and I start apartment hunting tomorrow. But I appreciate your hospitality, Son." Claire smoothed her hair. "Let's stop at a grocery store, huh? I've peeked in your fridge, and I don't think we can cook dinner with only milk and a couple of sticks of margarine."

"Margarita could," he said, grinning. "That ol' gal could make mud taste good."

"Yes, she sure could," Claire said. "But now you're stuck with your mother. And despite the fact I have a culinary arts degree, I need a bit more to work with."

Early September in Texas was normally bright and sunny and served as a nice transition from blistering summer to what often was the nicest time of the year. Unfortunately, the weatherman played a cruel joke this year and predicted a warm front from the gulf would meet up with an early line of cold air mass, creating potential for severe weather in the Dallas/Fort Worth metroplex.

Despite the warnings, Jana Rae pushed Claire to follow through on their plans to find a suitable apartment. "Honey," she said, "Max has been more than patient. You need to get off that boy's couch and give him his life back."

"Max likes having us there," Claire said.

"Sure he does." Jana Rae tossed her purse in the backseat of the car and slid behind the wheel. "And he loves strawberry jam on his ham sandwich." She handed Claire a spiral-bound notebook. "I've made a list of possibilities. I think we should focus on Dallas first. Even though prices are higher over here than in Fort Worth, you'd be closer to restaurants that might be hiring."

Claire gave her friend an odd look and moved to the passenger side. "Glad my life is in good hands."

"What are friends for?" Jana Rae buckled up and inserted the key into the ignition.

The first place they looked at was in uptown Dallas, a wonderful three bedroom with a study overlooking a stunning garden with landscaping that reminded Claire of a naturalized riverbed. She loved it, but the lease price was far over what she could afford.

Jana Rae followed her back to where they'd parked the car. "I wish you'd reconsider and let me and Clark help you. I mean, the Urologist might be opposed to sharing our funds, but I have a tiny nest egg of my own that I could use to help you out temporarily, until you get on your feet."

Claire shook her head. "Absolutely not. Like you said, I need to get off Max's couch. And I need to move on . . . learn to live within my means. When I get a job, I still don't want my entire paycheck going toward rent."

She let that thought settle. *Get a job.*

She didn't let on to Jana Rae, but the prospect of finding employment skyrocketed her anxiety level higher than Reunion Tower, especially since she'd never had a job — ever.

As usual, Jana Rae zeroed in on what Claire was thinking. "Look, I know things are tighter than Spandex on a fat girl right now, but you can do this. We'll find you a place to live, one with reasonable rent. And then you'll land a job." A sly grin formed on Jana Rae's face. "You could always be a buyer for Neiman Marcus. Or a sales clerk!"

She pounded her hand on the steering wheel. "With your good taste and sense of style, you could sell nearly anything. Even nail polish to an armadillo."

"Ha, Tuck was the salesman in the family." Claire smirked. "And look how all that turned out."

They looked at three more places before she settled on a condominium within walking distance of White Rock Lake and a Whole Foods grocery. The kitchen featured stainless steel appliances and granite countertops. The carpets showed a little wear here and there, but Claire felt good that she and her mother would be living in a safe area and within her current budget. Still, the check for the six-month lease severely depleted her checkbook, a fact that worried her.

"When do you want to move in?" the resident manager asked.

"The moving company needs three days' notice." Claire looked around at her new place, trying not to think about Legacy Ranch and all she'd lost. "I think Wednesday afternoon would be ideal."

She thanked the lady, took a deep breath, and gazed out the bare window at the darkening sky. Perhaps when she got her own things moved in and hung family portraits on the wall, she might even convince herself this tiny condo located on a street filled with traffic . . . was home.

34

Despite falling into bed exhausted, Claire stared at the alarm clock face, watching the minute dial turning to a new digit every sixty seconds.

Two thirty-four a.m.

She lifted and punched the pillows, settling into a new position. For the next few minutes, she worked to consciously slow her breathing into a rhythm that might foster sleep.

Outside her bedroom window, she heard a low growl, which quickly turned to a cat's screech. She pulled the pillow over her ears, trying unsuccessfully to drown out the sound.

Finally, she gave up and clicked on the lamp. The first night in her new place was definitely not going well.

In the kitchen, she started a pot on the stove to heat water for tea. A guest on the *Dr. Oz Show* said herbal tea had — what did she call it? Natural sedative properties.

Realizing she was a bit hungry, Claire pulled a small cardboard cup wrapped in cellophane from the pantry. She'd never eaten ramen noodles, but even at this age she was game for new things.

Minutes later, she sat at her table with her tea and noodles and let her mind wander. She'd have to find a job soon. Between the rent and the small fortune it'd taken to stock her kitchen, even as careful as she'd been, her financial resources were dwindling faster than she'd hoped.

She had to get employed.

There was a time she'd have shelled out her monthly rent amount for one night in a fancy hotel and thought nothing of it. But thanks to Tuck, everything had changed.

At one point in her life, she'd loved to cook. Despite her mother's urging otherwise — "Oh, honey, be practical. People like us don't cook" — Claire had majored in culinary arts in school.

In fact, she was the only one in a class of over twenty who had whisked her yolks into the pan of hot butter slowly enough that the hollandaise didn't break. Everyone else's sauce separated into what looked like scrambled eggs in grease. The memory caused her to smile, thinking back on how proud she'd felt when the instructor pointed out her accomplishment.

She blew on the hot noodles and slipped a bite in her mouth. Hmm . . . not bad for thirty-five cents.

If she had to work, perhaps she could cook. Better yet, she could work for an event planner and do large weddings and social gatherings. If she knew anything, it was how to put on a party.

"Claire, you up?" Her mother scuffled into the room, the bottom of her styled hair wrapped in layers of folded toilet paper held with bobby pins, her method of keeping her curls in place while she slept.

"No, Mom. I'm not up — I'm sitting here sleeping."

Her mother waved off the comment. "Oh, you know what I meant."

"Yeah, I know." Claire grinned and offered her mom some tea. "I can also make you a mean cup of noodles."

"Claire, dear, how are you ever going to live without a housekeeper? Who's going to cook?" Her mother wrinkled her nose. "And do toilets?"

She raised her eyebrows. "Well, I thought you might —"

"Oh no." Her mother raised her hand like a stop sign. "I gave up housework years ago."

"When you left my father," Claire added.

"That's right. And I'm not about to turn back now." Her mother watched as she moved to the cupboard and retrieved a mug. "Do you have a teacup, dear? Those mugs are so heavy."

"Sure, Mom." She exchanged the mug and pulled a cup and saucer from the shelf, then opened a tea bag. "You hungry?"

Her mother shook her head. "No. And you shouldn't be eating ramen. Those packaged noodles are filled with fat. You're going to have to stay trim to attract another husband, you know."

Claire rolled her eyes while filling the cup with hot water. "Who says I intend to look for a husband?" The minute the words left her mouth, she regretted opening the door to what she knew was an invitation for her mother to pontificate further.

"Of course you're going to marry again. Otherwise your only future is this." Her mom made a sweeping motion with her hands.

"What's wrong with living simply?" she challenged.

"What's wrong with it?" Her mother huffed. "You're my daughter, that's what. You were meant for so much more."

Claire stared across the table at the woman

looking back, at the toilet-papered hair and the face she knew had been heavily creamed before bed. "Mama, I had all that. Look where it landed me."

Suddenly she felt exhausted. She placed the steaming cup in front of the woman who likely meant well but whose attitude had helped shape Claire and park her here in the first place. "I don't mean to be rude, but all of a sudden I'm so tired I can't keep my eyes open." She kissed her mother's cheek. "Good night, Mama."

"Sleep tight, Claire. But don't brush off what I'm telling you. You're going to need a good man."

The following morning, Claire walked to Starbucks and grabbed a newspaper. Nestled in an overstuffed chair, she opened the *Dallas Morning News* and flipped to the Life section. Over the next half hour, she created a list of the caterers mentioned in the articles. Later she'd google the names and call for appointments. Surely, with her background, she'd have a job in no time.

The thought buoyed her spirit. Claire had a plan, and for the first time in months she felt in control of her life. In fact, she should celebrate by splurging on a second salted caramel macchiato, venti sized.

Smiling, she shuffled the paper into a neat pile on her lap and folded it in half. Then she saw something that made her breath catch.

She pulled the paper closer, staring at the front page, which displayed a large color photo of Reece Sandell, his arms around a perky-looking gal with short, cropped hair. The woman wore a stunning strapless cocktail dress in shell pink. A Badgley Mischka design, according to Claire's estimation. Below the photo, the headline read, "Polls Show Sandell Climbing Back."

Claire downed her remaining drink and read on.

The senatorial race in Texas is heating up and heading for what many believe will be a photo finish in November. Reece Sandell, plagued by his former engagement to the daughter of Theodore "Tuck" Massey, seems to have successfully distanced himself from the man who bilked investors of millions in a cattle investment scam.

"I strongly commend the US Attorney's Office for their work pursuing criminals who steal," said Sandell. "The scope of Theodore Massey's illicit activities is a serious concern. Each year, hundreds of millions of dollars are siphoned off unsuspecting investors to line the pockets of white-collar criminals, hurting our economy as a whole.

"Today Theodore Massey sits in prison. This action is an important step in our fight against fraud and abuse in the commodities markets. It is my sincere hope that these law enforcement actions will serve as both a warning and a deterrent to others that Texans are not to be manipulated for personal gain."

Claire slowly closed the paper.

Two tables over, a man leaned to the woman sitting next to him. On their table lay the newspaper. They stared at Claire, whispering.

She looked at her hands, feeling her brave facade crumble.

No matter how many times she tried to move on from the familiar story, the shame of what Tuck had done still stripped her confidence.

Worse, she knew the article would leave Lainie emotionally naked as well.

Lainie closed the newspaper, her eyes burning with tears. She tossed it across the dining table, sending a glass of juice spilling over. "How dare he take back up with Miss

Perky," she muttered under her breath.

A woman in a black uniform and white apron scurried from the kitchen, rag in hand. She busied herself wiping up the river of liquid running over the side of the table and puddling on the floor. Lainie grabbed her linen napkin and bent to help, giving the woman an apologetic look.

"What have we here?" Sidney McAlvain entered the room, wearing a suit and tie. He glanced between Lainie and his housekeeper, his eyes narrowing as he assessed the situation. "Thank you, Gladys," he said, reaching for the scattered paper.

Lainie straightened, wishing she'd curbed her reaction. Too late now. Without a word she moved to the buffet and poured herself a cup of coffee from the silver tea service. She turned as Sidney finished reading. He tightly folded the paper and placed it on the table.

"Did you sleep well, Lainie?"

She sat. Using a spoon, she stirred the coffee, hoping to cool it down. "Yes. And you?"

He eyed her with appreciation, even at this early morning hour. "I have several meetings this morning. At three, my car will pick you up and bring you to meet me at my hangar at Houston Executive. We'll be flying to Dallas tonight." Sidney's face broke into a slight smile. He reached in his pocket and set a black velvet box on the table in front of her. "I'd like you to wear this."

Curious, Lainie reached for the oblong box. Inside, a bracelet laden with diamonds sparkled back at her. "Oh my! It's beautiful, Sidney. Thank you."

"Just a little something for my princess," he said, using her daddy's pet name. "Later this morning, a dress will be delivered. I took the liberty of having something designed for my gal."

She averted her eyes. "I — where are we going? I mean, I have my own things. I'm sure I have something that would work." She liked the extravagant gifts, but she knew it was highly unlikely Sidney McAlvain's tastes matched her own. "I appreciate it, really I do — but I like to pick my own clothes, Sidney."

"The dress is a Fiona DeLacey — designed special for tonight." He looked at her with a chilly smile. "I insist."

Lainie grew uncomfortable under his stare. "Uh — sure. If you really want me to wear the dress, then of course."

"And why don't you wear your hair up tonight? Leave that pretty neck bare." He moved next to her, gathered her hair in his sausage-like fingers, and buried his face in it, breathing deeply.

"Sidney?"

"Yes?"

"Where are we going? Tonight, I mean."

He pulled back and remarked casually as he headed for the door, "A charity fund-raiser. A dinner at my good friends' home . . . the Sandells."

His words punched Lainie's gut. She stood, frozen. "No . . . I can't, Sidney." She shook her head. "That's not a good idea. There'll be photographers and —"

"You misunderstood, Lainie." He glanced at the velvet box, then back up at her with a steely resolve. "I wasn't asking."

35

Claire shifted in the uncomfortable arm-chair, trying to decide which looked more professional — reading a magazine, *Businessweek* perhaps, or reading emails on her phone. Or maybe she should just sit with her hands folded.

Yes, she'd do that.

She cleared her throat and focused on the music piped in from a speaker in the ceiling. A familiar tune, but off somehow. Orchestral renditions of Fleetwood Mac songs just didn't cut it.

She waited, letting her thoughts turn to Lainie. Claire hadn't seen her daughter since the night she'd called them all back to the house. Her girl hadn't even come home to say goodbye to Margarita. "Please don't be mad at me. I just can't, Mom," she'd said.

So it was good to hear her daughter's voice on the phone that morning, even if she was a bit evasive when Claire asked where she was staying. "With a friend," Lainie said. "Don't worry about me. I'm fine."

"Honey, let's go to lunch soon. Talk over things. And I want to show you my new place. It's not much, of course. But it'll work until I catch my breath and get back on my feet."

Lainie declined, saying she couldn't possibly fit anything else in right now. But soon, she promised.

"Claire Massey?"

The voice from behind the receptionist counter startled her. Claire stood and smoothed her skirt. "Yes?"

"Mrs. Craig will be free to see you soon. First, let's have you complete this questionnaire." She pushed a clipboard toward her.

Claire smiled. "Thank you." She returned to her seat and looked over the pages, printed on fine linen paper with a gold and navy logo and "Judith Craig Recruiters" at the top. She'd come to the right place, no doubt.

After filling out her basic information and contact data, Claire moved on to the employment history section. Her palms grew slightly clammy, making holding the pen difficult. She took a deep breath and steadied her nerves. Gripping the pen a little tighter, she carefully printed *None.*

She turned her attention to the next section — skills. With pen poised, she moved down the checklist.

Accounting . . . *None.*

Supervision . . . *None.*

Word processing . . . *None.*

Claire continued down the items one by one, checking the boxes indicated. With each pen mark, her spirits sank lower. About the time she'd talked herself into sneaking back out the front door, the receptionist called her name. "Ms. Massey, Mrs. Craig will see you now."

Too late to turn back. Claire followed the receptionist down a short hall lined with photos of Judith Craig and local dignitaries. The first was a pose with the mayor, then another with the CEO of American Airlines. Another shot showed her shaking hands with Jerry Jones, owner of the Dallas Cowboys. At the very end, she stood in front of Abundant Hills Church with Pastor Richards.

Oh, great, this is going to go well, Claire thought. She extended her hand to the polished woman, who shook it and invited her to sit.

Judith Craig had red hair, lots of it. And a tiny waist. She wore cream-colored slacks and a turquoise sweater. Her wrists bore multiple chunky silver bracelets.

"So," she said, looking over leopard-print reading glasses. "What have we here?" She scanned the forms, her head nodding slowly as she read. Once finished, she placed the stapled set of papers on the side of her desk. "Clearly you've not been in the job market for some time." Mrs. Craig pulled her glasses down and folded them. "And I suspect we have other challenges as well."

Claire forced herself to straighten in her seat. She looked Judith Craig in the eyes. "I think we both know I bring rather unconventional baggage to the table. My history is fairly known, I would guess."

The woman nodded. "Look, I'm the best there is in this field here in Dallas. Your lack of recent skills doesn't worry me all that much. I have a way of positioning candidates and highlighting features not otherwise apparent. My firm boasts a 97 percent success rate. I play both sides of the table, working for candidates and employers. And I only represent the cream, if you know what I mean."

She nodded, willing herself not to look away.

"I'm also a straight shooter. I wouldn't be doing you any service not telling you the truth here."

Claire leaned forward. "I'm willing to take an entry-level position. I'm a hard worker. I was hoping to find something where I could use my training in culinary arts."

Mrs. Craig scowled. "That was in college — how long ago?"

Claire hated how this woman echoed her insecurity. She swallowed. She needed a job and this woman's help. "I realize on paper I must look like a lost cause, but I assure you that —"

"It's not that." She steepled her fingers. "The truth is, your husband bilked most of Dallas in some manner or another. I'm not sure there are any positions available where I could convince people to hire Tuck Massey's wife."

"Well, I see," Claire said briskly. She stood. "I guess I'm wasting time here then."

The woman with the bright-colored top and dark disposition also stood. She gave a dismissive shrug. "I'm very sorry. Really, I am."

Later that afternoon, when Claire recounted the meeting over a glass of sweet tea, Jana Rae had a fit. "Well, that really blows. Why did she even have you come in then?"

Claire raised an eyebrow. "I have to answer

that one for you?"

Jana Rae vigorously stirred more sugar into her tea. "How small. I mean, really." She plopped her spoon onto the table. "People who think they know everything really annoy those of us who do." She pounded the table with her hand. "It's just not fair."

In spite of how Claire felt, she couldn't help but smile. "I have a lingerie drawer full of 'not fair.' "

Her friend threw her head back, laughing. "Ha, good one."

Claire took a sip of her tea. "Yeah, I learned my sense of humor from the best."

On the sidewalk, a young woman passed by their table wearing a long beige skirt, a gray tank top, and what looked like Army boots. She pushed a stroller carrying a toddler. Around her body, she'd wrapped an infant in a sling.

Jana Rae leaned over and whispered, "Who's her designer? Goodwill?"

Claire suppressed a laugh. Jana Rae swore a person's insides were based on what they wore on the outside.

To most people, Jana Rae had a catty side. And Claire supposed she could see why so many assessed her in that manner. But she'd discovered the hidden side of her friend, who spent every Tuesday in a soup kitchen for the homeless. That was the real Jana Rae.

"Look, here's the deal," Jana Rae said, staring at Claire. "Forget this employment nonsense. You need to start your own catering business, become an event planner."

She smiled wryly. "With what? My good looks?"

"I talked it over with the Urologist. I want to lend you starting capital." She held up her palm. "No. Don't be stubborn. Let me help you, Claire."

"No way," she said. "I'll think of something. I like the idea, and there are banks, you know." Claire threw Jana Rae a devilish look. "And if the banks won't lend me money — I can always go work at Goodwill."

36

Cars lined the street surrounding the Sand-ells' stately two-story home in Highland Park. As Sidney McAlvain's driver approached, Lainie leaned against the plush leather seat, picking at her fresh manicure. Sidney reached over and covered her hand with his own. "You look lovely tonight. A real knockout," he said as they pulled into the circular drive.

Turned out the dress Sidney had delivered was stunning, a simple tight-fitting sheath in pistachio. The perfect cocktail dress, and Lainie knew she looked beautiful in it. Given the opportunity, she'd use her appearance to her full advantage.

If Reece was even here tonight.

Months had passed since her former fiancé had broken off their engagement at the Arboretum. The early weeks after had been grueling. She'd simply lost her footing.

By the third week, friends had noticed and pushed her to get back out in the social scene. "The best revenge is to get even," one had said.

Her chance to get even occurred later that evening, when her father's very rich friend walked through the lobby of the Joule. Sidney McAlvain invited her to join him in the bar, where he bought a bottle of Barrique de Ponciano Porfidio, an expensive tequila costing nearly two thousand dollars. The liquor went down smooth, and Sidney's advances were even smoother.

The next morning, Lainie woke in the penthouse suite.

At first she felt disoriented and a bit ashamed. Sidney McAlvain was her father's age, for goodness' sake. And not all that attractive, if you wanted to know the truth.

However, the idea dawned that Sidney could be the answer to a lot of her problems. He had money, a lot of it. When word got back to her father eventually, she'd pay him back for ripping everything out from under her feet, for abandoning her. She'd buy Pride back from the trustee. And the icing would be the look on Reece's face tonight. If she got lucky.

Lainie stood at the door, Sidney's hand at her back. The same door she'd knocked on after the arrest.

She lifted her chin. None of that mattered now.

If she couldn't marry a senator, being the wife of one of the richest men in Texas — in the whole United States, for that matter — wasn't a bad second. Besides, after what her father had pulled, her options were limited, at best. At worst, she'd live her life a nobody.

And that was never an option.

The massive front door swung open. Andrew Sandell stood on the other side. "Sidney, so glad you could make it. Come on in." His arm made a sweeping motion, inviting them inside.

Lainie had barely crossed the threshold when the host's eyes met her own. "Evening," she said, tucking her arm tighter into Sidney's.

Reece's father raised his eyebrows. "Lainie. What a surprise." He looked back at Sidney, a knowing look spreading across his features. To his credit, he said nothing more.

On the other hand, Reece's mother threw a fit when she stepped into the front foyer to greet Sidney. "What is *she* doing here?" Glory Sandell hissed.

Her husband firmly grasped her elbow. "Lainie is here with Sidney, Glory."

Sidney stepped forward and gave Glory a tight hug. "Been following that boy of yours in the polls. Looks like he's finally pushing forward." He released her and slipped his arm back around Lainie. Then he pulled a monogrammed cigar case from his jacket pocket. "Mind?" he said.

Glory opened her mouth, but her husband quickly answered. "Of course not, Sidney." He snapped his fingers and a man wearing a suit and white gloves scurried over. "Get our friend a light."

Lainie gave Reece's mother a satisfied smile. Few people had the power and position to override Glory Sandell, but likely Sidney was a major contributor to Reece's campaign. And he definitely had the power to bring down her son's success, if he had a mind to. She knew from watching how her own father worked that the idea of elections being determined by citizen voters was a mirage, promulgated first in school and then by the media. The real swing votes came with dollar signs — lots of them.

It was that fact that forced a smile onto Glory Sandell's face. "So glad you could join us, Lainie. How's your mother?"

She let a smile break across her face and decided to play along. "Mother is the epitome of grace and dignity in every situation. Despite recent difficulties, my mother is doing splendidly."

However, Mrs. Sandell was a master at this game. At dinner, she seated Lainie directly across from her son and Miss Perky.

"How are you, Lainie?" Reece asked politely.

"Never better," she responded, dishing up her own plate of civility.

By the end of the salad course, she learned Miss Perky had a name — Hilary Goddard. Last spring, Hilary had graduated magma cum laude from Harvard Law School. She would be working at Bright McKee, one of the premier environmental law firms headquartered in Washington, DC.

How convenient, Lainie thought. *And aren't those pearls just lovely — if you're my mother's age.*

On purpose, she kept her eyes averted from Reece. She hoped that would drive him crazy. With any luck, the little pistachio number would do its job. Certainly there was no competition with that dreadful black lace thing Hilary wore.

For good measure, Lainie gave her rapt attention to Sidney as he argued the dual role of maximizing development of oil and gas resources while also protecting public safety and the environment.

Surprisingly, Hilary agreed with Sidney's positions. "With your growing global footprint, it's more important than ever that companies assemble a multidisciplinary team to address environmental issues. I'm impressed with the approach you've taken, Sidney."

Boy, she's good.

Not only had Reece's companion won favor at the Sandell dining table, but likely she'd cemented a future client for her firm.

Noticeably, Reece didn't enter the conversation. Lainie allowed herself a quick glance in his direction. As soon as she looked over, their eyes met and held, as if each of them was challenging the other to be the first to look away.

She steeled herself, but a familiar longing circled the pit of her stomach. She stared into his eyes. She loved their soft gray color, the tiny flecks of slate that gave him a certain air of importance. Without much thought, she could remember the smell of his hair and the fresh, soapy fragrance of his crisp ironed shirts.

She let herself smile ever so slightly. He smiled back, and she knew then that he missed her too.

Reece's mother saw it as well, because Glory took that exact moment to tell everyone that Reece had an announcement.

Hilary beamed.

Lainie shot another look at Reece, dread forming.

He dropped his gaze and tapped his linen napkin at the corners of his mouth. "Yes," he said, slipping his arm around Hilary. "I — uh, we're planning on a spring wedding. And hopefully" — he laughed — "we'll both have a job in DC after the election."

Oh no. No!

Andrew leaned back in his chair, looking pleased. "The handlers are telling us we shouldn't make a public announcement until after the election. An engagement would be too distracting at this juncture." He glanced around the table. "I trust as good friends and supporters, y'all will keep this quiet for now."

Lainie drilled her eyes at the floral arrangement, the russet mums and yellow sunflowers. Congratulations drifted from around the table like faceless voices floating on thick fog. Her mouth went dry and she reached for her water glass.

Glory Sandell smirked.

Hilary rested her head against Reece's shoulder. She grinned, showing off a set of tiny white teeth.

Lainie swallowed — hard. Her hands

dropped to her lap in defeat.

Sidney reached under the table and took her palm in his. He squeezed — a little too hard.

All anyone saw, including Reece, was Sidney McAlvain pull the cigar from between his teeth and smile.

37

Claire couldn't remember the last time she'd set foot inside a bank. Much had changed. Many of the desks sat empty, no doubt a casualty of the online age. She remembered tellers being impeccably dressed, with professional appearances and very little jewelry showing. They were trained to say "Ma'am" and "Welcome to our bank" with wide smiles, customer service utmost in their minds.

Claire stepped to the counter, marveling at these young employees wearing jeans, some with tattoos even. Suddenly she felt older than her forty-nine years.

"Hey." A black-haired girl with thick eyeliner greeted her. "Can I help you?"

She stepped forward. "Yes. Thank you. Could I speak with your manager, please?"

"The manager is over at our other branch this morning."

"Oh." Claire mentally chastised herself for

not calling for an appointment. "Will he — or she — be in this afternoon? I need to talk to someone about a small business loan."

The teller stopped chewing her gum. "Hmm . . . I think Nouri might be available. Let me check." The girl slipped through a door. Claire heard voices, and in less than a minute the black-haired teller reappeared, followed by a young guy not much older than Max.

He reached to shake her hand. "Hello, I'm Nouri Amir. And you need a loan?"

Claire followed him past a fake palm and a large aquarium filled with brightly colored fish to a semiprivate cubicle, the kind with fabric walls that stood a little taller than she did. She took a seat where he indicated and watched him rip a form from a pad. He grabbed a pen from the cup on the desk.

"Name?" he asked.

"Della Claire Massey."

"Address, Ms. Massey?"

Claire let out the breath she'd been holding. He didn't seem to recognize her tarnished name. Relieved, she recited her new address, her phone number, her Social Security number, and other basic information, hoping the young man had authority to approve a loan of this small amount. She didn't have a lot of time to waste.

She'd already made a list of the equipment she'd need to start. Just the very basics. She could add more when she turned a profit. As far as Claire could tell, she could run the business end from home and rent a commercial kitchen as needed. She'd need a Mac, and Jana Rae told her she needed to purchase accounting software. By far, her largest expense would be a truck to transport food.

"Now, let's talk about your financial needs today." The loan officer looked at her and waited.

Claire explained her plans, how she believed she could start small and grow the operation, utilizing all the contacts she'd made over the years. There wouldn't be any need for costly print advertising. She'd have Max help her with a basic website, and last night she'd studied how to create a business page on Facebook. Word of mouth would be her mainstay. At least initially.

She dug in her purse and handed a sheet of paper across the desk. "This is my starting budget. At the bottom, you'll find the cash I think I need to start."

Nouri Amir scanned the numbers. "Well, that seems reasonable." He stood. "I'm assuming this will be an unsecured loan?"

Claire looked at him, confused.

"No collateral," he explained.

She hadn't thought about that. Without giving a second thought, she pulled her wedding ring from her finger, the one piece of jewelry that had been exempted from the confiscation process. "I can use this."

The banker raised his eyebrows and took the ring. "I'll run this form through our system and be right back."

"Your system?"

"Yes, we have a central approval center. We do everything online."

"Oh, okay. Yes, sure." Claire folded her hands in her lap and waited.

Barely five minutes later, Nouri Amir returned. Claire scanned his face, looking for some sign as to how things had gone.

He sat behind the desk. "I'm sorry, Mrs. Massey." He handed her ring back.

Claire felt her spirits deflate. Of course they'd turned her down. The shadow of Tuck's illicit financial activities had followed her yet again.

The loan officer explained something about high credit risk and low FICO scores and potential civil litigation. Yes, yes, she understood, she told him when he apologized again.

Still, tears pooled as she collected her bag

and headed for the door.

Without those funds, she was dead in the water. Jana Rae would push to help, but Claire knew Clark Hancock still fostered resentment, and she understood why he'd feel like that. Their retirement fund had vanished, thanks to Tuck.

She might as well give up. Goodwill might actually be her only option, it seemed.

She thought of the many years she'd never given any thought to finances. She'd spent recklessly, with extravagant retailing adventures all over the world. Tony at Neiman Marcus was on her speed dial. A week after the arrest, Tony had put her on hold for the first time. Soon after, she'd received a polite letter on engraved stationery from the director of shopping services. Her account had been closed and her membership revoked in their exclusive Personal Shopper program.

A puff in the wind . . . all of it.

Just like her thirty-year marriage.

Now she didn't have any money. Her employment options were severely limited. And she couldn't get a loan to start her catering business.

Jana Rae would tell her to pray, but she hadn't been back to church since that awful meeting with Pastor Richards, not even after he'd sent a card telling her he was sorry to hear of Tuck's extended sentence and was praying for her family. Honestly, it felt like God had turned his back on them. Who could blame him? They'd all walked on from him a long time ago, even before Tuck's arrest.

No, she was going to have to figure out something on her own, and quick.

She pushed through the door and nearly planted her face in a man's chest. Startled, she pulled back. Her bag dropped to the floor, scattering her cell phone, lipsticks, pens, and sunglasses case at his feet. "Oh no. I'm sorry." She bent to gather her things. As she did, her head butted into his upper thigh. Embarrassed, she glanced up. "Excuse me. I seem to . . ."

The man knelt. "Let me," he offered. He quickly scooped up her possessions and handed them to her.

"Thank you." With a heavy sigh, she stuffed the items back in her bag.

"Everything okay?" He helped her to her feet.

Claire nodded. "Yeah. Just one of those days."

A warm, easy grin formed on the guy's face. "Yeah, life can deal a few of those."

He was tall and broad-shouldered, dressed

in faded jeans and a button-down shirt open at the collar. When he smiled, the corners of his eyes fell into well-worn lines, like someone who did a lot of it. Smiling, that is.

"Well, take care. Hope your day looks up." He held the door open, still smiling.

She thanked him and stepped into the beautiful September day, letting the sunshine chase away her foul mood with its warmth. Summer was literally a hot topic in northern Texas. When early fall arrived, cooler temperatures carried their own welcome mat.

Inside her car, she pressed the key in the ignition and turned.

Nothing.

Oh no. Please start.

Claire tried again. Still nothing.

She leaned against the seat, closed her eyes. Now what?

She climbed from the car and looked at the hood, not even knowing what to do next. Henry had always driven her everywhere. She didn't even know how to open the silly hood.

"Hey, what's up? You having trouble?"

Claire turned. The man from the bank moved in her direction — still smiling. She rubbed her forehead as he approached. "Par for my day. Won't seem to start."

He reached out. "Keys?"

Thankful for the help, she dropped them into his large, calloused palm. He slid into her car and turned the ignition. Nothing.

"Looks like a dead battery." He climbed out from behind the wheel. "Are you a member of Triple A?"

Claire gave him a blank look. "Uh, no. I don't think so."

"Don't worry. I'll call my service." He pulled an iPhone from his jeans pocket and made a quick call. "They'll be out within the hour and you'll be good to go."

"I don't know how to thank you."

He slid his phone back into his jeans and tilted his head in the direction of the Starbucks across the parking lot. "You could join me for a cup of coffee."

"Uh — sure," she stuttered. "I mean, I'd be happy to." She hated the way her voice sounded tentative and uncertain. What would it hurt to have coffee with him? He'd been kind, and she was simply thanking him.

Inside, the rich smell of coffee mingled with jazz drifting from the overhead speakers. They made small talk, and at their turn at the counter, he ordered coffee. Black.

She'd decided upon a salted caramel macchiato.

While waiting for their drinks, she learned his name was Brian Magellen. He lived on Parker Road, just outside Plano, where he built custom homes for a living. He was a musician at heart, and he used to hang out with Boz Scaggs.

They collected their drinks and headed for a table.

"You know Boz Scaggs?" Claire asked, intrigued.

"Yeah, he used to live in the area. Our sons were friends back in junior high and we became acquainted. We'd hang out in his garage and play while the kids practiced throwing footballs around in the backyard." Brian took a drink of his coffee. "He lives in northern California now. Started a winery with his son."

Claire glanced at Brian's finger. No ring.

"Divorced," he said, noticing. "Nearly ten years."

She nodded and stirred her drink, embarrassed she'd been so obvious. "I'm . . . getting one. A divorce, I mean." The words clogged in her throat. She'd never spoken them aloud to anyone but Jana Rae. And, of course, Tuck.

"Understandable."

Claire quit stirring her macchiato.

Brian's eyes held hers in momentary silence, and she realized he knew her history. Shame covered her like a thick blanket, one wrapped too tightly, and she felt the heat.

"Hey, look," he said in a reassuring voice. "Far as I can tell from all the media coverage, you were a victim. Just like the investors."

"Some feel differently." Claire scooped a tiny bit of whipped cream into her mouth.

"Yeah, well . . . you can't live your life as a mirror, reflecting everybody else's view. Sometimes you have to be willing to embrace your own reality and move on, not caring what others think."

"And keep the television channel turned to *Dancing with the Stars* and off the news."

"There you go," he said, grinning.

Over the next minutes, they chatted easily, no longer mindful they were waiting for the car service to show up. Brian's relaxed nature made her feel . . . safe.

Claire let down her guard and opened up. She described the night Tuck had been arrested, how it felt to learn her husband of thirty years had committed such a betrayal.

She told him all about Garrett and Marcy. About Max and how much support he'd been. She even confided her concern about her daughter, that her instincts told her Lainie had lost her footing. As a mother, she barely knew what to do to help any of them in the aftermath of what Tuck had done to their family. She had a hard time just making her own way through.

As they talked, the blanket of shame lifted. By the time Brian's phone rang, alerting him the car service had arrived, Claire knew she'd made a friend.

When her car engine started, he opened the car door and helped her inside. "Look, I've really enjoyed this afternoon. Could we maybe — I mean, if you're not busy Friday night, would you join me for dinner?"

The request instantly left Claire a bit unsettled. A hint of loneliness knocked, yet she couldn't open that door. She was still married.

"As friends," he reassured her.

She considered Brian's invitation. Why the hesitation? There was no good reason she couldn't have dinner with him — as a friend. She managed a smile. "Thanks, Brian. I've been a little adrift lately. I'd enjoy the company."

They exchanged phone numbers and he said he'd call.

As Claire pulled from the parking lot, she

glanced in the rearview mirror at her new friend leaning against his car, arms folded. Even from a distance, she saw something in Brian Magellen's smile that told her he was glad they'd met.

Despite herself, Claire smiled as well.

38

"You're going on a date? But you're married."

"No, Jana Rae. I'm going to dinner . . . with a friend." Claire loaded a plate into her dishwasher. "Women and men can be just friends, you know. Don't you watch *Oprah*?"

Jana Rae pulled a Twinkie from her purse and unwrapped it. "Yes, and I also watch *Downton Abbey.* Y'all better be careful." She took one of the little cakes from the package and pushed the remaining one across the counter. "Want some?"

Claire scowled. "I thought they quit making those things."

Jana Rae took a bite. With a full mouth, she gave a cream-muffled reply. "And there are people who think Texas is Baja Oklahoma. But stores are still selling Twinkies, and I don't care what you tell your pretty little head, you're going on a date."

It was pointless to argue. Instead, she changed the subject. "The bank turned me down. Something about potential litigation and blah, blah, blah . . ."

Jana Rae's eyes turned sympathetic. "Ah, I was afraid of that. Our offer still stands, you know."

"I know, but I'll figure something out." Claire wiped down the counter.

"Look at you." Jana Rae licked her fingers, grinning. "You've become the queen of domesticity."

Claire sighed. "I admit, I really miss Margarita. Not just that she cleaned my toilets. But I miss her enchiladas." Claire closed her eyes, recalling the way the melted cheese and tangy sauce blended perfectly with just the right amount of heat. No one made enchiladas like Margarita.

"That's it then." Jana Rae popped off the barstool and grabbed her purse. "Let's go."

"Where?"

"I'm taking you to Joe T's," she said. "For Tex-Mex."

Claire folded the dishrag and placed it in the sink. "How do you possibly consume all that food you eat and stay a size 4?"

Jana Rae gave a sly smile. "I have a high metabolism. Besides, God must love calories because he made so many of them."

■ ■ ■ ■

By Friday night, Claire's nerves were on high alert. Despite protesting this was not a date, she couldn't deny how often she'd thought of Brian since they'd met.

In some ways, not only had the feds slipped handcuffs on her husband's wrists all those months back, but with each click, her emotions had been taken captive as well. At no time since Tuck's arrest had she felt able to relax, to feel normal. Her brief time with Brian Magellen the other day suggested she was able to forget, even if only for a little while. With him, she felt like someone new.

New was good.

Her doorbell rang promptly at five thirty, just like he'd promised when he called. Claire checked her hair one last time in the mirror and moved to open the door, surprised by her sudden insecurity. He'd said to dress casual. Still, she hoped she hadn't underdressed by wearing slacks and a light sweater.

When Claire opened the door, Brian stood wearing jeans, a polo shirt, and a wide smile. Turns out she'd chosen just right.

"Hey," he greeted her, his eyes sweeping

across Claire appreciatively.

"Hi, Brian." Acutely aware of his appraisal, she invited him inside. "You'd be floored to learn how long it's been since I've done anything that could be called fun. I'm really looking forward to getting out of the house."

He looked around. "Nice place."

"Thanks. It's small, but then there's only me. And my mother."

As if on cue, her mother's bedroom door opened, pouring out two yapping Yorkies. She followed, dressed fashionably in a Bob Mackie pantsuit and flats.

Brian bent. "Well, what have we here?" He grinned and petted the dogs dancing at his ankles.

Claire cringed. "Uh, those belong to —"

"You must be Brian." Her mother extended her hand. "I'm Eleanor Wyden, Claire's mother. I'm *so* glad to meet you." She smiled widely and shook Brian's hand, then scooped up Puddin and Nutmeg. "C'mon, girls. Let's let these two lovebirds have time alone."

Claire scowled at her mother.

Her mother winked on her way back down the hall.

For days, Claire had tried to avoid telling her mother about Brian. Short of meeting him somewhere (and the thought definitely sounded appealing), she knew she had to find a way to broach the subject with her mother eventually. Still, she waited until the last possible moment that morning.

"Mama, I won't be here for dinner tonight, so you'll have to cook something."

Her mother stopped playing Angry Birds on her iPad and looked up. "Where are you going? These walls are getting a little cramped, and maybe —"

"Sorry, Mama. Not this time." Claire chose her next words carefully. "I'm meeting a friend."

Her mother raised her eyebrows. "A friend?"

She took a deep breath and confronted the annoying situation head-on. "Mama, look. I'm a grown woman and my social life is my business. I don't have to tell you where I'm going, or who with."

"Why are you getting so testy?" Her mother's eyes suddenly popped wide open. "Oh! You're meeting a man." She pointed her finger and grinned. "I'm right, aren't I?"

Claire tried not to react, but even when she was little, she couldn't hide her feelings from her mom. Not really.

"Oh, admit it, Claire," her mother said,

beaming. "You've taken my advice."

She fumed. "No, Mother. I didn't take your advice. He's simply a friend I met when I was at the bank earlier this week." She rushed on, telling her mother about the spilled purse, the dead engine. Why did everyone assume something romantic had to be involved?

Her mother patted the sofa next to her. "What's his name?"

Claire ignored her and remained standing. "Brian Magellen. Anything else?" she asked, not bothering to hide the sarcasm from her voice.

"What does he do?"

"Mama, stop with the third degree." Time to put an end to this nonsense. "I'm going to the store. If you want something for dinner, speak up now."

Still smiling, her mother asked her to get one of those Healthy Choice microwave dinners. Something with pasta and chicken. "I'm not too old to watch my figure, you know."

When Claire returned from the store, her mother held up her iPad and reported she'd looked Brian up.

"You're kidding, right?" Claire asked, unpacking the bags in the kitchen.

"No." Her mother followed her into the

kitchen and slid onto a barstool at the counter. "Did you know he owns a construction company?"

Claire pulled out the romaine from one of the bags and placed it in the refrigerator. "Yes, he told me."

"Good girl. Is it his money, or family money?"

She groaned inside. "Mama, what difference could that possibly make?"

Her mother grabbed an apple from the bowl on the counter and wiped it with a napkin. "You don't want to wait until the ol' in-laws die off before you can have all the assets moved into your name, do you?" She asked Claire for a paring knife. "I'm just glad you're getting back out there."

It was just like her mother to ignore the fact she was still married. Of course, Eleanor Wyden viewed marriage as a gold-digging enterprise, and she was the queen excavator.

The only thing she could hope was that Brian would understand.

"Sorry about that. She's — well, what can I say about my mother? It's complicated."

He chuckled. "We have all night for you to tell me about it."

Brian drove a silver Infiniti convertible, a sporty little number that reminded Claire of the man who owned it. A sensible model hinting of adventure, with a modest price tag that didn't quite reflect what was under the hood.

When they pulled into a winding drive bordered with lush landscape, Brian explained he had a little surprise planned.

"At the Gaylord?" Claire asked as they passed the sign to the spectacular hotel overlooking beautiful Lake Grapevine.

He tilted his head back, his eyes softening with laughter. "Ah, no. Not the Gaylord."

She looked at him, puzzled.

"Patience," he said, teasing her.

They parked at the Silver Lake Marina. He turned off the engine and turned to face her. "I hope you like picnics. I figured the last thing you needed was to be photographed out to dinner with a strange guy." He pointed to a waiting party barge. "Food's in the boat."

Claire's eyes widened. "Thank you," she said. She hadn't even considered the risk. Brian was right. In this day of cell phone cameras, she couldn't be too cautious.

Brian helped her from the car and guided her across a metal gangplank. She boarded, filled with excitement. "I can't believe you came up with all this. I love it."

Her comment seemed to bring him genuine pleasure. "The thought crossed my mind you might not share my enthusiasm for the water, but I took a chance."

Claire found a comfortable seat and watched as Brian started the engine. He pushed the throttle forward and accelerated the motor, sending the boat gliding gracefully away from the dock and across the water, leaving a quiet wake in its path.

They rode in comfortable silence until Brian cut the motor and anchored near a secluded shoreline, allowing the boat to drift from a generous length of rope.

"I hope you're hungry." He pulled a large cooler out onto the deck of the boat.

"I'm starved," she admitted.

Brian laid out the food, and they ate while watching a stunning sunset — a feast of corn cakes with tomato and avocado salsa, roasted asparagus wrapped in prosciutto, and chilled jumbo shrimp. Then they topped off the meal with chocolate chip cookies washed down with minted lemonade.

"That was absolutely marvelous." Claire rested against the white leather seat, feeling full and happy. A white egret stood in a patch of marshy grasses at the edge of the lake. As the boat drifted closer, the bird flapped its large white wings and lifted gracefully into the air.

"Beautiful." Brian followed the bird with his eyes before taking the seat opposite Claire's. He leaned across his knees with folded hands. "Unlike most bird species, it's the male great egret who chooses a site and builds a platform of sticks and twigs. After he builds the nest, he selects a mate."

Claire sipped her lemonade. "Let's hope a scandal doesn't wreck their happy nest," she said nearly under her breath. She hated that even here, Tuck's actions intruded into her happiness.

"You have a right to feel bitter," Brian remarked. "Just don't let the past rob you of a bright future."

Using her phone, she snapped a quick shot, then settled back against the seat, enjoying the warm evening air against her face.

Brian climbed over the cooler and sat next to her. They sat in comfortable silence for several minutes before he dropped his gaze to his feet. "Do you miss him?"

The personal question caught Claire off guard. She nodded. "Yeah, sometimes," she said. She studied Brian's face, his thoughtful eyes. "Sometimes I feel like a widow. Except the man I lived with for all those years isn't dead. He's sitting in a jail cell. And I'm in a condo living with my mother."

Brian chuckled. "At least you're not alone."

Claire looked at him in disbelief. "You're kidding, right?" In some ways, she was in her own prison, and her warden wore designer clothes and had bottle-blonde hair and Yorkies.

With a heavy sigh, she looked toward the sky. "You know what's been the worst thing about all this?"

"What's that?"

"So many people thought I knew. The woman living by his side, sleeping in his bed, had to be complicit." She didn't really have the words to describe what those early days were like — never revealed how frightened she was every time she opened the mail to find another letter with threats against her and the children. "I read in the paper that a man two days from retirement lost five and a half million. There were a lot of investment trusts and company funds invested. But many of the victims were just ordinary people. Some were our friends."

Claire ran her fingers through her hair and stared out across the water. "Phil and Carol Johanson lost forty million. Dan and Cindy Taylor lost over ten million — so did the Hessings, the Camerons, and Albert Kensington. The Fenways, the Leonard Liptons, and Jeramie and Angela Ausmus all lost between ten and five million. Larry and Heidi Claar lost 4.6, Jonathan and Amanda Rivera 3.2, and eighty-year-old Mrs. Shannon 1.5. That doesn't include our church fund of over twenty million, my best friend's retirement funds, and my own mother's estate."

Brian raised his eyebrows. "Wow, that's some serious cash."

"Ha — serious cash? Not even. Before Tuck's arrest, we were worth over a billion dollars, at least on paper. We had homes, jewelry, antiques. I had couture designers on speed dial, an unlimited account at Neiman Marcus, and over four hundred pairs of shoes. And where did all that money come from?" Claire's eyes teared. "From them — the ones Tuck stole from."

Brian blinked. "I had no idea."

Claire shook her head. "No wonder they hate me. I was stupid and blind."

Brian's hand moved to her chin, his thumb gently sweeping her jawline. "You're not stupid. You were a victim, just like everybody else. His eyes drilled into her own, willing her to believe him. "Are we square on that?"

As he slowly let go, Claire nodded, embarrassed she'd lost control of her emotions.

As if reading her mind, Brian slipped her hand into his. "I'm glad you're comfortable enough to open up and share what you're feeling inside. One of my favorite quotes is this: 'It's okay to look back, just don't stare too long.' "

"Wise words," Claire said, wondering how someone she'd known so briefly made her feel so safe.

Acutely aware his eyes watched her every move, she slipped her hand from his and fingered her hair. "Thank you for such a lovely evening," she said. "I've really enjoyed everything about tonight. Especially our visit."

His lips curved into a smile. "My pleasure." Brian lifted the linen napkin from her lap. His fingers brushed against her bare arm in the process. He smelled like the detergent aisle in the grocery store, a clean and dependable scent she found enticing.

Claire stared toward the horizon. "I'm afraid I went on and on about myself."

"Not a bad topic," he said.

"But I want to know more about you."

Brian leaned back and folded his hands behind his head. "What do you want to know?"

"Well, you said you were married?"

He stared into the sky. "Yup. But I screwed it up."

Everything stilled. His comment hung in the air until Claire asked, "What happened?"

"I drank too much," he said, indulging her curiosity. "Put her through hell, if you want to know the truth of the matter." He passed his hand over the back of his neck. "We're friends now. Carly got remarried. Eventually we shared custody until last summer when Trenton turned eighteen."

"I'm sorry." Claire desperately wanted to assure her new friend she understood, that she found his candor refreshing. "That must've been hard for you."

Brian studied the pattern of the wood-planked floor. "In the days right after Carly left, I couldn't bear the loneliness. I stayed drunk." He shook his head, the edges of his mouth curling into a slight smile. "Don't recommend that." He lifted his chin. "The whole thing was a big wake-up call. I've been sober almost eight years now. Worked hard to piece together a life worth living after mucking everything up so badly." His eyes took on a flinty look of determination. "That's what I mean by not letting the past define what's ahead. Life's too precious for that."

Claire nodded. "I believe you."

Over the next hour, they talked freely and easily, as if she and Brian had been friends all their lives. No topic seemed off-limits.

Brian confided that even though his home-building business enjoyed success, he secretly wished he could fold up the entire operation and focus on his music. Nothing would beat playing in small-town venues across Texas, the kinds of places where musicians could really connect with their audience.

When Claire asked why he didn't just go for it, he said he had a son to put through college. "I need to be there for him now," Brian explained.

Claire secretly dreamed of cooking. Maybe owning a bakery. Not your typical shop that put out standard cookies and cakes, but a quaint aroma-filled store offering freshly baked apricot bread and tarts filled with thick hazelnut custard.

A light breeze kicked up, and Claire brushed a strand of hair from her face. "That's what I was doing the other day in the bank. I want to start a catering company."

"And they turned you down."

"Yes," she quietly admitted. "Apparently, I'm not a great credit risk these days."

"I know someone," he offered. "A woman who extends venture capital to women starting businesses. Let me introduce you."

Claire's hand went to her chest. "Would you? That would be wonderful."

"Happy to." Brian rewarded her with a wide smile. "A first step toward that new future of yours."

In no time, it seemed, the sky dimmed and the lights from the Gaylord Resort lit the horizon with a warm glow.

"Guess we'd better head back in." Brian stood and squeezed her shoulder. "Are you chilly?" He grabbed a sweatshirt from a zippered bag and draped it across her back before making his way to the side of the boat, where he lifted the anchor.

Minutes later they were on their way. From his perch behind the wheel, Brian studied Claire as the pontoon slowly chugged toward the marina under the guidance of his capable hand.

The evening was nearly perfect — until they walked across the parking lot and Brian unlocked his car door.

"Hey," a voice shouted from the darkness. A camera flashed.

"What the —" Brian swung around. He held up his hand to shield Claire. "Wait here."

He raced in the direction of the commotion, but at the same time, two more guys stepped from behind a nearby vehicle and clicked photographs.

Claire's heart sank.

By morning, she'd be in the newspapers again. Only this time, not for Tuck's poor judgment, but her own.

39

"Looks like quite the date." Jana Rae slid the newspaper across Claire's table.

Claire pulled the towel tighter around her shoulders. "I told you, last night wasn't a date. I simply spent some time with a new friend who happened to be a male."

Jana Rae laughed. "Tell that to the reporters."

She groaned. "That may be, but please watch what you're doing with my hair."

Few things had been harder to let go than Claire's beauty appointments. In the past, she'd spent hundreds — no, thousands — on hair extensions and color, facial peels, waxing, and Botox injections. And that was just for starters.

Now, with the constraints of living on a modest budget, all unnecessary expenditures had to go. She'd collected drawers filled with expensive cosmetics and facial treatments over the years, a supply that would last for some time. She could buff her own heels and paint her own nails. But coloring her hair . . . well, that was another story entirely.

Thankfully, Jana Rae had a knack for doing hair, something Claire took full advantage of back in college — and now.

Jana Rae yanked back a section of graying roots. "Boy, you're right. The bloom's done gone from this rose." She gave the plastic coloring bottle a final shake and squeezed hair dye along Claire's scalp. The cool sensation made her shiver. "Good thing it was dark when you went on that boat ride. I'd hate to think you let Lover Boy see these roots."

Claire grunted. "What are you, in junior high?"

Her cell phone rang, and she reached across the table and checked the face. Her breath caught. "It's Garrett," she whispered, as if her oldest son might hear her somehow.

Jana Rae paused her work. "Well, answer it."

Nodding, Claire clicked the phone on and pulled it to her ear. "Hello, Son?"

"Mom, have you lost your mind?"

Her heart sank at the anger in her son's voice. "Well, hello to you too."

Jana Rae set the color bottle on the table

and sank to a chair, scowling. Claire frantically motioned for her to continue applying chemical. The last thing she needed was a hair disaster.

"Have you seen the newspapers this morning?" Garrett asked. "What were you thinking?"

Claire drew a sharp breath. "I beg your pardon, Son. Those photos shade the truth." She huffed, her emotions bruised. "Besides, I don't have to explain what I choose to do to you or anyone else."

"What? Are you going to get a divorce and start dating? When were you going to let your family in on that decision?" The edge in Garrett's voice drew blood. "Besides, I thought you loved Dad."

She rubbed her forehead. "I will always love your father, Garrett. But I have to live my life."

"But —"

"No buts, Garrett. Last night was *not* a date. And who I make friends with will not be open for judgment. Not by you or anyone else."

Claire clicked off the phone and tossed it on the table, surprising even herself with her brisk reaction.

Jana Rae pulled the plastic gloves from her hands. "Whoa, honey. What was all that?

I mean, maternal is not my skill set, but something tells me your son lost his binky."

She grabbed the hand mirror from the table and examined Jana Rae's work. "Not the first tantrum he's thrown over the years." She lowered the mirror and bit the tender flesh inside her mouth, fighting a fresh flood of tears. "Oh, Jana Rae. I didn't want Tuck to see the end of our marriage sensationalized in the papers. Or the kids."

Jana Rae stood and checked a lock of hair to see if the color had fully taken. "Tuck's a big boy. He'll survive. But you already know what I think on the matter." Her brows pulled together in serious thought. "You're done. Your hair, I mean."

Claire moved to the sink and bent her head down so Jana Rae could rinse the dye from her hair. Her friend might be right about Tuck. He had twenty years in prison to adjust.

But her children? Even though they were adults, learning of the divorce was bound to sting.

Is that why she hadn't personally told them before now?

She remembered the day her mom had walked into their farm kitchen with the painful announcement. She knelt on the faded linoleum, looking Claire in the eyes.

"I don't expect you to fully understand at your age," she'd said. "But someday you'll realize what I'm doing is for everyone's best."

Her own mother was flat wrong. Claire never recognized any good coming from splitting her family up. Even now she found the idea a tragedy. Sure, people divorced every day. But when it happens to you — to *your* family — everything turns different.

Perhaps that was why Claire hadn't called an attorney quite yet. As far as she could tell, there was no hurry, and she wasn't particularly anxious to get back in a court-room anytime soon. Maybe after the first of the year, let things settle a bit. Then she'd file and make things official.

There was only one thing of which she was certain — she hadn't planned on finding her life in shambles. She had no choice but to collect the pieces and move forward.

Lainie rubbed tanning lotion on her legs and arms before leaning back on the chaise lounge. With any luck, the late afternoon sunshine would provide for a perfect nap before she had to get ready for the Oil Barons Ball.

"Miss Massey?"

She shaded her eyes with her arm. "Yes?"

An older woman in a uniform stood at the edge of the pool. "Mr. McAlvain would like to see you inside."

Lainie sighed. "I'll be in shortly. The sun's perfect right now, and I'd like to enjoy some rays."

"I think Mr. McAlvain meant for you to come now." The woman's voice communicated guarded authority. "What would you like me to tell him?"

Frustrated, she sat up. "Tell Sidney I'll be in —" She paused. "Soon."

The woman nodded. "Yes, Miss Massey. I'll tell him."

Lainie collected her glass of sweet tea and the October issue of *People* magazine and made her way to Sidney's den, where he sat behind his desk. Still dripping, she asked, "You needed me?"

He scowled at the puddle at her feet. "Yes. I hoped you'd have a glass of wine with me before we dress."

"Now?" she said. "But it's —"

"And maybe give me a back rub." Sidney stood, his meaning clear. He placed his cigar in the ashtray. "By the way, have you seen this morning's newspaper?" A sly smile formed on his pudgy face as he pushed the paper across the desk.

She frowned and picked it up. A large

photo of her mother with some guy helping her into a silver convertible glared back. The headline read, "Wife of Famed Cattle Crook Moves On."

Lainie's gut kicked.

Apparently, she wasn't the only one with a secret love life.

40

The final days of September arrived, and along with them the Texas State Fair. In former years, Tuck and Claire had packed the children up and hauled them to Fair Park near downtown Dallas to ride the Ferris wheel and eat fried peanut butter and jelly sandwiches, an annual favorite of fair-goers.

Claire hadn't attended the fair in years, not since the kids were grown, certainly. Crowds strolling the midway and crying toddlers with cotton-candy hands weren't exactly her idea of a good time.

So when Max called and extended an invitation, she initially turned him down, instead urging him to consider an afternoon trip to the Crow Collection of Asian Art, where they were exhibiting treasures of jade and objects of art from China's imperial dynasties.

"C'mon, Mom. Let's go have fun. Just the

two of us," Max said. "I'll even follow you around the quilt exhibit. Huh, what do you say?"

What could she say? She'd park on the moon to spend time with one of her kids, even if it meant going to the fair. Besides, her mother would be out all afternoon at the groomers with those dogs. "All right. But you're buying dinner."

"Deal." She could almost see Max smile over the phone. "Pick you up around noon tomorrow."

The fairway was dirtier than she remembered. The people bumping into her sported more tattoos. But the greasy, sweet smell wafting through the air was exactly as she recalled.

After wandering the midway a bit, they headed for the food concessionaires. Max followed Claire's lead and ordered a corn dog swathed in yellow mustard, the way Tuck used to eat his. They made their way to a small table with an umbrella, which had a great view of the well-known cultural icon, Big Tex, the fifty-two-foot-tall mechanical man who welcomed fairgoers with his friendly loud drawl, "Hoooowdy, folks!"

"I'd forgotten how good these are," Max said, licking dabs of mustard from the corners of his mouth.

Claire smiled. "You hated them when you were little. Cotton candy and caramel apples were the only things you'd eat. If we tried to push anything with nutritional value — and I use that term loosely — you'd scream."

For the next few minutes, she and Max ate in comfortable silence, watching the faces of the little children light up when Big Tex boomed his greeting.

"I went to see Dad last week."

She stopped mid-bite. "You did? Why?" The minute the awkward question slipped from her mouth, she was sorry. Of course Max could visit his father. He didn't have to explain his reasons. "Son, I'm sorry. I didn't mean that like it sounded." She sighed. "Well, maybe I did. But I — you have every right to see him if you want."

"You know, Mom, I've turned what happened over in my head a thousand different ways. No matter which way I look at what Dad did, I just can't make sense of it. So I had to go. I needed him to help me understand."

Claire spotted a tall man wearing a tank top with a beer logo. He smiled at her, revealing yellowed teeth. "What did he say?"

Several seconds passed. "He claimed he's sorry." His voice caught. He cleared his throat and looked up at Big Tex. "And get this — Dad's joined a Bible study in there. Says he prays for each of us every night. Especially you."

A space inside Claire hollowed out. So Tuck had seen the light in prison and now clung to religion. How was that for a cliché?

Ignoring her own emotions, she swallowed her food — and her bitterness — and placed a consoling hand over her son's. "I suppose that's understandable, honey. He was an elder at Abundant Hills, don't forget."

Max shook his head in disgust. "An elder who stole the church blind," he said. "Along with most of the members."

Claire quietly finished the last of her corn dog. She wiped her mouth with a paper napkin, then folded it carefully and laid it aside. "You know, a friend told me something the other night. He said I had a right to be bitter, but not to let that shadow my future."

"That the guy in the newspaper?"

Her face flushed. "You of all people should know not to believe everything you read in the news."

"Dad said you want a divorce. Is that true?"

"Yes. I think so," she said. "I haven't seen an attorney yet. At times I want out, and yet in many ways I find it hard to let the past completely go." Claire brushed crumbs from her capris. "A year ago, who'd have imagined my home and everything we owned would be gone, my husband would be in prison convicted of federal crimes, Garrett and Marcy would be in Houston working for her dad, and your sister would be hiding out in places unknown?"

This time Max reached for her hand. "I want you happy, Mom."

"I know, Son. I plan to be." Claire turned her face upward, letting the sun warm her skin. "I called my friend Brian and took him up on his offer to connect me with a lady who makes money available to women who want to start a business and don't have the financial resources necessary. I'm thinking of using my degree in culinary arts and opening my own catering business. Small at first. Build from there."

Max grinned. "That's great."

"I googled catering businesses and submitted dozens of employment applications, expecting to hear good news. Unfortunately, my hopes dampened when no calls came. Potential employers view me as a liability, I suppose. Even Abundant Hills wouldn't hire me to cater their annual missions gala, the event I used to chair. The new person in charge thought it might ruffle too many feathers — under the circumstances." Claire propped her elbows on the table and gave her son a wistful smile. "I'm hopeful this lady with the investment capital turns out to be everything Brian promises. Because frankly, I don't have a lot of other options."

"Mom's starting a catering business? Are you serious?"

Max zipped his Jeep around a dump truck and accelerated. He adjusted his Bluetooth. "You heard me, Lainie. She's meeting with some lady who sets up women like Mom with needed financing when banks won't make a loan."

"I can't believe Mom's going to work."

Max rolled his eyes. His sister could be so shallow at times. "What do you think she's going to do without any money? She doesn't exactly have a lot of options after what Dad did. I mean, short of taking up with some wealthy dude, she has to earn a living." The phone went silent for several seconds. "Sis, you there?"

"I'm here," Lainie said quietly.

"Well, I've got another bombshell for you." He drummed the steering wheel with his fingers. "I went to see Dad."

She huffed. "You're kidding, right? Why

would you do that?"

"Funny, that's what Mom said."

"You told her?" She sounded shocked. "How did she respond to that?"

"Ah, you know . . . at first she was surprised. Then cautiously supportive." Max glanced in his rearview mirror, then signaled and switched lanes.

"Well, what did Dad say? Did he even know you were coming?"

"Among a lot of things, he asked about you. I didn't know what to tell him." Max slowed behind a lagging sedan driven by a white-haired woman whose head barely reached above the steering wheel. "Where are you, Lainie? Time to end the hiding-out act, don't you think?"

He could hear his sister sigh. Or was she . . . ?

"Lainie, are you crying? Sis, talk to me."

It took several seconds before she responded. Finally, she whispered in the phone, "Oh, Max. At age twenty-three, I never expected to feel this tired."

41

At exactly two o'clock, Claire walked into the lobby of the north tower of The W, a hotel complex with luxury condominiums in downtown Dallas. Her heels clicked against shiny cream-colored tile flooring as she admired the sophisticated modern design and furnishings of the posh and beautifully appointed venue, a place she and Tuck had often patronized before life went into a tailspin.

The concierge directed her to the bar, where Brian waited. Even though they'd had to wait a few weeks for her potential benefactor to return from a trip abroad, as promised, Brian arranged for a meeting with Maybelline Knudsen, Dallas's real estate grand dame — and, if things went well, the woman who would provide funding for Claire's new business.

When Brian disclosed the identity of his "friend," Claire had immediately balked.

Unlike her, Maybelline had not relied on any man's wealth. And most certainly the woman some claimed to now be in her eighties had never lived through the kind of financial debacle Claire had faced these past months. She was savvy and had a no-nonsense approach to life. At least in the articles Claire had read over the years.

So much was riding on this meeting. Claire's nerves betrayed the confidence she hoped to convey as she and Brian rode the elevators up to the top penthouse condominium where Maybelline lived.

"Look," Brian said, pressing the button to the top floor, "Maybelline made her fortune in the early seventies, when men ruled the real estate market in Dallas. You think she doesn't know what it's like to be sold down the river for money?" He gave her a reassuring smile. "Why do you think she's so motivated to help women get ahead in the business world? I promise there's nothing for you to worry about."

Claire didn't feel so convinced. "I bring a lot of baggage."

Brian gave her arm a little squeeze. "Maybelline knew everything and she wanted to meet you. So relax."

Brian's friendship had been a pleasant addition to her life. Despite the trouble the media tried to cause, he was a sweet spot after months of turmoil. At first, guilt over how quickly she'd connected with a man other than Tuck overshadowed her budding affinity for Brian, the easy way they talked and supported one another. Claire quickly moved past that frame of mind. There was nothing inappropriate about simply enjoying a friendship she very much needed.

Following his instruction, she took a deep breath and tried to be calm. "You're right," she said. "Thank you for brokering this meeting, Brian. I appreciate what you've done for me."

Before he could respond, the elevator slowed and a melodic chime sounded. The doors shifted open, revealing an elegant white-haired woman smartly dressed in a nautical pantsuit standing there waiting for them.

"Brian, right on time, as always." Maybelline Knudsen leaned forward and Brian brushed her cheek with a kiss. "This boy is like a son to me," she told Claire while guiding them into a living area with walls of glass overlooking the city.

In the center of the room, several plush leather sofas in shades of lemon-yellow and sage created an inviting seating area. Claire was no stranger to exquisite homes, but

Maybelline's place topped the charts on lavish living. Despite her host's age, the condominium was surprisingly modern, no doubt assembled by designers with superior taste. Even the carpets screamed *luxurious.* Claire's shoes sank in a good two inches with each step.

She wanted to ask who furnished her home, then she remembered. It didn't matter. She no longer lived in that world.

Maybelline sat across from her. They were served tea and small cookies filled with raspberry crème on delicate plates with lacy edges. After a few minutes of small talk, their host turned to Claire. "So, Brian tells me you want to start a catering business?"

Claire swallowed her nerves and described her plans. With Brian's help, she'd assembled the necessary financials and marketing proposal. "I intend on starting very small and building from there," she explained, handing the woman her business plan.

Maybelline nodded. "With my help, you're going to do just that."

Claire returned home that day battling a mixture of feelings. She'd been elated when Brian's friend leaned forward, placed her diamond-laden hand over hers, and said,

"Claire, I've got your back. I'm happy to provide the start-up capital you'll need to launch this effort . . . on a confidential basis, of course. Funding will come through a company I've set up for this very thing. Long-term success will depend on you." She looked her squarely in the eyes. "Honey, you up for the challenge of making it on your own?"

Claire assured her she was. She'd done her homework, put together a reasonable budget, determined equipment needs. All she required now was clients, and that would be the one thing that might hinder her enterprise, at least initially. The circles she and Tuck had run in were prime customer targets, but most held grudges for losses they'd endured, or they had climbed onto personal judgment seats rendering anything connected to the scandal unsavory and not worthy of association. Or both.

She adjusted her earlier thoughts. She'd have to go outside those circles, which wouldn't be easy. She knew from years of experience that a caterer worthy of his or her salt (and every other spice in the rack) was hard to find. She'd have to build trust through word of mouth. And that would take time. Precious time she didn't necessarily have.

Despite Maybelline Knudsen's generous support, Claire would have to turn a profit and make a living . . . and soon. If she wanted to eat and have electricity, that is.

She shared those concerns with Brian over dinner that evening, quietly nestled in a booth at an out-of-the-way burger joint. One that served homemade onion rings dipped in light batter and fried to a delicate golden crisp — the kind of meal she rarely ate. Not if she intended to stay a size 6.

"You worry too much." Brian squirted ketchup from a red plastic bottle onto his open bun. "I learned a few years back to live in the moment. Don't dwell on the past, don't worry about tomorrow."

Claire sighed and slid a slice of raw onion from her burger, placing it on the edge of her plate. "I know you're right. It's just hard to not think about what I might face. Despite the assurances I gave Maybelline, I've never stepped out on my own before. Tuck handled the business and financial end of things." She cut her burger in half. "Throughout most of my marriage, I never paid a bill, bought groceries, cleaned house, or maintained a checking account. I'm afraid I feel a little overwhelmed at times. I mean, who do I think I am starting a catering business?"

"So . . . you're paying bills, right?"

"Right."

"You're buying groceries, cleaning house, and maintaining a checking account?"

"I see where you're heading." She grinned and reached for the ketchup bottle.

Brian reached across the table and took her hand. "You are a beautiful and capable woman. Success is in your future. I promise."

Claire found herself unable to pull her eyes from his thoughtful gaze. Had he just called her beautiful?

"Bet you say that to all the girls." She playfully whacked at his hand, ignoring the way her heart raced. In an attempt to redirect the conversation, Claire put ketchup on her burger and chattered about her plans.

"I'm going to need an industrial kitchen, fully stocked. My big ticket items, to start off, will be the portable ovens and hotboxes, and I'll need a transport van. Of course, I can go with a used vehicle. So long as the thing is mechanically sound. I can't risk breaking down on the way to a job. That would be a disaster."

She lifted her burger to take a bite but stopped. "You know, I think the only permanent staff I'll need will be a kitchen manager and a driver. I could offer Margarita, my former housekeeper, the kitchen job. Henry can be my driver — well, Henry's fairly old, but I still want to put him on my regular payroll, if at all possible."

Claire paused. He was staring again. "What are you smiling at?"

"You." Brian leaned back against the red vinyl booth, his clear green eyes looking at her the way Tuck often had. "I'm looking at you."

Claire drove home with a bad case of indigestion. Not from the greasy meal she so seldom ate, although the thick burger and onion rings likely contributed. No, she knew her stomach roiled in large part because of that look in Brian's eyes.

She wasn't sure how it had happened so quickly, but things between them had taken an abrupt turn. At least on Brian's part. In her mind, she'd been careful to draw a line between friendship and romantic interest. Brian, on the other hand, single-handedly used a giant eraser tonight and left the line blurred.

She wasn't a schoolgirl, for goodness' sake. Claire had no business flirting with this kind of danger. She was a forty-nine-year-old *married* woman. She'd assured everyone, most importantly her children, that her friendship with Brian was just that — friendship.

She startled as her cell phone rang. Without checking the caller ID, she picked up. "Hello?"

"Claire? It's Brian."

A motorcycle whizzed by Claire's vehicle, driving dangerously fast. "Brian?"

"Look, I sensed I made you uncomfortable tonight."

"No — uh, I just —" Claire frowned and slid her foot to the brake. She slowed her own vehicle as the motorcycle crowded into the lane in front of her. "It's just that I'm still *married.*"

"I know, and that's why I called to apologize. I had no right to place you in that position," he said. "But at the same time, I can't live my life in any other manner than absolutely honest. Took a lot of years and many hours in rehab and AA, but pretending is what makes us all sick inside. So I'm not going to claim that I'm not attracted to you, Claire. I'm not going to deny I lay in bed at night thinking about you, that my waking hours drag until we meet for dinner." He gave a nervous laugh. "I feel like a kid sitting behind the prettiest girl in class, wanting nothing more than to get a whiff of her hair."

"I — I'm attracted to you as well, Brian." Claire couldn't believe she said those words, knowing there was no way to take them back. Still, Brian's honesty was refreshing after Tuck's lengthy deceit, and she felt compelled to reciprocate. As she'd learned, no relationship worth having could be built on pretense. "But like I said — I'm technically still Tuck's wife."

Despite the disappointment clouding his voice, Brian assured her he understood. He admired her respect for her marriage. Regardless of what feelings were building, they agreed the only relationship viable at this juncture had to be platonic.

Brian seemed relieved Claire didn't cut him off entirely. How could she, after all he'd done for her?

Besides, if she *really* wanted to be honest, she had to acknowledge her loneliness. Since Tuck's arrest, Claire's bed had been a tomb, a sad monument to a relationship once alive, now dead. How could anyone expect her to wait twenty years to resurrect that part of her life?

Tears formed, so close to the surface they almost spilled. She remembered how a man's skin felt against her own. She ached to be held again — to be wanted, desired.

Her emptiness needed to be filled.

Her hands tightened on the steering wheel as she turned her car into the parking garage of her building, maneuvered into her spot, and cut the engine. She sat in the dark for several minutes, letting scenes flash in her mind.

An image of Tuck waiting at the end of the church aisle, wearing a suit and a wide grin.

His hands carefully placing Garrett in his infant seat for the first time before he drove them home.

His red-rimmed eyes as he confided he'd let his mother die all alone.

Claire leaned her weary head against the seat back, pushing the memories from her mind. She couldn't let the past shadow her future. Isn't that what Brian said?

With trembling fingers, Claire wiped her tears. Her crumbled marriage was not her fault. She'd made those wedding vows never expecting her husband would betray her and tear their life to shreds. She could never have known that "forever" included twenty years apart because her husband committed federal crimes and sat in prison.

Sure, she'd had second thoughts since telling Tuck it was over. But she couldn't be expected to continue a marriage under these circumstances.

She deserved to be happy.

Before she could change her mind, she reached for her phone and quickly dialed the attorney she'd decided to use. When the receptionist answered, Claire took a deep breath.

"I'd like to make an appointment with Rhonda Kates, please."

42

Three weeks later, Claire made the big move into commercial kitchen space, with the help of Brian and some of his construction crew. Maybelline Knudsen pulled in some favors and expedited the perfect location, a tiny brick building east of the downtown arts district. From the street, the storefront wasn't much to look at, but the inside was a caterer's dream.

The prior lessee, also a caterer, went defunct after a party of five hundred got salmonella poisoning from cross-contamination. A worker had chopped up chicken wings and used the same knife to slice cucumbers.

Regardless, Maybelline negotiated a deal on her behalf that included leasing the property and all the equipment for an amount far under what Claire budgeted, which allowed her to spend extra for signage, a bright green banner that read "Della

Claire Catering."

"I think you should call the place Hugs and Quiches," Jana Rae had proposed when they'd shopped for linens.

"Nah," Claire said. "Too cutesy." Brian suggested Meal Appeal, which also quickly garnered a rejection. In the end, it was Max who suggested she simply use her full name.

Della Claire was the perfect name for her new catering business.

When Brian's crew finished the heavy lifting, she dismissed them all, thanking everyone profusely for their help. Brian promised he'd drop back in later, after he met with a rogue homeowner's association wanting him to replace fifty oak trees with flowering magnolias at a cost of nine thousand dollars. "You going to be all right until I get back?"

She assured him she had a lot to do. She'd be just fine.

Claire spent most of the morning organizing. She lined up the votives and vases on one shelf. She unpacked the linens and table skirts and stacked them neatly in the designated closet. The serving dishes and display stands were moved to a lower shelf, making room for insulated coffee and tea carafes.

By afternoon, everything was in place. She felt tired but satisfied. Who could imagine work could be this fun?

The first deliveries started just after lunch, a parade of trucks dropping off food staples like flour and spices, paper goods, and condiments. Many food items would be custom ordered, depending on the event. The trick would be to properly estimate amounts, factor in costs, and establish proper profit margins. She couldn't slip up. She needed to pay back Maybelline's loan as soon as possible.

Brian returned minutes after the last truck pulled away. "You really made progress, Claire," he said, nosing around. "Looks to me you're ready to open for business."

Pride filled her. "I'm so excited," she said. "You know, seems like my entire life I've relied on Tuck. Going forward, I'm dependent on my own ability. Succeed or fail, it's all up to me now. Not my mother, not Tuck. Just me." She looked at Brian warmly. "I should be filled with fear, I suppose. Instead, I'm so looking forward to what's ahead I can hardly stand myself." Claire placed her palm against her cheek and grinned. "Do you know how foreign that feels after these past months? To wake up and feel good?" She tucked her hair behind her ear. "I have you to thank. None of this would've been possible without you arranging to get me financed. I sincerely appreciate everything you've done to help me, Brian."

Brian's face flushed. "Helping you has given me great pleasure, my friend." They both knew he'd chosen to label their relationship according to their earlier arrangement. Still, his eyes communicated deeper feelings. He clapped his hands. "I think this calls for a celebration, don't you?"

Claire leaned against the counter she planned to use as her baking station. "What do you have in mind?"

He popped up on the opposite counter, letting his feet dangle. "Dinner out. I'm talking steakhouse with all the fixin's." He grinned. "Huh? What do you say?"

Claire should have been tired, but exhilaration buzzed throughout her body. Exhaustion would eventually come, but Brian was right. They should celebrate. She was now officially a businesswoman.

"Okay!" She grinned. "But consider yourself warned. I'm starving."

Brian wanted to splurge, so they headed to Pappas Bros., a popular Dallas steakhouse started over sixty years ago that offered rich dark wood and leather decor and steaks unsurpassed in quality. Brian ordered a New York strip, medium well. Claire had a harder time making up her mind. She scanned the large board menu and finally settled on a tenderloin wrapped in bacon.

The waiter left the table with their order, and Claire positioned her linen napkin in her lap. She looked up to find Brian's eyes lingering in her direction. "What?" she said, smiling.

"I'm proud of you, Claire."

She wrinkled her nose and grinned. "Thanks. But the real work is ahead of me."

She told him about her new website, how she couldn't decide on the feel until Matt Jones, her designer, showed her the perfect theme — one with inviting colors, elegant fonts, and photos that would make even the most weight-conscious person want to gorge themselves.

"What do your children think of this new endeavor?"

Claire fingered her utensils. "Max, of course, is thrilled for me. He tells me he's working on getting me some free ads in the *Longhorn Weekly.* I haven't talked to Garrett or Lainie lately. But I'm sure they'll be excited for me as well."

Eventually she'd tell Brian how her oldest son had failed to embrace their new friendship, and that Lainie had gone dark, not answering calls or texts, after Claire warned that no further money would be coming her way and Lainie would have to get employed as well.

But she wouldn't confide these things quite yet.

Her children were still finding their way through the aftermath of their father's actions. They needed time to heal, to get their feet back on solid ground. Even if they moved forward in baby steps.

"Hey, I think that lady is waving at you." Brian pointed across the room.

She directed her attention to the window where he indicated. A woman dabbed her mouth with a napkin, then stood and headed their way. Only then did Claire recognize Glory Sandell.

Reece's mother had lightened her hair. She was dressed impeccably in tan slacks and a white blouse. The gold bangles at her wrists were likely the ones Lainie had suggested Reece purchase for his mother last Christmas. The whole look was very Jackie Onassis — appropriate for the mother of a future senator, she supposed.

"Claire," Glory purred, both hands extended. "It's so good to see you again."

Claire eyed her with suspicion. The Sandells had lost a lot of money, and nearly an election, when Tuck's crimes became known. Had the woman moved on so easily?

She grasped Glory's hands with tentative reception. "Hello, Glory. How are you?"

"Oh, we're grand. The election is less than two weeks away and Reece's numbers are strong."

Claire forced a smile. "I'm sure the campaign worked hard and must be relieved the end is in sight."

Glory peeked around her to where Brian was sitting, watching with silent interest. "Hello," she said. "And who's this?" She cocked an eyebrow at Brian.

"Oh, excuse me." Claire apologized and made introductions, feeling compelled to add, "Brian is a friend."

Glory waved her husband over, who appeared as happy as Claire with this chance meeting. "Hello, Andrew," Claire said when he approached. "I hear the campaign is going well."

What else was she going to say? *Glad my husband bilked you of millions and so happy your son broke my daughter's heart as a result?*

"Claire." Andrew gave her a nod, clearly uncomfortable. "Nice to see you again."

Seemingly oblivious to everyone's discomfort, Glory continued. "So, I guess you heard the big news."

Claire gave her a tight smile, pushing a strand of hair behind her ear. "No, no I haven't." She tried to keep her tone light, especially given the mischievous smirk emerging on Glory's face.

Glory leaned forward and cupped her hand at her mouth. "Well, it's not public yet, but Reece is getting married." She dropped her hand. "I imagined Lainie would have told you. We announced it at a dinner party at our home a few weeks back."

Claire's brows tangled in confusion. "A dinner party?"

Satisfaction dawned on Glory Sandell's face. Despite her husband's hand gently pulling at her elbow, her face flushed and her eyes shone.

Their eyes locked and Claire found it impossible to look away.

Glory tilted her head. "Frankly, both Andrew and I were a bit worried how Lainie might take the news. But, well . . ." She looked to her husband and shrugged. "When she showed up with Sidney, we realized our worries were unfounded."

"What do you mean, 'with Sidney'? Sidney McAlvain?" Claire asked, putting niceties aside. Brian reached for her hand, but she pulled away. She thought about how Lainie had failed to pick up the phone when Claire called, how every text she sent went unanswered.

She tried her best to shake off the notion. "Look, Glory, I don't know what you are implying, but —"

"Oh, I'm not implying." Glory's lips curled into a triumphant smile. "And believe me" — she looked at Brian — "they definitely didn't claim to be *friends.*"

43

Claire drove all night and arrived in Houston only hours from dawn. Brian wanted to drive her, but she'd declined his offer. When he couldn't change her mind, Brian tried to talk her into waiting until morning. "You could leave before the sun comes up and arrive refreshed and ready to confront the situation."

That idea presumed she could sleep after hearing the news about her daughter.

Her mother tried to talk her out of making the trip as well. "Oh, darlin', you're overreacting, don't you think? Lainie's a smart girl and —"

Claire's dark look cut her mother off and communicated she was in no mood to argue the matter. She was going, and that was that.

Sidney McAlvain lived in the exclusive River Oaks area seven miles west of downtown Houston. Thanks to her GPS, Claire could find her way to the stately mansion with Greek-style columns and manicured lawns. She pulled her Escalade into the massive circular driveway lined with trimmed hedges and roses, and waited until dawn. At the first sign of daybreak, she got out and made her way to the front door.

She rang the bell and waited. A uniformed woman answered. "Yes? May I help you?" She looked past Claire to the driveway, clearly wondering why someone would visit at such an early hour.

"I'm Lainie Massey's mother."

The older woman nodded, approval showing in her eyes. "Please come in. I'll alert Mr. McAlvain you are here."

Claire waited in the entry foyer and watched as the woman ascended a massive circular stairway with a wrought-iron rail. In the adjoining living area, heavy gold draperies hung at floor-to-ceiling windows looking out over a collection of pools and waterfalls.

She had been in Sidney's home only one other time. Years ago, she and Tuck attended a party Sidney had hosted for the Houston Philanthropic Society. The event was a favorite for many well-known celebrities and CEOs and had raised millions.

"Claire Massey. This is a surprise."

She looked up. Sidney descended the

stairs, wearing a silk smoking jacket. He puffed on a cigar even at this early hour.

"Where's Lainie?" she asked, not bothering with polite greetings.

Sidney lifted his chin. He blew putrid gray smoke in the air above his balding head. "How's Tuck? I take it prison is treating him well?"

She jabbed her finger in his direction. "Cut it, Sidney. This isn't about Tuck. Where's my daughter?"

Sidney reached the bottom of the stairs. He leaned forward and said in a low voice, "Of course this is about Tuck."

"Mama?"

Claire jerked her attention to the top of the stairs. Lainie stood on the landing, wrapping the ties of her bathrobe. Her long blonde hair remained tousled from sleep. "Mother, what are you doing here?"

Claire brushed past Sidney and climbed the stairs, adrenaline propelling her up at a surprising pace for a woman her age. "Get your things," she barked. She grabbed Lainie's elbow. "I'm here to take you home."

Lainie pulled back. "Excuse me? What home — your apartment?"

Below, Sidney puffed on his cigar, clearly amused by the tense exchange.

Claire's breath caught and she turned

back to her daughter. "Lainie, what are you doing?" she implored. "You were never meant to be arm candy for some fat old rich man."

There was a time she would never have said such impertinent things of Sidney McAlvain, no matter what she thought of his lifestyle. This time he'd crossed the line. He deserved no respect.

"Claire, I realize you are emotional," Sidney said in a melodic voice of reason. "But our Princess is an adult. One capable of making her own decisions."

She bristled at the comment. Unless the pompous buffoon of a man had birthed her, raised her, and loved her for twenty-plus years, he had no right laying claim to Claire's baby. She continued her desperate plea. "Sweetheart, he's your father's age. This isn't what you want."

Lainie's soft blue eyes turned steel-gray with determination. "I know what I *don't* want. I don't want to be married for thirty years and have my husband do what Daddy did to you. I don't want to believe someone loves me only to find out that someone sold me down the river because of a drop in his polls. I don't want any more illusionary relationships." She pointed down at Sidney. "That man may not be your idea of a great catch, but he doesn't pretend to be something he's not. And he can give me a life that doesn't include baking cupcakes for weddings."

The force of her daughter's insult knocked Claire against the rail. She struggled to breathe against the emotional punch. "Do you know what they call women like you, Lainie?"

" 'They'? You mean the people who look at me like I'm pig feces because I'm Tuck Massey's daughter? I no longer care what *they* think."

Claire violently shook her head. "I won't have it." She jabbed her finger. "I didn't raise you to —"

"Sure you did, Mama," Lainie spat. "Just go home to your new boyfriend."

Claire clenched her fists. "Brian Magellen is *not* my boyfriend. He's a friend, one who's helping me start my little *cupcake* business."

Lainie's chin quivered and her eyes glazed with tears. "Yeah? So you're no different than me if you really think about it."

Those words haunted Claire all the way back to Dallas.

44

Claire's first booking was a small garden tea hosted by Governor Jackson's wife. Despite the risk of associating with a Massey, the lovely older couple remembered Tuck's past help, highlighting the difference between politicians and statesmen.

Claire busied herself piping sweet dough, which would later become her signature crème puffs, onto a baking sheet. Despite the exhilaration of landing this job, her joy was tempered by her fight with Lainie.

Her mind couldn't help but scroll back through the horrible exchange. Emotions had run high, and both she and Lainie lost their tempers, saying things they shouldn't have.

"Mrs. Massey? Which serving platters do you want moved into the truck?"

Claire looked at her former housekeeper, now her catering assistant. "Let's use the cream-colored ones with the tiered racks. I think they'll match the fall mums perfectly."

Margarita placed her fingers on Claire's arm. "Lainie's a good girl. She'll turn around. I promise."

Tears pooled in Claire's eyes. Her old friend always saw right through her. "I keep wondering where I went wrong. Lainie and her brothers were given the world, every advantage. We loved them and tried to raise them right — even took them to church."

"Ah-yee, I agree. A person can't pray one way and live life another. Lainie will soon discover she's on the wrong path. And when she does — we'll all open our arms to her. Just like Jesus."

Claire hugged Margarita. "I'm so glad you're back."

She slid the baking pans into the industrial ovens and set the timer. Margarita was right. Lainie had walked away from her morals and anything related to faith. A long time ago, really. So had all her children. None of them made going to church a priority.

A twinge of guilt poked its unwelcome head inside Claire. She supposed she'd been the first to set a bad example. She wasn't sure when, but going to church had become just a ritual they did on Sundays. Then when Pastor Richards declined to support

Tuck — well, that was the tipping point. Claire had easily released that part of her life and moved on.

She envied Margarita's sure knowledge that nothing came into her life without first being sifted by God's hands, that her Maker loved her. That was enough to keep Margarita from being anxious about the unfairness of life.

And as Claire had learned, life could be very unfair.

Her cell phone rang. She wiped her hands and picked up. "Hello?"

"Mom?"

Her heart skipped a beat. It was Garrett. "Is everything okay?"

"Yeah," he assured her. "And I'm really sorry about that telephone call. I had no right to climb all over you. Of anyone, I should understand that life's choices are not always black and white."

Claire let out the breath she was holding. "Oh, honey. I've missed talking. I'm so glad you called. How's Marcy? And our little one?"

"That's why I'm phoning, Mom. We had an ultrasound. It's a girl!" Garrett's voice filled with pride. "I'm going to have a daughter."

"Oh, Garrett! Congratulations, baby."

They talked for several minutes. Garrett told her about his wife's cravings and mood swings, and how Marcy wanted to do the nursery in soft apricot. "Looks like orange to me," he said. "But what do men know?"

When they ended their conversation and Claire hung up, she rejoiced in the fact Garrett had finally reconnected. And her heart soared at the news the next generation would emerge with a baby girl — her granddaughter. The thought both thrilled and terrified her.

She was far too young to be a grandmother.

But, oh . . . a baby girl.

Lainie wandered the mall alone with a fistful of Sidney's credit cards. He'd been tied up with work for days, something about a merger. Regardless, she was restless. Even Saks failed to provide any entertainment value.

Lately, melancholy had draped over her like a bad curtain, especially since her mother had charged into Sidney's place, her moral guns blazing.

"Lainie, what did you expect Mom would do?" Max asked when she'd relayed what had happened over the phone.

"It's such a double standard. Garrett and

Marcy sure weren't saints, and nobody said a thing."

Max laughed. "You're kidding, right? First, Garrett wouldn't put mayonnaise on his sandwich if Mom or Dad didn't want him to. Second, I agree with Mom. Sidney McAlvain is old and creepy. And if you thought you were in the right, why hide?"

He had a point, Lainie supposed. She could make the argument she didn't want to invite the trouble she knew would come. But the truth?

She was deeply ashamed.

Lainie wanted to show them all — her dad, Reece, everyone — that she was tough. Their wounds could not pain her for long. Only, she never counted on her own choices bloodying her soul.

She ruffled through a rack of fall sweaters, the colors blending together as she focused instead on her mother and how mad she'd been. Lainie said awful things meant to hurt her mother. The cupcake remark had certainly hit the target.

She'd taken things too far. Her mother didn't deserve more hurt, even if she'd pushed Lainie into a corner. Truth was she loved her mom.

She needed to call and apologize. But something held her back. Perhaps the knowledge she'd severely disappointed her mom, that her mother was so disgusted by her choices.

Why had she ever thought hooking up with a mean creep like Sidney McAlvain would fix things? If anything, his demeaning treatment left her feeling dirty and used — and broken inside.

Depressed and feeling trapped, she wandered out of the store and headed for Starbucks, stepping in line behind a young family. The man had his hand on his wife's back. She was pregnant and held tight to a toddler carrying a Veggie Tales stuffed toy, similar to the one Max used to own as a child.

After they ordered, Lainie stepped forward. "I'll have a venti iced hazelnut macchiato." She paid for her drink with Sidney's credit card, then moved into a chair to wait. She checked her texts. Finding no new messages, she leaned back and watched people. An older gentleman reading a newspaper and drinking coffee. A table of college-aged girls drinking Frappuccinos and chattering about a physics class.

She looked out into the open courtyard filled with seating areas and potted plants and again spotted the young family. The man guided his very pregnant wife to a chair. Taking great care, he held her hand as she lowered herself into the chair. Then he knelt, slipped off her shoes, and massaged her swollen feet while their little son stood nearby, watching.

The sight twisted Lainie's gut.

She wanted *that*.

If she stayed with Sidney McAlvain, she'd never want for any material thing. But Lainie knew deep inside that trading her affections for monetary security would never be enough. Worse, it would eventually break her soul.

Her eyes filled with tears.

How could she have settled for a muddy pond when she was meant to ride the waves of the ocean?

45

With the success of Helen Jackson's tea event, word quickly spread about Della Claire Catering. In the days following, the phone rang and Claire's calendar filled, to her extreme delight.

By far, her most ambitious booking was the upcoming Women of Dallas Philanthropic Society Debutante Ball, an annual event steeped in tradition. The Women of DPS, founded in 1954 as one of the primary charity funding organizations in the Dallas/Fort Worth area, enjoyed hundreds of members — Claire being one of them.

This year's black tie ball would be held at the Meyerson Symphony Center, with the price tag for presenting running well over three thousand dollars and individual tickets in the hundreds.

Claire tried not to think about the pressure as she and Margarita sat to plan the menu. The key was to offer something different and yet much the same. Not exactly an easy feat. In the end, she relied on her instincts. She'd attended many of these events and was not exactly new to the "ball" game.

She would serve butternut squash bisque for the first course. The entree — dry-aged filet of beef, grilled medium rare and covered with a coffee-infused sauce. That would please the fathers and grandfathers in attendance. For the women and vegetarians, she'd need something lighter. This is where she could stray from convention. After digging through numerous cookbooks, Claire decided to serve two sides — braised artichokes and smoked fingerling potato puree. Top that off with a dessert of cherry walnut tarts with pomegranate caramel sauce, and Della Claire Catering would make its mark.

No doubt the menu would be tough to price with much profit margin, but the business magazines Claire had been reading all said you had to spend money to make money.

She would dip into her marketing budget for the additional kitchen help she'd need, for servers, and for the high cost of food items. With any luck, she'd ace this dinner and, as a result, drum up business for months to come. The holiday season was right around the corner, so nothing could be more time sensitive for a start-up catering enterprise.

As she'd told Brian last night, this function was the big break she needed, and she wasn't going to blow it.

So important, in fact, she'd called and rescheduled her appointment with the attorney until after the holidays. She just didn't have the time right now. Or, more truthfully, the emotional stamina to deal with launching a new business while ending her marriage.

On the day of the big event, she arrived at the kitchen at three o'clock in the morning. Margarita was already inside, packing glasses for transport. Claire rolled up her sleeves and worked all day alongside the staff she'd hired, cutting and peeling, baking and stirring under Margarita's careful eye.

The trucks arrived promptly at three o'clock. Claire's former trusted driver, Henry, was now on staff as her transport director. She gave him a warm hug. "I knew I could count on you to be right on time."

She raced home for a quick shower before heading to the Meyerson. While she brushed a little color on her cheeks, her mother stood in the doorway of the bathroom, her arms filled with Yorkies. "I don't understand how you can serve those people. You can't be peers and the help all at the same time. Don't you see how mixed up that seems?"

Claire looked at her mother's reflection in the mirror. "You act like I have a choice, Mama. Life — all of it — got turned upside down with Tuck's arrest. My high-society days are over. I'm a working gal now."

Her mother frowned. "Only temporarily, dear. Until you give in and get serious with that nice construction fellow."

Jana Rae had a similar attitude about her working the ball. "I, too, have plenty of friends I don't like. But you won't see me kissing their —"

"Jana Rae! I thought you were a God-fearing woman?"

Her friend huffed. "I was going to say kiss their *shoes,* gutter mind."

Claire arrived at the Meyerson Concert Hall two hours prior to the start time. Margarita had done a beautiful job seeing the tables were set with linen tablecloths and white service ware. The entire feel — if done correctly — was meant to create the austere look of purity. Every cotillion event she'd seen was done in a similar white-upon-white theme.

All the girls would be wearing white gowns with full skirts — no mermaids in this group. Claire knew from going through the process with Lainie that the fifty girls had undergone months of debutante training, learning how to walk perfectly erect, to ballroom dance, and most important, to curtsy in a perfect Texas Dip.

That had been one of the hardest efforts for Lainie. Every time she'd stretch her arms straight out, bend, and tuck, she'd end up lopsided. It took hours of practice for her to get the traditional bow down perfectly.

In the service kitchens, the additional staff Claire had hired for the evening were busy plating the entrees under Margarita's watchful eye. She looked over her list several times, from sheer nerves.

Wine — check.

Beef — check.

Sauces — check.

Guests began arriving in earnest by six thirty, and soon the cloakroom looked like a fur storage vault. Generations of family and friends gathered, eager for the festivities and the chance to applaud their debs.

Claire couldn't help it. Her mind wandered back to Lainie's coming-out party. Unlike her own, where the ball served as an unveiling of young women available for the marriage market, Lainie's deb ball had been more about making connections in society that would last a lifetime . . . unless your father pulled off white-collar fraud, that is. Federal crimes could certainly tarnish one's social standing.

When Lainie debuted, Tuck had already sold fake inventory. What ran through his mind as he escorted his daughter through the crowd, wearing his red sash and tails? On the stage, when he passed her white opera-gloved hand off to her two brothers, who served as her Honor Guard escorts, did he consider that his actions could be a lethal injection to their Dallas aristocracy?

Never mind that now. Claire needed to be thankful. With this opportunity, she'd be able to pay her electric bill for the next six months.

Hours later, at exactly nine o'clock, the chimes rang, calling the guests to their proper places for the grand promenade. Dinner had come off without a hitch — no small thing. Claire had already heard that Cindrette Sloane-Wisner, one of the co-chairs, was thrilled with the food.

The servers had cleared the tables and were quietly placing dessert plates when the lights dimmed. In front of the stage, rows of empty chairs waited for the fathers after their stage duties were done. The deb moms were seated on the aisle seats of the orchestra floor.

The master of ceremonies tactfully advised the audience that a show of appreciation for each deb was welcome — to a point — reminding them that decorum should be followed at every point. He then acknowledged the Honorary Chair and thanked the co-chairmen for their support.

That was when Claire heard the commotion.

She turned. At the back of the room, Margarita apologized profusely to a woman in a lavender gown. The white linen tablecloth was spotted with deep brown spots, and the woman was dabbing furiously at her lap with a napkin. Margarita held a silver coffee service, her face nearly white.

Claire hurried to the scene.

"What's the matter with you?" the woman spat. "Look what you've done — you — you — get away." She pushed Margarita back, causing the old woman to lose her balance.

Margarita knocked into the lady sitting directly behind her, sending her coffee cup flying. "Oh my — watch out. What are you doing?" she said loudly enough for nearby guests to hear.

Margarita's face paled further. Her eyes shone brightly with tears.

"Hey, there's no reason to be mean." Claire glared first at one woman, then the other. "Obviously, what happened was an accident. There's no call for your horrible behavior toward this woman." She tried to keep her voice low, but her temper was boiling. How dare those rich, cast-iron witches treat Margarita in such a manner!

Heads were now turning. A woman with blonde hair piled high on her head and diamond earrings dancing from her ears gave them a dirty look. "Shh," she said. "Pipe down."

The woman with the coffee spots stood. She threw her napkin down. "I know who you are, Claire Massey." Her eyes became slits. "And I'll see to it that you and your little cooking business are done in this town." She marched away in a huff.

And she was right.

By the end of the week, Claire received a number of calls, all canceling. Her once-crowded calendar now sat nearly empty.

Her one big shot had turned out to be a tiny pop on the social horizon, and she now had a severely depleted marketing budget.

Worse, utility bills kept coming in the mail.

46

Utility bills weren't the only things in Claire's mail. On Tuesday, the morning of the big election, she found a surprise in her mailbox — another letter from Tuck.

She didn't open the envelope right away. Instead, she slipped the correspondence into her nightgown drawer. She didn't have time for distraction. She'd bought a mailing list from a vendor who put on the local bridal show each year at the Dallas Convention Center (Brian's idea), and later this morning she was meeting with the designers who created a flyer targeted to people with upcoming nuptials.

After the deb ball fiasco, Claire set her mind and decided she would never again work society events. Her bread and butter, so to speak, would come from regular folks, people with manners and regard for human beings.

It embarrassed her to recall how she'd

often acted much the same as those horrible women. Barking orders at the help. Complaining and acting like the queen of Sheba, all because she had money.

As it turned out, it wasn't even her money, but funds stolen from the retirement accounts of some of those same hardworking individuals all bustling to make her life easier.

Shame on those women at the ball.

Shame on her.

With any luck, and with Margarita's prayers, Della Claire Catering would soon be a thriving business — one with heart.

It was well after dinner when Claire turned her attention to the waiting letter. She should know better than to open it. Likely the contents would just make her lose much-needed sleep. But she also knew she'd have a hard time slumbering not knowing. So she bid her mother good night, took a hot bath, and slipped into a pair of wonderful flannel pajamas, then retrieved the letter.

In bed, she leaned against the pillow.

Dear Claire,

I don't know where to begin. There's so much I need to say, things I'm sure you need to hear. I do not write to change your mind about the divorce. I simply need to express how sorry I am.

I have no excuse for my actions. Somewhere along the way, I lost sight of everything good and right. My greed took me severely off course. No one is responsible for what happened except me.

I've spent the last months looking deep inside myself. With the help of godly men who visit and hold weekly Bible studies — guys who mentor me — I've seen my true nature. Deep down, fear drove everything I did for the past thirty years. And now, in God's mercy, he let the thing I feared most come true. I am stripped of everything I hold dear. And in that state, I'm learning God is enough.

My sweet, precious Claire. I'm not writing to ask for forgiveness. I simply want you to be happy. You are so beautiful — inside and out. I treasure the memories of our years together and will spend what time I have left inside this place praying for you and our children, and learning to forgive myself for what I did to you all.

Tuck

His words blurred as tears pooled. With

trembling fingers, Claire slowly dropped her hand and the letter to her lap. In her mind, she could imagine Tuck leaning over a metal desk, pen in hand. She saw the downy hair on his earlobe, the familiar freckle on his cheek. Closing her eyes, she remembered the way his arm bulged just below his shoulder and the way his rough palm felt against her own.

Despite her resolve, she ached. For him . . . for herself.

Life was too short to stay bitter.

Clearly Tuck was now sorrowful over what he'd done. His words somehow untied the knot of anger that had tangled her emotions over the past months since his arrest.

Yet how could she forgive and live alone for twenty years, without a man's touch? Without someone across the dinner table at night and by her side when her granddaughter blew out birthday candles each year?

Claire thought of Brian. They may be only friends at this juncture, but at some point she'd have to release the old in order to move on and embrace someone new — Brian or otherwise. There was no way around that.

Her fingers swept the words on the lined paper.

Now tell that to her heart.

She carefully refolded the paper and slipped the letter back inside the envelope. She climbed from bed and placed Tuck's correspondence safely back in place, next to a gown that had been one of his favorites.

Determined to move the melancholy from her mind, she grabbed the remote and turned on the small television on her chest of drawers.

Reece Sandell's face appeared. Below his photo, a banner scrolled: "Sound victory lands Sandell as the youngest senator from Texas."

The camera cut to a shot of a hotel room filled with supporters. In the background, Glory and Andrew Sandell beamed. Claire clicked the television off.

Although it may have been several years since the last time, she bowed her head. She asked God to watch over Lainie tonight. The election results would no doubt stab her baby girl's heart.

And then Claire did something totally un-expected.

She prayed for Tuck.

47

Claire sat in her booth at the Dallas Bridal Show, watching girls and their mothers wander the aisles. From what her vendor friend said, people who attended these shows were often the ones who couldn't afford expensive event planners. Finances forced these families to scour shows like these, trying to mimic high-society weddings on low budgets — people Brian gently explained were now her target market.

Just as well, Claire thought. No more running into investors who'd lost money with Tuck. No more catty attitudes, no more pressure to create the perfect foie gras, fly truffles in from France, or order lilies of the valley out of season. Frankly, she was happy to step outside those circles. Helping typical families celebrate their life events appealed to her renewed sensibilities.

A woman with gorgeous auburn shoulder-length hair, dressed in a stunning green top that flowed over her petite frame, manned the booth next to hers. She sold gowns. "Leave everything to me," she assured a rather big-boned bride-to-be. "I'll make sure you look stunning on your special night." The girl's eyes lit up. She turned to her mother, who smiled back at the vendor with appreciation written all over her face.

Kindness went a long way.

"Claire? Claire Massey?"

She turned to find a young woman standing in front of her booth with one of her flyers in her hand. "Do you remember me? I'm Daisy Anheuser."

She stared at the blonde, trying to place her. Finally, she shrugged. "I'm so sorry. You look familiar, but . . ."

Daisy smiled. "Well, I can't blame you. I'm dressed — uh, a bit differently. We met at your barbeque. I was with Sidney McAlvain."

Claire's breath caught. She took a closer look. "Oh, oh — of course! I'm sorry I didn't make the connection." Certainly this girl had toned down her attire. She now looked like a farmer's daughter from Kansas, not an arm candy bimbo for some fat man.

Claire shuddered. No, now that was Lainie.

Remembering her manners, she extended her hand. "Well, it's good to see you again."

Daisy glanced at the brochures displayed at the booth counter. "So, you're a caterer?"

Claire smiled. "Yes, I own Della Claire."

Daisy's eyes lit up. "Are you expensive? Your party was so wonderful. I — I'd like your help. If I can afford it, that is." She leaned forward and whispered, "I'm on a budget."

"Oh, I think we could work something out." She grabbed a thick three-ring binder she'd assembled with potential menus and table decoration ideas. "When's the big day?"

Daisy giggled. "In two weeks. My guy's a soldier stationed at Fort Hood. He deploys soon, so we don't have a lot of time."

"I see. Well, tell me what you've got in place so far. Venue?"

"We haven't decided where yet. We don't even have a minister lined up or anything."

"Tell you what, you come by Della Claire in the morning, say about ten o'clock, and I'll have some ideas for you then." Claire glanced at the woman in the neighboring booth. "Leave everything to me, Daisy. I'll make sure you have a wedding to remember."

■ ■ ■ ■

Planning a wedding with Daisy was pure joy. Claire soon found that the young woman was not at all the Betty Boop with nothing between her ears. Instead, she was warm and funny and so appreciative of everything Claire suggested. And she was kind to Margarita, which placed her on the top of Claire's best client list.

Daisy needed an inexpensive venue, so Claire reserved a quiet little park in the town of Mansfield, a small community in the southern part of the Dallas metroplex. At the back of the park, a quaint pond would provide a great backdrop to an archway, where the vows would be exchanged. They would set up a white tent and leave one end open to the view.

Jana Rae's brother, the pastor, agreed to officiate gratis. Mike's little girls would even serve as flower girls. Jana Rae insisted on buying their dresses. "They'll wear them over and over. No sense Daisy dishing out the money. Let me."

Daisy gave Claire full rein as long as she stayed within her meager budget. Oh, and she didn't want daisies in the floral arrangements, for obvious reasons. "Growing up, I was forced to wear one in my hair every day. I hate 'em," she said.

To save money, Claire planned to forego a sit-down dinner. Instead, she'd pass hot hors d'oeuvres, which would be perfect for the small guest list and the outdoor venue. Mushrooms stuffed with gorgonzola cheese and prosciutto with chopped fresh rosemary. Shrimp skewers and grilled pineapple rings glazed with Kahlúa. Potato skins topped with sour cream, cheese, and bacon bits. Scallops wrapped in bacon.

Claire baked homemade crackers to serve with a terrine of five different cheeses molded into the shape of a heart. She assembled a massive antipasto tray with varieties of olives and tiny marinated carrots and cauliflower florets.

For dessert, chocolate-covered strawberries and vanilla cupcakes with passion fruit frosting. And, of course, wedding cake.

She talked Daisy away from using colors, urging her to go with a slate of cream and chocolate brown, with russet and yellow accents. "It'll make for an elegant fall ceremony. Your portraits will be gorgeous." Then she added, "From the flatware to flowers, lighting to linens, everything should compliment the overall look to create a unified experience."

Daisy clasped her hands and nodded. "Like something out of a magazine," she said with reverence.

Never before had Claire felt so in her skin. She always enjoyed cooking and putting on parties, but this was so fun she should be paying Daisy for the entertainment value.

"Claire, you are really gifted at this," Brian said more than once.

Jana Rae agreed. "Yeah, just think. Up until now, you were living with only half your burners turned on."

Even her mother had caught the change in Claire, the way she got up in the morning filled with anticipation. She told Max, "Your mother's little hobby seems to be agreeing with her."

"What do you mean, Grandma?"

Claire's mother sipped her coffee and raised her brow in Claire's direction. "Yesterday she came home with flour in her hair. When I told her, she didn't even comb it out. Instead, she just smiled and gave me a hug."

It was true. In many ways, she was happy.

On the day of Daisy's wedding, everything came together perfectly. Beneath a wedding arbor decorated with cream-colored mums, white lilies, and tiny French roses the color of vanilla, the groom, Trevor Rudd, watched as Daisy made her way down the aisle to join him. His eyes had that soft look as the wonder of the moment washed over him and he realized he was the luckiest guy on the planet.

Claire knew that look.

When Daisy reached her place up front by her fiancé's side and the last note of "Pachelbel's Canon" quieted the crowd, Jana Rae's brother Mike stepped forward.

"Dearly beloved, we are gathered here today to witness the joining of Daisy Anhauser and Trevor Rudd in marriage. Unlike any other institution, matrimony was established by God. He is the author and the sustainer of this covenant relationship that is meant to be an earthly depiction of his relationship with his bride, the church. Hopes, dreams, and expectations of a good and happy marriage can be shattered when a husband and wife fail to walk in God's precepts for this holy union."

Mike's words formed a bubble of unexpected emotion around Claire's heart, a deep sadness despite such a happy occasion. She'd never wanted to be one of those statistics. Yet what choice did she have?

Daisy and her groom looked so happy. So ready to commit their lives to each other. But could they really map the road ahead and know "forever" would pan out?

Mike instructed the couple to grasp hands, then said, "When I was fairly young, I spent a summer working on a horse farm about an hour or so south of here. Not far from the farm there was a blacksmith shop. One afternoon I was sent in to get a broken cattle gate welded. When I got there, the blacksmith, a rather hefty guy with a black beard, told me he'd fix me up. I could even watch if I wanted. Fascinated, I stood nearby as the blacksmith welded together two pieces of metal.

"First, he stoked the fire until it was glowing red. Then, when it was so hot I could feel the heat on the other side of the shop, he shoved two pieces of metal into the middle of the fire and made the fire even hotter with his bellows. Next, he took the two pieces of metal out of the fire, laid them on the anvil, and pounded them together with his hammer again and again. Then he shoved the metal, now one piece, into the fire again.

"Over and over he did the same thing. Fire. Pounding together. Fire. Pounding together. Finally, when he was satisfied, he plunged the metal into a bucket of water. Then he turned to me and said, 'This old-fashioned way of welding together two pieces of metal into one is the strongest weld known to man. The metal may fracture in other places, but the weld will not break.'

"Trevor and Daisy, in a very real sense, this is a holy moment. God is the master blacksmith. As you recite these vows, he is taking two individuals and creating one. And you are promising before these witnesses never to break that bond."

Claire's eyes teared up. Certainly she and Tuck had been through fire and they'd both ended up fractured. Now, out of desperation, she'd decided to break their marriage bond.

Jana Rae's brother told a nice story. But the application didn't apply in her situation.

A part of her would always love Tuck. She might even forgive him. But what kind of marriage remained when he was incarcerated? Under such unique circumstances, her decision was more than justified.

Wasn't it?

Regardless, it didn't do any good in life to pine for what she could no longer have. Like so much of her former life, her marriage was over.

As if reading her mind, Margarita, who was standing near, pulled her into a hug and whispered, "Mrs. Massey, God makes all things possible."

48

Lainie had lived life fairly sure of herself. She had the ability to evaluate life and formulate a plan to get what she wanted. Lately, though, her resolute nature seemed to be pulled into a riptide of conflicting emotions.

She'd been so convinced moving in with Sidney would restore what her daddy had ripped away and get her out from under the shadow of losing her role as senator's wife to Miss Perky.

Now she knew differently.

She pulled herself from the rumpled sheets and glanced at her watch, a Cartier she'd bought at the mall the other day to console herself. Sadly, not even a Patek Philippe, at a price tag well over six figures, could have raised her spirits these past weeks.

She would tear up over the silliest things. Election night, of course. But she'd also

438

choked with emotion when she pulled a sweater from the closet. Daddy had said that shade of blue reminded him of the sky.

She'd picked up the phone to call her mother, then remembered their explosive exchange and the haunting disappointment in her mother's eyes, and she'd changed her mind.

Lainie slipped into her robe and headed for the bathroom. She turned the water on to fill the tub, then moved to the sink and gazed at her reflection in the mirror.

Since that day in the mall, she knew what had to be done. Problem was, she'd burned a lot of bridges, so to speak. Where would she go when she left Sidney?

How could she face her family now?

Despite her bruised pride, she had to find a way out of this mess she'd made.

Lainie hated to admit it, but the person looking back at her in the mirror with the dark circles under her eyes was not so different from most women who'd bartered their self-worth.

She longed to be cherished.

And because of that need, she was quietly coming undone.

49

Thanksgiving came and went, with only Max and Claire's mother staring at her from across her tiny kitchen table — a far cry from the elaborate family events of prior years. She no longer wrestled with her changed lifestyle — well, at least not as often — but there had never been a holiday without her entire family present. That, she'd never get used to.

Claire tried, as the weeks passed, to bury her mind in the busy Christmas season. There was a Christmas tea for a woman she'd met in the beverage aisle at Whole Foods. She catered several office parties, and when she wasn't preparing for an event, Margarita helped her bake and deliver Christmas cookies, homemade peanut brittle, and fluffy pink divinity.

On the evening that was to have been Lainie's wedding night, she tried to call her daughter. Sidney McAlvain answered. "Yes, hello, Claire. I hope you enjoyed Thanksgiving."

His voice grated on Claire's nerves. "Is Lainie there, please?" she asked with as much patience as possible.

"No, I'm afraid she's gone shopping and left her phone behind. I wouldn't have picked up except that I saw it was you. Would you like to leave a message?"

Claire couldn't stand Sidney's pretense, his phony disregard for their nasty encounter. "No. Just that I called."

Max complained he'd been unable to reach Lainie as well. He'd wanted to talk some sense into her after learning about Sidney McAlvain, and Claire wanted him to succeed where she'd failed.

Now it was a week before Christmas, and still nothing. No doubt her daughter was still smarting over Claire showing up, and perhaps that had been a bad move. Lainie was never one to be told what to do. Even when she was a child, her temperament required molding and rebelled at being pushed.

Claire's mother urged her to quit worrying. "Lainie is young and free-spirited. Like I was at that age." She clicked the channel to *The Price Is Right.* Over the years, she'd admitted to watching every morning because she had a secret crush on Bob Barker. Now she likely watched out of habit. "Perhaps Lainie and that man of hers plan to go to Paris for Christmas. Don't impose a guilt trip on the poor girl."

Never had Claire wanted so badly to take her mother down a peg or two.

"Mama, why did you divorce my father?"

Her mother's eyes darted from the television to Claire. "What kind of question is that?"

"Did it ever give you pause to dump me off in San Angelo and spend the holidays apart?" she challenged. "I was only eight."

Her mother waved her off. "Of course not. You were with your father. He loved you."

"Then why did you keep us apart?"

"Why, Claire, I'm surprised at you. I did no such thing."

Claire huffed. "You didn't make it easy for us to spend time together." She felt her eyes fill with sadness. "It nearly killed him, you know."

"Don't blame me for wanting a good life. I simply don't know what's gotten into you lately." She lifted from the couch and shook her head. "I made my choices. Lainie is making hers. I suggest, for your sake, you get on with yours."

■ ■ ■ ■

"Give me some advice, Brian. I keep thinking I've stuffed my life back into a box labeled 'happiness,' but no matter what, I see something or something is said that pulls me right back out and lands me on the table." Claire looked at Brian sitting on the floor in front of his fireplace, a smile playing at his lips. "Oh, don't look at me that way. You don't know what this feels like."

"Yes, I do," he assured her. "There were days in my early sobriety I thought I'd never stand on solid ground."

"What did you do?"

He grinned, then leaned back and wrapped his arms behind his head. "I just kept running toward what I wanted."

Claire sat up straight, her legs crossed beneath her. She studied him wistfully. "Maybe that's my problem. I don't know what I want."

"Sure you do," he said, popping up and heading into the kitchen. "You just won't let yourself have it."

She watched him open a bottle of chilled LaCroix water and pour it over two glasses filled with chipped ice. "Need some help?"

"Nah," he said as he delivered the drinks. "Tonight I'm serving you." He returned to the kitchen and from the counter pulled a tray filled with cheeses, olives, and delicate crackers. "The guy in the deli told me the Havarti was aged to perfection, said the cheese tastes like butter."

They ate in front of a crackling fire, talking very little, just enjoying each other's company. Their friendship had grown quickly over the past months, and Claire realized somewhere along the way they'd developed the ability to be silent with one another.

Brian was a good man. She was lucky to have his friendship. At times, she even expected she'd let the relationship take its natural course and move into something deeper. After the divorce.

Her mother would be pleased, do doubt.

Ellie Wyden believed a stellar husband was defined by his balance sheet. As her daughter, perhaps Claire had unwittingly embraced that kind of thinking.

Tuck claimed he felt pressure to provide a certain lifestyle. Had she contributed in some way to his awful choices? She didn't think so, but she couldn't be so sure she hadn't. She'd certainly enjoyed the wealth too.

Sadly, she was now left wondering if she'd passed along that illusionary attitude to her own daughter.

Amazing what women will grasp and label as happiness.

Brian reached out and tucked a strand of Claire's hair behind her ear. "You look sad all of a sudden."

"Not sad, really. Just mulling a lot over these days."

Brian placed his arm around her shoulders and pulled her close, making her feel warm and safe. He was not as tall as Tuck. Tuck used to rest his chin on top of Claire's head when he held her.

"In AA, we're taught we can't do anything about the past and we can't control the future. We need to focus on the present."

She smiled. Yes, he'd said that before. She needed to remember his sage words and apply them.

Brian slowly traced the side of her face with his calloused finger. His eyes bore into her own. Claire thought she should pull back.

She didn't.

In a bold move, he leaned forward and she felt his hands go to her waist. Claire's heart pounded as she felt herself melting into him, folding into the comfort of his embrace more eagerly than she would have liked.

"Now would be the time to ask me to stop," he whispered in a husky voice.

She swallowed, then brought her fingertips to his jaw just as their lips met for the first time. Soft and gentle.

She felt his fingers in her hair, heard him gasp for breath when he pulled back slightly and whispered, "Claire."

His voice, soft and reverent, shook her to the core.

Before she could respond, he pressed into her mouth again, this time with an urgency she too felt. She'd forgotten what it was like, and Claire found herself unable to stop trembling, unable to pull back, even though a part of her mind flashed a yellow warning light.

Her heart thundered against her chest. For a moment she let herself forget she was married. She'd been alone too long. She missed him.

His fingers grabbed her shoulders and pulled her against his body. She felt his beating heart. His hot breath on her neck. Heard him groan.

"Oh, Tuck . . ."

Suddenly everything stopped. Brian gripped Claire's wrists and gently moved her back. His face clouded and his breath came in gasps, as though he'd been running.

Claire's eyes scoured his face. "What . . . why did you stop?"

"I'm Brian."

Confused, she brushed her cheek with the palm of her hand. "I know that." She leaned into him, but he stopped her.

"I'm Brian," he repeated.

Then Claire realized. She dropped her head, sick at her slip. "Brian . . . please, I'm so sorry." This was her friend, someone she cared deeply about. She hated what she'd done to him.

"Claire, you are a beautiful woman," he whispered.

She sat frozen as he smoothed her hair. For one heart-stopping second, his hands lingered, then he dropped them. "There," he said, his eyes searching hers.

She couldn't speak, could hardly breathe.

In the distance, she heard her cell phone. Disoriented, she glanced around to locate where the ring was coming from. Then she remembered she'd left her phone in her coat pocket.

Jolted from the surreal, she stood and scurried for the coat closet. After opening the door, she pawed through the pocket

until her fingers scooped around the ringing phone. Without looking at the face, she
pulled it to her ear, never moving her gaze
from Brian. "Hello?"

Too late. She'd missed the call.

Frustrated, she moved her fingers across
the face and scrolled to missed calls — Max.
Her phone dinged, alerting that he'd left a
voice mail.

"Mom, where are you?" Max's voice
sounded frantic. "Something's happened
and I need you to call me. It's Garrett and
Marcy's baby."

50

Brian held open the door, and Claire rushed into the hospital lobby. Jana Rae and her brother Mike followed close behind.

As they approached the front information desk, a whirr of a vacuum strained from some distant hall, almost muting the voices coming from the television mounted on the wall in the nearly empty sitting area. Far across the room, near a massive Christmas tree, a young woman chased after a toddler, who stayed steps ahead of his tired-looking mother.

"Munchkin terrorist," Claire heard Jana Rae mutter under her breath.

A round-faced woman with deep dimples and hair that formed a curly bowling ball looked up from the information counter. She lowered a coffee mug that said Licensed to Pill. "Yes? How can we help you?"

"I'm Claire Massey. My daughter-in-law was brought here this afternoon." She fought back tears that threatened to form yet again. "Her name is Marcy."

"Oh, you betcha. Let's take a look right here." The woman set her mug down and swung in her chair to the computer on the left wing of the desk. She plucked at the keyboard, then cocked her head. She made a tsking sound and turned her head back in Claire's direction. "Now, how are we spelling that tonight?"

The lady's got to be kidding. We spell it the same way we do every night. Fighting to hide her impatience, Claire responded, "M-a-s-s-e-y."

"Oh, you betcha. Here we are. Right here." She displayed a smile ripe with satisfaction. "She's in our OCC unit — obstetric critical care. Fourth floor."

"Thank you." Claire turned to leave, then realized they didn't know where to go.

Before she could ask, Brian stepped forward and cleared his throat. "Can you tell us where —"

"Oh, I'm sorry. It says here they don't take visitors this time of night."

"Well, you don't understand," Jana Rae said. "We just drove from Dallas, and her son called and told us to come."

Claire looked at the ceiling and back at the woman behind the desk, heaving a sigh.

"It's urgent."

"Oh, you betcha. Then let's just have a call up there and see what we can do." She smiled and picked up the telephone receiver, leaned it against her ear, and quickly pounded out a number. Claire did her best to smile while the woman reported the urgency to the person on the other end of the line, at which point Claire noticed the volunteer pin on her sweater, decorated with holly leaves and red berries.

"Okay, honey. They're waiting for you. The elevators are over there." She pointed past the large fake ficus tree at the other end of the waiting room.

"Okay. Yes. Thank you." They all turned and took several hurried steps across the room before Claire caught her reply.

"Oh, honey, you betcha."

Lainie sat in Sidney McAlvain's media room, her eyes riveted on celebrities dancing on the television screen. From her spot on the sofa, she delved into a bowl of hot, buttery popcorn and brought a handful to her mouth.

Sitting in a large leather recliner, Sidney peeked over top his reading glasses and let the documents he'd been reading fall to his lap. He reached across the table and slid the bowl out of her reach. "Perhaps that's enough, Lainie. If you're not careful with what you put in your mouth, your legs will soon not look like those dancers."

Her face heated, and she pulled the bowl back. "What are you? My dad?"

In a flash, Sidney's hand grabbed her wrist. His grip bit into her skin, but she didn't flinch. Instead, she glared back at him.

His eyes narrowed. "Careful, Lainie," he said, slowly releasing his fingers. "I am a patient man, but there is an end to what I'll tolerate."

Her breath caught.

Despite the uneasiness creeping up her spine, she continued to challenge her overly controlling benefactor in a visual duel. No matter what, Lainie would not be the first to look away.

Finally, Sidney reached over and clicked off the television. He slowly pulled his glasses from his face, folded them, and placed them in their case. Then he slid the documents back in their folder and laid the file aside.

He gave her a menacing look, drew a deep breath, and slowly raised himself from the chair. He glanced at the watch on her arm with disdain, the one purchased using his funds. "When you depart in the morning, leave the watch and the credit cards behind on the guest room bedside table." He squared his shoulders and turned for the door. Suddenly he stopped and fished in his pocket. He pivoted and tossed a phone — her phone — onto the sofa next to her. "You'll need this to call yourself a cab."

Lainie wanted to scream at him, *What are you doing with my phone?* She didn't need to. She already knew.

She held her breath until he exited the room. Shaking, but relieved to be free, she retrieved her phone, trying not to consider how close she'd come to fatally wounding her future.

Her fingers trembled as she checked her cell. There were messages. Lots of them.

She scrolled and listened to the last one — from Max.

"Lainie, where are you? You need to meet us at Skyview Hospital. Marcy's losing the baby."

Upstairs, on the fourth floor of Skyview Hospital, a nurse nearly half Claire's age was waiting as they stepped off the elevator. "Ms. Massey?" Claire nodded and stepped forward. The nurse cupped her elbow. "I'm Heidi Strauss, the floor nurse this evening. I

453

talked with Dr. Elliott's PA on the telephone about fifteen minutes ago. Your daughter-in-law suffered a rather severe placental abruption, followed by a significant bleed. She's in surgery now."

Again Claire nodded. "But how are they? Are Marcy and the baby going to be all right?"

The nurse's face grew sympathetic. "Dr. Elliott is the best in his field. Your daughter-in-law is in very good hands." She paused, the pause that tells you the person is now going to say something that reverses the good news they just delivered. "We don't know yet what any of this means in terms of outcome. But she's getting the best care."

Claire bit the inside of her cheek, hoping to stop the quiver she felt erupt in her lower lip. Jana Rae gave her a quick hug. Brian touched her shoulder.

She thought of Marcy and sent up a quick prayer.

The nurse patted her back and led them down the hall through a large circular area. In the center was a nurses' station with bleeping monitors mounted on the counters. Beyond were individual areas cordoned off by glass walls. Those with patients were dimly lit. Some were darkened and had empty beds, neatly made up for the next people unfortunate enough to need them.

"Y'all can wait in here." She pointed to a small private room to the left filled with mostly empty chairs. A tiny plaque was mounted on the wall near the door that read "Family."

Claire spotted Max. He looked up as they entered. Across from him sat Jack and Emily Karstan. Marcy's parents looked wrecked with worry.

In the chair next to them sat Garrett, his head buried in his hands.

51

Claire and the others settled in to wait. Brian and Mike passed out Styrofoam cups brimming with coffee that had been left on the Bunsen burner too long, while Marcy's mother filled everybody in.

"Marcy complained of slight cramping right after breakfast," she said. "Garrett alerted me and I urged her to get checked, but she was reluctant at first." She looked to her husband. "She thinks I worry too much. Anyway, we came right over, and by that time her pain had turned severe. We all knew fairly quickly our girl was in trouble."

Jack shook his head. "Got her here as quick as we could."

Garrett brushed his hand through his hair, leaving a strand sticking up. "She started bleeding on the way," he added in a tired voice. Worry created deep furrows in his brow, and her son's eyes were filled with a desperation that made Claire ache inside.

Max moved to his brother's side. He placed his arm around Garrett's shoulders. "She'll be all right, Bro. You'll see."

A commotion out at the nurses' station pulled everyone's attention to the open door. Lainie's voice drifted from the hallway. Through the open door, Claire saw a nurse point in their direction, and she watched as her daughter scurried to where they waited.

"Oh, Garrett. Is she all right?" Lainie rushed to her brother's side and clutched his hand. Her lips pulled into a tight line and her neck pulsed in the way Claire knew happened when she got stressed. "And the baby?" Lainie looked at her. "How's the baby?"

Claire moved to her daughter and gently squeezed her shoulder. "We're waiting to hear."

Lainie seemed like she couldn't help herself. Her daughter turned and embraced her. With tears brimming, Claire hugged back and kissed the top of her blonde head.

When Lainie finally let go, Jana Rae brought her up to date on the situation while Mike poured her some coffee. "I'm Mike, Jana Rae's brother," he said. "You take anything in it?"

She shook her head. "No, black is fine." He handed Lainie a small white cup filled

with steaming liquid. "Thank you." She
gave Jana Rae's brother a grateful smile.

Claire caught Brian watching her. She
shook her head, realizing she'd neglected
her manners. "Everyone, this is a friend of
mine. Brian Magellen." She didn't know
exactly what to say after that, how to act.
This was not the way she'd envisioned
introducing him to her family. In fact, truthfully, she'd never really imagined that step.
Even now it was hard to think of Brian
around a dinner table with her adult children.

Max was the first to extend his hand.
"Hey, nice to meet you."

Lainie gave Claire a tentative look before
she nodded at Brian. "Yes, how are you?"

Garrett stumbled through his despair long
enough to shake Brian's hand.

Out of the corner of her eye, Claire saw
Jana Rae retreat to the corner. She lifted
her eyebrows and gave a silent whistle.
Clearly she'd assessed the tension in the
room.

So had Mike. He clapped his hands together. "Hey, anybody hungry? I bet I can
find the cafeteria."

Jana Rae gently reminded him it was after
midnight.

"I'm sure they have vending machines,"

he told her. He turned to Lainie. "I may need some help. Donuts and packages of Planters are heavy, you know."

She hesitated. "I'm not sure I should —"

Overhead, a loud voice crackled in the speakers. "Code Blue — OCC. Code Blue."

Garrett flew out of his chair. He darted to the open door.

Claire's throat tightened.

Outside the waiting room, medical personnel rushed past the glass windows. "Who called it?" one of them shouted.

"Surgery suite," another said.

Garrett followed after them until a young black guy with a stethoscope draped around his neck stopped him. "You have to stay here, man."

Inside the waiting room, Emily reached for her husband. "Oh no, Jack . . ." Marcy's mother knew, just as they all did, there was likely only one surgical procedure being performed at this hour.

Lainie and Max grabbed each other and hung on.

Mike dropped his head, his lips moving silently. Jana Rae shifted next to her brother and joined him in prayer. Claire quickly added her own.

Her heart pounded. Once again her family was in crisis. Marcy and the baby. Her sweet, tiny granddaughter. She might never get to meet her.

Claire shuddered, wrestling her mind back from dreadful possibilities. Regardless, a feeling of helpless terror slugged at her gut.

Brian moved to her side. He folded his hand over hers, sending the silent message he was there — for whatever she needed.

But in that moment, there was only one person she wanted by her side.

Tuck.

52

Nearly an hour passed before a man with graying hair at the temples entered the waiting room wearing scrubs. He was followed by two women, one with a clipboard and deep-set eyes that scanned the room, taking inventory of those seated and waiting for information.

Jack and Garrett stood simultaneously. Garrett rubbed his stubbled chin, then quickly extended his hand. "Dr. Elliott?" His voice revealed how grueling the wait had been for him.

"Let's everybody take a seat." Dr. Elliott gripped Garrett's hand in a quick handshake, then pulled a chair from a nearby table and sat. He pulled his surgical cap from his head. "First, Marcy is out of danger. At least for now."

Garrett's hand went to his mouth and his eyes welled up. "Oh, thank God."

Emily buried her head, and her emotion,

in Jack's chest. He patted her, his eyes filled with relief.

"And the baby?" Claire ventured.

The doctor nodded. "She's a fighter. A team of specialists are preparing to transport her to Texas Children's. She'll be under the care of Dr. Claudia Mathis, one the most respected neonatologists in the Houston area."

Claire clung to the doctor's words like a lifeline, letting the brief information buoy her hope. Both Marcy and the baby were alive.

Dr. Elliott explained that Marcy had coded during the emergency C-section. "We encountered a disseminated intravascular coagulation event due to increased thromboplastin." He looked at Garrett. "In layman's terms, that means your wife failed to clot properly and hemorrhaged severely during the procedure." His eyes grew focused. "I'm afraid we had no choice but to perform a hysterectomy."

Garrett shook his head. "Doesn't matter. She's alive. That's what's important."

Dr. Elliott stood and patted Garrett's shoulder before exiting.

The woman with the clipboard stepped forward from where she'd been standing. "Mr. Massey, we'll need you to sign these consent forms for the transport. It's urgent we move your daughter as soon as possible."

Garrett nodded and took the pen she offered. Without looking over the paper, he scribbled his name. "What are we dealing with? Can I see her?" He lifted his chin as if steeling himself for a blow, which quickly came.

The woman handed off the signed consent to the other woman, who scurried from the room with the document in hand. When she turned back, she introduced herself. "I'm Dr. Liz Nyles, head of NICU here at Skyview. Your baby girl had a very rough birth. Marcy's placental abruption caused what is called asphyxia, a disruption of fetal blood flow in the womb. She was born with very low Apgars, and her umbilical arterial blood gases — another determinant of fetal metabolic condition at the moment of birth — also gave indication that she was oxygen deprived for a period of time."

Claire's heart pounded and a dull ache formed at the back of her neck. She rubbed at the base of her skull. "What does all that mean?"

Dr. Nyles gave her a sympathetic look. "It means she's going to have to be carefully monitored to keep her out of further danger. A highly experienced staff, skilled in the latest advances in evidence-based treatment at a level 4 neonatal intensive care unit — one of the best in the country — will be following her progress and helping her to make it through this rough start." She turned back to address Garrett. "None of these factors are sure indicators of future developmental issues. But your infant is in what we call the danger zone. She's four weeks early, and that complicates matters. But again, I assure you she's in the best medical hands available."

Garrett rubbed his forehead. "Thank you. And, Doctor?"

"Yes?"

"My baby girl — her name is Emmy Claire. After her grandmothers."

Dr. Nyles smiled. "That's a great name. Now, I need to excuse myself and help the transport team." She shook Garrett's hand and headed into the hall.

Claire moved to her son's side. "I love her name, sweetheart."

Emily wiped tears from her eyes. "Me too."

"Look, why don't you, Jack, and Emily check when you can see Marcy," Claire said. "I'll head over to Texas Children's to be with Emmy Claire." She liked how the name sounded when she said it. She had a granddaughter, and nothing was going to keep her from being near that little one.

Jana Rae gave Claire a hug, then Garrett. "When they're ready, Mike and I will take Lainie and Max with us. We'll book some hotel rooms nearby and get some sleep. You have my number if anything develops or you need us."

Grateful, Claire agreed. Jana Rae knew better than to include her in the group that would be sleeping tonight. She looked to Brian. "Why don't you get some sleep as well?"

He shook his head. "No. Let me drive you over to Texas Children's. We'll play it by ear from there."

Texas Children's Hospital was located forty-five minutes away by car, even with no traffic at the early pre-dawn hour. On the way, Claire leaned back against the leather seat and closed her eyes — only for a second.

It seemed like no time at all and Brian's hand gently shook her arm.

"Huh? Oh." Claire sat up, feeling disoriented. She hadn't meant to drift off. "That was quick." She gave Brian a weak smile, then folded down the car's visor and smoothed her hair.

As they walked through the parking garage, Brian surprised Claire by slipping his fingers through hers. Not that she didn't want him to, only that the gesture felt . . . what? She was too tired to even put her feelings into words. Her relationship with Brian could be sorted out later. Right now her focus needed to be on her baby granddaughter — on tiny Emmy Claire.

The horizon outside the garage had turned a soft lavender, hinting that daybreak would soon follow. Claire glanced at Brian. "When's the last time you pulled an all-nighter?" she asked over the whirring HVAC system.

"Been a while," he conceded while checking the web on his iPhone. "Looks like we need to head to the fourth floor." He pushed the elevator button.

Even at this early hour, the hospital buzzed with activity. They made their way to the guest services desk, and Claire gave her name. Unlike the woman at Skyview, the representative quickly directed them to a bank of elevators to the left. "I'll call and let them know you're on your way up," she said. She turned to Brian. "And you are?"

He introduced himself.

"Are you family?"

He shook his head. "No, just a close friend."

"I'm sorry, you'll have to wait down here."

Claire gave him a quick hug and headed for the elevators.

On the fourth floor, she followed the signs, turned left, and walked several feet down a long hall that ended with large double doors and a sign that directed her to push the button. She did and a voice responded, "Your name?"

"Claire Massey. I'm here for Emmy Claire Massey. My son Garrett called and made arrangements for me to see her."

The door buzzed and then automatically opened to an area where Claire scrubbed in for the requisite three minutes and placed protective coverings over her shoes. With those precautions complete, she was shown into a spacious area lined with tiny Isolettes, many filled with infants. Monitors beeped, a stark contrast to the soft lighting and color schemes. To the left, a young Hispanic woman sat in a rocking chair, cradling a tiny baby with electronic cords tethered to a screen that charted the child's body functions second by second.

A woman in pink scrubs stepped forward. "You must be here to see our newest little one — Emmy Claire."

Claire loved that this nurse knew her granddaughter's name, that she wasn't just some nameless patient. "Yes, can I see her?"

The nurse gave her an encouraging smile. "Of course. Follow me. Dr. Mathis is expected back on the floor anytime, and she'll give you a status report."

She trailed close behind the nurse until she stopped in front of a metal Isolette. A tiny baby in a little pink diaper rested on a white baffled blanket. No booties covered her perfect, tiny toes. No cap hid the silky brown hair. Her tiny palms lay open with fingers extended.

Claire nearly stopped breathing. Emotion overwhelmed her, and her eyes filled with tears. In awe, she whispered, "Can I touch her?"

Without pulling her eyes from the perfect little being, she heard the nurse say yes. "Little Emmy Claire, let me introduce you to your grandmother."

Like many women, Claire had never wanted to announce she'd aged with that label. But right now — no word could be sweeter.

She reached out and gently caressed the baby's palm. Immediately Emmy Claire wrapped her itty-bitty fingers tightly around her own.

In that moment, Claire lost her heart.

53

Lainie paid for her Snickers bar and placed the change back in her purse. There were times nothing but chocolate would alleviate what she felt inside. "Thank you," she told the gift store clerk.

She stepped into the busy hospital corridor, needing to find a quiet place to think, to sort out the last twelve hours and make sense of everything. Her current situation was a bit shaky at best. Lainie Massey always had a plan, but not this time.

She had what she now owned in her car, as well as a horse with a boarding bill that would need paid. When she painted the bottom line on this thing called her life, the fact was she was homeless. Max would let her crash at his place temporarily, but she would need a job and a place to live. She'd need to make things right with her mother . . . and eventually her daddy.

But right now she wanted to be here for

Garrett. No matter what had transpired over the past months since Daddy's arrest, they were all still a family. She knew that now.

She turned left and followed a wide corridor with large framed portraits lining the walls. These were the ones with the financial means to contribute and have surgical wings and pediatric floors named in their honor.

She tried not to think about what she would have worn for a similar portrait had life turned out differently. Instead, she drilled her eyes ahead and kept walking, past a drinking fountain. Two women walked by, both in uniforms with stethoscopes hanging from their necks. The younger of the two looked at her and smiled.

Near the end of the hall, a small oblong sign mounted on the wall read "Chapel." Lainie paused when she reached the door and peeked in the tiny window. Empty.

She looked both ways before slowly pulling the door open, then stepped inside.

The room was tiny, filled with five rows of padded benches. Bibles were placed in racks on the back of each pew. At the front, a large plain wooden cross was mounted on the wall in between two backlit stained glass windows, which featured scenes of creeks running through green meadows with large, inviting trees. *Very pastoral,* Lainie thought.

Just like in the movies.

She moved into one of the pews and let her eyes focus on a plaque on the wall.

Come to me, all who are weary and need rest.

Lainie closed her eyes. She knew tired. For months she'd attempted to quench a raging fire with no water. The effort had left her scorched. Her stubbornness had been her downfall more than once, but this time she'd really made a mess of things.

She needed a fresh start.

Several minutes passed before she heard the door click at the back. She turned as Jana Rae's brother stepped inside.

"Oh, I'm sorry," he said. "I didn't see anyone. I can come back later."

He turned, but Lainie invited him to stay. "You're not bothering me, if that's what you're thinking."

He nodded and shut the door. "Care if I sit by you then?"

She patted the place beside her and Mike took a seat. He leaned back in the pew. "Sometimes I like to just escape to a quiet place, know what I mean?"

"Yeah, I do," she said. "It's nice in here. I was just contrasting this small chapel to the church we attended as a family, where Daddy was an elder."

"Where was that?"

"Abundant Hills in northern Dallas. Aptly named, by the way. Large fountains in the foyer. Massive auditorium, seating over five thousand on a Sunday, with three services and a screen rivaling a movie theater. Golf carts chauffeuring members from parking lots filled with hundreds of cars."

"Sounds . . . big."

Lainie smiled. "Max called it a country club for Jesus."

Mike laughed. "I see."

"Oh, don't get me wrong," she said. "Lots of nice people, and a lot of them loved God, I suppose. I mean, you can tell those who practice what they preach, know what I mean?"

"Yeah, I sure do." Mike grabbed a Bible and randomly flipped through the pages.

Lainie's face reddened. "Oh yeah. Of course. I forgot — you're a pastor."

"Soooo — do you still go? To church, I mean?"

She sighed. "No. Not for a long time."

"Oh? Why's that?"

Lainie wondered how she should answer. Should she tell him she'd lost interest in all the rules and platitudes? Say she'd wanted to go shopping instead of listening to Pastor Richards preach about all the ways she'd never measure up? Or, yeah — update him on recent months with Sidney McAlvain.

Current-day Christians may not stone women who fell short in the purity department . . . but there would always be some holding fast to their rocks.

She stared forward. "Oh, no reason, really. Just skipped a Sunday here and there, and pretty soon — well, you know how it is."

"After my wife died, I rarely went to church," Mike said. "Which is a bit of a problem when you're the pastor."

"Why did you quit going?" Lainie realized the question was a bit probing, but he'd started down that path by asking her first. "I'd think church would be the first place you'd want to be after — well, after something like that. Especially when you're a pastor."

Mike shook his head. "Nope. Frankly, I was spittin' angry."

She lifted her eyebrows in surprise.

"Sorry, did I offend you?" he asked. "I was only being honest."

Her face broke into a wide smile. How refreshing — a gut-honest pastor. "What made you go back?"

"To church? Oh, I guess — well, when you give your life to Jesus, you're always his. Know what I mean?"

473

Lainie wasn't sure she did. Still, she nodded.

"That, and my big sister hounded me half to death. Jana Rae can get pretty pushy."

She laughed. "Yeah, no kidding."

He laughed as well, then grew more serious. "I wrestled for a long time with how someone who was supposed to love me could let me suffer like that. I didn't understand. Took a long time, and a lot of honest talking with him, to realize he didn't promise I'd never go through hard things. Only that when I did, he'd go with me."

"What was she like, your wife?"

Mike's eyes lit up. "Ah — well, I think she was like a Tootsie Pop."

Lainie gave him a puzzled look. "The candy?"

"Uh-huh. Her outside was sweet, but boy, on the inside?" His eyes sparkled. "At her center, she was pure sugar."

She tilted her head. "So, you still miss her?"

He nodded. "Every day." He clasped his hands on the seat in front of him. "I have my girls. They remind me of her in big and small ways. My ten-year-old has her eyes. Like Susan, she looks at even the ugliest situations with compassion. And my little one has her quick sense of humor and easy laugh." He turned and looked at Lainie. "I loved Susan very much. Always will, I suppose. But, as they say, life goes on." Mike placed the Bible back in the rack. "Truth is, I'd be open to meeting someone else someday."

Lainie grew pensive. "I hope you do," she said quietly.

"You'll find somebody again too," Mike said. "The right man will come along, the one God planned for you."

She rolled her eyes. "You mean God has a dating service?"

"Ha, good one. What I meant is God wants good things for you, Lainie."

She didn't respond. Instead, she watched the candle on the table up front flicker, casting shifting shadows across the room. "Why?" She turned to face Mike. "Why do you think he'd want good things for me?"

"His goodness doesn't depend on yours. The moment you want him, he'll be there. Until then, he's too polite to barge in."

Barely breathing, Lainie stared at the cross on the wall, then dropped her gaze down at the swirls in the patterned carpet. "I don't think I'm church material anymore."

Mike reached out and covered her hand with his. "What liar told you that?"

Lainie wasn't sure if she believed him. She

wasn't even sure what he said mattered. But strangely, she felt drawn to the possibility that what she'd believed might not be congruent with the truth.

Her future was wide open now. Someday she hoped to have what Mike had described — to find that kind of love. To feel that valued.

She'd always wanted more.

Her daddy had tried to give her the world and failed. On the other hand, God had created her heart.

Who was more qualified to satisfy what she craved?

54

By midafternoon, Marcy's condition had improved enough for them to expect she'd be released before Christmas, which was only five days away. She'd be sore and need to take things easy for a while, but the doctors projected a full recovery.

Under the care of the medical professionals at Texas Children's Hospital, Emmy Claire underwent a groundbreaking therapeutic hypothermia treatment. The thin white blanket Claire earlier noticed her granddaughter lying on was used to lower the baby's body temperature from 98.6 to 92.2. The lower temperature would be maintained for three days, then slowly raised to normal. According to Dr. Mathis, a post-cooling MRI was expected to confirm she wouldn't have any long-term cognitive problems due to the lack of oxygen.

"We are very hopeful," she said. "The results of these treatments have been profoundly effective in averting the kinds of catastrophic neurological and developmental deficits we've seen in the past. There is every reason to believe this medical intervention will ensure Emmy Claire a normal future in terms of medical prospects."

No news would make a better Christmas gift.

With the medical crisis nearly over, Jana Rae and Mike drove Lainie and Max back to Dallas. Brian got a hotel room and some much-needed sleep. Then he too said goodbye and headed north. "I'll see you in a few days," he said. "And I'll call you every night."

Despite the busy holiday week ahead for Della Claire Catering, no one could talk Claire out of leaving Houston. "Go ahead and stay as long as you need, Mama. I'll help Margarita out," Lainie said as she hugged Claire goodbye.

"What about here in Houston?"

Lainie shrugged. "That's over." The look in her daughter's eyes was so raw it surprised her. "And, Mama?"

"Yes?"

"I love you. And I'm sorry."

Claire pulled her daughter into another embrace. Into her hair, she whispered, "I know, baby. I love you too."

■ ■ ■ ■

In her hotel room, Claire had just woken from much-needed sleep when her phone rang. Still groggy, she picked up, not recognizing the phone number. Suddenly she remembered the doctors could be calling about either Marcy or the baby, and her heart lurched.

"Hello?" she said, her heart pounding.

After a couple of strange clicks, the voice on the other end answered. "Claire, it's Tuck."

She felt herself stop breathing. "Tuck?" she said. "What —"

"Don't hang up. Just listen, please. I — I, uh, Max called and told me about Marcy and the baby." He paused. "Are you all right?"

Claire's eyes welled with tears. "Yes," she whispered. "I'm fine." Several long seconds ticked by before she added, "She's beautiful. The baby."

She couldn't help it. In her mind's eye she saw a much younger Tuck standing in the Burger Hut by the jukebox in his crisp, pressed jeans and a white oxford-cloth shirt. Her heart raced.

"Claire?"

"Yes, I'm here," she said, her voice filled with emotion.

"Did you get my letter?"

She told him she had. "I —"

"No, Claire," he said, interrupting her. "You don't have to say a thing. I understand. I didn't call for any of that. Only to let you know I was praying for all of you, and that I'm glad Marcy and the baby are okay. And that you are as well. I was — well, I was sick with worry."

As hard as the past twenty-four hours had been on her, she couldn't imagine what Tuck had gone through, not being able to call or be there with his family. There had been a time when that idea would have sparked anger. She'd rehearse his bad choices in her mind and claim he deserved everything he got. But not today.

Somehow, no anger remained.

"Tuck?"

"Yes?"

"How are you? Are *you* okay?"

"This isn't a bad place," he assured her. "For a prison. The inmate population is primarily nonviolent offenders, and I've made some friends. I go to Bible study and read." His voice dropped to a whisper. "And I think about what I did to all of you, and to those people."

Claire heard his voice crack.

"I'll spend the rest of my life wishing I could wind the clock back. I failed you, Claire, and I'm sorry."

He never mentioned the divorce. Neither did she.

It hit her, then, that she may have delayed filing on purpose, without even realizing it.

She supposed it was true — what God welded together couldn't be broken. She might be able to dissolve her marriage legally, but after thirty years, her union with Tuck could never be entirely disconnected.

They'd been through fire and she'd been burned. But she knew her true strength came from the father of her children — the man she'd loved for thirty years. She could go through with the divorce, but that would be like cutting off her arm. She'd live, but a part of her would always be missing.

A tone sounded, and a recorded voice warned them they had one minute to wrap up their call.

"That's the signal." Tuck sounded sadly resigned to accepting what he couldn't alter.

Claire bit her lip and picked at the hotel comforter. Realizing time was short, she gave in to the yearning she didn't quite understand. "Tuck?"

"Yeah?"

"I love you, you know." Claire's soft-spoken words hung in the air. He was quiet so long she wondered if he was still there. "Did you hear me?"

She heard him sniffle and realized he was sobbing. She pictured Tuck sitting in prison coming completely undone, and her heart thudded painfully.

"Listen to me," she said, choosing her next words carefully. "I'll go for days without thinking about you, and my life will be full and satisfying. Then, when I least expect it, you show up again in my head and I realize I can't let go. So the way I figure, we'll make it through even this," she said, struggling to make him understand her heart. "I only know one thing for sure. I'll always love you."

"I — I love you too. With everything I am," he choked out.

Then the phone buzzed and went dead.

55

On the morning before Christmas, Claire said goodbye to Garrett and Marcy and headed home to Dallas. The night before, she'd visited little Emmy Claire. "Oh, little sweet one. Grammy will be back to see you soon." She caressed the bottoms of her granddaughter's feet, cementing the soft feel in her mind so she could carry the memory home.

Emmy Claire's prognosis was surprisingly bright. The cooling treatment had worked just as planned, and although the medical professionals would watch her closely in the years to come, Dr. Mathis claimed she had every reason to believe there would be no neurological deficit.

The news was a huge relief. Especially to Garrett and Marcy, who would enjoy Christmas while staying with Jack and Emily.

In Dallas, Jana Rae offered to host the

holidays for both her brothers and Claire's family, including Claire's mother and her new boyfriend, a retired aeronautical engineer who had lost his wife ten years earlier.

"Where'd you find this one, Ellie?" Jana Rae asked when Claire's mom shared the news. She said she'd found his profile on Match.com and they'd instantly hit it off. Both Jana Rae and Claire suspected his generous pension was also a big hit.

Brian would spend Christmas Eve with his son. First he'd wanted to stop by for a few minutes. The doorbell rang right at the expected time.

Claire opened the door, dishcloth in hand. He leaned in and kissed her on the cheek. "Welcome home."

She gave him a warm smile. "I admit, it was pretty hard leaving that little one, but it is good to be home." She invited him in. "Can I get you something to drink?"

"Nah, I only stopped by for a few. I'm picking up Trenton and we're heading to the airport for a quick ski trip to Aspen, my Christmas gift." He glanced around. "Where's your mom?"

"Her *date* already picked her up."

Brian slipped out of his jacket. "Her date?"

Claire explained about the online dating match. "And get this. They're talking about marrying this spring. She says she thinks a Vegas ceremony sounds like fun." As soon as she mentioned marriage, she could've kicked herself. She turned abruptly and headed back into the kitchen. "What time does your flight leave?"

Brian moved to the counter and slid onto a barstool. "We're taking the red-eye. That way Trenton can have dinner with Carly and her mother tonight."

Claire nodded, suddenly feeling very self-conscious around Brian. She was going to have to tell him, but not tonight. Not on Christmas Eve.

He reached into his jeans pocket, pulled out a tiny jewelry case wrapped in a silver bow, and slid it across to her. "Here, I wanted to give this to you."

She frowned. "What? I thought we agreed no Christmas gifts."

"It's not a Christmas gift, just something I wanted you to have." He pushed the box closer. "Open it."

Her hands tentatively reached for the small box.

Brian was a dear friend. She wanted — oh, she wasn't sure what she wanted. Except that she didn't want to hurt him.

With slightly trembling fingers, she untied the ribbon and lifted the satin-covered lid.

Inside, a small pendant featuring a tiny picture of Emmy Claire rested against white velvet. She looked up at him. "Oh, Brian. It's beautiful."

"I had Garrett sneak in and take a phone shot for me," he said, watching her closely.

She couldn't help herself. Her eyes started to well. She hurriedly blinked several times, clearing away her uncontrolled emotion.

Clearly she'd made a horrible mistake in not telling him earlier. Over the phone hadn't seemed appropriate, under the circumstances. But he deserved honesty from her now. She took a deep breath. "Brian, there's something —"

He lifted his finger and put it to her mouth. "Shh . . . I know."

Her eyebrows lifted.

"And I understand." Brian stood and gently pulled the pendant from her hand. "Turn around," he said, then placed the delicate chain around her neck and closed the clasp. "Here, let me see how it looks."

She turned, not expecting to feel this much sorrow. She'd made the right decision, she knew. But Brian held part of her heart as well. "Thank you," she said, her voice choked with emotion. "For everything."

He pulled her to him and kissed the top

of her head. "You're welcome, Claire. For everything."

Claire pulled into Jana Rae's driveway and parked behind a shiny black Lincoln probably belonging to her mother's new beau. Jana Rae stood at the open doorway, waving wildly. "Get in here. You're missing all the fun."

Inside, the party had definitely started without her. Clark gave her a quick hug and pushed a cup of eggnog into her hand. "Merry Christmas, Claire."

She hugged him back. "Merry Christmas."

Two little boys dressed in suits and ties raced past, yelling at the top of their lungs. "Hey, you two. Pipe down," Jana Rae called out as she pulled Claire into the living room where the crowd waited.

Claire looked over her shoulder and mouthed to Clark, "Who . . . ?"

He pointed to a young guy sitting next to Mike, looking a bit uncomfortable in what appeared to be a new dinner jacket.

Ah . . . Jay. Jana Rae's *other* brother.

Past the sofa, a beautifully decorated tree filled the corner of the room. The only thing bigger than the fresh spruce was the mountain of packages beneath.

Jana Rae slipped beside Claire and handed

her a soda. "Afraid I'm just a gambler in front of a slot machine during the holidays — once I start, I can't seem to stop. Besides, Christmas only comes once a year." She grinned and nodded at Jay's kids, still running through the house, then winked and stepped back. "Hey, y'all. Time for dinner. Let's head to the dining room." She leaned toward Claire and whispered, "The Urologist cooked the turkey, so if the meat's on the dry side, you know who to blame."

When they'd all gathered, Clark bowed his head and blessed the meal.

Claire looked around the table. Her mother positioned a linen napkin into her new friend's collar. When he patted her hand in appreciation, she beamed. She looked up then and caught Claire watching. Claire smiled ever so slightly. Her mother lifted her chin in response.

Across the table, Lainie chattered with Mike's little girls. For the first time since Tuck's arrest, her daughter looked genuinely happy.

Jay adjusted his tie. He told his boys to sit up straight and quit fidgeting or they wouldn't get to open presents later.

Max helped Clark bring in a platter carrying a turkey the size of a small suitcase, and Jana Rae followed with another platter filled with sliced ham.

Claire took a mental snapshot, stashing the images in her mind. Max carried himself differently now, with an air of maturity of the man he'd become. She'd remember the contented look on Lainie's face, how her daughter seemed to have finally let go of striving for something always out of reach. She'd take the laughter and the good friends who stuck by her side no matter what — she'd wrap this and more and hide it all in the corner of her heart to share with Tuck. She'd carry these memories with her.

Margarita was right. God was indeed good.

Years from now, their family would sit at a holiday table similar to this, perhaps at Garrett and Marcy's house. Emmy Claire would have learned about all that had transpired this year. What would Claire tell her about it all when she asked?

She caught Max's attention and they smiled.

She supposed she'd tell Emmy Claire that the Masseys were a family who knew how one day could shift your course and catapult you into a series of events never intended to be lived. She'd explain that they'd all stumbled and lost their footing, but in the end they found their way — together.

Yes, they'd been rich. But at what cost?

And she'd make sure her granddaughter knew one more thing.

Claire Massey was still a woman of great fortune.

EPILOGUE

Nearly Twenty Years Later

BREAKING NEWS

Vice President Reece Sandell, whose rise to political power included being elected the youngest senator from Texas, resigned today, leaving office amid scandal.

Sandell announced he was stepping down at a grim appearance on the steps of his Washington, DC, office, less than forty-eight hours after being caught with a high-priced prostitute, leaving the public stunned and angered.

With his wife standing next to him, he said he was leaving political life to concentrate on his family.

In other news, Theodore Massey, former cattle broker and financier who was arrested and incarcerated on multiple counts of cattle fraud and federal racketeering charges, served his sentence and was released from prison today. With his family by his side, Mr. Massey says he is extremely happy to be released and is anxious to go home.

DISCUSSION QUESTIONS

1. In *A Woman of Fortune,* Claire Massey experiences a life event in which her security shifts beneath her feet. Have you ever felt a similar blow? Describe how you made it through.
2. Claire enjoys a fabulous life until her husband betrays her and his actions put everything she holds dear at risk. Why do you think she didn't see it coming?
3. Describe Claire. What are her strengths? Her weaknesses?
4. In what ways does Tuck remind you of the white-collar criminals often seen in the news? What characteristics make him different? Why do you think he perpetrated these crimes? Why does he continue to hide the truth of his crimes even after the initial settlement?
5. Claire's situation in this story is not

unlike many politician and celebrity wives who face public humiliation and have to decide whether or not to support their husbands. If you were faced with a similar situation, would you stand by your man? Why or why not?

6. Couples often carry baggage into their marriages. What did Tuck and Claire cart into their relationship?

7. Do you think Claire made the right decision to stay in her marriage? Or do you think she should have pursued her relationship with Brian? Why?

8. Describe the scenes that most reveal how Lainie's emotions are particularly bruised by her father's actions. In angry desperation, have you ever made decisions that made everything worse? Were you surprised at Lainie's choices?

9. As the events in the story unfolded, describe how Tuck's criminal actions affected each member of the Massey family. How did these events change the characters by the end of the story?

10. Brian tells Claire she shouldn't live her life as a mirror, reflecting every-

body else's view. Describe ways you think Claire does that.

11. If you were in Jana Rae's shoes, would you continue to support Claire? Why or why not?

12. Women have incredible influence. How did Ellie Wyden impact her daughter and granddaughter and their choices?

13. Men also have influence. Describe how Tuck molded his sons.

14. List the ways you think the Masseys' faith, or lack thereof, plays into their struggles.

15. While shopping, Lainie encounters a poignant scene of a man and his pregnant wife in the mall. Seeing the man rub his wife's feet moves Lainie to crave a different kind of relationship than what she's been pursuing. Why do you think that is?

16. Shortly after, Lainie acknowledges she's been swimming in a muddy pond when she is meant to ride the waves of the ocean. Why do you think so many young women settle for less than what they really want?

17. The story concludes with the author giving readers a quick peek twenty

years later. How would you write the rest of the story?

AUTHOR NOTE

In late 2008, many of us watched as master financier Bernie Madoff's story unfolded. I couldn't seem to pull my eyes from the television as this man, accused of swindling thousands of innocent victims — including family and friends — out of billions of dollars in the world's largest Ponzi scheme, was taken from his posh Manhattan apartment in handcuffs and his family became vilified in the media.

The events held particular interest for me. In my former role as a legal professional, I helped unravel what was then the largest cattle fraud in the United States. I interviewed dozens who were caught in the betrayal and who found themselves and their businesses floundering as a result.

These stories fascinate me on many levels, but in particular, I'm intrigued with the families behind the scenes. What is it like for a wife to learn her husband is a criminal?

What happens to children when they face that kind of shame?

We know at least in part what transpired in the Madoff family in the aftermath — fractured relationships, family devastation, and suicide. As a novelist, I yearned to explore what might happen if the converse were true. What would the story look like if a strong woman protagonist bucked the odds and stayed in the marriage? What if the family lost their footing but in the end landed on solid ground?

On a personal level, I know that even people who love one another can encounter marriage struggles. On more than one occasion in my own long-term marriage, there were times that deciding to stay was often much harder than leaving. I'm sure if you ask my husband, he could say the same.

I don't stand in judgment of any marriage or any person's decisions regarding their relationships. I'm simply acknowledging, through this story, that there are no pat answers when it comes to marital issues, but sometimes blessing can come if you work through the difficulties.

My own marriage stands as a testament to that truth.

Sadly, my own life also reflects Lainie's struggle to find security and love in the wrong places. My early adult years were spent a bit off track. But my life is living proof that Jesus is the Good Shepherd who comes after his lost sheep . . . and sometimes carries those of us with broken legs until we learn to walk again.

Kellie

ACKNOWLEDGMENTS

I'd like to thank a few people who granted me their time, knowledge, and support. My career as a novelist would most certainly be flatter without regular morning telephone chats with my writing partner, Lynne Gentry. Beyond all the ideas I bounce off her before placing them on the page, she helps me process the ups and downs of the writing journey, and life in general. You are very dear to me, sweet friend.

A big bowl of gratitude is poured at the feet of the team at Baker Publishing Group/Revell, especially Jennifer Leep, who shares my vision for the stories I want to bring to women. The hard work by the marketing folks, the art department, the sales team, and the editors shaped this book and created what you hold in your hands (or on your e-reader). I am honored to be published by such an amazing group of people, and my heart is filled with admiration and appreciation!

My gratitude also goes to my agent, Natasha Kern. Frankly, she is brilliant when it comes to this industry. Thank you for your amazing support and hard work on my behalf.

Special thanks go to a few people who provided technical support. Stanley D. Williams, PhD, writing coach and author of *The Moral Premise,* helped me early on in the development of this story. His stellar guidance helped focus the themes of betrayal, family, and losing your life to gain a better one. Thank you, Dr. Williams. And thank you to unnamed sources at various US Attorney's Offices and the federal court judge's clerk, for the criminal procedure and grand jury information, and for a behind-the-scenes look at how plea bargains really work.

I appreciate my good friend Carol Johanson, ICU Charge Nurse at Meridian Park Hospital in Oregon, for looking over the medical terminology (and for always giving me a place to stay when I'm on book tour).

Thank you to Lonnie Gentry, a Texas pastor. Although modified for this book, your wedding ceremony was *perfect.*

Thank you to the staff at the Adolphus for showing me around. Your hotel establishment is indeed stunning!

A big shout-out goes to Kathy Patrick and the Pulpwood Queens. Thanks for letting me hang out with you at Girlfriends Weekend. Who knew I'd ever wear hot pink and a tiara?

As always, I am filled with love and gratitude for my family — for my husband, Allen, and my boys, Eric and Jordan. For my sister, Jeannie Cunningham. For my daughter-in-law, Brandy, and my precious little grandson, Preston. And a new little baby girl, yet unnamed, who will debut about the same time as this book. For Jeramie and Angela Ausmus and beautiful little Jaslyn. You all make my life sweet and worth living.

Last, but not least, I want to tell readers how much I appreciate you. You faithfully purchase my books, share them with friends, and recommend them to libraries and book clubs. You send me emails and Facebook messages and post reviews on Amazon and Goodreads. Some of you even wear T-shirts with my book cover on the front (you know who you are). Thank you for reading my stories and for all the encouragement you send my way. You are foremost in my mind as I write.

ABOUT THE AUTHOR

A former legal investigator and trial paralegal, **Kellie Coates Gilbert** writes with a sympathetic, intimate knowledge of how people react under pressure. She tells emotionally poignant stories about messy lives and eternal hope.

Find out more about Kellie and her books at **www.kelliecoatesgilbert.com.** While you're there, don't forget to join Kellie's Reader's Club. As one of Kellie's VIP readers, you'll receive exclusive news about her books, exciting giveaways, and (shh!) maybe some travel opportunities made available only to Kellie's Reader's Club members.